This item is to be returned on or before the last date shown below.

SP
24/09/09

2 9 DEC 2010 EW

2 0 JAN 2011 EW

1 2 AUG 2009 KN

8 SEP 2009 EW

1 4 OCT 2009 EW

0 5 NOV 2009 EW

SEP 2011 EW

FEB 2012 ST

1 1 NOV 2009 EW

1 5 MAR 2012 ST

2 6 NOV 2009 EW

0 3 JAN 2013 ST

1 8 JUN 2010 EW

0 8 JAN 2013 ST

2 6 JUN 2010 EW

76

1 6 JUL 2013 DB

2 7 JUL 2010 EW

9 APR 2014 GE

1 8 NOV 2014 PW

1 9 AUG 2010 EW

0 3 MAR 2016

3 SEP 2010 EW

0 3 MAR 2016

1 OCT 2010 EW

0 6 MAR 2017

0 4 NOV 2010 EW

2 3 OCT 2017

0 9 DEC 2010 EW

the
Gathering
Night

Also by Margaret Elphinstone

The Incomer (1987)
A Sparrow's Flight (1989)
Outside Eden (1990)
An Apple from a Tree (1991)
Islanders (1994)
The Sea Road (2000)
Hy Brasil (2002)
Voyageurs (2003)
Gato (2005)
Light (2006)

the Gathering Night

Margaret Elphinstone

CANONGATE

Edinburgh · London · New York · Melbourne

For Caroline

First published in Great Britain in 2009 by
Canongate Books Ltd, 14 High Street,
Edinburgh EH1 1TE

1

Copyright © Margaret Elphinstone, 2009
The moral right of the author has been asserted

The writer acknowledges support from the Scottish Arts Council
towards the writing of this title

Scottish
Arts Council

British Library Cataloguing-in-Publication Data
A catalogue record for this book is available on
request from the British Library

ISBN 978 1 84767 288 9

Typeset by Palimpsest Book Production Ltd, Grangemouth, Stirlingshire
Printed and bound in Great Britain by CPI Mackays, Chatham ME5 8TD

Mixed Sources
Product group from well-managed
forests and other controlled sources
www.fsc.org Cert no. TT-COC-002341
© 1996 Forest Stewardship Council
FSC

www.meetatthegate.com

CONTENTS

THE PEOPLE

Bakar's family

Nekané	mother of Bakar
Alaia	sister of Bakar
Haizea	sister of Bakar
Amets	husband of Alaia
Esti and Alazne	daughters of Alaia and Amets
Hilargi and Sorné	aunts of Bakar
Sendoa, Itsaso and Ortzi	cousins of Bakar

Other members of the Auk People

Aitor, Hodei, Zigor	Go-Betweens
Edur, Zeru	hunters
Arantxa	mother of Osané, Oroitz, Koldo and Itzal

Members of the Lynx People

Kemen	hunter
Basajaun	Kemen's brother
Ekaitz	Kemen's cousin

First Night: River Mouth Camp

Haizea said:

Bakar's disappearance was my first loss. It's also where this story begins. If my brother Bakar hadn't gone, we wouldn't all be sitting here now. And you two boys – listen to me, both of you! If Bakar hadn't been lost, you two would never have become brothers. You might never even have known each other. And the lives of all us – of all the Auk People – would have unfolded differently. But I can't even begin to think about that. No one can undo the threads of a story once they're tied together. Not even the spirits can do that.

I was still a child. But I remember very well that terrible winter my family spent alone at River Mouth Camp.

There were only six of us at River Mouth Camp before Bakar went away in Yellow Leaf Moon. We became six again when my sister Alaia gave birth to Esti. After Esti was born we stayed on at River Mouth Camp, even though we'd been hunting there all winter. We were walking further every day to get enough dead wood for our fire. Alaia and I always managed to fill our baskets, but we couldn't get enough meat. Only Amets could hunt, now that my brother was gone. Amets has never failed us, but you all know it takes more than one man to feed a family well all winter. Once we'd finished the hazelnuts and acorns and lily-seeds, we had to dig for roots more often. We got reed-root from the marshes. Alaia and I pulled lily-roots out of the freezing mud at the bottom of the hill-loch: it's worst when you have to break the ice before you can wade in.

My mother kept going away. She didn't seem to want to be with us any more. She wouldn't tell us where she'd been.

In the Moon of Rushes the rest of us wanted to move on. Winter no longer held us; the wind from the High Sun Sky smelt of the coming spring. But now we were afraid my mother wouldn't go with us. We still didn't know what had happened to Bakar. That was the worst winter I ever spent. In the end we stayed at River Mouth Camp until just before Auk Moon. It seemed so long! I thought about running away. I knew how to find my cousins' Camp. I'd only been there by boat, but I thought if I walked down the shores of the Long Strait I couldn't possibly get lost. It would only have taken me two or three days . . . If Esti hadn't come I think I *would* have run away. But that winter Esti gave us something to be happy about, in spite of everything.

I think I was angry with my mother for not being there – I don't know. I certainly never thought of her going Go-Between.

I thought Go-Betweens were terrifying, distant men who spoke to the Animals about the Hunt. How could Go-Betweens be anything to do with my mother? I couldn't understand what was happening. None of us did. At least – maybe Alaia and Amets guessed, but I never heard them speak about it. My father – I think my father . . . My father was the wisest

man I ever knew. He understood everything. But he knew
how to be silent too. He never spoke to me about it.

Alaia said:

And so my mother became Go-Between.

I realise now that it started when Bakar was lost. I didn't understand at first what was happening. It was only when Esti was
born that Nekané really began to change. When my daughter
was born I lost my mother – that's what Nekané becoming Go-
Between did to me.

Esti was born in Thaw Moon. We had hardly any meat.
Haizea told you how we chopped and ground lily-roots every
day, and baked them in the ashes. We were getting mussels
and crabs and limpets, wading into the cold sea at slack tide
to pick them off the rocks underwater. Two nights before
Esti was born the traps were full of lobsters. We roasted them
in ashes of oakwood until the blue shells turned red. It was
a good enough feast for Thaw Moon, and maybe it gave Esti
the strength to come into the world. She took all night to
come. Amets and my father – as you know, his name isn't in
the world now – had gone hunting upriver. We were alone
in the winter house – just me and my mother and Haizea,
and the sound of the River. The River sings many songs at
River Mouth Camp, sometimes loud and angry, and sometimes in the gentlest of whispers. On the night of Esti's birth
the River sang with its whole throat. It told of snow melting
in the hills, of water under the earth stirring deep roots, of
white water filling empty streambeds, of overflowing banks
and flooded marshes. In Thaw Moon the River sings of its
own strength, and it's death for People or Animals to meddle
with it.

When Esti arrived no one recognised her. I knew who my mother hoped it would be, though she hadn't said anything about it. My mother didn't hide her disappointment when she saw that my baby was a girl. Haizea cut the cord with her own knife. It's good when the youngest does that. It makes a bond, and it's right for a child to have someone younger than her own mother bonded to her. There were barely ten Years between Haizea and Esti, and see what came of it: they've never let anyone part them. Haizea never thought that Esti should be anyone other than who she is.

My little girl lay across my stomach whimpering, taking her first breaths into her new body. I wanted to reach for her, but I knew what had to happen first. Haizea and I waited, and the little one twitched and breathed against my skin. At last my mother took the baby in her hands and turned her over. I watched my mother's face in the firelight. She looked into my baby's eyes. A pine log flared in the hearth. Outside the rain fell softly. I could see Nekané didn't recognise my daughter. All she said was, 'The child says, "I am not him. I am not him."' And so my Esti brought grief with her, because she wasn't the one my mother had hoped for.

My daughter had no name for two days. You mothers, you'll know what those two days were like for me. If she hadn't been recognised on the third day we'd have had to cast her out. Amets and my father had not returned. The wind howled and gusts of sleet blew in from the sea. Between the showers the Sun came out, but it was pale and filled with water. I couldn't go beyond the threshold because I had my baby in a sling. I dared not take her under the open sky when she had no name. My mother didn't look into her eyes again.

And then, just before sunset, the men returned. I heard voices outside: my mother's, Amets', my father's, Amets' again. Then Amets came into the winter house. He handed his wet cloak to Haizea, and looked across at me. I'd been sewing a foxfur into the back of my tunic to make a carrying pouch for the baby against my skin. I'd laid the fur down to feed the child, and when Amets came in I was holding her naked against my shoulder. I thought Amets might be angry that I was making preparations for my baby even though she had no name. Amets met my eyes.

He took his daughter from my arms. She lay still between his hands. He looked into her eyes. She felt safe. Amets said to his little daughter, 'I didn't recognise you at first, grandmother. I last saw you long ago, far away under the Sunless Sky. You are Esti. You've come again to bring sweetness into our lives.'

Because Amets recognised his daughter she was able to live. As the days grew longer she grew with them. She'd always be a newcomer among the Auk People because she had a name that was new to us. But she was welcome, just as Amets was welcome when he came to Gathering Camp looking for a wife. And now Esti is a name belonging to our family as well.

But all the while my mother was becoming Go-Between and I was losing her.

I hated it. But if she hadn't, I don't think you Auk People would be sitting round this fire listening to us now. That's why this story we're telling you is so important. Listen, and you'll hear how fiercely the spirits tested the Auk People. You'll see how close we came to being broken apart for ever.

But when my mother went Go-Between it was hard. Usually women who live to be grandmothers want to help with a new baby. Itsaso, you're always complaining that your mother wants to help too much! I think you're lucky. Even a woman who doesn't like her daughter often wants to love her grandchild. My mother became more distant than ever. Even if she was present in body she was often far away from us. And sometimes even in the body she had to travel, so we saw little of her.

Haizea said:

I think Amets should speak next.

Everyone knows Amets, of course! But perhaps some of you younger ones don't know how Amets came into our family. Amets came to us from the Seal People under the Sunless Sky. He met my sister Alaia at Gathering Camp. Amets could have found a place in any family among the Auk People where there was a daughter looking for a man! Lots of Auk men wanted my sister too, but it was Amets, the stranger, who finally got her.

Alaia's hair is thick and curly like mine, only, as you can see, mine is the colour of dead grass while hers gleams like the seaweed forests that shine gold in the Sun at low tide. While I was as skinny as a stick, Alaia was all curves – but for all she seemed a soft armful, I can tell you she was hard to please! If her face is good to look at, why then so must mine be, because women always say how alike we are. Men used to make fools of themselves just looking at Alaia. She'd look back at them out of those clear blue eyes, pitiless as the sky at noon in the middle of a drought. Except when she smiled – only I never saw her smiling at any men. But then, I was too young to go to High Clearing Camp. That's where she found Amets. She brought him straight back to our hearth at Gathering Camp. She didn't ask anyone; she just brought him. And he's been in this family ever since.

Amets said:

I last hunted with my wife's brother Bakar at River Mouth Camp, three Moons before my daughter Esti was born. We left Gathering Camp at the beginning of Yellow Leaf Moon.

The Sun was getting old, but he wasn't tired yet. It was mild when we arrived at River Mouth Camp. A circle of hills shelters it from all the winds. For those of you who've not seen it, our River flows down through many little gorges into a wide valley where it winds among the marshes, always heading for the Sunless Sky, until it reaches the salt flats and open water. River Mouth Camp lies on dry ground at the foot of a craggy hillock. Every Year we clear the saplings from the top of Lookout Hill so we can see out over the marshes, through the Narrows to the Open Sea, and the islets off Sand Island.

There were still plenty of berries, hazelnuts and crab-apples when we arrived. There'd been a lot of rain, and on our first day the women's baskets were overflowing with every kind of mushroom. It looked as if we were going to live well. Our family was very small – too small – but I was looking forward to hunting with Bakar through the winter. We needed meat to store and furs for our winter clothes. He and I planned to hunt in the hills, as much as the Winter would let us, between Swan Moon and Moon of Rushes. The best hunting grounds I know for winter pelts aren't far from River Mouth Camp, and you can trap small Birds and Animals from River Mouth Camp itself. That was just as well because I had to stay close to home after Bakar was gone, and yet I also had to get enough furs to clothe the whole family. My wife's father said we should never let River Mouth Camp go out of our hands because the hunting was so good. He was right, and I've kept my word to him.

Bakar and I had hunted together for a Year and two Moons. Haizea just told you how I took his sister Alaia when I first came to the Auk People's Gathering, and after that I went with her family. I come from the Seal People under the Sunless Sky, but I couldn't find a girl there – I'd plenty of cousins but not one that was far-off enough. Though Bakar and I first met as strangers, by now we knew each other well. We trusted each other.

Two days after we got to River Mouth Camp Bakar and I set off before dawn. We took spears and knives, a bark-rope to make a trap and a basket of broken mushrooms. We left the marshes behind us and turned towards the Morning Sun Sky. We climbed through oak-woods, and followed the course of a small stream rushing to join our own River. We had my dog – the one who came into Alaia's family with me – he was a great hunter. He'd soon made himself the leader, but now he was getting old, and wasn't so fast any more. We had Bakar's good dog, two bitches who were reliable and a young dog in training. First we went to the marshy pond where the pigs wallow to see if there were any around. Sometimes when we arrive at River Mouth Camp the wolves are in our hunting territory and the pigs have gone inland to get away. The wolves always retreat when we come back with our dogs.

Above River Mouth Camp there's a hollow like two hands cupped together where the trees begin to thin. It holds a shallow lochan in its palm. Some pigs had drunk at the lochan the day before. We followed the path they'd made. Three sows had passed that way, heading uphill, yesterday afternoon, with a couple of half-grown piglets. The boar's tracks were fresher; he'd come down to the pool in the evening, and gone back a little later. We found a good place for a trap under an overhanging birch tree. We hung the noose across the path, and fixed the weighted rope to the branch. I scattered the mushrooms I'd brought as bait. Then we went on very quietly, taking the pigs' path uphill, the old dog leading. The path led over rocky broken ground, crossing swollen streams and bright mosses.

We came to a clearing. Saplings were shooting up in the light where an old birch had fallen. Brown fungi grew out of the dead tree, and it was all overgrown with brambles and old man's beard. Flies danced in the patch of sunlight. We skirted the thicket, following the pig path.

The lead dog barked.

The other dogs cocked their heads – so! The thicket was still.

When the first dog barks to the stillness, he barks to wake the sleeping Animal – that's when the Hunt begins. In one heartbeat we all wake to the Hunt at once: dogs, men and the still-hidden Animal.

That dog was the bravest dog I ever had. He knew what was in that thicket – he could smell it plainly. If I'd known what he knew, I'd have hesitated – this wasn't one of the great hunts of Deer Moon. This was just Bakar and me, and a hand-full of dogs. But that brave dog of mine never held back. As soon as I raised my hand – like this – he ran round the thicket to flush the pigs out. Bakar's dog and the two bitches followed. I kept the young dog with me. I didn't trust him. One to the left and one to the right, with the thicket before us, Bakar and I crept in close – like this – spears ready. Bakar whistled. The dogs barked. They pushed into the thicket. A pig crashed in the brambles. The dogs barked, but kept their distance. The thicket swayed and rustled. I balanced my spear. We crouched, waiting. The brambles parted.

It was the boar. Not a sow. A full-grown boar – this big!

The boar rushed out. My heart was in my throat. And there was my brave dog coming up behind – like this! – lashing out at the boar as he rushed towards me. That wily boar suddenly twisted in his tracks. My dog was too slow. The boar had him by the throat. He let go and tossed him high into the air. I ran forward. My dog yelped when the tusk pierced him. He hit the ground and lay still. The boar charged me, head lowered. I jumped out of his way, and before he could turn I thrust my spear.

My aim was true. I caught him under the shoulder. My spear went deep.

Bakar ran to the twisting boar. He thrust his spear in below the other shoulder. Three brave dogs began to bite, tearing at the hide. The young dog ran round us, barking. The rest of us held on. We kept on holding. The boar writhed and fought. The blood from his wound ran down my spear and into the earth. The shaft slid in my hands, leaping up and down as if it were alive. The ground under our feet was slippery with blood and mud. We held on. We held fast, and slowly, very slowly, the great boar died. He thrashed and lay still, and together Bakar and I let our spears drop before the dead weight broke them.

We eased our spears out of the boar's flesh. The dogs licked up the blood round our feet. The barbed point of Bakar's spear was broken, snapped into three pieces by the boar's straining muscles. Bakar shrugged and said, 'So there's work for tomorrow, as if I needed it.'

I went to my old dog and rolled him over. His body was limp, and there was a great wound in his stomach where the boar had gored him. The soul had gone out of his eyes. The other dogs watched, tails down.

Bakar and I put our hands into the wounds we'd made, and smeared each other with the hot blood. We cupped our hands where the blood flowed, and drank. The Boar's spirit was with us, and our hearts were his.

I took embers from my pouch, unrolled the damp moss and blew sparks on shavings of birchbark. While I got our fire going, Bakar slit the boar down the belly-line and pulled the guts aside. He cut out the liver and heart. We cut strips, held them in the flame to seal the blood, then wolfed them down. We threw the lungs to the dogs. The hunt had made us hungry, but as soon as we ate, the life-warmth of the Boar flowed into our veins and made us strong.

Bakar knew I grieved for my dog. He helped me weave a

platform out of saplings and lay the dog high off the ground where the spirits would find him. We did that as if he were a man, because I knew the soul of that brave dog would wish to be among People, just as his life with me had been.

Bakar cut another sapling and we lashed the boar to it. It had taken less than half a morning to walk uphill to the Boar's Thicket, but it took from before midday until sunset to carry the dead boar back to River Mouth Camp. Although it was downhill, we had to rest often. We changed places, and shifted the weight from one shoulder to the other. He was as great a boar as two men alone could kill, let alone carry, but that day Bakar and I did both.

When we got back, the women had known – though how you women always seem to know these things is beyond me – to line the pit and heat stones in the fire. The dogs ran ahead, barking our success. The women came out to meet us. They noticed at once that my dog was missing. Alaia cried out, wanting to know what had happened to him. We took no notice. To tell the truth I doubt if we could have carried our load another step, but we wouldn't show weakness in front of the women. So we marched right up to the fire without speaking, and dumped the dead boar beside it.

Alaia glanced at me once, and didn't say another word about my dog, then or ever. Alaia is a good woman.

Bakar looked at the cooking pit and the hot stones waiting in the embers, and scowled. 'So you thought someone would bring back meat, did you? Ah well, you're sadly mistaken, as you see. All we've got is this puny bit of a pig for you. That won't do you much good.'

'Ah well,' Alaia grinned back at him, 'that's very sad. But I think if you scrape the bottom of the cooking pit you might find some old limpets. You must be hungry for your supper, after such a disappointing day.'

'Not so hungry as your man here. I had nothing to do but carry the pole. That was easy, because as you see all we had was this poor half-starved pig. But you should know it was your man who caught it on his spear first. Not that I'm jealous, since there's hardly enough meat to flavour a limpet, now I get a chance to look at it. Are you going to take first cut, Amets, or are you too ashamed of this small day's work to set your knife to it?'

I smiled. 'I'll conquer my shame,' I said. 'But admit it's your shame too, Bakar. Because I think that little needle-prick on the other side is your work. If we can call it work. These women might have made a better job of it, but they won't say so, because they're too kind. Isn't that right?' I was addressing Alaia, but I could see Haizea giggling at her side. I was fond of her, but of course I couldn't speak to my wife's little sister directly. 'You won't shame us by pointing out what a miserable supper we've brought back for you, will you?'

Haizea giggled. 'I don't mind eating it,' she said to Bakar. 'But then there mightn't be any left for you, if I eat all I want!'

So we went on, while Bakar and I laid the boar on its back. Bakar cut away the jaw while I cut the ribs apart. Alaia put the brain and kidneys to roast quickly in the ashes because everyone was hungry. I threw a hind leg to the dogs. Alaia put the hot stones at the bottom of the pit and laid the cut ribs and shoulders over them. Bakar and I hung the rest of the carcass in a tree. Alaia covered her pit with turfs so the meat would roast slowly. It soon began to smell good! One thing about being by ourselves at River Mouth Camp: we didn't have to give any of our meat away. That night we feasted by firelight while the stars swam towards the Evening Sun Sky, until the first streaks of dawn spread across the Morning Sun Sky. There was Moon enough to eat by, and on a night of plenty, who needs more?

That was the last hunt, and the last feast, that I shared with my wife's brother Bakar. It was a great boar who gave himself that day. See these tusks – the ones I wear round my neck – these are his. If I spread my fingers wide – see – the long tusk reaches right from my first finger to the fourth. See that mark, that's where his skin came to. Look how worn they are – sharp as an arrowhead! Go on, you can take them if you like – go on, pass them round – I don't wear these tusks because I've anything to say about my own skill. I did very little that day. I wear them so as to remember my good dog – the bravest dog I ever had. Look! See how the dogs are listening to me! They remember. They know.

Nekané said:

My son Bakar went out alone at the end of Yellow Leaf Moon. He wanted to train the young dog, so he left the other dogs behind. He had his bow and nine arrows. No spear. His spear had been broken the day Bakar and Amets killed the boar by the High Lochan. Though he'd started to make a new one, he still had to finish the barbs. That last hunt had been worth breaking a spear for! We were very happy that evening when Bakar and Amets came back to River Mouth Camp with the dead boar slung on a pole. We had the cooking pit ready, so they singed the skin at once, butchered the meat by firelight and gave it to us to cook right away.

After that it rained for three days. We cut up the rest of the boar and hung the strips of meat to dry in the shelter. Bakar and Amets cleaned the boar's skull and wedged it into the crook of River Mouth Hazel. We all stopped what we were doing while they told the Boar how we'd eaten his meat, and now we were happy because we were his children. Then Alaia and Haizea went back to tending the fire of rotten birch logs that smoked under the drying meat. Bakar walked over Breast Hill to collect pine branches. We have to walk a long way from River Mouth Camp to get pine. He was soaked through when he came back; I hung his leggings and tunic to dry in the meat shelter.

Bakar propped up the tent flap to make himself a shelter, and squatted under it, wearing nothing but his loincloth while his clothes dried. Raindrops dripped off the door flap and ran down his back. The marks of Auk and Wolf and Bear written across his shoulders gleamed as if they were alive, prowling in the secret hunting lands of a man's dreams. Bakar untied the bundle of pine lengths, chose the straightest, and stripped off the bark. He took a flint core from his pouch and chipped off a new blade. My son nearly always got just the blade he wanted at the first strike – nothing wasted. He flicked out the knife blade he'd used for cutting the boar meat, and carefully glued in a new blade. Then he shaved his pine lengths into supple wands; at the tip of each he carved rounded heads. As he finished each bird arrow he balanced it on his finger, testing the weight. He fletched each one with crows' feathers. He looked up when Haizea came back, dripping wet, lugging a big eel in a basket.

'Is that my dinner? It looks as if it's been in a fight!'

'It has. I had to bash its head right in to get it out of the trap. Are you making new arrows? What will you do with the old ones?'

Bakar was always teasing his little sister. But he was kind to her as well, in his way. 'Now why would you be asking me that? Surely you don't want any? All right' – Bakar shook three old arrows out of his quiver – 'here! You can try to mend them if you like.'

'My bow isn't big enough for these arrows.'

'*Your* bow? What's wrong with a sling?'

'*Babies* use slings and pebbles! I want a proper bow!'

'The finest hunters test their skill on slings! Don't let the spirits hear you getting above yourself, Haizea!' But Bakar was always soft-hearted. When Haizea trailed away, looking upset – as well she might – he called her back. 'Here, take the arrows, stupid. You can cut them down to fit your bow.'

When he had made his arrows and re-strung his bow, Bakar went back to mending his broken spear. While he cut the barbs and smoothed them with pumice, I used the rest of the pinewood to make the fire hot, and smothered the eel in the ashes. When it was roasted I pulled it out of the fire and cut it into juicy slices of delicious white meat.

'Eat now while it's hot! You can finish binding that afterwards, Bakar. It won't run away!'

Bakar propped his half-mended spear against the Hollow Oak, and laid the leftover piece of antler next to the tent. As soon as the Sun came out Bakar went out with his bow, his six new bird arrows and three flint-tipped arrows. He meant to teach the young dog to retrieve birds. He had his knife at his belt. He was wearing his deerskin tunic and leggings – without any cloak, because the Sun was hot. I filled his pouch with roasted hazelnuts. That was all he had with him.

He never came back.

The dog didn't come back either. Yellow Leaf Moon passed, and Swan Moon. The days grew shorter. Day after day I searched for my son. I walked the shores of River Mouth country, and wandered among the marshes. I followed the deer paths through the oaks, and climbed high among birch and juniper. I often climbed our Look-out Hill. I scanned the marshes, and the open water of the estuary beyond. I searched the ridges of the protecting hills that surround our River Mouth. I walked over the hills until I saw the snow-covered cone of Mother Mountain far-off under the High Sun Sky.

Day after day I, who had always provided so well for my

family, brought nothing home. Alaia and Haizea gathered roots, hazelnuts, acorns and mushrooms until Swan Moon. It was they who set the bird traps, collected shellfish and speared flatfish, and dug for roots among the reeds. They cooked the food and roasted the nuts, and fed the men when they got home. My man and Amets hunted small game, and sometimes went after the deer who come down to graze in the marshes when the days grow shorter. No one needed me. Never before had I taken more than I gave.

Day after day I searched for my son. I slept alone under the stars, and in the mornings my cloak was stiff with frost. I didn't stop to find food, but I felt no hunger. I journeyed far from River Mouth Camp. I followed the shores that faced the Evening Sun Sky. I borrowed a boat and crossed to Cave Island; my sister Hilargi's family hadn't seen my son. I followed the shore of Mother Mountain Loch and asked at every Camp I came to. No one had word of my son. I crossed Mother Mountain Island to the shore that faces the Morning Sun Sky, and I walked the coast of Long Strait. None of our kin at any of the winter Camps had seen my son. The tides had washed the sands clean, and I found no trace of him. I turned inland towards the Long Loch. As I wandered among the oaks I found the tracks of deer and pig, bear and beaver, fox, lynx, marten, cat and wolf. But there were no human tracks among them. I never found a trace of Bakar.

Swan Moon came and went. Now it was Dark Moon. The snow came. The days were too short for travel. I was forced to go back to River Mouth Camp.

I heard the ring of stone on stone long before I reached our clearing, and when I got there I found Amets using a wedge to split birch logs from the tree the beavers felled, and Alaia, with her big belly, stacking firewood under the shelter. A fresh deer hide, a seal hide and two beaver pelts were stretched on frames to dry. My husband and Haizea were sitting together on a log by the door, their heads bent over some work.

They all stopped what they were doing when they saw me. My man smiled at me kindly; Amets and Alaia seemed subdued. Only my younger daughter jumped up and hugged me. No one asked about my journey. Haizea has never been able to give her mind to more than one thing at once. She dragged me over to where my man was sitting: 'Mother, look! See my new bow! I made it! Actually Father helped me make it. We went upriver to find juniper yesterday, and we carved it and greased it with ochre – see! And today we strung it. Now we're making arrows – we're just gluing the arrowheads. I made the glue myself – look!'

It was warm and dry inside the winter house. While I'd been gone they'd stripped the walls back to the bark during a dry spell, and built fresh turfs over it. Amets and Alaia had laid new birchbark round the smoke hole, and lined the inside walls with hides. Haizea had cleared out the old pine twigs and strewn new ones across the floor. She and Alaia had climbed into the hills and brought back juniper to lay under the birch boughs in our sleeping places. The beds on both sides of the hearth were covered with winter furs. Firewood was stacked almost to the roof, and there was even more under the shelter between the oaks outside. Haunches of deer and beaver meat hung from the roof, and a string of saithe dangled in the smoke above the fire. Baskets of reed-roots, lily-roots, roasted hazelnuts and orange earth-mushrooms were lashed to the walls. I saw Alaia's hand everywhere. I wanted to praise her, but somehow the words came out wrong. She seemed angry that I should mention her work at all.

It was the season when an old woman should make herself comfortable by the hearth. I had the promise of Alaia's child to rock in my arms before the winter was out. But I cared for none of these things. I was starved with cold and hunger from my long wanderings. You'd think I'd be glad of food and shelter and the warmth of the fire.

But it was all ashes in my mouth, because Bakar was lost, and I'd found no trace of him.

Young men must die.

When we meet at Gathering Camp there's always news that young men have died. They die at sea when they fish far out; they die hunting bear or boar or a stag in rut; they die in spring when they climb the sea cliffs; they die killing one another. When they kill each other it's either because of a woman, or in a brawl at the Gathering. But when Bakar was lost the Gathering was long over and we were all in our winter Camps. There were no women to be had when we were alone at River Mouth Camp, and no groups of young men to goad one another into foolishness. Bakar wouldn't have strayed into another family's hunting grounds from River Mouth Camp. Why should he? There were plenty of Animals where we were, and if he had gone further, why then he'd have had to carry the meat all the way back home, and what would have been the point of that? And if others had come into our winter grounds, then surely I'd have found signs of them in my wanderings.

Young men must die.

But not my son! Every mother thinks that: 'not my son!' Some mothers have sons to spare. My sister Sorné has five sons, and never lost one. I had only one, and he'd gone.

If young men didn't die there'd be too many. If some didn't die People would grow dangerous, subject to the violent spirit of youth. Young men must die, just as young Animals must die when we hunt them. If there weren't so much death we'd all perish, and not be able to come back. I'd always known that young men must die. But not my son!

In Dark Moon, after Bakar was lost, the world grew strange around me. I began to see things that had been hidden – small movements out of the corner of my eye, shadows of other presences. Sometimes I stretched my hand out into the dark, full of longing – for what I didn't know – but whatever it was slipped from under my touch. In every breath I took I heard an echo. The more I strained to hear, the faster it faded away. The chat and clatter of my family grated on me. I couldn't listen – I couldn't watch – I couldn't answer the call I heard so clearly in my dreams. I had to get away from other People. Something new was happening to me. But I never thought – I was only an old woman – the wife of my husband – the mother of my children – what was I, after all? I never – not yet – not then – I never thought, 'Go-Between'.

Alaia said:

When Bakar didn't come back, my mother kept going away, often for several nights. She never brought back food or firewood. She grew haggard, and would hardly speak to us. We all mourned Bakar. But my mother made it difficult for us. I felt guilty because I ate and slept. She made me feel I oughtn't to gather food, or scrape hides, or prepare the winter house, or even talk to my father or husband or sister, because Bakar wasn't there. She made me feel as if I oughtn't to be alive.

I felt as if I didn't have a mother any more. I was afraid of dying. I was pleased – of course I was pleased – that I was carrying Amets' baby. The first Year we were together I didn't get pregnant. I was glad when at last I did, but as the winter drew on, and my belly grew bigger, I began to dream about dying. I knew that if *I'd* been the one to die, not Bakar, I'd have been like a stone that sinks with scarcely a ripple. Every young mother dreams about death, and sometimes it turns out to be true. I wanted my mother to care about me. I've known some women whose mothers never left them alone when they were pregnant, always giving advice and bringing in special foods. You remember when Itsaso left her family and went away with her man's People after the Gathering because she couldn't stand her mother fussing over her? Haizea and I never had a problem like that. But when I was waiting for Esti, and my mother was mourning Bakar, I was angry that she didn't seem to care at all about me, or my baby. I even thought that if I died giving birth she'd be sorry she'd neglected me.

But I didn't die, and after Esti was born everything else began to happen. Once I had Esti I didn't feel sorry for myself any more. Now, when I think about my feelings that winter, I feel ashamed.

One day in Dark Moon we'd been sitting in the house all morning, close to the fire, while gusts of rain flung themselves against our turf walls. We were passing round a hunk of dried boar meat, slicing off bits with our knives and chewing them slowly. Sometimes, when the meat came round to him, Amets would slice off a particularly meaty bit and toss it over to me. There are some good things about being pregnant! We had plenty of food, so there was no need to go out before the weather cleared. It was about midday when my mother stood up abruptly, took down her foxfur cloak and pulled it tight round her shoulders. Then she lifted the skins that hung down over the doorway and stepped outside.

'Where's she going *now*?'

I shrugged. I could no more answer Amets' question than he could. 'Father,' I said, 'it'll be dark soon. Shouldn't you stop her?'

'*Stop* her?' He was outraged. 'Alaia, you're speaking of your mother! Have you no respect?'

'But *you* could!'

'I? Why would I interfere? For what reason?'

'The weather . . . If she stays out she could die!'

'True,' said my father. He stared into the fire, still absent-mindedly rolling twine against his thigh. A log fell sideways, and small flames began to crackle. My father sighed. He hadn't mentioned his son's name since Bakar left us. Perhaps he'd been certain from the beginning that my brother's name had already left this world. And yet my father wasn't known among our People for understanding hidden things. He liked everything to be clear and plain. But I knew him, and I privately thought he noticed more than my mother did. My father had never gone to look for his son. He'd never referred to Bakar's absence. Bakar was a grown man. Soon he'd have married and left our family anyway. He was free to go where he wished and also, if that's where his path led, free to die without asking permission.

It worried me that my father would let my mother go just as easily. But when my father withdrew from the talk and stared into the fire like that, there was nothing more I could say. I met Haizea's eyes and saw fear in them. She was only a child. I put my arm round her. 'Don't worry. I'm not going away and nor is Amets. And you know our father will never leave us.'

Haizea whispered, 'He might not be able to help it, one day.'

It was true that our father was getting old. He was older than our mother. I knew what Haizea was thinking. Even as I put my arm round my little sister I felt the baby kicking inside me. My baby was reminding me that I couldn't make promises either because I mightn't be able to keep them. There's always danger, and mine was growing very close.

Suddenly I jumped to my feet. I shouted at my father: 'My mother has no right to do this! Just because Bakar's gone' – I was so angry I *would* name him as if he were a living man – 'she's no right to inflict her misery on us! We're *all* sorry! We *all* miss him! You *must* be angry with her, Father! You should be! Oh yes, you should be! She makes it seem like you don't care. That *you've* not lost *your* son. Oh no, you're not to have lost your son, and I haven't lost my brother, and Haizea hasn't lost hers! None of the rest of us is supposed to feel *anything*! She makes it seem like we don't care, just because we go on living. She ought to care about *us*! Supposing I die – because I might – I might easily – where's my mother going to be when I need her? And Haizea needs her? She won't care about us! Or about you either! If she came back and you were dead, and I was dead, she wouldn't care! She—'

My father dropped his twine. He stood up and struck me hard across the face.

I fell back on the piled-up furs, my hand to my cheek.

Amets looked at my father, and at me. He stood up, and reached for his cloak. 'I'm going to check the traps,' he muttered, and turned to the door.

'Let me come with you!'

We all froze. Amets looked at my father. Surely he'd interfere in this! Haizea realised what she'd done almost before the words were out. She clasped her hands over her mouth in horror. Then she flung herself on the bed, sobbing as if her heart would break. Neither of the men moved. It was I that knelt beside her and put my arm round her. 'Sweetheart, it's all right. No one will punish you. If mother had been here it would never have happened! We'll forget it, let it go.' I looked at my father and spoke to him firmly, although I was quaking inside. 'Father, Haizea didn't mean to speak to Amets. Amets is *my* husband, and I think nothing of it. My sister's upset because Bakar's lost, and now her mother's gone too. That's why she forgot. She's only little. So be kind and forget, won't you? Won't you?'

I could hear my mother's voice very clearly inside mine, telling my father what he should do. I quailed in my heart, but I stood facing my father, and met his eyes. I knew how my mother stood up to him, and gave as good as she got. *She* never quailed for any man. When my brother and I were little we used to cower under the furs in our sleeping place as the battle of words stormed over us. And here was I, speaking to my father in my mother's own voice, as if I had her power inside *me*!

He must have heard it too, because suddenly he threw back his head and roared with laughter. 'What a pack of women we have about us, Amets! Where did they learn to order us about like this? How did they get to be so unruly? I hope you'll keep your family in better order than I've been able to do, young man! Look at how my women behave, telling us what to do, and speaking out of turn! I'll come with you to the traps, Amets, and let's hope they'll rest their tongues and do a bit of work for a change while we're gone. Or maybe they've grown too uppity to want to feed us any more!'

Amets grinned, and held back the skins for my father to go out. Before he followed him outside Amets looked back at me, and winked. I knew the wink was for Haizea too, and that when the men came back everything that she and I had said would have been forgiven. I also hoped that, although my father would never refer to the matter again, what I'd said to him about my mother would not be entirely forgotten.

Amets said:

As the winter Dark slowly gave birth to another Year, I thought about what I should do now Bakar was gone. 'Next winter,' I thought, 'if Nekané comes back, I'm building a separate winter house at River Mouth Camp for my family. Never mind if we have to keep two hearths. Alaia and I will have a child of our own, or so I hope' – I stretched my arms up to the spirits even though I'd not spoken aloud – 'if I have Alaia and a child, then

I'll certainly build another winter house for us here. And if . . .
if that's not going to happen, and it's the worse for me' – I
could hardly bear to think of it – 'supposing Alaia is gone and
I have to take Haizea . . .' I didn't finish the thought. Already
I greatly missed Bakar. My wife's father was a good man, but
he was getting old. Bakar had been my friend, but he'd been
gone too long – three Moons now – for me to hold out any
hope for him. Alaia was my woman. I didn't want the child
Haizea – if I had to take her I couldn't do anything with her
until she was grown, but I'd have to feed and clothe her all
the same – and I certainly didn't want to be the only young
man in the Camp.

I can't say I'd been thinking much about my wife's mother.
The days had been quiet without her. There's little for a man
to do in the long dark except sleep, and if his sleep is disturbed
– well, maybe that's a sign of too many women in a house.

One evening we sat by the outside fire. It had been a clear
day with the smell of snow in it, and hoar frost glittering on
the grass. The bare oaks were black against the sky. I'd found
a young pig in my trap that morning. Dark fell as we feasted.
While I sat chewing the meat off the bone, I thought about
everything in a way I never had before. I now belonged to a
winter Camp with one old man, my woman and a girl child.
'If that's how it is next winter,' I decided, 'I won't come back.
Even if I have Alaia and a healthy child of my own, I won't
come back if I'm the only hunting man. Alaia works better than
two of most women put together' – yes, that's what I thought
about my wife then, and I still do. I saw how well Alaia looked
after everything even before I took her. In fact that's one of the
things . . . But not the *only* thing, I'll give my word on that! But
this is what I was thinking: 'My wife's father still brings home
meat. He set traps, and he shoots small game. He still fishes
from his coracle. But he can't trek far inland after deer or boar,

and certainly not bear or wolf. Next winter he'll do even less. No,' I decided, 'without Bakar this Camp makes no sense. Before next Gathering I'll speak to my wife's father. Either we bring in others from Alaia's family – she has plenty of cousins – or he must find a man for Haizea – one who'll be prepared to wait for Haizea to become a woman in return for having a place in this family.

'If my wife's father says no . . . He can't say no!' It dawned on me that I was now the one who'd say how things were to be. If I refused to come back, this family would have to give up River Mouth Camp and let others take it over. Now that Bakar was gone, I was the only hunting man. They couldn't live here – they couldn't go anywhere in fact – without me.

Now I'd started thinking, a host of new ideas crowded into my mind. 'Unlike some men,' I thought, 'I don't talk a lot about what I can do. I don't need the whole Gathering to tell me I can hunt, or fish, or dance, or make love, or sing or do anything well at all. I've never fought other men if I could help it. Even when I was a boy I didn't squabble or fight much. Since I took Alaia, and lived in this family, I've watched them argue but I've never said much myself. But the fact is, now Bakar's gone, I'm the one who's in charge here. Of course I'll not shame my wife's father in front of his daughters. I'll show him proper respect, but' – this was another new thought – 'he must know as well as I do how matters stand.'

I glanced at my wife's father, who was splitting the pig's thigh-bone to suck out the marrow. His eyes were downcast and he seemed absorbed in what he was doing. I was staring at him without realising it. When he suddenly looked up and caught my gaze my eyes dropped at once. Even so I'd seen the look he gave me. Old he might be, but his eyes were as piercing as ever. I felt the hot blood redden my cheeks, and hoped it didn't show in the firelight. Because in that look I read that not only did he know exactly what I was thinking, but he'd thought of it all himself, long before any of it had occurred to me.

Nekané said:

All winter I searched in every place I knew, right to the edges of our hunting grounds. I went down Long Strait beyond Boat Crossing Camp. When I got to my sister Sorné's winter Camp the men were away hunting in the hills. But Sorné sees everyone: she told me that no one for far around had seen my son that winter. I realised by now that I wouldn't find Bakar alive, but I needed to know what had happened to him. If only I could *know* it would be easier, or so I felt.

The others seemed to have let him go. At first they mourned almost as much as I did, but as the ripples fade and vanish after a fish has leaped into the Sun then disappeared again into deep water, so too did the memories of Bakar fade from the minds of his family. Only I, his mother, never ceased to think of him.

In Dark Moon the nights become dangerous and powerful and almost swallow up the days. For half a Moon the days were so starved and shrunken it seemed as though they could never recover. Day after day the wind was from the Sunless Sky. Blizzards and hail came down with the wind, and blotted out the weary Sun. For seven nights we saw no stars. On the eighth night the wind died. The snow lay still at last; it had grown so thick it reached almost to the top of the door. We'd piled thick logs across the doorway to keep it out. The clouds died with the wind, and when Amets dug away the snow so that we could step outside everything was quiet. We heard a big branch snap under its weight of snow. The sky blazed with stars.

I trudged over the frozen snow. Once more I climbed Look-out Hill. I read the shape of the hills in the darkness where there were no stars.

I looked up at the River of Milk that spurted from the breast of our First Mother – the white River that spans the sky and dims the farthest stars. I saw it as a sandy strand where a man might easily walk. Although the air was freezing I stood staring, and I saw how the stars were as many as the grains of sand on the shore. It was as though the hide of an immense beast had been hooked back from a huge door. Inside a house one can see no further than one can stretch out one's hand and touch. A house holds us close, like children in the womb. But when the hide is lifted from the door you can see across the world to where the sea meets the sky. And sometimes in the winter Moons it's the same when you look into the sky: everything is sharp and clear and bright, and there are more stars in the sky than you'd ever see on a summer night.

I looked into the stars, and I saw the shape of my son Bakar. I saw him stand above the River of Milk with his bow over his shoulder and his knife hanging from his belt. Red spirit-lights flickered round his head. His wolfskin cloak streamed across the sky, green as the sea. And I knew that I must search for him in places more different than I'd ever dreamed of.

On every cloudless night after that, I went up Look-out Hill and watched the stars. As the Sun got tired the nights grew strong. One by one new stars peered over the Morning hills, ready to begin their winter journey. Each night they climbed higher before they dropped into the Deep Sea under the Evening Sun Sky. Slowly the Hunter shook himself free of the horizon. Soon the timid Marten followed him, crouching low, ready to run back to his cave before day came and put him out. As the Sun grew weak the dark grew strong. I was glad. Like the winter stars, my journey belonged to the night, and the braver the dark grew the more I welcomed it.

One day a Dark Moon will come when the nights will swallow the days for ever, and when that happens our world will end. Every person who was ever born must have wondered if the last Dark Moon would come in their lives, but it never has, and now I have travelled far enough to know that there is much more still to come, and many more lives to be lived, before the Sun dies.

But that winter my eyes were on the dark. The days were an empty waste. I lay in the sleeping place and turned my face to the wall. When my family all danced in the melting snow to greet the light I wouldn't raise my head. They thought I was ill, and so perhaps I was, for what is ill? I don't know if I ate or drank or slept. I only know that slowly the days passed, and each one was far too long.

Each night, when the dark came, my man lay down in his usual place beside me. I ignored him, and when his breathing told me that he slept I slid from under the thick bearskin and crept away from my family, where they lay in their bed places round the hearth, all fast asleep. I pushed aside the hides that covered the door, and stepped into the freezing night. Did I wrap a fur round me? Did I put on my sealskin boots or my hood? I don't remember. Perhaps I stood under the icy stars with no protection at all. Perhaps not. But the small things we do every day to protect ourselves – the way we take care to be warm and dry in winter, cool in summer – the way we eat when we're hungry and drink when we're thirsty and sleep when we're tired – the way we enjoy and comfort one another – none of these things seemed to matter any more.

In Thaw Moon Esti was born, and her father recognised her. I should have been very happy to see my daughter a mother and I still as strong as ever, and able to travel as far as I liked. I knew that much of my life still lay before me. Ever since I'd seen Bakar outlined in the stars, I knew that the next direction would be new and strange. As the Sun recovered its strength, I did too. I began to go out in daylight again, and to eat and drink with the others. I could see they all hoped that whatever illness had struck me down in Dark Moon had gone away for ever. I knew I hadn't been ill. I came back into the world only for a breathing space. I had to gather my strength for what lay ahead.

Alaia said:

Slowly the Sun came back. The days grew longer and milder. Most of the gulls had gone to sea, but we were woken earlier every day by the blackbirds in the thicket, telling us that spring was on its way. Catkins dangled from the hazels; birch twigs took on the purple tinge that promises green leaves. Rising sap filled birch bark and pine bark with the delicious flavours of spring. Celandines lay like stars along our paths, and the trees overhead were filled with song. The oaks were black and bare against blue sky, but even their buds were beginning to swell if you looked closely enough.

The Marten disappeared below the High Sun Sky, but even though the stars were telling us it was spring the dark still brought the frost with it, and we spent many evenings by the inside fire. One evening, when my mother appeared to be sleeping, my father said to Amets, 'We won't go to Flint Camp this Year.'

My hands were still. Not go to Flint Camp? Not meet our cousins, and gather flints, and fish for saithe among the islets in the loch, and build big fires with fresh firewood, and feast in the dusk on sea-fish and seal meat? I'd been thinking about Flint Camp all through Limpet Moon. I'd been holding on until the meltwater spate was over so we could launch the boat and paddle towards the Morning Sun Sky, round Hidden Shelter Point, along the Sunless shore to Flint Camp.

I'd been scraping an otter pelt in the light of the fire. When my father spoke I pressed the soft red fur against my cheek as if that could bring me comfort. Esti lay sleeping; I felt her warm skin against my back. In the silence after my father spoke we heard the rain swishing on the wet ground outside, soaking our already-sodden walls. Daylight filtered in at the smoke hole, mingling with the firelight. The fire ate away at the end of a long oak branch whose cold end stuck out way beyond the hearth circle. The flames licking round the wood sounded like water trickling across the floor. Haizea dropped her scraper, and the bone made a little clunk against one of the hearthstones. With our hearts in our throats we waited for Amets to speak.

'What about firewood?' said Amets at last.

'It's spring,' said my father. 'The sea will let us through. You and I can take the big boat along the shore and fill it with wood from further off.'

Amets moved the oak log further into the fire. After a while he said, 'We've only three flint cores left. I doubt if there's more than a hand-full of good blades left in them.'

'Flint won't go away,' said my father. 'We can get it later. There's an old Flint Camp at Boat-Hazel River. We can go there and find what we need for now.'

Amets was silent. Then he said, 'I could get us much more meat at Flint Camp. I wouldn't have to hunt alone.'

'We are few,' said my father. He held his left hand up with all five fingers spread, and his right forefinger. 'That's all. The brown trout are rising already. We can catch those. We can set more eel traps. And if we stay here Alaia and Haizea can still get roots from the marsh. And now the days are longer there's nothing to stop them getting sea-roots from the shore, and more shellfish.'

Amets looked at the ground. I felt my heart beat in my chest, but I couldn't speak. To be eating eels and shellfish and sea-roots right through the Moon of Rushes, when a bare day's paddle away our family would all be feasting together, with plenty of meat for everyone! I didn't want Esti to learn the Moon of Rushes as a season of wretched hearths and scanty food. I didn't want to go on living in our own dirt – it's unhealthy to stay in one place too long. But much more than that, I wanted to see my aunts and cousins. I wanted something done about my mother. There she lay, even as we sat by the hearth, with her face to the wall, pretending – in my anger I was sure it was all pretence – to be asleep.

'To fish for eels and river trout will be more work,' said Amets. 'I could take the boat and get sea-fish – I could get plenty for all of us – but you know how far I'd have to go to reach the grounds. The Moon of Rushes will rise tomorrow: we'd do better if we camped by open water.'

'Amets,' said my father, 'I'm thinking of Nekané when I say this.'

I lifted my head. 'Father, I know you want to help my mother. But it might be better for her – for all of us – if we get away and leave this sad winter behind us. My aunts and cousins are expecting us! We agreed when we left Gathering Camp that we'd all meet again at Flint Camp in the Moon of Rushes! My aunts might help her more than we can.'

'I might have known these women couldn't keep quiet,' said my father to Amets. 'I don't know what I did wrong, but these daughters of mine don't seem to have learned any respect.'

'I have no fault to find with your daughter,' said Amets, smiling. 'I'd like to hear what she has to say.'

'You would, would you? That's asking for trouble. But if Alaia gets uppity you'll be the one that has to live with it.' My father turned to me. 'So you think I'm making a mistake, little daughter?'

I looked him in the eye. 'You're speaking to the mother of your granddaughter, remember. Perhaps I've learned something, even though I haven't lived as long as you.

'I think my mother's sickness would be cured if we took her away from this place where my brother was lost. Flint Camp would remind her of all the good things in our lives. It would be better for us too. We've been away from the others for long enough. We've suffered, and we're tired. We need food and warmth and company. If we stay here it'll be like a bad dream.' I added boldly, 'That's what my brother would say, I know.'

'Alaia,' said my father, speaking directly to me, quite gently, 'all that you say is true. For a woman you're learning to be Wise. But there's more in this than you understand.' He sighed. 'Yes,' he went on, as if he were speaking to himself, 'it will be like a bad dream, because that's exactly what it is. Alaia, Haizea, Amets . . .' He looked round at us all as we gazed at him in the firelight. A gust of rain swept against the house, and a spatter of drops came through the smoke hole and hissed in the fire. 'I've known Nekané for longer than any of you. She's done all that a woman should. She's given me five children. Three lived, and she taught them to look after themselves. Two little ones died here at River Mouth Camp. We wrapped them in birch-bark and hung their bodies from a high tree when the snow was on the ground. The spirits took them home. She's provided well for all of us. But now there's something else . . . She's wandering in places that I can't see. The possibility was always there, like a seed in dry ground. And now our son's gone . . . Alaia, you tell me that you're a mother now and not my little daughter. Your mother lives, but you don't need her any more. We have to let her become what she will.'

Haizea gave a little sob. 'But *I'm* not grown up. Why can't we take Mother to Flint Camp and let her get better with our family there, and then we can all be happy again?'

'You have Alaia,' my father reminded her. 'You've been lucky to have two mothers for so long. So that's enough!' He turned to me. 'You're right, Alaia. If we took Nekané to Flint Camp no doubt we could bring her back into the good world of familiar things where you and I will always dwell. But if we did that, there's something in her that would be unsatisfied. And for our People too – what would we become, if there were no dreams? If there were no one to Go-Between?'

'Go-Between'. The word was said. My hands flew to my cheeks. Amets looked up under his brows, his hands – he'd been plaiting twine in the firelight – suddenly still. Haizea looked from one firelit face to another, trying to understand. Even Amets' dog stirred and growled in its sleep. This was the thing hanging over us, which we'd all been dreading. 'Go-Between'. Not in our family, no! We'd lost my brother – why did we now have to put up with this?

'If that's how it is,' said my father, 'then for the sake of all our kin we must accept it. That's why we must stay here for now, and let her be.'

So my father had the last word, and after that we let the days go past when we would have launched the boat and gone down-river. Soon my mother went away again. We waited for her to come back.

I'd never seen spring at River Mouth before. The first crumpled hazel leaves unfurled. The birches turned from purple to pale green, and the sallows put out stiff little catkins. Only the oaks still stretched their empty twigs towards the sky, while the ivy clinging to their trunks looked dusty under the new Sun. When we dug for roots the brown marshwater was almost warm against our legs. We chewed fresh garlic leaves as we walked through the woods, and when we pushed aside the scrub with our digging sticks we found violets hiding under the birches like little bits of sky. We gathered sorrel and silverweed, while all along the River toads basked in the first heat and mayflies danced above eddies of still water. Our winter fire seemed to dwindle in the Sun, and when I went inside the tent everything was dark and green as if I'd dived into deep water.

The heat on my back was like the touch of a spirit; all day the good light fell round me in a shower of birdsong. Winter was past: we'd all lived. Esti was born – she had a name – she lived. In spite of these good things I was unhappy. Even when everything has gone well for a small family, it's good to see the others after the long cold Moons when the family is splintered into little pieces at the winter Camps. It's like being made whole again. That was the hardest winter I ever lived through. I felt the loss of my brother. I wanted my little daughter to find her kin as soon as possible. That was all the more important because she was Esti, and came from her father's People. It couldn't be too soon to plait the careful threads that would bind her to the Auk People. But my father had decided, and so we stayed on at River Mouth Camp.

Haizea and I fished for the brown trout that were beginning to rise from the bottom of the pools. At first we lay on the banks upriver and caught them in our hands. When the Sun grew warmer we grew wary of fishing the upland pools, because these were given to the bears, not us, in Moon of Rushes. Amets killed a young bear that came out to fish in High Tarn. He set the skull in the tree next to the boar skull, so we had both Bear and Boar to watch over us.

Haizea and I scraped the bear hide clean, and stretched it on a frame. We rubbed it with the bear's brains and ashes, and propped it downwind of a smoky fire. We kept on rubbing it every day until the hide was as soft and white as a swan's feather on the inside. It's a beautiful pale-brown pelt – that winter cloak should last me all my life. Once the bears were on the move, hungry after their long sleep, Haizea and I went downstream and fished for trout with lines and baited juniper hooks, though sometimes we sneaked upriver in the early mornings and took the headless bodies of the fish the bears had thrown away. We cut hazel wands and willow withies, and made more eel traps. Every day we walked the shoreline at low tide, taking turns to carry Esti on our backs, and dug for sea-roots. Once the sap began to rise we collected strips of birchbark for tents and baskets. We scraped all the inner bark clean and mashed it up with the sea-roots. We weren't hungry – I can't say any better than that.

At last my mother came back. She came into River Mouth Camp at twilight. Haizea and I had caught enough trout to fill a small basket. We were rolling them in sea-root paste, and roasting them on twigs at the outside hearth. As fast as they were cooked we were all eating them, burning our fingers and then licking the juice off them. Esti lay against my heart, eyes half open, watching the firelight flicker, suckling sleepily while I turned the fishes. She was growing firm and round, alert as a wagtail. Haizea was never far from my side, watching over her.

Haizea said:

I was the first to see Mother come back. I just looked up from the fire and there she was, standing at the edge of the clearing. She looked white like a dead person. I screamed. Everyone looked round. Alaia leaped to her feet, holding Esti to her heart.

My father didn't get up. He said in his usual voice, 'Welcome back, wife. There's not much to eat – these girls have managed very badly without you – but we can offer you a small fish if you're hungry enough.'

My mother smiled and stepped forward. The fire shed its warm light on her and she stopped looking so pale. I hadn't seen my mother smile since my brother was lost. She said, 'They look like fine fish to me, a very good catch for the hungry Moons. You should be grateful for your clever daughters. And grateful to the woman who taught them, too!'

I hadn't heard my mother speak with a laugh in her voice since my brother went away. I felt as if my real mother had been dead all this while and now she'd suddenly come alive. I jumped up and ran into her arms and hugged her. I'd missed her so much. I was only a child, remember. My mother was hugging me, and I was laughing and crying all at once. She spoke to me in the old way: 'Yes, yes, little one. I've come home. It's all right. Everything is changed and it's going to be all right.'

I didn't know what she meant by 'changed'. I don't know if she had any idea then of the troubles that lay ahead, or of how she was going to deal with them. But this I can say: although Nekané has travelled so far and done so many things for our People, although she became Go-Between and could never be with us in quite the way she was before, she's never again rejected her children or been unfaithful to them. After she came back she couldn't be the sort of mother I'd had before. But that was all right: I was growing older myself, and I had Alaia, and later on Osané. So no one can say I've ever been short of a mother, except in that bad winter after Bakar was lost. I don't even like to remember it. I think we should pass over all that now, and go on to what happened two Moons later, in Egg Moon, when we were at White Beach Camp.

Nekané said:

Before we do that, I'll tell you how I left behind the woman I'd been before, and how I was born into a world that was new to me. I can't say everything because it would destroy you to hear it. But the story I'm about to tell won't hurt you, so there's no need to look afraid.

I'd wandered far inland, past the Long Loch and the Boat Crossing Path, and by hunters' paths into the hills around our Mother Mountain. At River Mouth Camp the Year was already beginning to grow strong and green, but it was too young to have reached the hills. I walked back into the old Year, right up into the high snows. I climbed beyond the oaks, through the birch and scrub willow, past juniper and myrtle, up into the empty places where People are not meant to go until the Year has opened the way for them. There was no food up there. It was very cold. I didn't care. I was thinking only of Bakar. It was in the old Year that he went away, so only by returning to the old Year could I follow him.

When I reached the bare rock, Mother Mountain was hidden in mist and I couldn't go any further. I squatted down, leaning forward with my arms between my knees to rest my aching back. I stayed there in the shelter of a little cliff while the cloud swirled above my head, sometimes dipping down to smother me. It was too wet and cold to sleep much. I had no food. If I'd had no purpose I'd have died, but my purpose burned inside my ribs and kept me from freezing.

I waited for days and nights and then a dawn came when everything came clear. The cold Sun struck the rocks and made them gleam. I looked at the little cliff above me and saw a place where I could climb up. Lichen and mosses grew among the boulders, but the bloom of the new Year wasn't on them. I was glad of that, because my purpose lay in the past. I came to the top of the hill. The air was still and cold. A greater world than I had ever seen glimmered at my feet. I saw beyond the lands of our People and the lands of our People's kin. I saw range upon range of hills, from our own lands which we know, into the far blue where there are no more names.

I saw the Sun cross the sky and set behind an unknown horizon. I saw the stars move through the circling Year. Yet again I saw the Sun cross the sky. I watched it travel through the high paths of summer and the small paths of winter. I saw the Moons wax and wane. I saw how the Years were born, and how they died and came back again, and how everything that lives follows the pattern of the circling Years through all the births and deaths from the Beginning.

As I watched I died. No living creature can see all the Years and live. I died. My body lay on the hill. Ravens came and pecked out my eyes. They tore my belly open and ripped out my guts and ate them. Lynx drove away the ravens, and feasted on my stomach and my heart. Wolves came and devoured my limbs, splitting open my bones to eat the marrow. And last of all came Bear, who tipped up my skull and licked out the meat inside it.

As the Sun sank into the far-off sea, a Dolphin came out of the water and swam through the sky. He leaped joyfully through the waves all around the high hill where my body had once lain. I heard him call. I sat up. My Dolphin swam so fast I couldn't look into his eye, but I could see how he was watching me. His glance was kind. I heard him laugh. In my old life I thought the sea Animals spoke without making any sounds that People hear, but now I often hear their laughter.

When my Dolphin dived into the deep again, sadness pierced me through, opening the wound below my ribs which I got when I lost my son. I watched my Dolphin go, and from the ripples of his dive I saw Swan rise into the air, flapping his wings to get free of the water. I'd seen that Swan before. In the world I'd left, I'd seen that Swan rise from the still water at River Mouth Camp. I hadn't known it was carrying Bakar's soul out of our world. Now I understood. Swan told me that while Bakar was out of the world Swan would accompany me instead. My Swan told me that he wouldn't leave me – although there would be many days and nights when I saw nothing of him – until the Moon came when he would bring Bakar back to us.

That's how Dolphin and Swan came to be my Helpers. I know some of you have seen them just as I do. Not everyone can see them. But every one of you knows them, because, through me, they are Helpers for us all. If we hadn't lost Bakar, they wouldn't have found their way to us. I can't say – none of us can say – how things might have been better or worse. All I can say is, 'This is how it is.' And that's as much about my path to Wisdom as I'm able to tell you.

SECOND NIGHT: WHITE BEACH CAMP

Haizea said:

Last night we told you how Bakar was lost and my mother went Go-Between. I can see it's going to take a while to tell this story. I don't know how many nights you'll have to sit here listening to us talk. The story's like a River: it flows as it will, and no one can make it go any faster. The Go-Betweens want us to tell you everything that happened after my brother was lost. They say it's the only way for us Auk People to decide about the Lynx names. So listen, all of you!

In Auk Moon a cold wind came from the Sunless Sky and blew away the cloud that had settled over us. Day after day the Sun shone down. Spirits woke in the woods and marshes. The gorse turned flame-yellow as if the Sun had showered down sparks of fire that fell like snow. The air smelt heavy as honey with gorse-blossom. From the shore we saw the first Auk flying over the shining waves. Joyfully we held up our arms to greet them. Sand Island looked near enough to throw a stone across, even though it was a day's voyage away.

My father watched the auks flying towards the Evening Sun Sky. He looked at them for a long while. He said that now we should leave River Mouth Camp, and go to White Beach Island.

I was so excited! The spirits who watched over my birth had been waiting for me at White Beach Camp for ten winters. Some People return to their Birth Place every Year; I don't think those People can guess what it was like to be me the day I first returned to White Beach Camp.

The sea only lets us through to White Beach Island in certain Years. Sometimes we go to Sand Island in Auk Moon; sometimes we move to another Camp on Mother Mountain Island. But in some Years a small cold breeze flows from the Sunless Sky and lingers under the young Sun. The wind from the sea gives way to it, taking the clouds with it. Sky and sea blaze blue, as if the stars are on fire and won't let the daylight put them out. Islands move in closer. Little sounds from far off ring across the water, clear as pebbles in a spring. The sea flattens into a bright path that beckons us into open water, further than anyone would want to take a boat in ordinary Years. Those are the Years when our families know they'll find each other at White Beach Camp in Auk Moon.

Day after day my father climbed Look-out Hill. Every day he stood there for a long while. He felt the wind against his cheek. He watched the birds flying over the marshes. He gazed towards the Sunless Sky, looking far-off through the Narrows to the place where our River meets Open Sea.

My father told us that the sea would soon be ready to let us through. We let the wind speak softly to the sea until the swell went down. The day we left, the sky was the colour of the bluebells under the birches, with swirly streaks of cloud high up, like blown smoke. We covered the hearth at River Mouth Camp with turfs. We left dry firewood inside the winter house. We stretched our arms up to the spirits who'd watched over us at River Mouth Camp. We explained to Bear and Boar that we were going away for a while. We gave our clearing back to the Animals, and told them that if we were still alive we'd like to come back to River Mouth Camp in Yellow Leaf Moon.

We floated our big boat. We loaded it with hides and birch-bark, furs, baskets of roots, bundles of bone and antler, and meat and water for our journey. Life is usually easy at White Beach Camp, but we take plenty of work with us, and do it outside during the long days when the Sun gives us as much light and warmth as he possibly can. We paddled downriver through reeds and grasses taller than a man. Our boat slipped past the birch that overhangs the stream – the tree with the mossy fishing-place where we lie along the trunk dangling our lines. We glided past our fish traps. The River widened and went mud-coloured. Reeds and bullrushes hid its banks. Moorhens paddled out of range as we slid past.

We came into open water. Geese grazed in the salt flats. The sea flooded into the estuary, pushing the River backwards as it tried to escape towards the sea. Brown river-water was lost in the flood like smoke in mist. In the Narrows the flood would be too strong for us. We paddled out of the current, between rafts of floating seaweed, towards the Morning Sun shore. It was almost the middle of the day. We laid our paddles across the lip of the boat, and waited for my father to say the word.

At last the Sun climbed as high as the young Year would let him. My father stared at the sky. He smelt the wind. He watched the water lapping higher up the shore. Now the tide was wetting the stones four fists below the line of dead leaves and seaweed which marked the height of the spring flood. Three fists . . . nearly two fists . . .

'Now!'

In a heartbeat Amets leaped into shallow water and pushed us away from the shore. He scrambled over the stern as the current caught us. The tide still flooded through the Narrows, but it was getting weaker. We paddled as hard as we could. Now we were into the Narrows. The sea ran swift and deep between low cliffs. The rocks on each side rose sheer as if the land had been sliced open with a knife. The tide grew weaker. The River grew stronger. Now the River was helping us against the tide. The Narrows opened out between rocky islets. Through our boat-hide we felt the pulse of the Open Sea.

Waves lapped our bows. The boat stirred at the familiar taste of salt. Its winter sleep was over; we felt it waken under us.

The men sat on the bundles of furs to paddle, with the spears and harpoons lashed alongside. Everyone smelt of seal blubber because Alaia had rubbed so much of it into our sea cloaks. She'd made me help her. I'd said I didn't think we need do *all* the cloaks every Year. But she was right as usual: we were soaked with spray long before we reached White Beach Camp. The dogs crouched uneasily on top of all the things. Alaia was our fire guardian now my mother was Go-Between. The fire guardian has to be someone who stays in this world and isn't likely to suddenly go away or forget all about it. Alaia carried the fire in a leather bag lined with damp moss, arranged so the oak embers wouldn't burn through the hide. We knew that whatever the weather brought us, our fire would be safe with Alaia.

The sea crinkled and sparkled under the Sun. Seals slept on the skerries beyond River Mouth, wet bodies gleaming. One or two raised their heads to watch us pass, but they didn't move. They knew that no Seal had agreed to give itself that day. The wind from the Sunless Sky touched my right cheek with its cold finger. We met it head on, paddling as fast as we could into the slackening flood.

I knelt in the bows between my father's knees. I paddled on one side and he paddled on the other. I'd made myself a new paddle because my old one was too small, and my father let me think that my hard paddling helped us along. When we'd cleared River Mouth and turned towards the Evening Sun Sky, Amets raised the mast. Soon the wind filled our sail. My father said I needn't paddle any more, although he never broke his own stroke for as much as a heartbeat. I dabbled my fingers in the shining water and watched Fierce Point grow nearer.

White gulls wheeled overhead. Rafts of auks in their new spring feathers slid over the waves. I felt that old Aurochs' hide come alive against the soles of my feet when he felt the sea against his skin. He saw how the Auks let the sea slide away under them, and he did the same. He hadn't forgotten he was Animal. Through his skin I felt the sea ripple against my skin. I flexed my toes against his frame, and I felt the strength in the hazel wands as they remembered to bend with the sea. Small waves made slapping sounds against his side. Our boat was Auk. We – Aurochs, Hazel, Willow, Dog and People – were Boat-Animal. We were Auk.

Slowly River Mouth country turned from grey-green to blue under the High Sun Sky. The cliffs of Mother Mountain Island were like rows of teeth snarling at us. White water curled over the reefs off Fierce Point: we kept well away. Now we were coming into different water. The tides met, tossing our boat to and fro between them. At the foot of each swell we couldn't see over the crest. Amets' young dog started whining. But the flood was slackening. My father had been too clever for it, and its strength was almost gone. We rounded Fierce Point at slack water into the great groundswell of the Open Sea. Now, far off under the High Sun Sky, we saw the soft blue shadow of White Beach Island.

The ebb tide swept us forward. The sea settled into a slow swell. Looking back under the sail, I saw the snow-capped mountains of the lands that lie under the Sunless Sky. Beyond those mountains Amets' family have their summer Camps. That's Esti's country, although our Esti hasn't been there in her present life. Ahead of us, White Beach Island turned from a hump in the blue distance to firm land with green grass and thickets of trees. Between us and the island lay islets surrounded by stretches of gleaming seaweed and drying reefs.

'Take down the sail!'

Amets obeyed my father at once. Our boat rocked in the swell. Seaweed rose and fell beside us, so close I tried to reach out and touch it.

'Stop that, Haizea! Amets, listen to me! We're coming into the channel. No, you can't see it yet. As we go through I'll tell you the sea-marks. B . . . my son . . . he knew the marks as well as I do. Now it'll be up to you. I'm not saying these women mightn't know something about it. Women are always listening to what doesn't concern them! But if you rely on your wife to tell you your sea-marks, you might as well cut off your balls now and be done with it. So listen, and remember!'

We all had to paddle as my father steered us through the seaweed-covered rocks that guard White Beach Island. My arms were so tired! But my ears were busier than my arms. White Beach Island was *my* Birth Place, long before Amets ever came among the Auk People. I listened just as hard as Amets to every word my father said. Some of you have every reason to be glad I did – but that's another story.

The sea turned from grey to green as our boat slid in with the waves over sandy shallows and waving forests of brown weed. Starfish scuttled away from the shadow of our boat. Shafts of evening Sun slanted across the island. Long shadows reached towards us from every rock and hummock, as if the island were stretching out its arms to its returning daughter. I stood up in the bows, eagerly scanning the shores of my Birth Place. As we slid into the bay the shadow of the island swallowed us. A cold finger of onshore breeze touched my shoulder. Then I saw a small boat in the hollow at the top of the beach. Whose was it? I caught my breath in excitement. But now the sand was growing so close I could see the ripples in it under the water, and little coils of worm cast. A wave caught us. We rode in on the curve of it and landed on firm sand.

As soon as we grounded I leaped ashore, clutching the hide-tail to pull the boat in, but I could hardly wait to hand it to Alaia, who jumped on to the sand after me, Esti bouncing on her back. I could see the camping place. I scrambled joyfully up the slippery dunes.

'Haizea, come back! There's work to do!'

'I'll be quick!'

It was at White Beach Camp that I came back into this world, and it's there I've been happiest ever since. I love the long days, and the nights that grow just dark enough to show the stars in their courses. I love the bright Moons of the still-young Year. The sound of the Open Sea was in my ears when I drew my first breath, and whenever I go back to White Beach Camp I greet it as my friend. I love the changing moods of the sea, and the rough days when there's no path back to where we came from. When the boats can't put to sea the island of White Beach Camp is the whole world, and when I first came back to it I thought it was just the right size: not large and difficult, but contained and perfect. Yet the thing that makes White Beach Camp the place that it is – the very reason why I love it so – is that even in the best Years of all we're only there from Auk Moon to Seed Moon. We come after the auks have arrived, and we leave before they do; otherwise there'd be nothing to eat on days when the sea's too angry to let us fish or seal.

After that long winter on our own I was excited about seeing our family again. And someone was here already! I ran past our shell heaps – the oldest ones were almost covered over with bright green turf – on to the soft turf of the Camp, still barely trodden. A small fire simmered in the hearth. Someone had laid wet seaweed over the whitened drift-logs to keep it in.

And someone had pitched a tent – a small hunting tent with a wolf-fur flap over the door. Using wolfskin for a door flap! That was showing off! I knew who it was. It would be like him to arrive early, maybe with one of his younger brothers. The hide was hooked back from the door to let in the morning Sun. But the Sun was looking the other way by now.

'Haizea is here!' I shouted. 'And my father' – I called out his name – 'and Amets! And Nekané, and Alaia! And Esti! We have a new cousin for you! We have ESTI!'

No one answered. I pushed the dogs aside and peered into the dim tent. When I looked into the small space I felt the boat still rocking inside my head. A big bearskin was spread in the sleeping place. I knew that bearskin! I remembered very well how six men had carried that bear into Gathering Camp, and I also remembered the great feast, the Go-Between's chant to Bear – which had really frightened me – and the dancing that had followed. There were no baskets inside the tent – that meant they'd gone out for food.

I ran back to the top of the beach. Already our gear was piled up on the sand. 'Father! Mother! Alaia! Cousin Sendoa is here! With someone else, but I can't tell who! It's SENDOA!'

'Haizea, come down here at once! D'you think there's no work to be done?'

I went down to help with the loaded baskets.

'Perhaps your daughter thinks she's already one of the Wise,' said Amets, laughing. 'She thinks she doesn't have to carry gear like the rest of us!'

'She's no good,' agreed my father. 'You'll bring yours up

better. Give her a good beating sometimes. It's never too soon to start with these women!'

My mother and Alaia were laughing, but I wasn't. I was at the age when I was beginning to want some sort of respect which my family weren't prepared to give me. All this talk of beatings made me feel like a child. It was stupid, anyway. My father had never beaten me, nor Alaia either, and he never would. I'd heard enough stories at Gathering Camp to know that in some families it was different. The trouble was I'd grown old enough to pay attention to what the men and women were always saying to each other, and to realise that I would have to be a woman too, quite soon, so all this was going to have something to do with me. But I was still young enough to resent it when the joke seemed to be against me.

Amets said:

I was pleased to find Sendoa at White Beach Camp! Sendoa is one of the best hunters of the Auk People. We pulled up the boat, and carried up the gear. Alaia dumped her baskets, went straight to Sendoa's tent and disappeared inside it. I wondered what she was doing. When she came out she said nothing, but her mouth was set in a hard line.

'Ah,' said my wife's father, as he stood at my shoulder. 'She was hoping to find some sign . . . Young men, travelling together . . . Sendoa's winter Camp is on the Long Strait . . . He could have gone that way . . . But no, she's found nothing.' He turned away. 'Ah well . . .'

We all stood round the hearth while Alaia put our fire with the one that was already there. Our spirits saw our fire and came to join the others who were already at White Beach Camp. We held up our arms to them and thanked them for bringing us safely across the sea. Then Haizea was sent to gather shell-fish to eat with the rush roots we'd brought across. Alaia and I went to find our old tent poles in the dry hollow above the dunes, while Nekané peeled back the turf from the inside hearth. The poles were in good condition. I lashed twine around one weak place, just to be sure. Then I helped Alaia put up the frame, and I tied the wands together at the smoke hole. I'm telling you this because I want you boys to know that I'm not ashamed to help women with their work sometimes. I hope you're all listening to me: you don't always have to do nothing, just to show a woman how clever you are! Anyway, Alaia's shorter than I am so it's easier for me to reach. I unrolled the birch-bark round the smoke hole and tied it down. Only then did I leave Nekané and Alaia to lash the rest of the frame. My wife's father and I carried the heavy rolls of hide up from the beach, and dumped them by the tent frame.

We strolled back to the beach. The tide was at the turn, lapping the stern of our boat. 'It's enough,' said my wife's father. 'When Sendoa comes he'll help us pull her up further in case the weather changes. Like this, she's all right.'

I felt I must speak, and called him by name.

'Yes, Amets?'

'Alaia – when she went to look in Sendoa's tent just now, you said . . . You mean she's still hoping for some sign of her brother? She doesn't make any fuss about it. But Nekané – before, in the winter, she was always looking. And now . . .'

'And now – she's not? That's what you're asking me, isn't it? You're asking why Nekané has stopped searching for our son.'

'Because – forgive me if I'm upsetting you – because—'

'Because she knows she'll find nothing.'

'I'm sorry, I – I . . .'

'You don't upset me, Amets. I knew it long ago. I'm not one of the Wise. I never needed to struggle after knowledge as

Nekané has had to do. What someone has to go through to become Go-Between – no, I never had to worry about any of that. But I knew about my son . . . Amets, I've seen a great deal. See here: a young man leaves his family. He may be far away and alone, and the dangers are very great. You know that: you were travelling alone when you came to us, looking for a wife. Young men are foolhardy, too.'

'Your son was *not* foolhardy.'

'No. That's true. But he was no coward either, and, as we both know, the dangers are very great.'

'Do you have any ideas about what happened to him?'

'Only simple ones, Amets. An accident, a fall, a fight . . . who knows? Perhaps you'll have a son one day. But you know already: the dangers are very great.'

Just then the dogs barked in welcome. We heard a shout from along the beach. We turned and saw two men, one running full tilt towards us, his dogs leaping at his side, the other lagging a little behind.

'Sendoa!' My wife's father hugged him, slapping him on the back. Then Sendoa turned to me, and we slapped our hands together in delight. I vowed to the spirits, then and there, that I would never again pass a winter without a man of my age for company. And indeed I never have.

'And who's this?' My wife's father was frowning. I looked up, and saw that the man standing by was not any kin that I knew of, but wholly a stranger.

Well, you all know who I'm talking about. But back then none of us knew that this stranger was part of our story. When I first laid eyes on him, no spirit whispered in my ear, 'Remember Bakar!' Or if one did, I didn't hear it.

'All is well.' Sendoa took the young man's arm and pulled him forward. 'All is well' – he spoke to my wife's father by name – 'This is Kemen, of the Lynx People who live under the

Morning Sun. Although he's not of our People, he's kin of mine, and therefore of yours, because his grandfather's father was from the Auk People. He was called Basajaun, and he married a woman from the lands under the Morning Sun long ago. So when Kemen and some of his family travelled this way they came seeking us, the Auk People, because they knew us for their far-off kin.'

'Basajaun?' My wife's father frowned a little less. 'Yes, that name has been among us, though not in my family.'

'Kemen came towards the Evening Sun with his brother Basajaun,' said Sendoa. 'So you see a name from our People still lives among theirs.'

'And where is this brother Basajaun now?'

'We parted,' said Kemen. I was startled by his voice: his tongue was different from ours and he spoke his words strangely. 'Four of us came to this coast. We met another People, the Heron People, that way' – he pointed towards the High Sun Sky, and my wife's father nodded – 'and one of my cousins took a woman there, so the others decided to stay as well. But I came to look for the Auk People because I didn't want to settle with a woman before I'd found kin of my own. Because I had none. So I travelled on alone, and I met Sendoa's family at their winter Camp. I told them who I was, and they took me in. Then Sendoa and I decided to come early to White Beach Camp because we'd seen a lot of auks about already, and we wanted to be at the cliffs early.'

My wife's father was silent, looking Kemen over. Kemen politely avoided the older man's gaze. I watched Kemen too. I liked what I saw. He had thick dark hair and blue eyes like Alaia's; it wasn't hard to believe he was her kin. He wasn't as tall as I was, but he looked sturdy. On this warm day he was only wearing his loincloth and a deerskin tunic without sleeves, so I could see how strong his muscles were. If he had skill to go with his strength he would be just the sort of man one would wish to hunt with. I liked the way he stood up to my wife's father's scrutiny, standing there as tall as he could, with the confidence of one who had nothing to hide.

'Why do you say you have no kin?' asked my wife's father abruptly. 'How can that be? Didn't you leave kin behind you in the lands under the Morning Sun Sky?'

A shadow crossed Kemen's face. 'I expected you to ask that,' he said. 'I have a terrible story to tell. This winter – it was like no winter that ever happened since the Beginning. No, I have no kin, except for the three I left among the Heron People.'

My wife's father looked at Sendoa, as startled as I was. Sendoa nodded. 'It's true,' he said. 'Kemen, tell them!'

'No!' My wife's father held up his hand. 'If a man has no kin . . . This is indeed a terrible thing to hear, before you even begin to tell your story. But we must . . . Before we go back to Camp, just tell me this: you're not saying "I have no kin" because you've been cast out, are you?'

'Before all the spirits who live in your lands,' said Kemen, stretching both hands towards the sky, 'I say to you that I've done nothing wrong. My kin loved me as I loved them, and the terrible thing that happened was none of my doing. Look, let me show you that I'm telling you the truth!'

Kemen untied the strings of his tunic and pulled it off. He swung round to show his naked back. Five blue lines curved round one another and wrote something that was swift and lithe – an Animal stilled in a heartbeat of flowing movement – an Animal that knew how to creep, climb, hide, stalk, spring . . . something shy and fierce – an Animal we'd never seen written on a man's back before, but which we all recognised at once: Lynx!

'That reads true,' said my wife's father, 'though your word should have been enough.'

'I have no lies to tell,' said Kemen. 'But I want to tell you how—'

'You shall. But you'll also tell the Wise among us. Come!'

My wife's father turned on his heel and strode back to White Beach Camp. I glanced at Kemen and gave him a small smile, which he could read as he pleased. Sendoa slapped me on the back and linked his arm through mine. He seemed happy, but I couldn't help wondering if Kemen was telling the truth. Supposing he *had* been cast out? Had he murdered a kinsman, or raped a sister, or a cousin? How could a man say 'I have no kin' unless his People had sent him away? I didn't say anything though. Sendoa and I walked together and Kemen followed us, and so the three of us followed my wife's father back to Camp.

Kemen said:

This was the story I told them as we sat round the fire that evening at White Beach Camp. I told it as well as I could but it was difficult: their tongue was different from mine. I tried to speak as they did so they'd understand. But sometimes my words didn't work with them, and we had to seek for other words as I went along. Now, of course, I can tell you very easily. Nor could I know, then, that I was part of a story that began many Moons before I arrived. I'd never heard of Bakar – I knew nothing of the Auk People's loss.

So I began: the Year was eight Moons old, and my family were at our Fishing Camp, which lies – lay – at the mouth of a River. Where I come from, the land is low-lying, covered mostly with oaks and birch and hazel, which grow taller than they do here. All along our shores we have sand dunes – we *had* sand dunes – and long beaches. We don't have the bird cliffs you have here. That's why, when Sendoa described White

Beach Camp to me, I wanted to come with him at once to try my hand at this new sort of hunting. Anyway, our Camps are bigger than yours. The Lynx People lived quite close to each other, all down the shore and along the Rivers. We have *big* Rivers in my country. We fish all the Year round, and still the fish keep giving themselves. There are so many fish that many People don't even bother to go inland to hunt. We young men go, of course, but often some of the family stay at Fishing Camp all the Year round.

My brother Basajaun and I were at the age when we were often up at Hunting Camp with cousins like ourselves. Away from our families we could move fast across country and go where we liked. Basajaun is older than me, and always very daring. My mother used to say I was the cautious one. Basajaun would get us into trouble, and I'd be the one to find a way out. That's what she used to say, anyway.

Basajaun and I had just come back from a hunting trip. We'd killed an aurochs among the high birches, and we'd brought back our share of the meat – as much as we could carry. That got us a good welcome! We'd been back at Fishing Camp two days.

We were on the shore, Basajaun and I, a little way from our Camp, mending our boat. The hide was no good any more. It leaked. We'd stripped it off, and replaced some of the sinews that bound the hazel wands together. Now we were laying new hide over the frame. We'd already pierced the holes back at Camp, and we'd just started stitching the rawhide over the lip. Our dogs lay at our feet, disappointed because we weren't going anywhere. There was no hurry. The Year was past its prime, but the Sun wasn't too tired to burn the chill off the morning. There was no wind. The air was so clear we could hear children's voices back at the Camp, and the women laughing, and the rhythmic chink of stone on stone. Everything was ordinary, just as it should be.

But the dogs were growing restless. They whined and padded under our feet. They ran a few steps back to Camp, and whined again. 'Stop that!' Basajaun aimed a kick. The dogs cowered. After that they were quiet. When I looked up from my work again they'd gone. If they were bored they'd have headed back to Camp. I thought nothing of it.

We heard a far-off noise.

Basajaun stopped stitching and looked up. My hand, holding the needle, was still.

The noise was like thunder far away, only it never ceased. It was not above our heads. It came from under the Sunless Sky. I put down my needle, and stared out to sea.

Basajaun grabbed my arm – 'Look!'

The sands were growing bigger. I saw that first. No, that was wrong. The sea was shrinking. The tide was coming in – but the sea was going out. We saw, but also we couldn't see, because it wasn't possible. Out and further out – beyond the lowest tide. Sand we'd never seen before, pale and gleaming. Ripples like stars, and the frightened crabs scuttling over them. Fish flapping, madly trying to swim in this sudden world that had no water.

'Kemen! The sea! Look!'

I saw it then, far off under the Sunless Sky. A grey cliff, white-tipped. A cliff made of water. A noise like a mountain falling. My heart turned cold.

And the Camp behind us – my mother, my sisters, the children . . .

The grey cliff roared like a waterfall. Its sound filled the world. It raced towards us.

We froze.

The grey cliff crashing down. Our world ending.

'Kemen, run!'

My body came back to me. We raced back along the beach. The grey cliff screamed behind us.

Basajaun ran faster than me. He always could. I turned once. I saw the cliff made of water. All the thunder I'd ever heard was rolled up inside it. It flew towards me, faster than an eagle. I ran.

The trees bowed in the wind.

Basajaun glanced back. I smelt the water. It roared over us. It was swallowing my head. Basajaun ran back to me, and seized me by the shoulders. 'Too late. Hold on!'

The sea smashed down on us. Its roar swallowed us. It gobbled us like little fishes. Its belly was noise and whirlwind. We kicked and fought. No air. I was drowning. I died.

It was a kind of death, anyway. Because in that crashing sea my old life was swept away, and, in so far as I still walk the earth – I, Kemen, in this body – I've come back from the dead, so I must have been born all over again, out of that wave which swallowed Basajaun and me.

Because after I'd died – inside that whirling water-cliff – the sea spat us out.

We were tossing in rough water, still clinging together. There was air. I breathed air. I couldn't see. There was only water. Nothing else. Basajaun and I held on to each other. We tried to swim. He was stronger than me. I'd always been a better swimmer, but he was stronger. He held me up.

Something hit me in the back.

Basajaun cried, 'Hold on! Hold on!'

Before I knew what I did I held on. My hands clutched wet wood. It was an oak branch, sheered off at the end. We held on. It lay low in the water, but it rode the waves.

We were cold. If the Year had been any older we'd have died. The sea had just enough warmth in it for a strong man to live a short while. Basajaun and I were strong. We were together. That gave us twice the strength of one. We lived in that sea for a night and two days. We clung to our oak. We saw no land. We had no water. Our thirst was bad. It hurt to shout above the waves. The water grew calmer, but still we couldn't see. We were too low down to see over the waves – our land isn't high, like yours. There was nothing but sea, and sky.

The sky was kind to us. If the sky had been cruel we would have died. The sea had risen from its bed and tried to kill us. If the sky had done the same, and sent us bad weather, we would have died, for what's a man against the combined strength of sea and sky? But the sky was kind to us, even while the sea was cruel.

The sea forgave us. At last, as we rose to the top of the swell, we saw land: a blue line under the Evening Sun Sky. After that we watched for it whenever we came to the top of a wave. It looked so far away that there seemed little hope of reaching it. But Basajaun and I are strong, and we're brothers. Together we held our oak and kicked as hard as we could, swimming towards that distant strip of land.

Very slowly the land took shape. It turned from blue to green. At last we could see, from the top of the swell, a line of yellow sand. But we were so tired! Sometimes one of us rested, but never both at once, for fear of being swept back. Our legs ached with kicking. And now that we were working hard our thirst was growing. My dry tongue felt so huge I thought it would choke me. It was the thought of water, not of life itself, that kept me from going under. If we reached land there would be water. In the end I could think of nothing else.

At last we came to the breaking surf. A wave seized us. It hurled us forward. It was our friend. It dumped us, and drew away quickly as if the sea wanted nothing more to do with us. We crawled on to dry sand and lay face down like logs.

When I think of it I still feel the warmth of dry sand seeping into my body. I was so soaked in seawater that it came leaking out of my eyes as I lay. I stretched out my arms and let the sand sift through my fingers. It was grainy and warm, and almost dry. The spirits of the sea were done with us.

We had to find water. We didn't know where we were. When we stood up we were unsteady on our feet after so long in the sea. We saw at once that our troubles weren't over. There were no sand dunes. The sand we were on wasn't a beach. It was strewn with uprooted oaks, birches, alders and pines. Torn branches were scattered everywhere. We had to climb through. We couldn't take off our soaked deerskins and soften them – our naked bodies would have been ripped to shreds. As our deerskins dried out the leather grew stiff. It chafed our skin, which was already softened by seawater. Before long we had open sores. That was nothing. All around us the sea had uprooted the forest and flung it down like so much kindling. There must have been Animals here but their paths had all vanished so there was no way in. We found a dead pig impaled on a pine branch. Of People there was no sign at all.

There were no Birds. Can you imagine that? In all the lands I ever heard of, there was never a forest without forest-birds, just as there was never a coast without sea-birds. It's quiet now because night's fallen: your cliff-birds are all roosting, but how do you know when it's morning, before ever you open your eyes? You don't know how you know – you've never thought about it – but I, who have heard the silence, am the one to tell you that all your lives have been accompanied by the songs of your forest-birds or sea-birds or hill-birds – just wherever you happen to be.

Never in my life, before I came to that accursed place, had I breathed air that had no songs in it. Once the silence had thrust itself upon me I couldn't get rid of it. With each breath I breathed I felt the fear inside my lungs. And I had reason to be afraid, as you shall hear.

We found fresh water flowing across the sand: a stream that had lost its course, just as we'd lost ours. It was no deeper than my smallest fingernail. We had to lie down to drink, and then spit out the sand. We didn't care. We lay on the sand and sucked in water – it was too shallow to drink properly – until our thirst was gone. Then we slept.

In the morning Basajaun and I talked about what we should do. All the forest was torn apart. The soil was covered with fine white sand: we couldn't gather food inland. The whole shoreline had been washed away: there was nothing to eat there. My knife had been stuck in my belt while I was working with the needle – it seemed long ago now. Basajaun had laid his beside the boat, so now we only had my knife between us. It was enough to cut along the belly-line of the pig we'd found, and to cut up its meat when we'd skinned it. I used the knife as little as possible because we had no way of sharpening the blade, and nowhere to get new flint if it broke. While I prepared the meat Basajaun found an oak stick and a long sliver of pine, and made fire. One thing we weren't short of was firewood. We cooked all the meat and wrapped it in such leaves as we could find. Now that we had gut and sinew we weren't short of twine. We were ready to set off on our long journey.

We started walking along the broken shore. Below the new tide line the waves had washed the sand clean so we could get through. The Sun was already sinking when we came to a small River. There were smooth rocks scattered on the sand. When we came close they were not rocks but bodies. Their Camp had been swept away. We didn't recognise the place any more, but when we rolled over some of the bodies we knew them. They weren't close kin, but they belonged to our People. A hard lump came into my throat and tried to choke me. I was thinking about what we'd find when we reached our own family.

There was nothing we could do for the drowned People.

Some of the remains of their settlement were washed up on the shore, or scattered among the trees – tent hides, baskets, wooden hafts. Basajaun said we could use these things because our need was great. I was afraid. We'd done nothing to hurt the dead, but if we took where they had not given, they might be angry. I followed Basajaun reluctantly as he searched among the debris. I watched him turn over an old man's body. I knew that man, though I can't name him – all those names went out of the world when the sea took them. I covered my face with my hands as Basajaun searched in the old man's pouch. He drew out a flint core. We needed flint badly – we had no tools.

Basajaun said the spirits were telling us to take from the dead to save our own lives. When I hung back he said we could speak to the spirits before we went any further. We stretched up our arms and explained what we were doing. We asked the spirits to make things right with that old man's soul, and with his kin who'd made the other things we were about to use. The spirits showed me how the old man's soul had wanted us to come this way, so I promised that as soon as we'd made our knives we'd build a platform for the dead. I saw how the old man had wanted us to find his flint so we could make blades to cut the wands. We had to do what he asked before we made anything for ourselves. So we made a platform and laid the bodies on it. We didn't have enough twine to lash them, but I explained that to the spirits.

The spirits showed their thanks by leading us to a boat. It was stuck high in a thicket, and the hide was ripped. We managed to get it free without damaging it any more. We laid it on the shore, and set about replacing the broken wands. Basajaun said, 'This is what we were doing before the sea came. The spirits want us to go on with our lives where we left off.'

I said, 'But nothing can ever be the same again.'

'No,' said Basajaun. 'But *we're* still the same.'

'How can we be the same, without land or kin?'

'A man is his own self,' said Basajaun.

That seemed to me so wrong that I raised my hands to the spirits and silently asked them to forgive my brother. I knew it was courage, and not arrogance, that made him speak as he did, and I wanted the spirits to understand that.

We found hide, and wood already cut so we could make paddles. Then we spent one more night in that dreadful place, and put to sea.

We paddled out far enough to see the far-off hills so we could tell where we were. We thought the retreating sea had carried us towards the Sunless Sky, so we headed the other way, towards the High Sun Sky. We were right: after a long while we saw hills we recognised.

I won't tell you about our journey. I don't want to tell you what we found when we came to more places where there'd been Camps. I don't want you to see, as I still have to see inside my mind, the dead lying open-eyed on the broken shore with no one to prepare them for the spirits. I don't want you to smell the stench of death in the ruined Camps. Why should you hear about the few lost souls – children alone sometimes, or old men with blank eyes, or women weeping for their sons and daughters – that we found wandering, searching hopelessly for their families? We couldn't help any of them – we couldn't possibly build platforms for all the dead we found – so why remember them now?

Twice we saw other boats in the distance. When we saw the first one I wanted to paddle to them at once, but Basajaun said no. 'We don't know who they are.'

'But they're our People! They might be kin!'

'And they might not. We're not trusting anyone until we get to our own hunting lands. Everything's different now.'

I wanted to argue, but he wouldn't let me. We paddled further out to sea and the waves hid us. We did the same when we saw the other boat. My heart was heavy: those People might have been our kin. I didn't want to live in a world where I couldn't trust other Lynx People. I wanted Basajaun to be wrong about that. Perhaps he was.

But my People – my own family – Basajaun and I came to the place where Fishing Camp had been.

The shore was gone.

You don't understand me. We couldn't understand either. We paddled up and down. We knew this was the right place, but the land wasn't there. We found the River. It ended in a place that used to be far upstream. We paddled back to sea, and, now we knew where the River was, we worked out where Fishing Camp had been. The sea had taken it away. All my family were gone. We paddled inland – what had been inland – picking our way among floating trees and dead Animals. We got ashore and searched in mud and sand and broken trunks. We weren't even certain which of our places this new shore had once been.

We found one body. We thought it might be our sister's son. A child about that age, anyway. We tied a stone to the rotting corpse – we had no colour to adorn his body – and paddled out to where Fishing Camp had been – or where we thought it had been – and dropped him overboard there. We thought that, if it was him, his soul would know the place, and land or water would make little difference to the dead.

When that was done we headed upriver to our Hunting Camp. We'd left some flint there, and by now we needed tools very badly. At Hunting Camp we met two of our far-off cousins who were also fleeing from the dead lands. You can imagine how glad we were to find each other.

I held Ekaitz to my heart – his grandfather and mine were brothers – he was initiated only two Years before I was – we'd often hunted together. We wept for joy to find each other still alive. Ekaitz's youngest brother was there too. The sea takes what it will, and spits out what it will, and we People can see no pattern in it.

Now we'd found kin, Basajaun started making plans at once. Ekaitz was never one to argue. Even when we were all boys, he'd just look at Basajaun and smile. But Ekaitz has his own way of getting what he wants! He's – he was – one of our best hunters. Now we'd found Ekaitz, I began to look beyond my own shock and despair. As we sat round our Campfire that night, we all talked about what we should do.

Ekaitz and his brother had a couple of dogs with them. That meant we could hunt properly. But it was hard to see what shape our lives should take. Everything we knew or loved was lost. All our close kin had been born and lived and died on the ruined coast we'd left. We didn't want to search there any more – we wanted to go somewhere else. But where?

Then Basajaun started talking about our grandfather's father: how he also was Basajaun, and how he had come to the Lynx People from the Evening Sun Sky when he left the Auk People long ago. He first brought my brother's name to the Lynx People.

'I am Basajaun,' he said now. 'The Auk People live in my name and blood. I say we should go back to where I came from. You three are my kin. We are all of Auk blood. The sea has told us to go. Auk spirits are waiting for us! We should go back!'

Basajaun argued that in the Auk lands under the Evening Sun Sky, the sea wouldn't be angry. It would have stayed in its own place. In the end he persuaded us.

We stayed at Hunting Camp for a few days, working in our rock shelter out of the rain, making plenty of blades so we'd have spares to carry as well, and trapping small game to eat while we worked. Each of us made a knife, a short hunting spear, a bow, a quiver-full of arrows and a roll of twine. We repaired our clothes, and filled our pouches with flint cores, embers and meat for the journey. The morning after we were ready we filled our waterskins and set off towards the Evening Sun Sky.

We followed the deer paths over the hills – these were Lynx hunting lands, so the way was easy – until we came down to the valley of the Great Salmon River. The rain stopped. Mist wreathed over the hills and curled like smoke over the River. The glen smelt of too much water. We saw the smoke of a Camp and approached it cautiously. On the one hand, the Salmon People ought to give us food because we were kin: young men bringing gifts have always crossed the hills between Lynx and Salmon lands, looking for women and a place to hunt. On the other hand, there'd also been fights, and sometimes young women had been carried off. My younger cousin and I had never been this way before. None of the Salmon People could possibly recognise us, so we two walked in front.

Luckily we heard women singing before we met any men. We found a hand-full of them singing to the feather-plant roots as they grubbed them up with their digging sticks. I told them who we were, speaking as clearly as I could because the Salmon People's words are not always the same as ours. Two old women chattered together. We trembled when we heard the names they spoke, for we knew – and they didn't – that those Lynx names had already gone out of the world. But because they could name our kin, those women led us to their hearths. The Camp was full of People – many of them women and father-less children – who'd fled upriver from Camps on the coast. Everyone was talking about the Great Wave. The old women told us in slow words what they were saying: how the sea had funnelled up the estuary of the Great Salmon River and swept across salt marsh and forest to the very feet of the high hills. Many men were missing. The Salmon People were glad to have the meat we'd brought, but we had no other gifts, and they had troubles of their own. They didn't want us.

That night there was an argument. We couldn't follow the words but the meaning was clear: our two old women were saying that, because we were kin, the spirits said the Salmon People must help us on our way. The men were unwilling. In the end one of their young men hustled us through the glens of the Salmon People as fast as he could. We kept our knives close to our hands the first day, but on the second day he grew more friendly. He took us to the foot of the Loch of the Great Salmon River, where he let us take a boat and a basket of meat. 'Follow the loch into the heart of the mountains,' he told us, his hands working hard to make his meaning plain. 'You can leave the boat on the shingle where the River flows into the loch. We'll find it in the spring. Then you walk upriver to the watershed. From the pass you'll see the Grandmother Mountain of the Auk People. On the far side of that mountain lies the Open Sea that surrounds the world. That's where the Auk People hunt. To get to their sea you have to cross the hunting lands of the Heron People. Keep your course to the Grandmother Mountain; she'll show you the way.'

We were anxious about these Heron People – we had no kin among *them* – but the Salmon man was so keen to get rid of us that in the end he gave us his own and his father's name to trade with. 'Tell them you're our kin,' he said. If the Salmon People hadn't lost so much from the Great Wave that man would never had given us his name to pass on to a strange People! So though the Great Wave took away so much, it did now grudgingly give something back.

The Loch of the Great Salmon River is like an inland sea. We paddled, heads down, into driving rain, hugging the faint grey line of shore on our left. We were stuck ashore for four days while a gale swept in from the Evening Sun Sky. As soon as the wind gave way we struggled on. Spray leaped up and soaked us; rain tried to blind us. At the loch head we made a fire the length of our shelter so we could sit warm and naked, and dry out our clothes. The rain beat down on our boat-roof like a herd of deer hurtling down a gully. 'It's telling us about great hunts to come!' said Ekaitz. That made us laugh! The great hunts of Yellow Leaf Moon seemed very far away! We caught enough eels in the River to fill our bellies and forget we had no meat.

As soon as the wind gave way we struggled on. We left our boat at the head of the loch and climbed upriver among tumbled rocks, avoiding the precipices where the ravens wait. We travelled fast and ate little. Only one Moonless night lay between us and Yellow Leaf Moon. In the hills it was already winter. Mist lay over the watershed so we saw no Grandmother Mountain.

But no spirit had the power to turn us back now! We smelt salt in the sleet that stung our faces. Even as it tried to force us back the wind spoke to us of the Open Sea, and our hearts rose. We followed the stream into lower lands. We had no food left. But we were strong! We knew how to fast! At last the rain stopped, and the wind died down. We saw trees below us. Basajaun shot a stag as it leaped from the bracken. We made Camp at the kill, and feasted by firelight. It was good to taste that rich hot meat! The spirits were at last being kind to us! That made me think we might be drawing near to the Auk People.

The next day we saw Grandmother Mountain at last. She filled the Evening Sun Sky ahead, but we still had to cross the glens of the Heron People. We were lucky: the spirits led us to the fires of good People. We spread our arms wide to show we came as friends, and spoke the names the Salmon People had given us. When we swung the joints of deer meat off our backs and laid them on the ground before the headman of the family the Heron People put away their weapons and began to smile. When we said 'Auk,' one of them wrote in the mud of the loch shore with a stick. He showed us Grandmother Mountain, then marked out how the Auk People lived on the other side of Grandmother Mountain, over the sea towards the Sunless Sky.

The Heron People took us to a Camp at the head of a long loch, right under Grandmother Mountain, facing the High Sun Sky. We stayed two days because we needed to repair our clothes and tools before we went any further. On the second night they made a dance to show us why they'd welcomed us. We had no words we could share, but the dance was easy to understand.

In Seed Moon there'd been a big fight with the Otter People in the islands under the High Sun Sky. Nearly two hands-full of Heron men had died when the Otter People had sunk their boats. Now this family had women without men, and children without fathers.

The drums stopped beating and the song grew soft and slow. One of the women stood alone in the firelight. We were lying propped on our elbows beyond the hearth so as to watch the dance, and we had to look up to see her. She wore only her woman's skirt and the colours of the dance painted on her skin. The firelight played across her face and breasts, turning her skin sun-gold. Her eyes were like dark pools of deep water in hidden hollows of the hills. Ekaitz didn't need any more persuading; he jumped to his feet and said he'd take that woman. He'd have her that very night! Next morning he told us he wasn't going any further. He wanted to stay and hunt for the rest of his life with the Heron People.

I didn't mind that, but when Basajaun told me he had an eye on a woman too, and thought he'd stay for a while and see what came of it, I was furious. It had been Basajaun's idea that we come all this way! He was our link with the Auk People! I'd set my heart on finding kin of my own. These Heron People had treated us well, but we shared no blood with them.

'We can't stay for a while,' I shouted at him. 'It's Yellow Leaf Moon already! We'll be lucky to get across the sea as it is! If we leave it any longer we'll be stuck here all winter!'

'And why not?' Basajaun was laughing at me. 'Don't you want a woman to keep your bed warm, Kemen? You see how easily they give themselves here! You might find the Auk women more particular!'

I'd never been so angry with him before in my life. When I said I'd go on by myself he flew into a rage too. I shouted him down – I'd never done that before. I thought I was the one who should be angry!

But the Lynx spirits didn't want us to quarrel. I made myself calm, and spoke to him quietly. 'Basajaun,' I said. 'All we have left is each other. Now my path lies one way, and yours another. I hope we'll meet again in our present lives. When we do, you know what joy that will bring to me, your brother! But if we don't meet again in this life, what will the spirits say to two souls who lost so much, and then threw away the little they had left at the bottom of the basket?'

Basajaun smiled at that. In the end he stretched up his arms to the spirits, and asked them to help me on my way. He asked the spirits to let us meet again before we died. Then he held me to his heart, and I held him to mine.

I walked away from him without looking back. I left Grandmother Mountain behind, and followed the shores of a long loch. I watched fierce tides sweep into the loch and out of it, and I knew I was close to the sea. I climbed a little hill to see where I was. I looked towards the Sunless Sky and saw the far-off hills of a great island. You know what island that was! I looked at the sea that lay between and saw huge tide rips fighting one other. My heart leaped to my throat. That was the sea I had to cross! It was Yellow Leaf Moon already. I didn't have very long.

I found another family of Heron People. They'd heard about me already; they took me to their hearth and gave me food. I used my hands and body to tell them what I meant to do. They watched me and shook their heads. But their spirits were with me, and their kindness didn't run dry: they showed me where they'd coppiced the best silver hazel, and let me take as many wands as I needed to make myself a little boat. They gave me the raw hide of a well-grown hind.

I built myself a shelter above the high-tide line where I could look out towards the Sunless Sky. I gathered sea-roots and shellfish to eat. I slept two nights in my Boat Camp. At night I had strange dreams, sometimes about my old life that had gone for ever, and sometimes about matters I didn't yet recognise. During the day I worked alone on my boat in a quiet place where a little stream flowed out of the forest and stretched itself in glistening folds across the sand. The wands bent themselves willingly to my will. I sang as I bound them into a frame. I sang to the willow withies as I cut and wove them. I sang to the hide as I stretched it and sewed it over the lip with rawhide strips. As I whittled my paddle into shape I sang how we'd cleave a path through the waves towards the Sunless Sky, looking for the Auk People – the only kin I had left in the wide world.

As it was, I had to wait another hand-full of days because I needed a kind wind and tide to take me into the Auk People's hunting lands by daylight. I didn't go looking for food for fear of missing my chance. I bashed limpets off the rocks, and ate them with sea kale and silverweed. But then the wind dropped and the sea went down. A friendly breeze came from the High Sun Sky. It cleared away the mists so I could see the Auk People's Mother Mountain Island across the sea. The Heron People pointed out the headland I must steer for. They made it clear I must leave at first light so as to catch the tide where I needed it most. They gave me a basket of shellfish. Then I pushed my boat off, jumped in and paddled out to sea.

The Heron People had warned me about the terrible currents that sweep through the Straits. I paddled against the ebb as hard as I could. My heart was in my throat as I met the swell. It rolled in on my beam in great sweeps that reminded me of the terrible wave that swept away the whole world of the Lynx People. Each wave lifted my boat and then swept away under me. With every wave I felt I'd fall for ever, but soon I saw that all I had to do was keep paddling, and let the next swell take me. I came to waters so fierce I thought I'd tip over and drown, but the spirits were with me and my arms were strong. I was more than halfway across when I felt the flood tide tugging me towards the Sunless Sky. I did what the Heron People had shown me, and steered a paddle's length to the left of the head-land where I wanted to go. White waves washed against fierce cliffs. I couldn't see anywhere to land. The closer I got, the more the sea swept me towards the Sunless Sky. I was going so fast it was all I could do to steer my boat. I can tell you, I began to wonder if I really wanted to belong to you Auk People, if you did this sort of thing every day!

My boat raced round the headland, faster than a man could run, into Long Strait, which the Heron People said would lead me to the Camps of the Auk People. The Heron People hadn't been able to tell me anything about the waters beyond Wide Strait. 'The Auk People belong to the sea,' they seemed to say. 'They paddle across open waters where no other People dream of going. They know the currents that sweep between the islands. Once you're across Wide Strait you must find one of their Camps as soon as possible. You don't want to risk the Auk People's seas by yourself a day longer than you must.'

You're all smiling – I know what you're thinking. But I'm of the Lynx People, and I never saw seas like yours before, let alone paddled across them. But I found my way between the skerry and the headland, just as the Heron People said. After that I had no more words to guide me. I was glad to find the tide and I were in agreement: we both wanted to keep close to the shore of the Evening Sun, sheltered from the wind. The shore of the Auk People's Mother Mountain Island looked kinder now. Wintry woods sloped down to rocky shoals. Just as the tide was slackening I saw a stretch of sand where a boat could beach. I paddled cautiously into the bay. The wind didn't follow me into this sheltered place, and everything was quiet. A heron rose from the sea's edge and flapped away across Long Strait. I watched it go – it was a kind spirit from the Heron People leaving me. When the heron was out of sight I looked back at the shore, but the Sun had gone behind the hill and the slopes lay in shadow. My eyes were dazzled with looking at the bright sky. I shaded them with my hand.

When my sight cleared I saw a trickle of smoke rising over the trees, then bending towards the Sunless Sky before the breeze. My heart leaped to my throat. That smoke was telling me that here was a Camp of the Auk People. So now I must take my chance, whether to find kin, or enemies – whether to live at their hands, or die.

When I stepped out of my boat I realised how cold and stiff I was – hungry too. I carried my boat up the beach, and I found two others upturned above the shingle. I laid mine beside them. A path led through the trees. I looked at it warily. When we'd arrived at the Heron People's Camp at Grandmother Mountain there'd been four of us. Now I was only one. Without words I might not be able to explain myself. But I was cold and hungry, and I couldn't make a fire of my own without these strangers noticing. Besides, these were the very People I'd come so far to find. I seized my courage in both hands. I followed the winding path. And the rest you know – because I found myself in the winter Camp of Sendoa's family, and they told me that they were Auk People.

That's how I lost my kin, and my place in the world, and that's how I found it again. If you're not my kin now, then I have none. And if you are – if you say you are – then I've come home.

Alaia said:

Kemen didn't actually tell us his whole story – not on that first evening when we sat round the hearth at White Beach Camp. His tongue was still so strange, even though he'd spent a whole winter learning how to speak properly, that it was hard to listen to him. I think he told us as much as he could, and sometimes he's talked about his old life since. It's hard to remember exactly what anyone said on a particular day, and how much we've heard since, and how much is just the picture we make in our own minds when we listen and remember. But certainly he told us where he'd come from, and what had happened. When we'd been at Salmon Camp last Year these terrible things were happening in the Lynx People's hunting lands, and we knew nothing about them.

I was very troubled by his story. I didn't know then how much it would come to affect us. I was especially worried about the little boy whose body Kemen and Basajaun had dropped into the sea. What would happen to that child's soul now? Kemen seemed to think the Lynx spirits would understand what they'd done. Perhaps the sea didn't give food to the Lynx People in the way it does for us.

Later on, after Gathering Camp, I told Kemen my fears. He

didn't know what I was talking about at first. I had to explain how when Auk People are lost at sea we beg the sea spirits to bring the drowned souls back to land. Kemen didn't know that you shouldn't eat anything out of the sea for a full quarter of the next Moon or the sea spirits won't let the lost People come back. I told him he should beg the sea spirits to make sure he'd never taken any sea Animal that had once eaten one of his lost family. Kemen said that everything I said was new to him. But he didn't eat any food from the sea for a quarter of the next Moon – I said I was sure the spirits would understand why he'd been so long about it – and after that I think he felt better. I stopped dreaming about that little Lynx boy too, which was a relief to me.

But I had something else to worry about. Kemen first came to Sendoa's Camp in Yellow Leaf Moon, just a short while before we lost Bakar. His troubles were ending just as ours were beginning. I worked that out in my mind while he was speaking, and the terrible thought occurred to me that perhaps he'd brought bad spirits with him on his journey, and when these spirits reached the Auk People they'd abandoned Kemen and started to feast on us instead. I looked at my mother to see what she was thinking. If I'd thought of this, she most certainly would have done so. And, unlike me, she would probably know what to do about it.

Nekané said:

Next day I was sitting on the hillside opposite the high sea stack that lies under the Evening Sun, exposed to the open seas that come from the edge of the world. The inward side of the stack is sheltered by the island, facing the Morning Sun. That's where the guillemots and kittiwakes nest.

Amets and Sendoa were showing Kemen where to climb.

I watched the three of them gathering eggs. Amets and Sendoa moved quickly across the cliff-face, their bare toes feeling for cracks between the narrow shelves where the nests were. They collected the auks' eggs as they went, reaching out with one hand while clinging on with the other, with no more pause than a man makes between one step of a dance and the next. Sometimes they crept along the rock face so stealthily they caught a parent bird unawares. They didn't have snares with them – they'd only come for eggs today – but Amets reached out suddenly and grabbed a guillemot. He leaned into the cliff-face while he wrung its neck, then tucked it into his belt, where it hung limply by its head. I was pleased: it's good to have a taste of roast bird to season a feast of eggs. A few heartbeats later I saw Sendoa catch a razorbill the same way.

All the while the waves surged hungrily against the shore below my nephew and my daughter's husband. White sea-spittle licked round the rock-teeth, then withdrew with empty sucking noises. High on the cliff-face, Amets and Sendoa were well out of reach. They never bothered to look down.

Kemen had a basket strapped to his back just like the others, but his was still empty. He moved very slowly along the cliff-face, feeling for footholds. He trod on a nest. I saw a splash of yellow yolk as the egg smashed against the cliff. Guillemots rose in alarm, screaming. Kemen stood splayed against the cliff, one foot in the broken nest, his cheek against the rock, clinging with both hands. Slowly he twisted his head and looked down. After that he didn't move for so long that I wondered if something was the matter. Then, very gingerly, he brought his right foot across to join his left in the remains of the guillemots' nest. One hand edged along the crack in the rock above him. He took another step. At least he seemed to be trying to avoid the nests now. He reached out carefully with his left hand. A guillemot rose into the air, screaming alarm. Kemen's hand dropped back. Then he reached out again, shifting his balance. He felt along the ledge with his fingers. His hand closed over the egg. I found myself holding my own breath as the hand clutching the egg came slowly back. The egg dropped into the basket. Ten heartbeats passed. Kemen's left foot moved again, feeling for the next crack in the rock.

By now Amets and Sendoa had several birds tucked into their belts, and their baskets were almost full. All the ledges Kemen could reach seemed to be empty. The guillemots knew he was a stranger to the bird cliffs so they refused to give themselves.

Now I knew that at least part of Kemen's story was true. I knew he wouldn't be pretending: very few young men ever pretended to *lack* skill. I knew he'd be trying as hard as he could to keep up with the others, even if he couldn't beat them.

I thought about Kemen. He'd arrived among Sendoa's People early in Yellow Leaf Moon. My son had disappeared at the end of Yellow Leaf Moon. Kemen never encountered Bakar. He'd been with Sendoa all the while at a winter Camp far away from ours. We had Sendoa's word for that as well as Kemen's. We could trust Sendoa. If Kemen had brought evil spirits with him on his journey – and certainly his story showed that he'd come from a place where some spirit must be very angry – then he couldn't have carried them directly to Bakar, because he was never near him. But if Kemen had brought spirits powerful enough to fly through the air from one man to another . . . that was quite possible. He'd told us of spirits powerful enough to drive the sea out of its bed and sweep away the land. Spirits who were able to do that would certainly be strong enough to abandon one young man when they'd done with him, and fly as far as they liked in search of new prey.

All this Kemen might have brought upon us without meaning it. I found no guile in him – though I could have been wrong – how could I know the thoughts in a stranger's heart? But now I was Go-Between I had ways of finding out. More than that, it was now my duty to my People to discover what I could, whether I felt like it or not. I'd not been tried yet, but I was beginning to be aware of new responsibilities. Kemen was my first test.

I walked away from the cliffs towards the High Sun Sky, in the opposite direction from White Beach Camp. No one had used the way through the hazel woods since Seed Moon. Willow shoots, briars and brambles had grown into the path. I pushed them aside with my digging stick. I passed the narrow part of the island and climbed the little hill that's almost a separate island. I went up beyond the trees.

I sat looking at the glimmering waves. I gazed at the Open Sea until Near and Far had no meaning any more. The patterns of shifting light stopped being out of reach. They pushed against my eyes and forced their way inside me, rippling through my head so I was the sea too, in the sea, my smooth, striped body leaping joyfully through the waves as the light broke apart and showered down round me. I wasn't afraid. I was laughing. Dolphin was laughing as he leaped through the waves with me. He was with me, and he said no, no, *no*, you don't need to worry, no, life is good, and Kemen is a good man, and the evil spirit he brought with him is far away it will come it will come one day one Year oh yes it will come and you must be ready for it but not yet not yet. Not yet. Not yet.

I found myself sitting on the hill where I was before. There were clouds above my head and the light had gone out of the sea. I could see rain coming towards me from the Evening Sun Sky. I stood up, shivering, and pulled my foxfur cloak round my shoulders, hugging myself tightly to get warm. But though my outer body was cold, inside my ribs I blazed with delight, and also with the comfort that Kemen was a good man. It was safe to accept him as our cousin. Whatever harmful spirit had followed him, it was still far off, and Kemen had brought nothing in his own person that could harm us.

Amets said:

No, don't put any more wood on that fire. It's getting late – look how high the Moon is above Gathering Loch. Alazne's fast asleep, and those boys can hardly keep their eyes open. I haven't much more to say. I can see Alaia wants to speak too, but then we'll end this story for tonight.

As soon as we met Sendoa and Kemen at White Beach Camp I was happy again. We started hunting the sea-birds at once. Kemen hadn't done that kind of hunting before, but he was quick to learn. I explained to him how we leave the women to get puffins, because all they have to do is haul them out of their burrows. And a woman can get terns' eggs, gulls' eggs and duck eggs, just by walking over open ground. It's easy for them to do that. But it's a man's job to catch birds and collect eggs from the cliffs. I walked along the coast with him and showed him our best bird-hunting places.

'You see? The guillemots and razorbills nest in the ledges all across the cliff. All we have to do is climb down there, and they'll give themselves just as much as we want. Kittiwakes too: you'll find a lot of gulls' eggs as well as auks'. It's all the same – they're all just as good as each other. Then down below – just above the shags there, look, about a man's length above high tide – see there, where the waves are breaking over Flat Skerry – that's where the great auks nest. You've never seen one? We'll soon show you! There's enough meat in a great auk's egg to keep a man going for a full day's journey, even if he finds nothing else. They're big birds – one great auk will stop the whole family complaining they're hungry for the best part of half a day! Oh, we get good hunting, I can tell you, while the auks are here on White Beach Island!

Kemen stood beside me on the cliff top, looking down at the places I showed him. All he said was, 'We don't have any cliffs like these in Lynx lands. We don't hunt auks at all.'

I couldn't imagine what it would be like to have no auk season.

When we got back to Camp I showed Kemen how to make a snare from bark twine to catch auks. Kemen looped the twine to make a noose the way I showed him, and took his knife to trim the end.

'What kind of blades are those?' I kept my voice even. My head told me that Lynx stones might be different; my heart feared that the spirits had written the colour of blood on the blades of Kemen's knife for a bad reason.

'Just flint.' Kemen hesitated. Then he held out his knife to me, as if we were kin.

I held back for a heartbeat. Then I took his knife, balancing the haft between my finger and thumb. I kept my voice ordinary, as if nothing particular had happened between us. 'I've never seen flint that colour.'

'No? Yours is all like that?' Kemen pointed to my knife.

I handed it to him. 'That's Auk flint. Over there' – I pointed towards the Sunless Sky – 'where I come from, in the hunting lands of the Seal People, we have other stones.' I watched Kemen testing the blade of my knife against his thumb. I handed him a little stone core from my pouch. 'There's no blades left in this now. I don't know why I keep it. When I first came here, that's what I was using. You won't find any stone like this in Auk lands.'

Kemen took the core of dark-grey stone. He turned it over in his hand, and felt the smooth surface. 'That's good hard stone.'

'Only white-stone is harder. We get plenty of *that* in Auk lands. On the beach and in the rocks. You won't find much flint on Mother Mountain Island – we get most of ours from the beaches on Gathering Loch – but you'll always find white-stone here if you want it.'

'I've never worked with white-stone.'

'It's harder than flint or bloodstone. Do you know bloodstone? No? We get it at Gathering Camp – they bring it from Bloodstone Island. I've got some in Camp – I'll show you – well, you saw Sendoa's knife? Dark-green stone – tough to work, but it makes a good blade.'

We sat there for half a morning talking about stones. I won't tell you the rest because my wife is listening – it was all what she calls men's talk! You all know how Alaia keeps us men in order! She can work stone as well as anybody, but she only likes talking about People really.

Kemen handed me back the useless little core of mudstone I'd brought with me from the Seal People's lands, saying, 'I think you *do* know why you keep it.'

After that talk I didn't worry about giving Auk knowledge to Kemen. He knew about boats already, but he wasn't used to the fierce tides that rip around the islands. At first he thought that if there wasn't much wind or swell there was nothing to worry about. We had to teach him better before he went off and drowned himself! Sendoa and I had a private talk about our fishing marks.

'Are you sure it's safe to show him?' I asked. 'Remember his kin are staying among the Heron People.'

'The Heron People won't come here. They don't know our seas. Besides, I trust Kemen.'

'Why?'

'Because I've had all winter to get to know him. And because Nekané said he was a good man.'

'Nekané is Go-Between,' I agreed. 'And I'm telling you, Sendoa, I hope no one else in my family ever becomes Go-Between. I couldn't stand it!'

Sendoa chuckled. 'A woman too! Her man can't stop her getting above herself now!'

I laughed with him. 'But to be honest, cousin, she doesn't use it against him. Not since she came back after – whatever it is that they do – after it happened. Before that – oh, she was terrible. But now she does her work again and doesn't make much fuss. But after my wife's brother left, I tell you, it was terrible!' I slapped him on the arm. 'I was never so glad to see anyone as to find you here! One thing's certain: I'm not going through another winter being the only hunting man. Because' – I mentioned my wife's father – 'he knows a lot, but he can't keep up really. He's too old.'

Sendoa glanced at me when I said that. I guessed what he was thinking. 'Nekané going Go-Between won't help with the hunting anyway,' was all he said, 'because she's still only a woman – she was never initiated. I've never known a woman Go-Between before, though I've heard it happens sometimes. But a woman Go-Between can't have the right Helpers for the Hunt. Anyway, she wouldn't know what to ask them.'

But Nekané might have other uses, I thought. I didn't say so to Sendoa, but she'd already shown, over this matter of Kemen, that she had. 'Also,' I added aloud, 'she's past having children. That makes her equal to a man in many ways.'

'I can accept Nekané being one of the Wise,' agreed Sendoa. 'In fact that's what old women are for. They're not much use for anything else!' I laughed with him, a little nervously, because we were mocking at the Wise. 'It's having a woman Go-Between in our family. I'll get used to it, I expect.'

'She was able to tell us it was all right to have Kemen here.'

'Which brings us back to Kemen – telling him where to fish. Listen, Amets: even when everyone arrives we'll only have' – Sendoa held up his fingers one by one, thinking of the men in our family – 'eight hunting men. Old men' – he counted his fingers again – 'three. Women' – one by one he raised all ten fingers, and then another three – 'and then there's the children and dogs, who all have to be fed too. I think we have good reason to show Kemen our fishing grounds.' He glanced at me. 'He is our kin, though far-off, I agree.'

I nodded slowly.

'And also,' argued Sendoa, 'if he stays, he could have one of our women. That would make it right.'

I grinned, and suggested a name. We began to laugh. I won't repeat the things we said after that, because all the girls we mentioned have a man of their own now, and we know what happened with Kemen. But we ended up laughing so much we couldn't say another word. From then on we accepted Kemen as one of us. When the others arrived they found the matter already settled, and they soon accepted things as they were. Nobody discussed the matter any more.

Alaia said:

Of course when the other women came – everyone arrived before Auk Moon was half full – we talked endlessly about the loss of Bakar, and the arrival of Kemen, as we sat in the Sun plucking birds and grinding sea-roots. It was obvious that the spirits had taken one and given back the other, but we weren't able to see why. But that's how it is: the spirits have their own ways of working and we can't expect to understand why they have to hurt us.

It was so good to have the others to talk to, who weren't my mother, and who were in no way Go-Between. My aunts and cousins welcomed my baby. They passed Esti from one to another whenever she was out of my arms. They never tired of cuddling her and singing to her. I felt as if my Esti was safe at last: whether I lived or died, from now on the voices and scents of her kin would always be familiar.

As we sat together round the fire picking over dandelions, clover and chickweed, roasting sea-roots, eggs or fish in the ashes, or shelling shellfish, we played names with the new baby. Haizea would hold Esti up to face one of her kin, and we'd all sing together, 'Who's that, Esti? Who's that? Who's that? Who's that?'

And then we'd chant, 'That's Esti's cousin Itsaso! Itsaso! ITSASO!' Or 'Sorné' or 'Hilargi' or whoever it might be. My baby loved that game, as every baby does. She'd smile and chortle, and before we left White Beach Camp she knew all their faces, and I'm sure she already understood how every name and every face joined up to make that particular soul.

When we told the others what had happened with Bakar we had all our grieving to do again with them for company. Their sorrow helped me. The scar was still there, and always would be, but the pain of Bakar's loss began to heal. I could talk to my cousins in a way I couldn't talk to my mother, especially now she'd changed so much.

Now Amets was back with our cousins he wasn't silent and grim any more. When he was laughing with the others I realised how little laughter there'd been all winter. When we sang in the evenings I remembered how sadly we'd all gone to bed as soon as it was dark. And I'd had Esti to think of; I'd been pregnant and then I'd given birth, and now she was attached to me all night like a little limpet. Perhaps I'd been neglecting my man. In fact my aunts told me so: they said my mother should have warned me that the birth of the first child was dangerous in this way.

'Amets loves his daughter,' I said to them indignantly. 'I told you, he was the one who recognised her. Esti was his own mother's mother!'

'That's as may be,' my aunt Hilargi said, knotting a piece of twine and biting off the loose end, 'but look at what he had to put up with last winter. First your brother disappears – his only friend – and then my sister Nekané becomes even more impossible than she was before!'

'And it's not as if your father's much of a companion,' put in my aunt Sorné. 'I've never seen a man age so much in one winter. He looks half dead already.'

'Now if you had boys to train it would be easier,' remarked Hilargi. She reached across me for another bundle of twine-grass. 'But it looks as if Nekané's blood mostly produces girls. Maybe the spirits will give you a boy one day, or perhaps they'll give Haizea a son. That would improve things. I'm not saying it isn't better to have girls, Alaia. You're the lucky one, really! You bring up a boy, feed him all through the best part of your life – and don't they just eat a lot! I'm telling you, you clothe him, keep him warm in winter, teach him everything he needs to know – and then what? He can't wait to leave you and find a woman of his own, and you see him at maybe two Camps in a Year if you're lucky. No one knows that better than I do! But a family needs a proper balance if it's going to work.'

'*One day* is too far-off!' Sorné held up three, and then four fingers. 'That many Years far-off, at the very least. Our little Esti has to grow first. Would you snatch her mother's milk out of her poor little mouth, sister? You'd surely kill her! And Haizea's still as skinny as a stick. No point thinking about getting a boy just yet, Hilargi. Alaia, you'll just have to persuade your father to give up River Mouth Camp. Tell him you can come along with us to Big Pines Camp, and Amets can hunt with Sendoa and my sons.'

I let my work fall into my lap, and stared at her. 'Father won't agree to that! He and my mother have always gone to River Mouth Camp.'

'But there were a round hand-full of men in those days! Things change, Alaia. He must see that. You have to make him see it.'

'What! You'd have *me* tell my *father*...'

'Well, Nekané won't,' said Hilargi.

Sorné agreed. 'Nekané has no more sense than a beached jellyfish. Hold your hands up, Alaia, so I can coil this twine.'

'Never did have. Alaia, you listen to what we're telling you. If you don't do something about it, you'll lose your man.'

I flinched at the very thought. Lose my man! Lose Amets! That's the worst thing that can happen to a woman. If Amets went away, I thought, we'd have no one to hunt for us, and Esti would have no father to look after her. Children without fathers usually die. Besides, I wanted Amets for myself.

'Don't look like that, child. Your old aunts only say these things because they care for you.'

'And it needn't be so difficult,' added Sorné. 'If you look around, you'll always find that the spirits have provided, if you only have eyes to see. They don't always do it in the way you'd expect.'

'Why, Aunt, what do you see?'

'I see *Kemen*,' whispered my aunt, nodding her head significantly. 'What the spirits take with one hand, they give with another. But only to those who do a little thinking for themselves.'

I thought a great deal about what my aunts had said to me. A few days later I spoke to my little sister. We'd been collecting terns' eggs, and when we'd each got a basketful of pale-blue eggs we strolled along the shore above the beach. It was a relief to get away from the terns diving and shrieking and shitting over us. I'd left Esti with my aunt; it was good to walk with a light step and remember how it felt to be unburdened. The sea was wrinkly smooth, green over the sand and dark blue further out where the tides met. Haizea wanted to pick couch grass, so we sat down at the top of the beach. While I waited for Haizea, I absent-mindedly pushed my fingers into the warm sand, following the roots of the couch grass. On the surface each single blade of grass seemed to stand alone, but under the sand they were all joined together by long strands of yellow roots. It's like that with kin, I thought.

When Haizea had collected what she wanted, she came and sat beside me. I watched her plaiting her grass stems. Presently I said, as casually as possible, 'What do you think of Kemen?'

Clearly Haizea was only thinking about the twine she was making, because she just said, 'He can't do twine patterns, anyway.'

I tried again. 'What would you think about Kemen staying in our family?'

'Instead of Sendoa's?' Haizea didn't sound in the least interested. She twisted her twine into a circle and knotted the ends together. 'Nothing, really. Alaia, can you show me how to do Fish in a Basket?'

I saw it was useless, so I just said to her, 'I used to know. Give it here.'

At River Mouth Camp, when we were so lonely and bereft, I'd started thinking of Haizea as an ally, but now she was among the children again we'd stopped being close. She was often with her cousin Ortzi. He'd seen one more winter than she had; if there'd been boys his own age around he'd have had nothing to do with Haizea, but all the other boys at White

Beach Camp were much younger. Children must grow up, and I guessed – though she didn't – that when we got to Gathering Camp Haizea would lose Ortzi for ever. I encouraged her to go around with Itsaso instead. Itsaso was willing: she didn't have any girls her age at White Beach Camp either. Haizea liked Itsaso, but Itsaso wouldn't play games. She just wanted to hang around with the women. After River Mouth Camp Haizea wanted to be a little girl again. So she and Ortzi went off on their own adventures, and if Haizea did listen to anything we women said when we were out gathering, or sitting working at the hearth, she showed no interest. She'd only join in when we were singing.

After my aunts had talked to me I treated Kemen with great friendliness, offering him titbits from the food I'd gathered, and inviting him to sit on our side of the hearth when the smoke was blowing the other way. It wasn't hard, because I liked him. I encouraged Amets to go fishing and sea-bird hunting with him.

Towards the end of Light Moon everyone began to talk about where they'd make Salmon Camp this Year. My aunts and their children always went to Salmon Spirit Loch. They had their fish traps at the mouth of the loch, and the men hunted all summer in the hills around Mother Mountain. There'd be plenty of food there for our family as well. I wanted my father to see how wise it was to stay with my mother's sisters for a while. I feared he wouldn't listen, because our own Salmon Camp, which lies only half a day's sail from White Beach Island, is my father's Birth Place, and I feared he'd insist on going there as usual. It took me a few days to put another idea into his mind without him noticing.

I talked to my father when my mother was out one evening collecting gulls' eggs. He told me he'd been thinking that it was a long while since we'd let the Animals have our Salmon

Camp to themselves in Seed Moon and Salmon Moon, and perhaps we should go elsewhere for a change. He asked me if I'd mind making Salmon Camp with my aunts and cousins at Salmon Spirit Loch just for this once. I looked surprised and seemed to take a little while to think it over. Then I said yes, and I told my father how happy I was that he thought so well for all of us.

In all this I was encouraged by my aunts Sorné and Hilargi. If the men had any idea what we were up to, they gave no sign of it. Which meant that either they didn't notice – which was probably the case – or they thought – rightly – that life would be easiest if they just let us sort things out in our own way.

THIRD NIGHT: GATHERING CAMP

Haizea said:

Shall I begin the story tonight? Be quiet, boys! This is *your* story we're telling. Listen to us, and you'll soon find out how much these things matter to you.

At Gathering Camp my cousin Itsaso let me come with her friends. I always used to play with her younger brother Ortzi, but when we got to Gathering Camp Ortzi stopped speaking to me.

Oh, but . . . before we get to Gathering Camp I need to tell you how Itsaso became a woman at Salmon Camp. We had a feast for her there. We'd sent the men off to their Hunting Camp on Mother Mountain; the men couldn't wait to get away. Men are always terrified of the spirits who watch over a girl as she becomes a woman! But then – maybe some of you have noticed this – men aren't always as overflowing with courage as they want us to think! Ortzi wanted to go with the men. They said he was still too young. When they wouldn't let him, he went off fishing by himself. He came back when the food was ready though, and ate just as much as the other children.

Once we'd got rid of the men from Salmon Camp we spent

all day getting ready. My aunts took down bundles of reed and grasses – it so happened they already had just the right sort hanging from one of the wands that made their tent frame – and sat by the hearth plaiting them together into soft lengths. It took them all day to twine the plaits to and fro until they'd made a woman's skirt for Itsaso. Meanwhile the rest of us built up the fire and roasted salmon, trout and some ducks we'd snared in the shore traps. We stuffed the birds with charlock leaves and pignuts, and added yarrow, self-heal and water-mint, because that helps with bleeding. I went with my cousins and we picked meadowsweet flowers and raspberries, elderberries, hips, hawthorn berries . . . you never saw so many berries as we got that day!

When we got back to Salmon Camp my aunt Sorné had laid out a woman-stone and quartz on a piece of birchbark. She let me wet the woman-stone and rub it on the quartz to make red. We painted patterns on each other's faces, and our arms and shoulders too, and some of us even did our feet and legs – it was summer so there was lots of bare skin to paint. Itsaso plaited my hair into sixteen plaits.

Before the feast began, my aunts stood Itsaso between them, and wound the strings of her new skirt around her waist. The plaited aprons fell almost to her knees at the front and back. Now everyone could see she was a woman. It came into my head that before many more Moons had passed the women of my family would be plaiting a woman's skirt for me. I didn't want to think about it. I was standing next to Ortzi, and I was happy to think we looked just the same, each with a child's length of deerskin wrapped round our middle. That was quite enough for anyone to wear in summer. I wished with all my heart I need never change.

After the feast we danced right through the night, and sang all the songs about men that they never hear. The other children went to sleep, but I didn't. I was surprised that old women – even my aunts – even my *mother* – would sing those songs. I was still a child – I didn't know much at all! But I made sure I stayed awake, and I saw the other things too – the spirits know what I mean.

But yes – the day after we arrived at Gathering Camp I went with the older girls to get hazelnuts. There are so many Animal and People paths all round Gathering Camp I kept close to the other girls. I would be shamed for ever if I got lost! We walked past oak, aspen and birch, and quite a lot of hazel growing in their shade. We didn't bother with it: we were going to the hazel grove. Only hazel trees grow in the grove because at every Gathering the Auk People cut down the other saplings that try to get in, so as to leave more light for the hazel. That pleases the Hazel spirits, because without the other trees in the way they can reach the Sun, and now there are lots of hazel trees all growing together.

The others sent me up first to see if the nuts were ripe. I was a good tree-climber, and I was lighter than the rest of them. That was good: I needed to show I was the best at *something*, and not just Itsaso's little puppy. Hazel never grows very tall, even when it's allowed to grow alone and feel the Sun on its leaves, but we were high on the hillside, so from my tree I could look down on the treetops in the glen. They looked like the sea: oak and pine, aspen and hazel, rowan and birch making a pattern of greens like the ebb and flow of different-coloured tides. A hunting peregrine swooped and soared over the wood. Even as I heard its mewing cry, the small birds round me twittered into flight.

'Haizea, what are you doing? Have you gone to sleep up there?'

'Are there any nuts?'

I peered into the dark green leaves. 'Yes! The hazelnuts are ready for us! Come on!'

I sat in the fork of a branch and watched the others unroll the hides we'd brought and spread them under the trees. They scrambled up, two or three to each tree. Itsaso joined me in my tree. We started shaking the branches. Nuts pattered on to the hides below. Lots more nuts stayed clinging to their twigs. We swung our baskets round so they hung down in front of us, and started picking. As we searched out where the nuts were hiding we gradually climbed up to the highest branches that could only just take our weight.

Itsaso said, 'Look Haizea – two hazelnuts in one shell – that means a marriage. Do you know why?'

'A man and a woman under one fur?'

'No, stupid!' Itsaso dangled the twig under my nose. 'Two *nuts*!'

We giggled. A breeze soughed among the leaves, rocking us as we picked.

When our baskets were full we came down and gathered up the fallen nuts in the hides. We stacked everything round a tree trunk and tied leafy twigs over the baskets in case the squirrels came thieving. Then we climbed up for a rest before we went back. I sat on the highest branch, with Itsaso lying back on a branch below me, her arms spread wide, making sure we could all see she didn't need to hold on. A hand-full of others were there, some close cousins I knew quite well, and some far-off. I felt shy of the ones I hardly knew.

We were quiet for a bit, lazily picking any stray nuts within our reach and stuffing them in our pouches. We'd left the cracking-stones at the bottom of the tree. Someone suggested fetching them but no one could be bothered. Above our heads the leaves stirred, making the light move like running water over our bare arms and legs. Squirrels scuttled among the leaves, their fur glistening like hazelnuts. Doves cooed; the other birds were resting in the heat, except for a woodpecker that kept knocking on a birch trunk. A red dragonfly settled on my knee, polished his long front legs together, and then took off again. I rubbed the soles of my feet against the rough hazel bark; it felt good. Perched high on my branch, I could hear the spirits breathing as they drowsed.

My far-off cousin Zorioné broke the silence. 'Is it true, Haizea, that your mother's Go-Between?'

'Yes,' I said reluctantly.

'Well!' Osané said, 'I never heard of a woman Go-Between!'

I didn't answer. Osané had been a woman for three winters, and she seemed quite old to me. I only knew her from Gathering Camp, and I'd hardly spoken to her before. Everyone said she was pretty. I admired her because she could walk on her hands, turn cartwheels without stopping and lean over backwards and grab her own ankles. She had rows of blue lines tattooed on her hands and feet – lots of women had those, but Osané's were the best – and she could climb trees almost as well as I could.

'It can happen.' Zorioné cracked a fresh nut between her teeth the way my mother had warned me not to in case I broke a tooth. 'But my uncle Zigor is very angry about it. Does Nekané know that?'

'I don't know.'

'Of course Nekané knows!' Itsaso said. 'She's Go-Between, isn't she? She knows everything!'

Zorioné spat out bits of nutshell and said thickly, 'She doesn't know as much as my uncle. He's been Go-Between all his life.'

'You can't be Go-Between all your life,' pointed out Itsaso. 'Zigor must have been a child once.'

'Well, since he was initiated anyway.'

'No, that's impossible. Because a boy would have to—'

'But the point is,' Osané interrupted, 'that he *was* initiated. I mean he's a man. Nekané can't speak to the Animals about the Hunt!'

'So?'

'*So*, that's what the Go-Betweens are *for*, isn't it?' retorted Zorioné. 'To speak to the Animals about the Hunt! That's why we're all *here*!'

'No it isn't! We've come to the Gathering for *lots* of reasons.' Itsaso held up her hand with fingers spread. 'Like seeing everyone, and hearing what's happened, and People getting married – and . . . and . . . like us here now. We've come to be with our kin.'

'But that's not what it's *for*. The only thing it's actually *for* is about the Hunt. My uncle—'

'*My uncle*,' mocked Itsaso. 'My uncle says . . . my uncle is . . . *Your uncle* shits sunshine, I suppose.'

'Itsaso!' they all cried out at once.

'He'll *hear* you!'

'Are you mad?'

'Itsaso, Zigor is Go-Between!'

'Zigor could strike you dead if he wanted to!'

'If I tell my uncle . . .'

'If you tell your uncle on her, Zorioné, we'll *do* you!' I was startled to hear Osané sound so fierce. 'D'you hear?'

'Forget she ever said it! Itsaso, make the sign!'

Itsaso looked defiant, but even so she made the sign. The others breathed a sigh of relief. 'But,' Itsaso said, 'what I'm still telling you is my aunt Nekané *is* Go-Between, and even if she can't speak to the Animals about the Hunt, she can speak to them about anything else if she wants to. What's more, she already has!'

I was pleased by Itsaso's loyalty to my mother, but also surprised. Itsaso and Nekané didn't like each other much. They were too alike. Later I understood how People in a family almost always stick up for each other at the Gathering even if they're not getting on by themselves. That's why things have to be really bad before a family brings its silly grievances to the Go-Between in front of everyone. I've always thought it was stupid to let things get to that state. All that happens is that everyone mocks you, and they tell stories and laugh about it for ever after. And the Go-Between asks horrible questions and shouts insults at you all. It always turns out to be everyone's fault anyway. No one goes away feeling as if they'd been right. I reckon that if I ever had trouble with my own family I'd just go with some cousins instead and not make a big fuss about it. In fact that's what Itsaso did in the end, and she and her mother get on quite well when they meet now.

'How has she spoken to the Animals?' demanded Zorioné. 'What did she do? Haizea, what did your mother do?'

I didn't want to talk to them about my mother, and still less about my brother. I'd answered enough questions about Bakar when we'd arrived at the Gathering. But now I didn't have to: Itsaso told them – even though she'd not been there – what had happened at River Mouth Camp, and how Nekané had found her Helpers, and how at White Beach Camp her Helpers had told her that Kemen was a good man. 'And he's been with us ever since,' finished Itsaso. 'And it's true. He's all right.'

'How can you be sure? Anyway, he'll have to come before the Gathering.'

'My uncle Zigor will find out if he's bringing any bad spirits.'

'Your uncle—'

'My mother says,' Osané interrupted, 'that there *is* a bad spirit, because Kemen came just after your brother was lost, and that means—'

'It doesn't!' cried Itsaso. 'Nekané would have known if it did!'

'Well, it'll still have to come to the Gathering,' declared Osané. 'I'm not saying my mother is right. She usually isn't. I'm just telling you what they're saying.'

'What do you mean, "she usually isn't"?' I was glad Itsaso

had asked; it was a new idea to me that anyone would think her mother was usually wrong.

'Oh,' Osané sighed. Then she sat up so quickly her branch shook and she had to grab hold. 'I *hate* my mother!' she burst out. 'She just does everything my father tells her – she lets him tell her that I . . . But she's *wrong*!'

'So? Why should you care? You're a woman; she can't make *you* do anything.'

'Is that what you think? Itsaso, you don't know anything! You just think with your belly! And that's so stuffed up with your feast – which you keep going on about as if most of us here hadn't had one too – it's not telling you anything at all!'

'All right, all right,' said Itsaso, too curious to argue. 'So what's your mother doing to you?'

Edur, you may not want to hear what I'm going to tell next, but it's the truth.

'You know Edur?'

'*Him*!'

'The one who raped—'

'They're not trying to make you—'

'But he *raped*—'

'I don't know that! Who?'

'Don't *touch* him!'

They clamoured like rooks, while I looked from one to another, trying to make sense of what they said. My brother had told me Edur was the greatest living hunter among the Auk People. Listen, you boys, and I'll tell you what he was like back then. Actually he's not changed much since: I'm the one that's changed. Even in summer Edur wore a thick bearskin tunic that came from a bear he'd killed when he was hunting alone with just a couple of dogs. He was more tattooed with signs of dangerous Animals he'd killed than any of the other men, and when he wasn't hunting he was all hung about with amulets made from the teeth and antlers of Animals that had given themselves to him. I'd always thought he was admirable.

'Tell me!' commanded Itsaso. 'I didn't know this! Who got raped?'

The other girls looked at each other. 'If we tell you, don't say anything!'

'All right.'

'I mean that.' Osané looked at Itsaso severely. 'She's his first cousin. If the men knew . . . She's not married yet. And it wasn't her fault.'

'Did she go with him?'

'She didn't know. He was her *cousin*. She admired him. But if the men knew . . . If I tell you, Itsaso, you must *never* say. Not even when we're all married! *Never!*'

'But doesn't her mother—'

Osané spat loudly. 'Her mother's worse than mine! And now *my* mother keeps telling me I must take Edur. He is after all' – she mimicked her mother's voice – '"the greatest hunter among our People, and he'll always bring back plenty of meat, even in the very worst seasons". My mother wants him for our winter Camp, and that's all there is to it!'

'But your mother can't decide what man you take! Why don't you—'

'Oh grow up!'

There was another pause. Then Itsaso said tentatively, 'At least you were going to tell me her name.'

'You'll never tell?'

Itsaso balanced on her branch and spread her arms wide. 'Before all the spirits, I'll never tell!'

'Lean down!'

Itsaso swung round and hung down, holding on to her branch with her legs. I saw Osané whisper into her upside-down ear.

Itsaso's eyes grew round. She swung back to her place without a word. I could see she had something new and alarming to think about.

I lay looking up into the leaves. They turned green and then white and then green again as the wind moved them, changing like the colours of a dance. A few leaves were already brittle and brown at the edges. One leaf broke away and floated down just past me. It was the first leaf I'd seen fall in that Year.

'I reckon the Go-Betweens will search this Kemen after the Animals capture the boys,' said Zorioné, breaking the silence. 'Anyway, they can't speak to the Animals about the Hunt until everything's cleared up. And I mean *everything*, not just this Kemen man.'

'You mean about Edur and—'

'Hush! No, no, that mustn't come to the Gathering! I told you.'

'*That* wouldn't matter for the Hunt,' said Zorioné dismissively. 'No, I just mean the *important* things that have to be dealt with before the Go-Betweens speak to the Animals about the Hunt.'

Kemen said:

It was much easier sailing up the Long Strait with the Auk People! The tide surged under the boat-hide ; I felt it singing through the soles of my feet. It filled my body with its strength. It found its voice in my breath as I sang the paddling songs of the Auk People with the others. Since I'd first landed on Mother Mountain Island – eleven Moons ago now – the Auk People's words had become mine. I understood their speech. The Lynx People's songs lay silent in my heart, hoping that one day they would find a new voice. Now the Auk People's songs were finding a space in my heart beside those silent songs. As we paddled up the Long Strait in Gathering Moon, the Auk songs and the Lynx songs lay with one another inside my heart and a small hope was born: that one day all the songs I knew would find their voices in one People. That hope drew its first breath as I sang. It had no voice: it wouldn't find a voice for many a long day yet.

I thought of my lonely voyage into Long Strait last Yellow Leaf Moon, and shuddered. My life was very different now! There were more than two hands-full of us at Salmon Camp, and we met as many more at Boat Crossing Camp, all preparing to sail up the Long Strait to Gathering Camp. If I'd met so many Auk People in one place in Yellow Leaf Moon I'd have feared for my life. Now, coming as I did with Sendoa and his brothers, I felt mostly excitement, with only the faintest tinge of fear.

We paddled out of the bay at Boat Crossing Camp and Sendoa raised the sail. I looked back the way I'd come in the autumn. I saw two high peaks standing alone between the Morning Sun Sky and the High Sun Sky. I couldn't help exclaiming, 'There's the Heron People's Grandmother Mountain!'

Haizea, facing me from the bows – she'd chosen to travel in Sendoa's boat that day – blazed up at once. '*Heron People's*? What do you mean? How can you say that! That's our very own Grandmother Mountain! That's where the spirits gave life to our People at the Beginning. How could you not know *that*?'

Sendoa pulled the sail rope tight. 'Kemen's right,' he said mildly. 'Grandmother Mountain belongs to the Heron People too. You know that, Haizea!'

'Of course I know that!' Haizea fixed her gaze on me. '*Surely* you know that Grandmother Mountain had *two* daughters. They lived with her – right there, on the Mountain. Then a man came from under the Sunless Sky, and he took one daughter, and they were the Father and Mother of the Auk People. And then another man came from under the High Sun Sky, and he took the other daughter, and they were the Father and Mother of the Heron People. And so the two sisters were parted. But from the Beginning the Grandmother Mountain has kept watch over both her daughters, and over all their children from the Beginning until now. That's why she stands where she does. We hunt here, on this side of her, and as for the Heron People' – Haizea pointed down Long Strait – 'they hunt beyond Grandmother Mountain, way over there.'

I paddled silently for a while, letting the songs flow past me. Wind filled the sail-hide, and the shore of Mother Mountain Island slid by easily. There was no point mentioning that I knew more about the Heron People than Haizea was ever likely to. The Heron People were nothing to me. I became a man a long way from here, among the Lynx People. Even the smallest Auk children knew the Ancestors in this land better than I did. I watched young Ortzi's back as he paddled in front of me. His skin was as smooth as a girl's, and, although I could see that his muscles were already strong, he was very skinny: all his ribs showed when he bent forward. He was only a boy, and yet in some ways I had more to learn than he had. Amets had also been a stranger when he first came to Gathering Camp, but his grandfather was from the Auk People, so although he came from far-off he'd already belonged more than I did. I guessed I'd be tested more severely, but how I didn't yet know.

That night we all camped on a sheltered beach behind a low-lying island. We were up before dawn to cross the head of Long Strait at slack water. That was my first sight of Gathering Camp Loch. I'd never seen anything like it! You're all used to the way it narrows and widens again; how the tide races through the narrows and slackens into broad stretches; how the loch curls like a snake, first one way and then another; how if the mist's down you have to read where you are from the colour and feel of the water because the bits of land you see will all try to deceive you. Gathering Loch knows how to keep strangers away! You're all used to dodging the rocks and islands that rise up to bar your way. None of you notice that the land itself is trying to stop you. It doesn't worry you that at every headland and island Gathering Loch pretends to come to an end, and then you turn the corner and there's a great stretch of sea still lying before you.

Neither was I used to the way the tide does your work for you – I was still frightened of being swept along so fast. Sendoa had told me we'd only sail with the flood every day. I soon saw why: there's no point struggling against the ebb in Gathering Loch. These days I'm happy to set up Camp for half the day along the way. I like having lazy days feasting with kin from other islands as we all make our slow way into the heart of the Auk People's hunting lands. But on that first voyage I was anxious to get there. I wanted to make my life among the Auk People, but I knew my test would be waiting for me at Gathering Camp. I wanted to get it over.

As the arms of the hills enclosed us, the sound of the Open Sea was left behind. The sail was no good to us any more. Sendoa rolled it up and lashed the mast down. We paddled over white-capped waves setting our course for Loch Island, as the flood flowed under us. As we drew close to the island I saw two stags on the shingle drinking from a River that flowed into the loch. I narrowed my eyes to see them over the shining water. Both Animals had rounded bellies and sleek hides. The old stag raised his heavy antlered head – tatters of velvet still hung from the points – to stare at us. The younger one – he was only in his second Year – stirred uneasily. The old one knew no Stag had agreed to give himself that day. The great Hunt of Deer Moon comes just before the Rut. Until Gathering Camp is over, all the stags have to do is keep out of the way.

Of course if a stag crosses a man's path before the Hunt, that man will take what the spirits have given. But for the little space before the Rut the stags are not part of the Hunt. In Deer Moon, men become Stags. Men roam the hills and watch the hinds. Men choose the hinds and circle them. Men take what the spirits have given. This is why men say that the great Hunt is the Rut that comes before the Rut. Because at Gathering Camp men are also choosing hinds – of a different kind! They watch them and circle them. They fight off their rivals. Sometimes they die. They're driving their slippery hinds into a different kind of trap. They'll take them if they can get them! Yes, you boys over there! You may well laugh! You know what I'm talking about!

My thoughts had drifted far-off. My heart had been filled with hopes when we set out for the Auk People's Gathering Camp. But the fear in the heart of that young stag flew over the water and wreathed itself round my own heart. The spirits of the Hunt are very powerful. If you get on the wrong side of them they're dangerous. Long after we'd paddled past, the image of that young stag lingered inside my eyes. I only gradually became aware of the talk going on around me.

'I thought we were going to beach on Loch Island?'

'We won't waste the flood. Not with a good wind like this. We'll take the channel, and keep going until slack water.'

'Sendoa wanted Hodei to see Kemen before we got to Gathering Camp.'

My ears pricked up at the sound of my own name.

Sendoa said, 'He's right: we can't waste this tide. We'll find Hodei later on, at Gathering Camp.'

'Who is Hodei?' I asked Sendoa.

In front of me Ortzi snorted. 'He doesn't know!'

Sendoa leaned over and boxed Ortzi's ears. 'Enough! You may be a stranger yourself some day! D'you expect the spirits of far places to be kind to you then, if you can't show them any respect now?'

Ortzi kept his sore head down, and paddled furiously. No one spoke as Sendoa steered us into a narrow channel, following Amets' boat in front. The tide surged through the narrow gap, sweeping us with it, past green and gold woodland on our left hand, and a craggy island on our right. A group of children were standing at the top of the crag on the island. They whooped and cheered as our hand-full of boats shot through the channel. Haizea yelled back, 'Argi! Argi! We'll see you at Gathering Camp!' I hardly glanced up; I could see water pouring over jagged rocks a bare paddle's length away. I still wasn't used to the Auk People's ideas about travelling!

When we'd raced through the channel into gentler waters Sendoa gave me an answer. 'Hodei's one of our Go-Betweens. He usually stays on Loch Island all summer. You can see how it is – no one can pass through Gathering Loch without the People on Loch Island knowing about it. It's Hodei's Birth Place. The spirits of Loch Island are very powerful. If Hodei decides in your favour, Kemen, you couldn't wish for a stronger friend.' Sendoa stopped speaking while we rounded a point on the High Sun Shore. I'd thought we were almost at the end of Gathering Loch, but now what seemed like a whole new loch opened up before us. When we were in open water again Sendoa went on, 'That's why I hoped to take you to Hodei before he leaves Loch Island. But while wind and tide are as kind as this I daren't anger the spirits by refusing their gifts. For your sake, Kemen, I want to keep the spirits of Gathering Camp on our side in every way I can!'

While I was thinking about Sendoa's words, Haizea shouted from the bows: 'I can see Sharp Peak!'

I looked where she pointed, and saw a far-off mountain peak. It looked like a double tooth, with a little dip in the middle of the peak. I felt another tremor run through the men around me, between one paddle stroke and the next, like a bowstring suddenly pulled taut. I gazed at Sharp Peak, and the mountain spoke to me of the great Gathering Hunt of the Auk People. It knew we were drawing close. A little shiver ran up my spine. If I'd known how . . . But the spirits had told me enough. When I next glanced up the mountain had hidden itself in cloud. A swathe of rain drifted across the hills around us, and pattered on the water as we paddled on.

Next morning's tide brought us to an expanse of shingle and salt flats where a River flowed out from the Sunless Sky. We could see the head of the loch at last. There were a lot of boats already carried up the flats and weighed down with stones. We laid our boats beside them and picked up our baskets and rolls of hide. I caught myself trembling, and drew in my breath to stop myself, hoping no one had seen. This Deer Moon would set the course for the rest of my life. I turned my back on the others and stretched up my arms to the spirits. I was a man and I would not beg. But as a stranger I humbly asked the Auk spirits to accept me. I told them that although this place was new to me, I wanted to belong here. I asked for the chance to show them – and these Auk men – how well I could hunt. I asked for the chance to show them – and these Auk women – how much I deserved a woman to take me into her family.

I expect my friends knew what I was saying. Although I was a stranger no one tried to stop me speaking to the Auk spirits. I looked round, blinking, and saw that everyone had set off towards the River. I took the hides they'd left for me to carry, and followed the others across the flats, picking my way from tussock to tussock of tough salt-grass. Little rivulets of shell sand ran between the tussocks, with broken shells and bits of seaweed stuck in the cracks. I walked towards the River: the spate had left a tangle of seaweed and brown leaves behind it.

The air was shrill with oyster catchers, and gulls wheeled, screaming, above my head. I looked back the way we'd come. The wind blew patterns across the ebbing tide, telling me that until it changed there was no easy way out. I stood still, clutching the rolled-up hides to my chest. I breathed deep, and smelt the kind air of Gathering Camp; it told me that I could easily become familiar with this place.

I'd seen so few People in Auk lands that I'd thought the lands under the Evening Sun Sky were almost empty. Of course I was wrong. The path upriver had been ground into mud by many feet. The air was heavy with the smell of People. The River wound between marshlands and reed-filled beaver lakes. I forded a chattering burn and found myself among oaks and hazels. Light slanted through the leaves; moss and lichen gleamed as if flames were licking up the tree trunks. Rapids gushed over rocks as the banks grew higher. Suddenly I was afraid. My friends had gone ahead of me, and the air smelt of many strangers. I saw light ahead of me, and ran towards it like a deer hurtling into a trap, the hides bumping on my back.

I stopped short at the edge of the clearing. Like a trapped deer, I wanted to turn and flee. There was nowhere to go. Never in my life had I seen so many strangers at once. You Auk People – you women who'll never leave your own lands – you boys who've never yet left your family hearth – you can't begin to know what it's like to come upon hands-full upon hands-full of strangers – People you've never seen before – whose names you've never heard in all your lives.

Through the wreathing smoke of my confusion I saw how the People's hearths formed a great circle with the Go-Betweens' mound in the middle. All the spirits of Gathering Camp clustered above that one green mound in the middle of the clearing. I felt a warning in my blood, as if I were coming close to a sleeping bear or hungry hunting wolves. As I watched, the fires on the green mound flamed high among crackling pine branches. Smoke billowed across the clearing. Looking up, I saw two cloaked figures through the smoke.

I was the stranger: these Auk People had nothing to fear. Children and dogs were scrambling up the steep sides of the Go-Betweens' mound. They'd catch sight of the cloaked figures of the Go-Betweens through the wreathing smoke, and slide back down, shrieking in delighted terror.

Then Sendoa pulled me over to the family hearth, and I forgot about the mound with its clustering spirits. Fear fled into the shadows. Everyone was greeting everyone else with roars of delight and much slapping of arms and backs. All around me women and men were hurrying from hearth to hearth so I couldn't see where anyone belonged. But with Sendoa pushing me forward, they all greeted me kindly. Some even brought out roasted hazelnuts from their pouches and insisted that I eat.

Gathering Camp is Auk all right! You can tell by the din! Gathering Camp is like all the Auks gathered together on the nesting cliffs of White Beach Island after their long winter out at sea. But Lynx is a silent, solitary Animal. I won't say our People were always true to Lynx in that – but the noise you Auks make when you're all together is enough to frighten away any spirits except your own!

But Auks are kind. They'll nest alongside kittiwakes and gulls. They take no notice of shags on the rocks below or rock doves in their hidden clefts, or pipits among the puffin burrows. No one at Gathering Camp seemed worried about me. And I was pleased to find, when I spoke to these new People, that they understood what I said. Since Yellow Leaf Moon I'd worked very hard to speak like the Auk People. But even today my tongue still tells strangers that I wasn't born under the Evening Sun Sky.

Later on, People told me about the journeys they'd made to get to Gathering Camp. In my country we don't sail across the Open Sea. Why would we? There aren't any islands, and a boat can – could – follow the coast as far as it wanted to go. But some of these Auk People had made long journeys across the Open Sea from distant islands, from which, they told me, the hills above Gathering Camp looked blue and far away, and very often weren't visible at all. Not all these far-off People come to Gathering Camp every Year – they counted a lot of kin who'd stayed behind – but I soon realised that although the Auk People are thinly scattered, they hunt under many skies.

As soon as we'd pitched our tents Amets took me round to show me what a good place this was. It didn't occur to anyone else that I wouldn't know my way. Ortzi and the dogs tagged after us. We took no notice of them, and Ortzi was pleased not to be sent away. Amets showed me the fish traps along the River and the paths that led up to the high Hunting Camps. Everywhere we went there were skulls wedged in the trees: Wolf, Stag, Lynx, Fox, Aurochs, Bear and Boar. Some were green and rotting; many still gleamed white. A hand-full were fresh kills. I could see that this land gave itself generously to the Auk People.

I was pleased I could say to Amets that Gathering Camp seemed a good place. I'd been embarrassed when Amets and Sendoa had taken me across to Flint Camp in Seed Moon. When we'd sailed into the wide bay the Auk men said we'd get enough flint there to last the winter – as if we had to collect all our stone at once! But we didn't find any flints that I'd even have bothered to pick up in Lynx lands. I knew my silence was as bad as an insult, so now I was very glad I could say good things to Amets about the hunting lands at Gathering Camp.

The land was full of birds: sparrows, tits and chaffinches scavenging in the Camp; pigeons, rooks, turtledoves and songbirds in the forest; and ducks, moorhens, geese and herons in the marshes. We certainly weren't going to be hungry! Amets showed me the beaver dam and the pool above it where someone was fishing from a coracle. He explained how we don't take beaver close to Gathering Camp because they look after the dams that hold in the trout pools, and they cut down trees that give us firewood for the whole Gathering. Amets led me uphill to the hazel grove. The trees were already laden with nuts, and the grove was surrounded by a circle of thicket where the hazel had been cut back to the ground to make clumps for wands.

I whistled under my breath, and Amets smiled. 'Your People do this?' I asked him.

'Yes, at every Gathering Camp. We'll come and cut what we need before we leave. You'll see.'

Amets led me further into the forest and showed me where there were bright earth-mushrooms. People had already been here with digging sticks, but there were plenty left. We picked some and chewed as we walked. As we ducked under the great branch of an old oak that reached sideways across the path Ortzi appeared between us and pulled Amets' sleeve.

'What is it?'

Ortzi pointed at a gash in the oak trunk, where a blackened wound told how long ago a storm had ripped a big branch away. 'Bees! There's a bees' nest up there!'

I squinted up at the trunk. The Sun was in my eyes, but now I saw the bees buzzing around the scarred wood. A black slit in the broken trunk could be a hole – I couldn't tell.

'Look, Amets!' The boy was jumping up and down with excitement. 'They're going in and out of that hole where the branch used to be. Can't you see?'

'You have your uses, Ortzi,' remarked Amets. 'Suppose you climb up and make sure?'

Eagerly Ortzi scaled the rough bark. He swung himself on

to a wide branch just above our heads, and stood on tiptoe, his hands against the trunk, peering upward. 'Yes, it is! Ow! There's hands-full and hands-full of them, going in and out! Ow! Amets, I think I can smell honey! *You* could reach it if you stood on this branch. Ow!'

'Come down! You'll get plenty more stings later!'

Ortzi swung himself round the branch, hanging by his hands. He edged his toes into the rough bark and slithered down the trunk. He stood beside us, rubbing his palms on his deerskins, and grinned up at Amets.

Amets took no notice of him. 'That's a new nest, Kemen! It wasn't here last Year. We'll come back with fire and baskets this afternoon. I think we might get something good! And Ortzi,' – Amets rounded on the boy – 'you keep your mouth shut till then. I'll flay you if your friends get here first!'

Ortzi shook his head hard, and stretched his open hands to the spirits.

There'd been plenty of Animals about, especially red deer, roe deer and aurochs. Already People had set ground traps for small game, and bird snares in the trees. Of course now the Auk People were gathering in great numbers the Animals would retreat, but not so far that we couldn't follow. As soon as the Go-Betweens had spoken to the Animals about the Hunt, the great Hunt of Gathering Camp would begin.

'Amets!' I spoke to him quietly when we'd gone a little way ahead, because I didn't want Ortzi to hear.

'Yes?'

'Will they let a stranger join the Hunt?'

Amets stopped and put his hand on my shoulder. He didn't answer at once. Then he said slowly, 'Only the Go-Betweens know what the spirits say. But a spirit already spoke to Nekané about you, and what she heard was good.'

'But a woman . . . will that make any difference?'

Amets shook his head. 'The Go-Betweens here won't listen to her, no. What could she say about the Hunt? But what I mean is, Nekané told us that the spirits think highly of you. The spirits don't lie. That means they'll tell the real Go-Betweens the same thing.'

I hadn't thought of it like that, but what Amets said made sense.

'Besides' – Amets shook my shoulder to emphasise the point – 'ordinary men can speak too. What do you think Sendoa and I are likely to say about you?' He smiled at me.

I smiled back: I was a man, not a child or a woman, and I hid my anxiety.

'Hush,' said Amets, 'here comes the boy.' He shook my shoulder again and let it go. 'Few People would argue with Sendoa, anyway,' he added lightly, as if our conversation had just been about that. 'Isn't that true, Ortzi?'

Startled, but very happy that Amets should speak to him, Ortzi nodded dumbly.

We went back to the bees' nest in the afternoon. Our grass hats were pulled down over our ears, and our sleeves tied tight round our wrists. We rubbed seal grease over our faces and hands and feet. We had fire, axes and mallets, and a basket each. Amets spoke to the bees and told them we wanted their honey. He said we knew they had plenty, because this was their winter Camp, and all their winter stores would be gathered in. Amets told the bees we wanted them to stay in this oak tree: we'd leave enough honey – they didn't have to give us everything. We stretched our arms up to the Bee spirits. They agreed to give themselves. We climbed up to Ortzi's branch. Our faces were on a level with the hole in the tree. Now I could see the bees plainly, going in and out of their nest. Ortzi scrambled on to a thin branch so he could watch what we did.

'You'll get stung if you stay there!'

'I don't care! I've taken honey before! I know what bees are like.'

'But you don't know what *these* bees are like – no one does – especially now they've heard you making so much of yourself!'

I glanced at the bees buzzing round Ortzi's head. My sister's son died of a bee sting – he'd lived two winters – Ortzi would never have lived this long if he'd been the same. I said nothing.

Amets took an ember from his pouch. My basket was full of dry grass and bracken. I passed Amets small handfuls. As soon as the tinder caught Amets put his face close to the hole, ignoring the stinging bees, and gently blew the smoke into the hole.

'Does that kill them?' asked Ortzi.

Amets was blowing smoke into the hole, and didn't reply.

'They'll think there's a fire,' I told Ortzi. I was glad to show this Auk boy that even Lynx men knew something! 'They'll eat as much honey as they can. Then they'll try to get away. They'll eat so much honey to take with them, they'll be too gorged to sting. At least – not sting quite so much.'

'I've got lots of stings already!'

Amets dusted ashes from his fingers. Two hands-full of heart-beats passed. He raised his axe. It thudded into the wood above the hole.

The tree was quite hollow. In a heartbeat we'd broken the scarred wood away with axes and mallets. Amets reached into the nest with both hands, one clutching his knife, his cheek against the rough bark. His hands came out clasping a great lump of waxy honeycomb. Bright yellow honey dripped between his fingers. Angry bees flew in his face, trying to sting him off. I held Amets' basket open. Two more shining handfuls and it was full.

I wriggled past him until I was leaning against the trunk. Amets held my basket. I didn't expect to fill it – *two* baskets-full would be too much to hope for. I groped in the darkness of the tree, my eyes shut so all my seeing went into my hands. Amid the stinging bees I felt the warm stickiness of honey. I cut through the nest with my knife, and eased my fingers through the waxy comb. I pulled a lump of honey away in my cupped hands and lifted it into the daylight. Rivers of sunlight oozed between my fingers. Thick honey clung to my hands, then slid reluctantly into the open basket. I licked my fingers. Sweetness sang on my tongue, full of light and memory. I shut my eyes to savour it.

I reached again into the dark hollow in the oak trunk. Once . . . twice . . . my basket was as full as Amets'. I felt around the hollow inside the tree with my sticky hands, but I couldn't touch the top of it.

'Is there more? Is there? Can I have a turn?'

Ortzi slid down in front of Amets. He had a woman's basket – his mother's I suppose. That boy always had large ideas of what he'd find! Amets didn't speak to him, but he held the basket open for him. Ortzi reached into the tree as far as he could. 'Ow! Ow! Ow!'

'What did you expect?'

'I don't care! I can feel honey! It's too far away! My arms aren't as long as yours!' Ortzi jumped up and thrust his shoulders into the gap. In spite of the angry bees settling on him he reached right in. 'I've got some! Ow! Ow! I've got some!'

'That's enough!' said Amets presently. 'Three handfuls.'

'But my hands are smaller than yours! There's more honey in there!'

'For the bees,' said Amets. 'You want to find them here next Year, don't you?'

'Even so,' said Ortzi when we were all on the ground again, licking honey from our hands and faces, and picking out the stings from our bare skin. 'I don't think anyone ever found this much honey in one nest before, Amets! And I found it! *You* wouldn't have seen it if I hadn't told you! D'you think I'll make a good hunter?'

'No, I don't! Stand still – look at me – let me get those stings off your face before your mother sees you. You sing your own praises much too loud, Ortzi! The Animals will be so frightened of you they'll all run away. Isn't that right, Kemen? This boy is going to have to learn how to behave properly before he learns to hunt anything, don't you think?'

That evening the Go-Betweens spoke to the Animals about the Hunt.

Alaia said:

It always takes me a day or two to get used to all the People at Gathering Camp. There's so much to do in less than a Moon. What with dogs barking, gangs of children running round yelling, fights breaking out, singing all night long – different songs on every side of course – bargaining, visiting, gossip, crowds chanting while the Go-Betweens heal sicknesses and quarrels . . . And that Year People were asking us about Bakar all over again . . . that was hard.

Also I had Esti to show to everyone. Her name was new to us, so they were all eager to meet this small stranger. Woman after woman came to hold her, and look into her eyes, and say to her, 'Welcome to the Auk People, Esti. You will always find food here!'

The Go-Betweens were going to speak to the Animals about the Hunt that evening. I said I'd stay in Camp with Esti and roast the hazelnuts as the women brought them to us. My aunt Sorné got back first. She tipped out her basket. As we spread the hazelnuts over the sand she was saying how Eguskiné had told her that Arantxa was full of some story about how Edur was going to take her daughter Osané. 'Which is not what I'd wish for any daughter of mine,' my aunt said, smoothing sand over the fresh nuts. 'He may be a great hunter, but meat isn't the only thing a woman needs in her life. Eguskiné thinks he'd settle down if he got Osané. I'm not so sure.'

Sorné helped me spread oak embers over the sand. She sat with me until we had a good roasting fire. Then she was off again – we'd be needing all the food we could get. Later I wished I'd taken my basket and gone with her. First I had a row with Agurné – their tents were next to ours and every morning their dogs were shitting on our ground, right next to my roasting pit. She said it wasn't their dogs – but I'd *seen* them. Oh, you know what it's like at Gathering Camp, but in our family we don't shout filthy words and throw dirt at each other. So when Eguskiné came over with the bloodstones I was still upset. I gave her blackberries, and hazelnuts still hot from the sand. We chatted for a bit before we talked about the stones, so I thought I was feeling better. But when she'd gone I opened the leather bag again and laid out the bloodstones, and realised at once I'd given two big flintstones for what was actually very little. It was too late now. I couldn't quarrel with Eguskiné. Her great-grandmother was also mine. And Eguskiné's hearth is always open, surrounded by songs and laughter. I didn't want to find myself shut out. And who knows when one of our family might need to go to Bloodstone Island to fetch stones, or get a woman? You never know. I've never been there, but I know the high mountains of Bloodstone Island very well – I often see them, far across the sea under the Sunless Sky.

I was trying to heat stones, split wood, scoop roasted hazel-nuts off hot sand and suckle Esti all at once, when Amets came back, sleek as an otter from bathing in the beaver lake, his hair dripping over his eyes. He laid down a basket of trout, and immediately wanted me to comb out his wet hair and plait it again. So I had to stop everything and do that. I put Esti down on a hide. She began to cry. Amets picked up his daughter and held her naked between his hands, facing him.

'Keep your head still or I can't comb your hair!'

Esti laughed in her father's face and pushed with her legs, dancing on his knees. She caught hold of a strand of wet hair and pulled it.

'Ah, you would, would you? Have you no respect for your father? What's your mother been teaching you? How dare you look me in the eye, little daughter?'

Esti chuckled and tried to grab his nose.

'What did I do, eh, to be surrounded by all these women who have nothing better to do than pull my hair and laugh at me?'

'D'you want me to stop then?'

Amets reached up, holding Esti with his other hand, and seized my wrist, laughing. 'You know I never want you to stop!'

He went away when I'd trimmed his hair with my knife and plaited it again. I was behind with my work now, but I felt better.

Anyway, we had plenty of food. Amets brought the trout, and my father had gone over the hills to the marshes with his dog and taken two mallard. I was pleased for him: he couldn't go hunting with the young men any more, but he could creep and hide in the rushes as well as ever, and I never knew anyone, man or woman, who could use a bow as well as my father did. The reason I remember so well is that this was the last day that my father brought home meat: he who provided so well for us all my life. Of course we'd been hungry in bad seasons – no one could avoid that – but with my father we'd never known real want.

Haizea and Itsaso had been fishing too, with lines. They'd got a basket of young saithe, and, believe it or not, an octopus. They couldn't have set an octopus trap from the shore, but I had more sense than to ask whose boat they'd used. The others brought in small birds and baskets-full of many-coloured mushrooms, endless hazelnuts and berries, and lots of different roots from woodland, marsh and shore. My aunt Sorné brought a basket of acorns and set them to steep in the River. I'd kept the fire hot so as to make a heap of smouldering ashes. I covered up the roots and fish, and skewered the birds on hazel spits. Other families were also cooking. The rich smell of many kinds of food mingled and rose into the air. Everything is plentiful in Gathering Moon, except in the worst Years, and this wasn't one of them. The spirits crowded above us, hidden behind clouds of flies, savouring the different tastes that floated up to them. There was all the usual to-ing and fro-ing between hearths, especially the children, offering and receiving the best titbits from each other's food. Everyone was laughing and joking; we were as noisy as rooks! Even Agurné came over with a big basket of mussels, cooked and ready to eat. I gave her one of the ducks – a lot better than mussels – which was all I had ready. I hoped this meant there'd be no dogshit at my tent door in the morning. Just when the food was ready, Amets and Kemen came back with a huge basket dripping with honey. Nothing could have been better! I sent the two girls off at once to offer honey to all our kin.

Itsaso and Haizea carried the basket between them, and I could hear Itsaso's ringing tones all round the Camp. She sounded just like her mother! My hand went to my mouth when she swaggered up to a Go-Between's hearth. At least she hadn't the gall to speak to Zigor directly, but I was near enough to hear what she said to his wife and nieces: 'Forgive us for inter-rupting you with such a sad little gift. You really won't think much of it. I don't know why my cousin bothered to bring it back. I know People like honey – but this! Well, it's not much good, but it could look worse, see' – Itsaso dipped the stirring-stick and let the honey flow off it in a thick golden stream flecked with sweet lumps of waxy honeycomb. 'Won't you be kind to my poor family and honour us by accepting some of this, even though it's not much good?'

Of course they could hardly wait. The birchbark basket they held out certainly wasn't the smallest they had, either. I didn't grudge them one mouthful. Honey sweetens the soul. As Itsaso poured their honey I realised the spirits were indeed looking after us. If there were one thing we needed to do above every-thing else it was to sweeten Zigor now. No fewer than three of my family were going to be tested at this Gathering: Nekané, Ortzi and Kemen. Itsaso was a clever girl: she kept on pouring honey until it was oozing over the birchbark on to Zorioné's deerskins, and they had to cry out for her to stop.

The girls came back to us with an empty basket. Only the children who were too young to understand the value of gifts minded. We gave them the basket and a cockleshell each, and let them scrape the thickly woven rushes clean. I smeared a little honey on the end of my finger before it was all gone, and let Esti suck it. She'd never tasted honey before. We ended up with some very sticky children!

The Go-Betweens started preparing the three fires at the top of their mound. As we ate and talked, we watched them walking round their fires, stretching up their hands, getting ready for the spirits. Most of the children had finished eating. They kept scrambling up the Go-Betweens' mound and sliding down again, shrieking with excitement. A hand-full of half-grown puppies barked and leaped amongst them. As always the Go-Betweens took no notice. The spirits see children like leaves blowing in the wind. Children can do whatever they like because the serious business of life has nothing to with them; not yet.

We had three Go-Betweens: Aitor, Zigor and Hodei. There was Nekané too, of course, but she hadn't been publicly accepted. Some People thought she never would be because she was a woman. Zigor was against it – his niece Zorioné made sure we all knew that! When the Go-Betweens came out of the shelter with their drums some of our kin glanced across to see how my mother was taking it. Nekané's face showed nothing. She knew better than to draw attention to herself when they were speaking to the Animals about the Hunt. She was biding her strength.

Only when the footsteps began was everyone quiet. As soon as the Go-Betweens heard the footsteps of the Animals they began to echo them with their drums so we could hear them too. The nearest People began to clap with the drumming. The clapping spread across the Camp. The last conversations ceased. Everyone stopped eating. Young women went round collecting the good bones into baskets, and flinging the rest on to the midden with all the empty shells. People wiped their mouths and turned to watch the Go-Betweens. Soon everyone was clapping the footsteps of the Animals.

Most of you remember Aitor in his last life. He was quiet and kind when he wasn't Go-Between, but when he was – oh, he was frightening! Aitor was a huge man with a big voice. When he came out of the Go-Betweens' tent, painted all over in spirit-patterns of Red and Yellow, with his wolfskin round his waist and Wolf's face pulled over his man-face – when he came out of that tent with his Drum written all over with secret marks, and its wolf-claws and sea-eagle feathers dangling from its frame – all the People used to gasp and cower away. Children burst into tears at the very sight of him. You think Hodei is a frightening Go-Between – it's true that Fox looks cruel and hard over a man-face, especially when the spirits have written Blue and Red over a man's body, and his Drum beats through your body like the heart of the land itself, and his cloak of feathers flies out behind him . . . But Hodei – I hope you won't mind me saying this, Hodei – isn't as terrifying as Aitor was.

Then Zigor . . . After the other Go-Betweens Zigor seemed light as a bird. He was always small and bent, even when he was young. Painted in his spirit-colours he seemed to turn spirit himself, caught in a beam of light and made suddenly visible. His power was like the whip of a hazel wand coming after the solid strength of oak. Zigor used to come out of the tent last, after the other two. Some People – especially the women – well, me too, I suppose – thought he was the most frightening one of all. Women often feel – I feel myself – the very thought of Snake makes us shiver, even on a sunny day when everything that's Go-Between seems to be fast asleep. Yet when Osprey soars over the Open Sea our hearts long to follow . . . Osprey opens up our dreams and makes our waking thoughts fly high and far. When Zigor's Drum awoke and began to beat, its voice was so cold and far away – that Drum was somehow the most Go-Between thing I ever heard. I tremble now, even just thinking about it.

Aitor began the song. Although the song has no words it tells of many things most of us will never understand. A cold wind creeps down my back every Year when I hear that song. The Go-Betweens sang to the Animals while we clapped their footsteps until our palms were sore. The Wise began to sing to the Animals as well. The younger men joined in, and last of all the young women. We sang softly at first so we could hear the Go-Betweens above the rest, and then louder. The song grew fast and fierce. Some People stopped clapping and drummed their fists on the ground until it shook. The song got so loud it wasn't just the People any more. The Animals were in it too, and so were the spirits that link the souls of People and Animals together, because at the Beginning we were all one soul, and inside everything else that happens to us we are still in the Beginning, and always will be.

The dark covered us. Out of it shone Deer Moon: a little sliver, no thicker than the paring of a thumbnail, still entangled in an oak tree top. The People kept clapping until Deer Moon came clear of the leaves and launched herself into the sky. She was barely big enough to dim the stars. The Go-Betweens' fires glowed above us on the mound. The Go-Betweens were lost in the shadows. We only saw the flash of tooth or tusk catching the firelight as they moved.

Other things moved in the shadows behind the fire. Now the firelight caught the curve of an antler, the sweep of a horn, and lost them again. The men around us were on their feet. The ground thudded with the footsteps of the Animals.

Sendoa leaped from our hearth. His brothers followed. As he passed, Sendoa leaned over me and grabbed Kemen by the arm, pulling him forward. The firelight fell on Kemen's face: I saw the startled question in his eyes. The brothers surrounded him, shoving him into the centre. Amets wasn't there. I hadn't seen him leave, but I knew why he'd gone. We couldn't see anything now. The darkness of many bodies hid the fire, and swallowed up our men.

We stood up so we could see better. We linked arms – Haizea was on one side of me and my aunt Sorné on the other. We swayed and sang, stamping out the footsteps of the Animals. Their song was our song. We couldn't see them because the Men hid them from us. The Animals crouched and hid, and began to creep and run away. The Men raised invisible spears and stalked them. All round the Go-Betweens' mound they crept and stalked. Whenever the light caught them they fled into the dark again. We saw them aim their spears.

Then we saw – over the heads of the men – caught in the

firelight – the spread antlers – there at the foot of the mound – where the song began – we saw them turn gold and black and gold again in the shifting light. They rose in the still heartbeat which is the beginning of the Hunt.

The antlers twitched. They turned one way and then the other. They twisted and ducked among the thundering footsteps of Men and Animals. The Dance turned around the antlers, just as the stars all turn round the one Still Star in the heart of the Sunless Sky.

Haizea jumped up and down at my side, trying to see over the heads of the Men. She was too young to know that even if she were as tall as an aspen she would never see what was hidden at the heart of the Hunt. I saw Deer Moon high above my head. I felt Esti a sleeping weight on my back. My hands and feet ached with clapping and stamping. I drew back and sank down on the big oxskin by our fire. We'd laid heather and bracken underneath it, and put a birch trunk at the back to lean on. In spite of the noise, or because of it, the young children were already asleep. I pulled Esti round to my front and lay propped against the log with her in my arms. The ground shook under me with the footsteps of the Animals. The heart of the earth beat through me. One by one the others joined me. Haizea and Ortzi were the last to drop. They'd forgotten they'd stopped being friends. Ortzi was frightened, both of what might happen next, and – worse still – of what might not happen. Child-like, he clung to Haizea as he never would again. They crouched at the edge of the spread skins, arms round each other's shoulders, and though the rest of us dozed now and then, as far as I know those two children never moved.

Later on I was cold. Drowsily I pulled my deerhide round myself and Esti. The Morning Sun Sky was streaked with pink and grey. I could hear the footsteps of the Animals, but now they were far away. I watched the men who were still dancing.

Their steps were slow and weary. Up on the mound the Go-Betweens' fires burned low. Just below the hearths lay three huddled shapes: the bodies of the Go-Betweens who'd given their lives to the Hunt. So all was well. Once again the Go-Betweens had saved us from the terrible bargain we make when we come into this world, because we have to eat up other souls in order to feed and clothe our own. Every child needs to hear this, so listen, even the little ones! For every soul we take, a soul must be given back. If our Go-Betweens didn't speak to the Animals about the Hunt, so they agree to die for us and come back, over and over again, the People would have to leave the world for ever.

I looked round at the family hearths lining the clearing. Women and children lay fast asleep all round me, though some had gone back to their tents. Haizea and Ortzi were curled up together on the edge of the oxskin. Sleep had swallowed up Ortzi's fears at last, but not for long.

Something crashed beyond the fires on the mound. Sparks flew. Drums beat. The footsteps weren't measured any more. They ran all over the place, as if all the Animals were fleeing or giving chase at once. A wild shrieking came with the foot-steps: the spirits themselves had turned Hunter and were screaming for their prey. The knot of men that hid the Go-Betweens scattered in all directions, running and yelling.

Everyone woke. Esti began to wail. Other babies were crying; little children screamed for their mothers. Haizea and Ortzi, startled from sleep, clung to each other like a couple of squirrels.

The Go-Betweens were on their feet. Animals flew from the empty air behind them. We weren't hunting them: they were hunting us! They rushed towards us. They had the bodies of Men – painted all over – and the heads of Animals. Women who'd often seen them still quailed and hid their faces. The air shook with shrieks as boys were snatched from their family hearths and spirited away. One Animal made straight for us – he had the head and upper jaw of a wolf, and a wolfskin flying at his back. His naked body was black as night and red as blood. Haizea screamed as he swooped. But it wasn't her he wanted. He ripped Ortzi from her side, threw him over his shoulder, and shot past us into the forest.

Haizea burst into tears. I took her in my arms and tried to comfort her.

'It's all right, it's all right. Ortzi will be fine. He'll be a fine man when he comes back. You'll be proud to call him cousin! Oh yes, you will. He'll be back before Gathering Camp is over – yes, and Amets too!'

'Amets?' Haizea sat up and looked round. She began to cry again. 'They took Amets too!'

'No one takes Amets!' I was sorry for her but what she'd just said was a slur on my husband. 'Amets is a man! But yes, Amets will come back too. They'll both come back before Gathering Camp is over.' I stretched my hands over her head towards the spirits. 'It happens every Year, Haizea, you know that! It's just that Ortzi was your friend. But you should be glad for him, you know. You must be glad!'

Haizea sniffed and sat up. 'I do know. It's just . . . It won't be the same any more with Ortzi, will it?'

'No,' I said, stroking my sister's tumbled hair. 'No, Haizea, it won't be the same any more. But then it never is.'

Kemen said:

We danced the Hunt. Sendoa brought me in. We were dancing. Far from the Go-Betweens' mound and then near to it: we were Roe Deer, we were Red Deer, we were Aurochs. I looked up and saw the long fires blaze above me on the mound. We were Pig, we were Bear, we were Wolf . . . Flames rose in my heart. We were Lynx, we were Lynx, and then . . .

They hurled me off my feet. They blindfolded me. They dragged me up a steep slope. From under the skin that bound my eyes I saw the fire flash by. Stones scraped my back as they dragged me. The footsteps of the Animals pounded in my ears. Under the band of skin I saw darkness. I smelt leather and sweat. They flung me down. The ground shook with the thunder of footsteps.

He gripped my hair and pulled my head back. I felt the blade against my throat.

He spoke so close to my ear I could hear him plainly over the noise of the Dance. 'You! Stranger! What have you done?'

'No wrong! I've done no wrong!' I tried to stretch out my hands, but they held me down.

'What have you done?'

The Dance echoed his words. It drummed them over and over in a multitude of stamping feet: 'What have you done, Kemen? What have you done?'

'I did no wrong! The sea swallowed us!'

'What have you done?'

'I did no wrong! Except that I lived!'

'What have you done to your kin?'

'I did no wrong!'

'What have you done to your kin?'

'They died.'

Whether I sobbed like a child in front of their eyes, or whether that was in the world he took me to, I don't know. Afterwards I feared I'd shamed myself, but if it happened in front of men in this world, no one ever mentioned it. But I dare to tell it now. Zigor knew. It was he that took me down.

Zigor dragged me by the hair. We went down. Into the heart of the sea he took me. I wept for my lost family. Zigor pulled the band from my eyes. I saw them – my father, my mother, my sisters, my cousins, all the little children – one by one they came and looked at me, the poor pale souls. Not one of their names had returned to this world.

'There's only one way they ever can.' His voice in my ear was as harsh as ever.

'I could run no faster! Even Basajaun couldn't run fast enough!'

'Basajaun!' He jerked me by the hair. The knife was still at my throat. 'What did Basajaun do?'

'Nothing! Nothing! We did no wrong!'

'You're lying!' The knife moved. Warm blood trickled past my ear.

'No! I loved them all! I did no wrong!'

The knife was gone. The blindfold bit into my forehead.

'That's true.'

I didn't realise at first what he'd said. There was no pity in his voice. But when he spoke again I heard every word. 'You did no wrong, Kemen. But wrong was done. For every soul a soul must be returned. If their names are ever to be spoken in this world again, it will be among the Auk People, and nowhere else. You hear me?'

'Yes.' Although the voice was cruel, relief flooded my soul.

'*Nowhere* else. Do you understand?'

I thought that I had, and his words filled me with joy.

'Turn him over!'

They held me down, my face crushed against the earth. Hands stretched my skin tight. I felt the graze of blades, then a stab like a bee's sting. The same hand stabbed again, and then again, across my shoulder blade. Cold fire ran through me. Stabs of fire crawled up my shoulder. They hit my collarbone and flared to flame. I let my breath go softly so no one heard me gasp. The stabs went back to my ribs and began to crawl again. I couldn't read the pattern from inside my skin. Slowly the pain changed: I felt calm inside it, even as I lay blindfold in the hands of strangers, as if this were how things were always meant to be. The warm blood running into the hollow of my back seemed like a caress.

The last island lay far behind us. We flew low over the swell. We wheeled and circled and dipped over our fishing grounds as if we were not many separate souls but one. The Open Sea was our hunting ground. On and on we flew, until the very edge of the world was before us.

He wrote my skin aflame. Careful and slow. His thoughts flowed into me. I felt the icy sting of colour, stab after stab. It no longer seemed like one after another, but all at once, burning a new message into my skin. I'd lost all sense of how long, when at last I felt the moth-like touch of cold ashes sprinkled over me.

Zigor's voice brought me back from far away. 'Auks have many enemies, Kemen. Auks use skill more than strength. They travel far across the sea where no one else can reach. Wherever you find one, not far off there'll be many together. The names of your kin will live among them, if you choose wisely.'

I turned my head sideways and managed to speak. 'I've already chosen.'

'No man can see his own back,' said Zigor. The laugh inside his voice chilled me more than words could do. 'What have you done to make you think it would be so easy? But the one man who can show you what's written on your back – he'll tell you the truth. Think of him as your brother, Kemen . . . let *him* be your brother, and your name will live among the Auk People. And *nowhere* else.'

Nekané said:

When the Go-Betweens spoke to the Animals about the Hunt it had nothing to do with me. I knew my test would come later. I expected it to be difficult. Zigor was against a woman becoming Go-Between. He couldn't say it wasn't possible. Everyone knows that in the Beginning no one was Go-Between because the spirits of People and Animals understood one another without needing to speak. After the Beginning women as well as men had difficult questions to ask. Women haven't been Go-Between so often because we don't ask our questions all at once. For the same reason, a girl doesn't need to be initiated: her initiation happens when her body's ready and she learns from her family what it means. It's the same when a woman becomes Go-Between.

I thought Aitor would be on my side because his mother was Go-Between; in fact she was the only woman Go-Between in living memory. Perhaps she taught Aitor what she knew. I didn't know about Hodei. I was sure that Zigor would stand against me. I've known Zigor since we first came to Gathering Camp as babies in the same Year. We didn't get on. Children will put up with most things from each other, but not whingeing. Zigor couldn't have kept up with the rest of us anyway: he was always ailing. People thought he'd be one of the boys who don't come back from initiation. His mother was frantic about him while he was gone – *she* wasn't Go-Between, she was a sad creature! But when Zigor came back he was as you knew him later – aloof, frightening, *dangerous*. Anything could have happened then. But, as it was, he went Go-Between very soon: he became dangerous *for* the Auk People, and not against us. So the spirits did their work. But now I was scared he'd be against *me*. It wasn't just his power as Go-Between – I was also scared he might remember the way I'd treated him when he was little.

I didn't want to be tested in front of the Gathering. I'd much rather have enjoyed being an old woman, sitting round the family hearths catching up with all my kin. I'd done my share of work. It was all very well to be counted one of the Wise, but I wanted no more than that. Of course when it comes to being Go-Between a soul has no choice.

The Go-Betweens had spoken to the Animals, so the men could set off for the Hunt. At least the men in our family were well prepared – no hurried making of blades, binding arrows, patching shoes, mending old spears or shouting at their women for not doing what they should have done long ago for themselves. Amets had already gone. My husband stayed behind. He said he was tired. If he found it hard to let go of the Hunt he never said so.

Only Sorné and I were up when the hunters left. We were glad to see them go. The morning sky was grey. The Sun had wakened us joyfully every morning since we came to Gathering Camp, but now he was resting. I came out of the tent to the whine of mosquitoes. Sorné pulled back the turfs and laid a green hazel branch on the fire. But today the mosquitoes and midges didn't mind thick black smoke. I decided I'd take my basket out as soon as I could: warm smoky Camps full of biting flies, weeping children and short-tempered women are something I can do without. I didn't yet know what the day held for me.

I heard the rustle of bracken from Sendoa's tent. I bent over the fire. Out of the corner of my eye I watched the men come creeping out of their tents, bodies still painted from the Dance, without waking their families. The dogs came from behind the tents, yawning and stretching, without so much as a growl. The men softly lifted their weapons and slung them on to their shoulders. The dogs waited, ears pricked. I made a great show of laying logs over the burning hazel branch, and blowing last night's embers into fresh flame. Sorné went off with the water-skins, keeping her back to the men. Very soon men and dogs disappeared into the forest, and we didn't have to pretend we couldn't see them any more.

'Peace at last!' said Sorné when she came back, laying down the heavy waterskins and stretching her shoulders. 'And a bit of *real* meat to look forward to!' When we were alone my sister and I didn't worry about tempting the spirits; we knew they didn't care much what we said. 'And now the young ones can get on with the work. We can sit around for a change and just be old women, Nekané! What a treat! Most women never get this far, but we grow from a strong tree, you and I.'

'I don't see you doing much sitting around! You should try it, though. Sit by the fire and look like one of the Wise!'

'What, like this?' Sorné made a prim face and we burst out laughing.

I never got my chance to sit around. Itsaso, Haizea and I, surrounded by clouds of flies, were scraping lily-roots to make a paste when Zorioné came to our hearth. The two girls stiffened as she approached. Zorioné seemed nervous, which was unlike her.

'Nekané! My uncle asks you to come to Arantxa's tent!'

'Does he say why?'

'Osané is sick. He asks you to come.'

So this was my test! No sooner were Aitor and Hodei away to Hunting Camp than Zigor had seized his chance. I had to admit he was clever. 'Why doesn't Zigor heal her himself? Why's he asking me? His skill is great, and I've none at all.'

'He said to tell you that in this case the spirits will speak only to you.'

Itsaso and Haizea exchanged glances.

'Very well. If Osané needs me I'll come.'

Itsaso and Haizea followed Zorioné and me across the Camp.

I ignored them. Up on the Go-Betweens' mound the great logs from two nights ago had almost burned themselves out. Flies buzzed in the warmth. The spirits were at rest. I passed by without saying anything.

Arantxa is, and always was, a fool. Osané's father – his name isn't in this world now – was worse than a fool. It's a wonder those children turned out so well. You two – Oroitz and Koldo – some call you fine men these days. I'm not so sure: you're a bit small and skinny – you'll never get over that – but none the worse, I suppose. The third boy – we know all about *him*! The girl, who's worth more than all the rest of that family put together, Arantxa almost killed with her greed and stupidity. When we reached her hearth, the silly woman was wailing and wringing her hands at the tent door.

'If your daughter's lying sick in there, this can't be doing her much good!'

Arantxa stopped in the middle of a sob and blinked at me, her mouth hanging open.

'Zigor sent for me,' I told her. 'Where is he? And where's Osané?'

She began to weep again. 'He left us! He went away! My poor girl's dying, and he wouldn't do anything for her! He left her to die! He—'

Zorioné broke in, 'That's not true! You know quite well what he said! The spirits told him not to meddle, and to fetch the woman! And I *have* fetched her, like he told me. Here she is!' Zorioné pointed at me.

'No, no, no! Go away! She brings bad spirits! They took her son! Now he's sent them to take Osané as well! Go away! Go away!'

I sighed. The men in this family weren't good for much, but surely between them they could have shut Arantxa's mouth and dragged her away. Only they were all at the Hunt. There was no one else at the hearth but a couple of frightened cousins and some snivelling children covered with mosquito bites.

I stretched my arms high and flung my head back. 'We come for Osané!' I cried in a loud voice. 'Take this woman away!'

My Helpers didn't need to stir themselves: they knew I could handle Arantxa on my own. No sooner did I call out than she threw herself on the ground, hands over her head, sobbing for mercy. I stepped over her, lifted the tent flap and went in.

It was hot and smelly inside. At first I couldn't see where Osané was. Empty shells and chewed bones were heaped over the cold ashes in the hearth. The sleeping platform was piled with moth-eaten furs. I stooped closer and smelt stale urine. There was a bigger pile at the back of the platform. I pulled away an oxskin. Underneath was a tangle of light-brown hair. I tugged away the skins; startled lice scuttled into the folds. She'd wrapped herself up so tightly it was like skinning a seal.

When I'd last seen Osané she was red-cheeked and laughing, on her way home with a basket of hazelnuts. That was three days ago. Now, when I held her under her chin and forced her head round to look at me, I was horrified. Her cheeks were grey and hollow as if she were dead. I saw no sense in her eye, only blind terror. The other eye was buried in a purple bruise. The string of her tunic was undone. I pulled the deerskin back. There were bruises on her swollen neck – I read in them the shape of fingers, four on each side – and a scarlet mark in the hollow of her neck in which I read two thumbs.

When I came out I found Itsaso and Haizea guarding the tent door. That woman who called herself a mother was sobbing by the hearth. The children grizzled beside her, chewing their knuckles. If she couldn't face her daughter she could at least have fed the little ones. Zorioné had gone.

'Haizea,' I said. 'Go to Zigor at once, and tell him we need fire in the Go-Betweens' hearths, and the shelter ready!'

She gaped at me.

'Quickly!' I gave her a small smile. 'Have faith, little daughter! It'll be all right! Now go!' I turned to my niece. 'Itsaso, run round the Camp. Use that voice of yours! Summon everyone to the healing! But first go to your mother. Tell her to bring clean skins to wrap Osané in, and to come here at once. And tell her . . .' – Itsaso stopped in her tracks – she was already on her way – 'Bring Hilargi as well: we'll have to carry Osané. Off you go!'

As I sat holding Osané's hands in that miserable tent I heard Itsaso's voice ringing round the Camp. 'Come quickly! Come quickly! The Go-Between is waiting! Come for the healing! Come for the healing! Come! Come! Come!'

I was too taken up with Osané to think that when Itsaso cried 'Go-Between' she meant me. I heard startled voices chattering like so many starlings – shouts – questions – then the quick patter of many footsteps.

Haizea called to me through the tent flap. 'Mother! I told him! He didn't say anything. But he's gone up the mound and pulled back the turfs himself, and laid kindling on the fire. He's doing it himself! But he didn't answer me – didn't take any notice of me at all! And they're coming – everyone who's here is coming!'

'Well done! Now go and spread the word: Osané's soul is already far away. Tell them we must get ready to call her back at once, or it'll be too late.'

And so my first audience was made of women, children, old men – and Zigor. Nearly everyone was on my side. If the men had been there it would have been different. To this day I don't know what was in Zigor's mind. I'm sure he didn't want to make it easy. Perhaps he simply did what his Helpers told him: it was right for Osané. Whether Zigor could see far enough to know where the healing of Osané would lead I don't know. All I can say is that Zigor was a powerful Go-Between, and in those days he didn't like me. It's also true that he never failed our People.

I'd never stood on the Go-Betweens' mound before. I'd never yet felt the heat of the spirit-fires. Now I came close I saw how the three rings of hearthstones overlapped, joining the Go-Betweens' hearths together like the segments of a caterpillar.

We carried Osané to the Healing Place halfway up the mound, just below the Go-Betweens' fires. Fresh pine branches crackled and smoked in two of the hearths already, billowing round us so that People could only see us through thick smoke. The sky was low over our heads, heavy with unshed water. Some People carried pine tapers to keep the mosquitoes off – I could see little dots of fitful light through the pall of smoke. Even the little children kept still. My family sat at one end, where they could see more clearly. I could feel their support rising up to me, and the coldness of Zigor at my left hand.

The air felt tight. When I took out my knife to carve a space round Osané and me I felt it pushing against the blades. I used all my strength to cut through the tear in the air. Then I went up the mound, behind the three fires and into the shelter. Three Drums hung from a withy screen. I swallowed, and summoned up my courage. I lifted the first Drum. I'd never touched a Go-Between's Drum before. It was very light. Faded red spirals were written on the hide. I read strength in them, but no harm. I turned the Drum over. The hide was stretched over hazel wands bound in a circle, and pulled tight with strings of sinew. I took down the second Drum, and studied the pattern on the hide. I couldn't read it. I picked up the hazel drumming sticks that hung beside the drums, and went outside.

I felt the gasp from the crowd. Without looking at Zigor I held out the Drum I hadn't been able to read, and the stick that went with it. The spirits had told me right: Zigor let me give him his Drum. Later I found out that the Drum I'd taken for myself was Aitor's. If I hadn't succeeded, Aitor would have seen me die. I'd never handled Drum or drumming stick before. I held the Drum in my left hand, the way I'd always seen it done. As soon as I touched the stick to the hide I was filled with power. Softly at first, then gradually more firmly, I began to drum.

I drummed alone. For long heartbeats I drummed alone. Fear touched my back with his cold finger. Then I was angry. Osané lay in the Healing Place at my feet. Would Zigor let her die? My head grew hot. I ceased to care. I stood up straight and drummed with all the fire I possessed, my head held high.

I remembered what to ask. At once I saw – even though we were far from the Open Sea – I saw to the very edge of the world where the water meets the sky. I saw my Dolphin leap through the waves towards me. I saw his painted side. His mouth was open, laughing. I drummed as loud as I could to show him where to come.

My drumming came winging back to me, stronger than it went away. The strength was coming from my left – from Zigor. As my Dolphin leaped through the water Osprey swooped over his head. She plunged into the sea as Dolphin leaped into the air. I saw a twin trail of white spray. Osprey surfaced, and soared into the sky.

I threw back my head and called my Helpers with all the sound my lungs could hold. I drummed and I sang, and the People chanted too, echoing the words we gave them. I heard my own voice, and the voices of my Helpers were inside it, making it strong. We began to sing for Osané, calling on her soul to come back.

I laid down my drumming stick but it was still drumming. The drumming was on my left. The singing filled the air. I jumped down to the Healing Place and put my arm over Osané, my Swan's wing to protect her.

I fell into darkness. This was where she'd wandered. I followed her down and down. The spirits mocked me. I wouldn't look into their eyes. I kept going down into the pit where her soul had gone before me.

I heard a short rasping bark. I flew to find my enemy. Then I smelt him:

Lynx!

The Moon ducked from under a cloud and gleamed in his yellow eyes. By her light I saw the broad cat-face – tufted ears – painted hunting-stripes – body tense as a hazel-whip, crouched to strike – all the pent power of the Hunt. I froze.

But now I had his name. I used it. I used all the powers I had and wrestled with him. I smelt raw meat in his hot breath. His teeth flashed in the Moonlight. But now I knew my enemy, and that gave me strength. Lynx shook Osané's soul between his teeth. With wings and beak and webbed claws I fought him for her. My strength was running out.

For a heartbeat I saw my Dolphin lying dry on a sandy beach. Seaweed was strewn along the high-tide mark. Alder and sallow willow grew at the top of the beach, and sea poppies in the dry sand. I looked into the dying eye of my Dolphin. The embers of a small fire and a smooth white pebble lay on the sand before his body. I picked up the white-stone pebble and put it in my pouch.

Lynx fought hard but there was nothing he could do. When he realised what I'd seen, the strength went out of him. His grip on Osané's soul began to slacken. I put my mouth to her neck and sucked him out of her. I made him let go. I swallowed him and spat him out. I watched him flee with flattened ears and tail towards the High Sun Sky.

Osané's torn soul drifted in the darkness.

I lay across her body and began to call her back. The People swayed to the rhythm of her name and took up the chant. 'Osané, Osané, Osané . . .'

Her soul heard. Watching her face, I saw her eyelid flicker. She opened her eye. The black centre had grown huge, with just a little rim of blue. The other eye was a slit in the swollen flesh. Osané blinked. Slowly I saw her gaze come back to me and fix itself on my face.

'It's all right, little daughter. You can come back now.'

I had her carried into the Go-Betweens' shelter. We cleaned her body, and put cold moss on her bruises. I gave her water, and after a while I persuaded her to eat some berries.

'We must keep her there until she finds a family,' I told Zigor later. 'She can't go back to her parents.'

I didn't know what he was thinking. Nor could I make my memory of the soaring Osprey join up with the thin man squatting beside me at the Go-Betweens' hearths. Zigor reached for his waterskin and took a long drink. He didn't offer me any.

Zigor wiped his mouth and said as he stared into his fire, 'So you found the first cause?'

'First cause?'

'Of her sickness! You surely had the wit to look for that?'

'I found the cause.' I felt as if I were fighting all over again. 'I'm not sure who strangled her – or tried to – she won't say a word – but I think I can guess.'

'You *think* you can *guess*! If you're Go-Between, Nekané, you neither *think* nor *guess*. You *find*, and *learn*. As to whose hands made those marks – does it matter? Or can you go no further than that?'

'It matters that she never goes back to her parents.'

'Then give her to Edur. His family can have her.'

'Zigor, do you remember what Arantxa was like when she was young?'

'Do I care what Arantxa was like, then or ever?'

'Perhaps you should.' It was difficult to say enough without saying too much. 'It might be better for the Auk People if Arantxa's daughter took a man who can't be related to her in any way.' I glanced at him. Zigor was clever: surely I need say no more? '*In any way*,' I repeated. He must have understood me now.

'Is that all you have to say?'

'No, it's not all.' He was Go-Between for the Auk People, and so was I. His Helper had come to my aid, and he must have seen my Swan and Dolphin. I told him exactly where I'd found Osané's soul, and everything that had happened on my journey.

I knew Zigor wouldn't praise me. What mattered was that he listened. When I'd finished he didn't speak for a while. I watched him tracing patterns with a twig in the ashes round the fire.

'Last night I read the mark of Lynx on a man's back,' said Zigor at last. 'I wrote Auk over it.'

'But the spirits Kemen brought with him are good! I saw that at White Beach Camp.'

'All spirits are good. You know that. But the good spirits of one People can be the enemies of another. When you followed Osané out of the world you met Lynx. Be careful how you read that Lynx. It might not mean what you think. There's no such thing as a bad spirit. *Your* beloved Helpers are your enemy's worst enemies. Never forget that.'

'*All* spirits? But . . . the sea that washed away the Lynx People's land and killed so many of them – how was that *good*?'

'Everything on earth is good.' Zigor spoke so bleakly he might as well have said the opposite. 'But the spirits of the Sea care nothing for People. Why should they?'

'So the Sea became the enemy of the Lynx People—'

'The Sea was not concerned with the Lynx People.'

'But why should Lynx be *our* enemy? Kemen is not . . .'

'No. We can use that.'

'How?'

'Give her to him.' Zigor bared his teeth in the semblance of a smile. 'That solves your other little problem too, I think.'

My thoughts ran fast. Remember I'd never worked with Zigor before. Now I know very well how far that man saw! That first day he surprised me. But yes – I could see it now. On my journey into the spirit-world Lynx had been Osané's enemy – *our* enemy. But all spirits are good . . . Lynx is also good. If Lynx is taking care of his own People, that might be the worse for us. The spirits that bring sickness can't be destroyed; you have to make them change sides.

And the first cause? I was beginning to understand: whoever attacked Osané had got caught up in this – we all had. Perhaps it was Edur who'd so nearly throttled her . . . Edur wanted Osané, and Arantxa had egged him on because she was frightened that her sons would go away after Gathering Camp and leave her to starve – all that woman was after was getting a good hunter into her family – maybe Edur had got fed up with Osané evading him and had tried to force her. I'd seen no signs of rape when we'd undressed her. That didn't mean much – she'd have cleaned herself up – girls usually do – which means you can never prove anything – but I wasn't sure it was Edur. All spirits are good, but to their enemies they become evil. In which case . . .

'The *first* cause,' Zigor repeated. 'You keep worrying about details. What do they matter?'

I jumped: had he read my thoughts? I answered as humbly as I knew how. 'I think that every small thing matters. But of course I don't know.'

'You want the girl to live?'

'Of course I do!'

'Then I suggest you don't mention again that she hasn't spoken to you.'

'You mean—'

'Everyone says you're a clever woman,' Zigor mocked. 'Someone tried to kill Osané. D'you think there's a man lurking among the Auk People who longs to be shamed in public? Who can't wait to be cast out? No? But there *is* a man among us who's tried to kill Osané. Where is he now, Nekané?'

I was angry that I hadn't thought of this. 'Osané's no weakling,' I said, working it out. 'There are women here with strong hands, but I don't think . . . She'd have fought back! She's small, but she's strong, and very agile. She'd have left a mark, anyway, and I don't think anyone here . . . I can soon find out. It's almost certainly a man. And if a man's strong enough to do that to her without her fighting back, he's strong enough to go hunting. So he's not here now. But he must know he didn't kill her. Osané's got a tongue in her head. He knows his danger.' I clenched my fists together. 'But how do I make him think she's told me, when she hasn't uttered a single word? How can I hide the fact that I *don't* know?'

'Easily. You don't need my help for that.'

I shook my head slowly. 'Not for *that*, no.'

I waited three heartbeats. Zigor said nothing.

If I didn't seize my chance now it would vanish. I crouched, head low, for three heartbeats, every muscle tense. Then I leaped: 'I said just now I didn't know. I don't know because I've not been taught. Every new Go-Between must have a teacher. That I do know!'

Zigor wiped out the patterns in the ash with one flourishing circle, then swept over it with the twig. He dusted the ash from his fingers, and reached for his waterskin. His lips drew back, showing stumps of blackening teeth. He was smiling. My heart sank.

At last he answered me. 'Have I so many words inside me that you think I want to waste them? You ask me a round handfull of questions, and still you ask me "Where is my teacher?"'

I stared at him, trying to take in what he said. 'When did you know this?' I asked at last.

'When did *you* know it, Nekané?'

The answers to that were piled in so many layers I couldn't seize upon any. Thoughts reeled round my head. I watched Zigor lean forward, pick up the twig he'd used to write and hold it in a flame. When it was burning he dropped it into the fire.

Presently I reached into my pouch and took out the white pebble I'd picked up on my journey. I gave it to Zigor. He held it in the palm of his hand and studied it.

'You'll know that place again,' was all he said.

'Yes.'

'This matter is up to you, Nekané: you made the journey. Will we give her to Kemen when he comes back from the Hunt?' He dropped the white pebble into my hand, and I put it away.

'All the winds blow that way.' I sighed, though I had no reason to be sad. 'I made the journey, but you saw what it meant.' I thought it clever as well as right to give him his due. 'It certainly answers a lot of questions. But where it will lead us in the end – that's what I can't see.'

'Surely you know, Nekané: that's exactly what we *never* see.'

Amets said:

Initiation Camp is high in the hills. We take the boys to the mountain-tops to teach them the lie of the land. We show them where the spirits live. It's good for the boys to hunt in the bare lands above the trees. If they can find food for themselves there, they'll find it anywhere. They need to learn what to do in cold and dangerous places. In the high places it can be winter in any Moon.

When I thought about it later I was pleased at how well the

boys did that Year, in spite of all the other things that happened. No one died, their cuts healed well and not one hurt himself enough to matter. I heard later that nearly all of them came back to Initiation Camp on the right day, with full stomachs and grins on their faces. The only one who was small and weak turned out to be clever enough to make up for it. I wish I'd been there to see them all come back.

I did see them half a Moon later, when they all returned to Gathering Camp. Not one had forgotten the words or the stories, and the tests ended in laughter, which is a good way of making People remember. I was proud of our Ortzi too, though I was careful not to let him know it.

But that was later. When the men reached Hunting Camp word came to bring the boys to the Hunt. The boys had just finished making their weapons. They'd wasted a lot of stone, but they'd all ended up with a spear and arrows that I wouldn't be too ashamed of carrying myself – if it were a dark night and none of my cousins was looking too closely. We led the boys up to the Hidden Place – no, I'm not telling you women – or you little ones either – where that is! We showed them the Pool of the Young Men. We mixed water and ochre on the flat stones round the Pool. The spirits of the water showed each boy the colours he must write.

We sent the boys off to get food. They weren't allowed to go below the tree line. When they understood that they had to get enough food from the high places for all the men coming to Hunting Camp, and have it cooked and ready for them, they went pale with terror. No wonder! I'll admit to you now – though I've never told any of you People before – that when we boys were put to the same test among the Seal People we failed miserably. It wasn't the beatings I minded, it was the shame. I thought the men would never forgive us. I only understood afterwards that forgiving had nothing to do with it; we just became a standing joke that got told again and again every single Year. We grew used to it after a while.

Anyway, these boys did neither badly nor well. They came to Hunting Camp with fat ptarmigan, snow bunting and plenty of smaller birds. Itzal had trapped a hare. Ortzi pointed out that men ought to fast before they hunt, and so, he explained, the boys had been careful not to get too much. I cuffed him round the ear, but not hard, because of course he was right. Ortzi was often quicker to get the point than the others.

The great Hunt of Deer Moon belongs to the high places. You little ones – you often see your fathers and brothers and cousins take their dogs and weapons, and quietly walk away from your hearths. You may not see them for many days. You know, wherever your Camp may be, that they're heading for the high hunting grounds. But you've never been there yet.

Shut your eyes and see my words inside your minds: you're climbing uphill through the trees – you've often done that. It's Deer Moon. The Sun slants through the leaves – green and yellow and gold. The ground's bright with fallen leaves and green mosses. You're clambering over slippery rocks, white with lichen. As you climb higher the trees grow smaller. The River doesn't sound like the wind in the pines any more. Its voice changes: it's rushing between the rocks, seeping through marshes or tumbling over broken boulders in little waterfalls. The trees are thinning out. They lean towards the Morning Sun Sky from the weight of the wind on their backs. The oaks are bent and spindly. Soon they give up. You're among birch and rowan and juniper. Clumps of bilberry and bog myrtle scratch your deerskins as you pass. Between the trees bees browse among the heather. You can't see the path – the scrub's above your waist – but your feet know where to find it. Now you see the mountain peaks above you, closer than you've ever seen them yet. They're guarded by the crags of the high corries. In the hollows of the corries the spirits have spread pastures of sweet grass and tender herbs. That's why the hinds are still there in Deer Moon. The Rut hasn't begun, and winter hasn't yet driven them down into the woods.

Hinds never leave the lands they know. The old ones know everything – just like the old women of the Auk People! The lead hind sniffs the wind and chooses the best places. Wherever the wind blows from, some old woman – People or Animal, they're all the same – will always remember a sheltered hollow where food can be found. The trick – if you're a man, that is – is to read what's going on inside her mind.

When the men arrived at Hunting Camp we were ready. The boys had slung shelters between the skinny birches and thatched the roofs with bracken and heather. They'd fetched wood and water. Heather and bog myrtle were trodden flat around the fire. The boys were busy cooking the meat. The men took no notice of them, but you can always see the eyes of the fathers flickering round the Camp to check their own boys are there. I was happy that, so far, no man had to face that grief this Year. I was also glad to see Kemen with Sendoa. Things must have gone well for him when they spoke to the Animals about the Hunt. When Kemen went off to the stream to refill his waterskin I walked with him.

'I'm glad to see you,' I told him.

'I'm glad to be here. But I'm hot!' Kemen squatted by the stream, filled his waterskin, then drank from the stream, water dripping from his cupped hands. I began to feel thirsty too. I knelt beside him, cupped my hands and drank.

'That's better!' Kemen wiped his mouth, stripped off his tunic and began to splash cold water over himself.

I stood up, and saw his back. The swift mark of Lynx still ran across his shoulderblades, but now it hid behind a mass of welts. Under the blistered skin I read three spirals of red smoke. Below it, raw and shining, the three blue curves of Auk. Through the welts I also saw what was not there: the red birth-line of Auk had been left out. When I cried out, Kemen whipped round at once.

'What is it? What do you see?'

'Nothing now. Turn round again!'

'You weren't at the Dance,' he said with his back to me. 'Didn't anyone tell you they'd done this?'

'No, but I read it now. We were doing the same thing where I was.'

'You were at Initiation Camp?'

'Boys must become men. And a few men have to change all over again in the middle of their lives. That's hard, but it can be good too. More good than bad in the end, sometimes – at least, that's what I think.'

'Amets! Tell me what he wrote! Because I can't see it.'

'Don't you know?' I stripped off my own tunic and turned my back to him.

Kemen was silent, reading what was written. Then he said, 'Almost, but never quite. And mine says the same?'

I turned to face him again. 'No man ever sees his own back. But you and I were both born under other skies. Now I think we belong in the same place.' I glanced at him. Since he'd been accepted into the Auk People I was free to say something I'd been thinking about for several Moons. 'The family I belong to is much too small,' I told him. 'I won't go back to our winter Camp this Year if I'm the only hunting man. I decided that after my wife's brother was lost. But River Mouth Camp's a good place. If we don't go back this winter someone else will take it. It would be a shame to lose it.'

'You think that I—'

'I can't offer you much. The hunting's good. But my wife's little sister is only a child. Otherwise there's only her parents. If you want a woman you'll have to take one before Deer Moon!'

We laughed, and I clapped him on the shoulder. '*If* you want a woman!'

Kemen looked at the ground, grinning. 'What do you think?'

'But you'll join my family?'

He seized me by the shoulders and hugged me to his heart. 'I ask nothing more!' He grabbed my hands and shook them up and down. Joy was written all over his face. 'Amets, I ask nothing more!'

'Not even a woman?' I asked slyly. After that we had to grip each other's shoulders to stay on our feet, we were laughing so much. And so the matter was settled. I was very pleased with myself, because I'd had it all planned in my head long before.

I asked Edur if he'd let Kemen go with him on the Hunt. I knew Kemen would learn more about Auk hunting lands from Edur than anyone else. Edur wasn't willing. I didn't blame him. It's hard enough to take a boy who knows nothing – who may kick a loose stone, or show himself above the skyline, or let the Sun gleam on his face – all the things that foolish boys may do when they first come to the Hunt. But to take a man who's already a hunter in his own country, but who's lost his place in the world – it's difficult to tell a grown man what to do. You can't just cuff him if he makes a mistake! But a useless man is a lot worse than a boy, and twice as dangerous. I didn't want to cast a burden on Edur that should have been my own.

'I didn't want to trouble you with this, Edur,' I explained. 'It's my family's problem, not yours. If I didn't have the boys to think of, I'd have taken Kemen with me. But I can't desert the boys at their first Hunt! I'd planned that you'd take Itzal – he did best of all the boys at Initiation Camp. He deserves to go with the best hunter in all the long memory of the Auk People. No, I can't ask as important a hunter as you to . . . Itzal should go with you!'

Edur stopped scowling as I spoke, and when I'd finished he

clapped me on the shoulder. 'If you want the best hunter for Itzal, Amets, he'd certainly better go with you! I'll probably lose my way – I expect the kill will be over before I even get a scent of a deer! Just because I had a bit of luck when I was younger, I wouldn't want you to expect too much. I'd be sure to disappoint you! I'll take this stranger for you. At least then I'll know if he's going to be any use to us!'

That evening, as we sat round the hearth making our plans for the Hunt, my heart was light. Itzal's face lit up when he heard he was going with me. I told Ortzi he would go with Sendoa. I could see Ortzi was disappointed – he and Itzal had been watching one another like two stags after the same hinds all through Initiation Camp. I feared that if they didn't become friends they'd be the worst of enemies. Of course that changed when . . . but that comes later.

A hand-full of us climbed up to the ridge at dusk. The wind was shifting towards the Morning Sun Sky. It told us of fleeing clouds and many stars. We listened to the wind. That wind had eddied round the high corries of Cat Mountain and Deer Mountain and far beyond. It whispered in our ears, telling us where the hinds would find shelter. We let that wind sing in our ears, telling us everything that we needed to know.

Below the lip of the corrie the waterfall gleamed like a white flame in the growing dark. Before the boys knew what was happening we'd leaped on them from behind as they sat warming their faces at the fire. We grabbed them by their arms and legs and ran towards the corrie. We flung them into the Pool. They were still spluttering as we leaped in after them. We washed ourselves under the waterfall. The boys knew better than to make a sound, but when we stood on the bank again we could hear their teeth chattering so hard we couldn't help laughing!

We scooped fresh colours – red and yellow and black – from the bark trays. We painted our clean bodies by firelight. Our skins became the colours of the land. We were the land. We put on our deerskins and sang the Hunt. We danced the Hunt until the boys had taken every step of it into their blood. The spirits of the Hunt watched what we did. The spirits of the Deer heard us when we asked them to give themselves. The spirits of the Hunt welcomed the Auk People, and held them to their hearts.

When the dance was over we sat silent as stones around the glowing embers. The clouds fled. Deer Moon shone from a clear sky. Deer Mountain and Cat Mountain lay bright as water, their heads against the stars. One by one men got up, took their weapons, and disappeared into the shadows, their dogs soundlessly following. Edur and Kemen were the first to leave. They had to cross the watershed right over to Long Loch and climb back up the far side of Deer Mountain to reach their place in the ring by dawn.

Each man left in his turn. Each one had his dog. Some had a boy following in their tracks. Each boy was desperate to prove himself. None of the men even glanced at them. But none of us has forgotten what our own first Hunt was like.

Sendoa, his dog at his heels, left with Ortzi. I heard Itzal's quick breathing at my side. I watched Deer Moon swing herself free just as Cat Mountain stretched up to spear her. I sniffed the breeze as it eddied round the clearing. Its breath smelt of the deep heart of the night.

I touched Itzal's arm. He was on his feet in a heartbeat. We slung our spears over our shoulders. My dog's nose brushed my heel. We climbed swiftly up to the ridge. Itzal sent a stone rolling. I felt his shame; I said nothing. I stopped on the ridge for a heartbeat. I sniffed the air. I ran along the ridge. The dog and Itzal followed me. I slid down the other side over smooth grass. Itzal had learned his lesson. Now he was quiet as a mountain cat. I turned my face towards the Morning Sun Sky.

Dawn found us in our place above the Black Corrie of Cat Mountain. We'd squeezed into the top of a crack that ran from the skyline, a man's length above our heads, right down to the corrie floor. The Moon had set. The Sun's first light fell past us on to the hills under the Evening Sun Sky. The rocks shone fiery pink only a man's length above us, but the light couldn't reach our cleft. Itzal held his breath to stop himself shivering with cold and hunger and excitement. He was still wet through from crossing the Grey River. I pulled my wolfskin hat down over my forehead so it hid my face. Itzal copied me at once. I didn't glance at him. We had a long way to go yet.

The corrie held the darkness like a hollow pool.

I peered into it. Rocks and grass slowly came free of the clinging dark. And Animals. The hinds were there, just as the wind had told us. The dark still covered them: I couldn't count. But even as I watched, the dark grew thin. It seeped out of the corrie like water from a basket.

I looked across the corrie. I saw Sendoa raise his hand, out of sight of the deer below. I sent a cautious signal back. Every man must be in his place by now, spread far across the hills.

Currents of wind flowed around the peaks like a braid coming apart. The corrie had a breeze of its own that eddied over the crags. The breeze carried the smell of the hinds up to us. I nudged Itzal as I sniffed the strong deer-smell, and he sniffed it too. If that boy had learned anything at all, the breeze would be telling him that the hinds wouldn't be aware of us until we started to climb down.

The dark lifted. Pipits started to chirrup in the rocks below us. I searched the floor of the corrie. I was looking for anything different. I saw a pale rock on a hillock. I knew that hillock: I knew it had no rock. I stared and stared at that pale rock. Suddenly, under my eyes, it turned into the lead hind.

She was looking around from her vantage point between the

scree slope and the other hinds. As soon as I'd seen her, the spirits opened my eyes and showed me the rest of the herd. I spread my hands and counted ten hands-full, including the calves. Some had their heads down, grazing in the growing light. I counted more than a hand-full of wise old ones, the same colour as the bleached autumn grass, their heads low. The old mothers are always the ones to watch! The young ones in their sleek summer coats – some good red hides there, waiting to give themselves! – those are the sort a man can trick more easily. I tell you, Deer and People are just the same, if you want to know where to seek wisdom in a woman!

I looked across to the hills under the Evening Sun Sky. An arrow of light struck the summit of Sharp Peak.

Now!

Rocks slithered and crashed. Men slid down the scree. Dogs barked.

The old mother bounded towards the lip of the corrie. Families bunched together, mothers calling their calves. The herd fragmented. The old mother was at the corrie's edge. Many hands-full of hinds came back into one herd. Some wise ones broke away. Their calves ran after them, through a gap in the net of men and out to open ground. All the others bounded after the lead hind. They vanished over the edge of the corrie.

We leaped from boulder to boulder down the scree. We ran across the corrie floor. Itzal passed me like a gust of wind. We stood at the lip of the corrie, looking down.

Men and dogs were spread across the hill. From above we could see the whole circle, like the noose on a snare pulling tight.

The lead hind hesitated. She ran for the open space on her left. She reached the top of the gully.

Deer hate gullies. They hate to feel crags all round them, and no way out.

The lead hind stopped. She headed the other way, across a fall of loose rock. The hinds bunched together, trying to turn and follow. Their hooves slid on the boulders. One calf tried to take the easier way, towards the gully. Its mother leaped after it. Some of the other hinds stopped, hesitating.

Just below the lead hind, men and dogs rose from the heather. Hodei and Oroitz leaped uphill over the rocks, yelling and waving their spears. Their dogs rushed to and fro across the space between the men.

The lead hind scrambled back on to the heather. We stood in front of her. We blocked the way to the corrie. We shouted, brandishing our spears. We closed in.

She turned towards the gully. There was light at the far end. A way out.

Hinds and calves streamed into the gully. Two old ones broke away, their calves following. They'd seen that gully before! They charged downhill between Oroitz and Zeru. Dogs snapped at their heels. Trampled by hooves, a young dog rolled down the boulders, yelping. The old hinds vanished into the trees below, their calves at their heels.

Hodei and Oroitz ran into the gully at the heels of the herd. I scrambled up to higher ground. Itzal shot past me. He waited for me on the crag.

The hinds thundered down the gully. We watched from above. The lead hind headed for that patch of light. A way out. The light vanished. A wall came up in front of her. She stopped. The thundering herd crashed into her, forcing her on. She could leap a fence of withies, only there were men on it. Men with spears. Dogs barking. No way out.

Her herd blocked the way behind her. They couldn't turn. She found the other gully. A grassy downhill slope. No way out. But no men this way. No dogs. No choice. She led her herd into the trap. No way out.

Spears rained down. Her calf fell. She smelt blood. High crags all round. Rocks falling. Calves screaming. The smell of blood. Slippery crags. No way out.

A boulder crashed. Her back cracked, and broke. Her legs buckled.

Her nose in the slippery bloodstained grass. The pain and the blood and the slow death. The smell of the blood on the grass, and the giving in.

We took many Animals that day – we counted three sets of two hands-full, and four more, including the calves. As soon as the trap was closed we leaped down and cut the throats of all the wounded Animals and let them bleed. After the Hunt the Wise among us broke open the old mother's skull and divided the warm brains between them. Every man and boy drank of her blood. There were more hearts and livers than all of us could eat. Our dogs gorged themselves on fresh lungs. We lit a fire and ate at the top of the gully. That old mother was kind and wise; she looked after her People until the end. No man should wish for more. We stretched up our arms and gave thanks to the spirits of the Deer. Once again they had given themselves that the Auk People might live. The blood of the Deer was now our blood, and our hearts were theirs.

We gutted the deer inside the trap. Flies buzzed over us, and settled in pools of blood. We piled the innards into rush baskets, swung them on to our backs and took them down to Hunting Camp. We stretched the carcasses on poles, ready to carry all the way down to Gathering Camp. Before our Hunters' Feast we washed ourselves under the waterfall. The mud we stirred mixed with blood and ochre from our bodies, turning the water brown. Before we'd all climbed out, the waterfall had swept away every trace of the Hunt. We looked down at the clear stones at the bottom of the pool; now we were as clean as they were. The spirits had forgiven what we owed the Deer, and our hearts were light.

After the Hunters' Feast I was meant to stay with the boys at Hunting Camp. Now they'd taken part in the Hunt they needed to study the high hunting lands with newly-opened eyes. Their last test lay before them. My heart was with them, but I also wanted to go back to Gathering Camp. I needed to tell my family about Kemen so he could come straight to our hearth. I told Sendoa what I was thinking. Sendoa offered to tell the family in my place, but I shook my head. 'No, it has to be me. Your mother has her own winter Camp. If Kemen's going to join us at River Mouth Camp, it has to be me that tells my wife's father – and Nekané and Alaia.'

The others heard us talking and asked what I was worried about.

Edur was in a good mood. He'd already told me that Kemen hadn't held him back at all. 'Of course, he doesn't know the land,' he'd said. 'Even a useless hunter like me was able to tell him quite a lot. But I don't think the Lynx People can have been such bad hunters either.' You can guess how much those words pleased me! Edur said now, 'Yes, you should go, Amets. You might have to argue with your woman – you never know – and Sendoa can't do that for you.'

Everyone laughed. Jokes flew to and fro about what Sendoa should or should not do to persuade my woman.

At last Edur wiped the tears of laughter from his eyes. 'I think you'd better go and look after your own, Amets! I can see how badly you want to get back into bed with Alaia. Why don't I stay here with these boys, and you go and deal with your family?'

'Do you mean that, Edur?'

'Would I say it if I didn't mean it?'

'But Edur,' someone called, 'don't you have a little matter of your own to deal with? A small matter of taking *your* woman?'

'What! He's taking *another* one!'

'Edur's taken as many women already as most men have trapped deer!'

'But Osané's *parents* want him! You don't believe me – it's true! They want him to join their family!'

'That makes a change!'

'Usually he doesn't even ask first! Did you ask this one, Edur?'

'Yes, tell us, did you ask Osané? Or did you just . . .'

At last the laughter died down, and I said quietly to Edur, 'If you're happy to do this for me . . .'

'I told you – I wouldn't have spoken if I wasn't! Don't worry about my girl. She's not going anywhere. It can wait.'

We told Aitor and Hodei what we wanted to do. They said the spirits wouldn't mind, as long as Edur and I exchanged everything we had until Initiation Camp was over. This would show the spirits that we'd agreed to become one another for a little while. So I put on Edur's deerskins and his heavy bearskin cloak, and he took my clothes – my tunic was stretched as tight as it would go across his chest! And my cloak barely reached his knees – you can guess how many jokes I had to put up with about that! But Edur did better with my bow and arrows – most of his arrows needed mending, and his bow wanted a new string. I was glad I'd be able to do those things for him before I gave them back. His spear was heavier than mine. At least it wasn't broken! The haft of my spear had snapped: one of the hinds had twisted so much she'd broken it in two. Edur and I exchanged our knives, and our flints and needles – even our tinder. So there I was, looking like the greatest hunter of the Auk People – all I lacked was his tattoos, and his ugly face! Isn't that right, Edur?

We carried as much meat as we could. We'd hung the rest from trees where no Animals could reach it. It was already drying in the wind. When our Hunting Feast was over, we walked by Moonlight through the long shadows of the forest paths. Gathering Camp was sleeping when we arrived. We laid our meat by the Go-Betweens' hearths, and stretched ourselves out to sleep at the foot of the mound, men and dogs together, until the dawn.

We were woken by the squeals of children. They crowded round while we began to divide the meat. We brushed them off like so many flies, but like flies they kept coming back. The women came out and woke the fires in their hearths, fetched firewood and water, and carried on as if they hadn't seen us at all. But none of them went out with their baskets. They hovered, pretending not to wait. Some were mothers, hoping to over-hear some hint about their sons. Itzal's mother, Arantxa, was the worst. She knew very well that no man could say anything until the boys came back to tell their own stories. I felt ashamed for Itzal. He'd done well: he didn't deserve a mother who made a child of him before other men.

We laid out the carcasses in the Dividing Place in front of the Go-Betweens' mound, from the largest to the smallest. We'd taken so many hinds it was easy to divide them: even with one for every hunter to take to his own hearth we had enough left over. We agreed – as always – that Edur had earned the biggest, for more hinds had given themselves to his spear than to anyone else's. I was proud when the men decided the next should be for me! When every hunter had his share we gave three calves to Zigor, who'd stayed behind as Go-Between. We gave extra calves to the Wise. There was still a little meat left over. Because our hearts were kind we gave to the hearths that had the fewest – or worst! – hunters, or the most children.

Everyone had enough meat to eat all they could for the next few days and still have some to dry for the journey home. Soon the trees around Gathering Camp would be filled with new skulls: the spirits of the Deer would stay and watch over our Gathering Place while we were scattered in our winter Camps.

As I worked the hide off my hind, I felt the rich meat under my fingers. My heart filled with pride. I'll never know why the others gave the second hind to me – how did I deceive them? Perhaps my friends mistook me for someone else; perhaps they were so busy making their own great kills they didn't realise how little I'd done! I handed the hide to Alaia. It was heavy with delicious fat. *She* thought I'd deserved this great prize! It's easy to deceive a woman about something she knows nothing about!

Nekané was sitting by the fire, spooning mashed up reed-root into Esti's mouth, when I carried my share to our hearth. I threw the meat at her feet. 'I'm ashamed to bring you so little,' I told her. 'But I'm not much of a hunter, as you know. The others were kind enough to let me take these bits and pieces. I hope our family isn't going to starve because I'm not much use to you.'

Nekané nodded. If she was surprised to see me back so soon she didn't say so. She let Esti have the spoon, and started poking at the meat. 'Hmm,' she said. 'I suppose we can make some sort of feast out of this, if we can make it go far enough. You might as well hang it from the oak; it won't weigh that thin branch down too much. I can't say we've missed you. But here's your daughter letting on she's pleased to see you again!'

I swung Esti on to my shoulder and she pulled my ears in delight. Kemen came up behind me with his share of the meat. Because he was a stranger he'd got a thin hind with a worm-eaten hide and very little fat – I'd noticed her lame leg when we stood at the lip of the corrie. Kemen only had a small share because he was new to the Hunt, not because he didn't deserve any better. Kemen dumped his meat at Nekané's feet. She couldn't hide her astonishment! I almost doubled up laughing, and Esti grabbed my hair.

'This family's got Amets so it doesn't really need me,' Kemen said to Nekané. 'He can do all the hunting you need without any help. But here I am, all the same.'

I didn't yet realise why Nekané was so astonished, but I saw the gleam of satisfaction in her eye. That pleased me.

My wife's father came out of the tent. I'd only been away five nights, but suddenly he seemed very old. He looked at our meat and smiled. 'You could have done worse, Amets! It could have been even less!'

'It *would* have been a great deal less.' I took Kemen's arm and pulled him forward. 'But now there are two of us. He'll hunt for us better than I can. At least he can't do much worse!'

I'd seen my wife's father give Kemen that piercing look before, sizing him up. Perhaps he wasn't so old after all: perhaps he did still have something to say. For a heartbeat I was alarmed.

My wife's father nodded at Kemen. 'So! The names of your kin are to live among us, it seems. You were told to choose wisely: you've set about it pretty quickly, haven't you?'

'*You* were—'

My wife's father laid his finger across his lips.

The word whipped round the Camp faster than the wind that Kemen had joined our family. So many women crowded round our hearth I could stand it no longer. 'Come on,' I said to Kemen. We strolled over to the Go-Betweens' hearths. Men came and slapped us on the back and shook Kemen's arms until he was dazed. The smell of cooking began to fill the air. The Sun climbed into the High Sun Sky and beamed into our clearing. Dogs gnawed noisily at deer legs, snarling at men and dogs who came too near. We felt drowsy after the long days and nights in Hunting Camp. There wasn't anything much for men to do now except sleep, so that's what we did.

When the Sun dipped behind the oaks we stirred ourselves. The feast was almost ready. We strolled back to our own hearths, but we'd barely reached them when angry shouts broke out from somewhere behind the Go-Betweens' hearths. Itsaso came running over. 'They're fighting!'

'Who?' I asked idly. Men are always fighting at Gathering Camp. If this wasn't about the meat it would be about some woman.

'Hodei and Zigor! He *hit* him!'

'*What?*'

'I tell you – they're at the Go-Betweens' hearths – and – and – I *saw* – he *hit* him!'

We weren't the only ones to rush to see what was happening. The whole Camp was gathering. Itsaso wriggled and pushed her way to the front, just below the mound. Kemen and I could see well enough over People's heads from where we were. Someone had wakened the fires in the Go-Betweens' hearths: they were filled with little licking flames from end to end.

We looked up through the wreathing smoke. Zigor and Hodei were circling one another like dogs waiting to spring. Nekané stood at the threshold of the Go-Betweens' shelter, arms stretched out as if to bar the way. Aitor came shoving through the crowd. He rushed up the mound, leaped over the Go-Betweens' fires and ran between Zigor and Hodei, pushing them apart. They turned on him in fury. Aitor shouted something back. After that they kept their voices low, but the air still quivered with their anger.

Aitor went over to Nekané. His head was close to hers. They talked. Zigor and Hodei stood far apart, watching them warily. Then Aitor took Nekané by the arm and led her over to the other two.

By now the children had drifted away, and some of the women had gone back to their cooking, but when Aitor called us the women came running back. No woman was going to miss a story like this!

Aitor spoke to us across the fire. 'A girl was healed while we were at the Hunt. Osané was brought back from death. Someone had tried to kill her.'

A low muttering rose from the men. When I looked at the women's faces they showed no surprise. I caught my wife's father looking at Kemen and me. He seemed the least surprised of all.

'It was one of the men standing here.'

We all glanced at each other.

'That man knows who I'm talking about.'

When we looked at each other again we saw only our own question mirrored in each other's eyes.

'Soon the rest of you will know too,' said Aitor. He pulled Nekané forward. 'There's more. This woman dared to use a Go-Between's Drum! What should we do with her?'

'Kill her!'

'Stone her!'

'Cast her out!'

If Nekané was frightened by the shouts and shaken fists she didn't show it. Aitor held up his arms and the men were silent.

'You're all wrong,' he said. 'If the spirits had been angry they'd have killed her then and there. D'you think I didn't know when she took my Drum? D'you think I couldn't hear it when it called me? If you think as little of me as that, then it's *me* you should cast out!'

That puzzled everyone into silence.

'Osané's soul was wandering far away,' said Aitor. 'The spirits of sickness had carried her close to death. Nekané followed her. She brought Osané back. My Drum showed me every step she took. This woman is Go-Between!'

I heard every man take in his breath at once.

'I know because she took my Drum. Zigor knows because when Nekané followed Osané's soul out of the world Zigor watched what happened. Hodei didn't see any of this. Hodei, what do you say now?'

The unwillingness in Hodei's voice was plain. 'If you accept her, and Zigor insists on teaching her, no doubt we'll soon find out if this is a gift or a curse! So, very well: let it unfold if it must, and we shall see. But there's another matter.'

Hodei turned to the People and raised his voice. 'Osané belongs to Edur. If anyone doubted whether Edur was a good hunter – and I don't think anyone ever did – then this last hunt will have taught them something! My sister Arantxa and her husband' – Hodei called Osané's father by his name – 'gave Osané to Edur, and Edur agreed that as soon as he got back from the hunt he'd join their family. I also gave my word on this.'

My heart leaped to my throat. Was Edur about to lose Osané? It was my fault that Edur wasn't here to speak for himself. I owed it to him to stand up for him. I began to clear my throat anxiously, in case I had to lend my voice to Hodei's plea.

Then Zigor spoke: 'Osané will not go back to her family.'

'Osané's my niece, not yours! You keep out of it!'

The angry shouts of the Go-Betweens were taken up by the People. A scuffle broke out in front of us, close to the Go-Betweens' hearths. Kemen plucked my deerskin. 'This isn't our fight,' he whispered. 'It's too early for me to take sides.'

I pulled him back. 'No, stay here. I know what you . . . you've not been here long enough . . . but you're in my family now. No one can get you alone . . . Besides, I may need—'

'Enough!' Aitor roared.

Everyone was quiet.

'Come now,' said Aitor, suddenly smiling. 'Let's have no more fighting! It's only over a woman, too. What are we coming to, that the whole People has to concern itself over such a little thing? And we have a feast tonight! What are we thinking of, wasting the evening like this? Is nobody hungry after all?' When People started laughing Aitor laughed with them. 'So let's get this business over with. Nekané, fetch Osané!'

Nekané lifted the flap of the Go-Betweens' shelter. As one, the crowd took in its breath, and held it. While Nekané was inside the shelter, silence settled over us, heavy as river-fog.

Nekané came out, leading Osané by the hand. I couldn't see much through the smoke. The girl stumbled, but followed where she was led. She stood next to the Go-Betweens, staring at her feet.

'This girl no longer belongs to Arantxa's family,' repeated Zigor in his dry voice.

'We agree to that,' said Aitor.

Hodei was silent.

A wild screaming broke out at the back of the crowd. There was a flurry of movement round Arantxa. The rest of us barely glanced round. Aitor raised his voice just a little. 'But someone must have her. Some man will have to take her, and bring her into his own family.'

Now was my chance to speak. I cleared my throat.

The smoke suddenly started blowing the other way. Now we could see across the fire. Osané's face was white as ash – it was easy to believe that Death had come close enough to breathe on her. Her face was lopsided, and all round her left eye there was a great red and purple bruise. In spite of the heat she had a squirrel-skin scarf tucked round her neck, right up to her chin.

'You're saying some man here did *that*?'

People looked round, but I never saw who'd called out.

'You'll know who it was soon enough,' Aitor repeated. 'Meanwhile someone must take her.'

'She's Edur's!' I croaked. No one heard me. But other men were shouting the same thing so it made no difference.

'Where's Edur?'

'Give her to Edur! Let him take her!'

'No, not Edur!' Suddenly Aitor swung round and pointed straight at us. 'Kemen!'

I never saw a man give such a start. I put my hand on Kemen's shoulder to steady him. He stared at me wildly, as if all this were my fault. As, in a sense, I suppose it was.

Aitor fixed his gaze on the pair of us. 'Kemen! You hear me! You know who you are, don't you?'

Kemen just gazed at him, mouth hanging open.

'Don't be a fool, man! Come here!'

Kemen seemed rooted to the spot. It was me that pulled him to the foot of the Go-Betweens' mound and shoved him upward. What would any of you have done? You'd have had to do the same! Kemen was my brother now, and the Go-Between was getting angry – what else could I have done?

Osané stumbled again as Aitor seized her from Nekané's sheltering arm and thrust her at Kemen. Kemen was forced to put out a hand to steady her, but he never took his eyes off Zigor.

'Take her! Go on, man, take her! What are we all waiting for? You want the names of your People to live? Do I have to tell a grown man what to do with a woman? Take her away, man, before we all die of hunger.'

Mind you, that wasn't quite the end of it. Arantxa set up such a howling you'd think a pack of wolves had joined our feast. Then Osané's elder brothers, Oroitz and Koldo, came over to our hearth and tried to make us fight. They threatened us with what Edur would do when he got back. That made me so angry I forgot I owed Edur anything. I don't like having thoughts that don't make sense sitting next to each other. Besides, we had a feast laid out in front of us.

Osané didn't even look at her brothers. She sat mute between Sorné and Hilargi, their arms protectively round her shoulders, hugging her squirrel-skins round her neck and staring into the fire.

Osané's brothers shouted at Kemen. 'You can't steal Osané! She was promised to Edur! You can't take her! She's ours!'

Kemen just sat there as if he hadn't heard a word. It was Itsaso who said to no one in particular, 'You know, all Arantxa's family wants is a good hunter who'll keep them fed in winter. Their own men are so bad at hunting they're all scared of starving. That's all it is.'

Kemen reached out and cuffed her. It can't have been very hard, because Itsaso just stared at him with her hands pressed to her mouth, then suddenly snorted with laughter.

Oroitz shook his spear at Kemen. 'You can't steal my sister! We'll get her back! You don't even belong here! How many enemies do you want, Kemen?'

Suddenly Kemen leaped to his feet. He swept past the women and grabbed his share of our feast from the fire. He seized a hide and flung the half-cooked meat into it. Haizea cried out, 'Oh no!'

Kemen strode across the Camp and dumped his meat at Arantxa's hearth. '*So* much for your daughter!' he shouted, and swept away the hide so the meat was all tumbled in the dirt.

It didn't stop them. Osané's brothers hurled threats and shook their fists at us. They called the spirits to witness that Kemen would be their enemy for ever.

I'd had enough. I jumped up and bundled my share of the meat into a hide.

'Oh no,' cried Haizea tearfully. 'Not *all* our feast!'

She needn't have worried. When Sendoa and his brothers saw what was happening they seized their meat from the women, and they too bundled up their share of the kill and dumped it at Arantxa's hearth 'because these great hunters of yours don't seem able to get you any'. Suddenly everyone began to laugh.

More cousins started joining in the game. More and more meat was laid at Arantxa's feet – far more than any single family could possibly eat. Arantxa's husband and sons were so shamed in the end they had to creep away into the forest until after the feast was over. Arantxa didn't know what to do with all that meat. She couldn't persuade anyone to take it from her. By now the whole Camp was enjoying the joke. Those who hadn't dumped their meat on Arantxa started coming over to our family with baskets full, and begging us to take a few sad morsels from their leftovers. They gave so much that Haizea said afterwards she'd got more food than if we hadn't given anything away at all.

So that's how Kemen got his wife, and paid for her too. And because of Kemen, Hodei the Go-Between and all his family were angry with my family. And because of Kemen my friend Edur thought I'd betrayed him. Oh, I had plenty to worry about! Even so, I'll never forget the sight of all that meat piled up at Arantxa's hearth. People still tell the story of that night. It was one of the best jokes we ever had: it still makes me laugh whenever I happen to think about it.

Fourth Night: Salmon Camp

Alaia said:

In Light Moon I carried the Fire to our Salmon Camp – the one that was my father's Birth Place. Salmon Camp is a place of many waterfalls. We fall asleep to the sound of water rushing through the gorge below. Two Rivers meet just above our Camp. One comes down from Mother Mountain, the other from Salmon Camp Hill. Many small streams have fed those Rivers and helped them grow strong. Wherever the streams cross the precipices that line the hillside they make more waterfalls, until the whole hill sings. At the foot of every waterfall there's a dark pool. The streams sing to the Salmon with many voices. When the Salmon hear the call of the waters they come in from the sea and leap up the falls. They jump from pool to pool until they lie in the lap of the hills. The high pools are the Birth Place of the Salmon, and their Death Place too. All the while we're at Salmon Camp we hear the Rivers sing to the Salmon. The songs of the water live in our hearts and become our songs too.

We'd agreed with my aunts in Deer Moon that we'd all make Salmon Camp together, but the weather had been so bad we weren't sure anyone would come. When we arrived my aunt

Sorné was already there. She had a basket of trout and shellfish ready roasted for us: she'd seen our boat coming through the straits between Cave Island and Mother Mountain Island on the far side of the loch. We always keep the saplings cut back on the steep slope below Salmon Camp; it doesn't matter being so open because the wind seldom comes from the Sunless Sky in summer. From our hearth we can see everything that's happening on the loch below.

My mother didn't seem particularly pleased to see her sister. Nekané can be ungrateful: Sorné had only come because she'd been thinking about us. It was kind of her to want to hear all about our first winter with Osané and Kemen. When I said so to my mother, Nekané just snorted, and went on cutting heather for our sleeping places, slicing through each stem as fiercely as if the spirits of the heather had offended her. Sendoa had brought his mother – that was because he wanted to hunt with Amets – and some of the younger cousins came with them. Our own family ended up staying at my father's Salmon Camp until Deer Moon went into the dark. Sorné was with us until the end of Salmon Moon. Most of her family had stayed at their Salmon Camp by the Boat Crossing Place. The River's much bigger there. I didn't blame them. I tell you, it wasn't the sort of Year when you'd paddle far if you could help it!

As soon as we got to Salmon Camp I unwrapped our embers and added them to my aunt's fire. Everyone stretched up their arms while my father called on the Salmon spirits and told them we'd come back. My father said to the spirits that, just as he'd come back to his own Birth Place, now we were waiting for the Salmon to come home too. My father spoke to the spirits for a long while. Behind him I could see a wave of cloud rising under the Evening Sun Sky, over the shoulder of the great cliffs where Salmon Camp Hill tumbles to the sea. I couldn't help thinking we ought to get the hides stretched over the tent frames before it rained. In less than a hand-full of heartbeats that great grey wave would swallow the Sun. Even as I watched, the Sun slipped into it and began to disappear. The air turned cold and smelt of coming rain. Still my father spoke to the spirits . . . what more could he possibly have to say? I had baskets of shellfish, eggs, shag chicks and flatfish we'd brought from Seal Bay. I needed to build up the embers into a good roasting fire if we were going to eat before dark. If only I could get the fire ready now, we could eat outside before the rain drove us into our tent.

I'm not like my mother and sister. There are many things I'll never know. I see so little that I find it hard sometimes to be patient with those who look further, and understand more. But the spirits don't despise me either. One thing I can say for myself: I've never – in all the Years I've looked after the fire, however hard the rain, and however wet the voyage – I've never let our family's Fire go out.

Next morning the men went down to Shellfish Narrows to rebuild the fish traps. Often the winter River is so angry it sweeps everything away; sometimes it's kind and leaves a few stakes still standing. This Year the River had not been kind. The men spent all day cutting and fixing new stakes. We women dug the withy fences out of the dry sand and set about mending them. No one had been at this Salmon Camp last Year; there was a lot of work to do to get everything mended. It rained all day, but at last the sky cleared. The red Sun shot its dying rays across the sea. Above us, Mother Mountain glowed purple in the last light. Hills and islands moved closer as, one by one, stars pierced the deepening sky like sparks rising from far-off spirit-fires.

That night we sang to the Salmon. Our song told the Salmon we were at the River waiting for them. We called on them to come back:

Come, Salmon, home to your River!
Your River is waiting for you
Come, Salmon, leap up the high falls
Your River is waiting for you
Death is looking out for you
Like a Mother watching for her young sons to come home
    from the sea
Come, Salmon, come to your River!
Your People are waiting for you.

We sang one song after another. Light Moon rose over the hill
where Salmon River springs. She was already waning, telling
the Salmon that soon Seed Moon would follow her, and they
must hurry towards the River where the People waited. The
evening light had barely faded when the morning began to glow
with the beginning of another day. Our last song trickled into
silence. Dogs and children had long been asleep, curled up
together in little mounds by the warm hearth. We brought furs
from the tents and covered the children up. Sorné laid damp
turfs over the fire. Men and women wrapped themselves in
their cloaks and stretched themselves on the ground to sleep
under the watchful eyes of the new day.

Until Seed Moon rose, we women were able to fish from the
boats every day. Our nets were full of saithe, and, on calm days
when we paddled out beyond Driftwood Island, some fine fat
cod as well. We wrapped them in dulse and roasted them, then
feasted off the delicious white flakes. Until the great storm lashed
the River into a fury, Haizea and Itsaso guddled for stray trout
in the pools below the falls. They didn't get many, and sometimes we had to send them to do more useful work collecting
sea-roots and shellfish along the shore. While we were fishing,
the men went off to their Hunting Camp on the side of Mother
Mountain, where Salmon River begins. The red deer calves were

still young enough to be run down with dogs, and twice Sendoa and Amets came back with hinds in milk as well, though that's always a tough kill – a mother, whether People or Animal, will always fight harder for her young than for anything else.

But before I can explain what happened next at Salmon Camp, I need to take you back to River Mouth Camp and tell you about the first winter that Osané spent with our family.

She didn't speak.

I don't mean she was quiet, or she didn't talk much. I mean what I said: she didn't speak. Not one word. When we left Gathering Camp, taking her and Kemen with us – we had to make another boat before we left, our family had suddenly grown so much bigger – she didn't say a word on the journey. I thought it would be better when we got to River Mouth Camp. I was wrong. She didn't speak all winter while we were there. Nor did she speak when we got to Seal Bay Camp. Not a single word for many Moons – two hands-full! Now it was Seed Moon, and Osané still hadn't said one word to any of us.

She was still saying nothing. Sometimes I wanted to shake her; I was sure she could speak if she tried. After all, I was the one that had put compresses of eel fat, plantain and yarrow round her neck every day until her bruises healed – no one knew better than I that there'd been nothing the matter with her throat since Swan Moon.

It wasn't that she was unhappy with us. I'd realised she was feeling better right back in Yellow Leaf Moon, when she started making herself new clothes. She'd brought nothing when she came to us except the deerskin tunic and woman's skirt she was wearing. She never fetched anything from her parents' tent, so she had no leggings, no shoes, no winter furs, no knife, no needles, no awl, no thread . . . Kemen made her a knife when we got to River Mouth Camp. I saw him carving the haft and I asked him what he was making.

When he told me I burst out, 'Osané's got two hands of her own, hasn't she? What kind of a woman doesn't even make her own knife! You know I'd have lent her mine to do it with! It's fair enough if you cut the blades – I can well believe they never taught her – but surely she can do the rest! You'll teach her the worst—'

Amets seized me from behind and put his hand over my mouth. 'I think it's *me* who's let my woman learn the worst habits, Kemen! It seems to be *my* wife who thinks she's in charge round here!'

I pulled his hand away, and pretended to grab him just where it would hurt. 'And so I am, Amets! Certainly I'm the only one with any sense! We all know what *men* think with!'

'Ah, *would* you!' He wrestled me round and got me in an armlock. After that I was laughing too much to say anything. Kemen just grinned, and went on carving a groove in the haft of Osané's knife.

At least Osané made her own sewing things with her new knife. I let her take whatever she wanted from the basket of clean bones. She chose a swan bone and made herself a needle case, then spent half a day decorating it with swirling patterns; I thought she'd do better to get on with making her needles. But I soon found out what a quick worker she was. I gave her such furs as I could spare before Amets and Kemen started bringing in new pelts – mostly hare and deer, but there was one thick foxfur. Osané scraped the hides until they were soft tawny-grey, and when her tunic was sewn she decorated it with everything she could get. I was astonished at how much she'd collected already: she had it all hoarded away in a little bark box. She kept adding new things – polished beaver teeth, otter claws, fishbones, feathers and grasses. She strung necklaces and bracelets for herself and Haizea out of seeds, nuts, acorn cups, cowrie shells and polished bones. She also made some for me, which strangely touched my heart. She even decorated her sealskin boots with otter claws. She used my foxfur to make a winter cap, and kept the tail hanging down the back. It showed off the colour of her hair. Osané might not have a word to say, but she knew just how pretty she was, and she knew how to make the most of it too. When Kemen brought back a winter hare from the hill she made herself white gloves – white *gloves*! – and a tippet for her neck. Even her leggings had swans' feathers threaded down the seams on each side. As for her hair, I never saw such a girl for washing and combing it – she even washed it in the River in *winter*. I told her she'd catch a chill and die of it: she just smiled and carried on plaiting it, threading in feathers and seedheads, and all the rest of it. But she never shirked her work – she certainly looked after Kemen's clothes as well as she looked after her own. And she wasn't vain: Osané just likes decorating things. Even now, she never so much as makes a birchbark bucket without carving swirling patterns all over it. It's never bothered me; I was glad to see her doing something that seemed to make her happy.

The spirits were kind when they brought us Osané. I was very happy when she got pregnant. I was quick to spot that glow – it made Osané look lovelier than ever. I didn't tempt the spirits by saying a single word, but Osané soon noticed that I was giving her the choicest bits of meat – liver, kidneys, hearts, fish roes and so on. She took them with a secret smile. I hoped all would be well: my little Esti was lonely at River Mouth Camp away from her cousins. If my brother had lived he'd have taken a wife, but I doubt if she'd have wanted to come to live with us. Not many women choose to leave their own families, though they usually get a good welcome if they do, especially in a family that doesn't have daughters. Anyway, sometimes I thought about how it had all turned out: how Bakar was lost, then Kemen came, then Osané came, and in the end it was through them that Bakar was given back to us.

When Osané got pregnant my mother had been away for more than two Moons. I wasn't looking forward to her return very much. I thought it would be better, now our family was getting bigger, if we had two summer tents instead of one. One morning Osané and I were sitting outside the winter house at River Mouth Camp sewing new soles on our men's sealskin boots – sometimes in winter we never seem to do anything else – when I suggested we use some of our extra hides to make ourselves a new tent. Osané gave a big smile, dropped Kemen's boot with the needle still in it, and jumped to her feet. We started looking through the hides at once.

'We'll have them ready to take with us in Auk Moon,' I told her. 'We'll have them scraped and cured before we leave, and we can make a frame as soon as we get to our spring Camp, and sew the hides there. We can get birchbark then too.'

Osané always looked as if she were listening. Now I'd got used to her I found it quite easy to do all the talking. After all, I'd had to listen to my mother all my life, and I hadn't always agreed with what she said. Osané usually did everything I suggested, sometimes better than I could. Of course, as she wouldn't speak she couldn't argue with me, but sometimes she'd set about things differently from how I'd told her. She didn't do that often, but when she did she sometimes turned out to be right.

My mother never came to Seal Bay Camp – that's where we went in Auk Moon when the sea wouldn't let us through to White Beach Camp – she went off across Long Strait some-where. So we only started using our new tent when we got to Salmon Camp. It was much better than the old one. If we'd known how little we'd see of my mother we mightn't have both-ered with another tent. When the weather was bad my father and Haizea spent their days in our tent anyway. When I suggested they sleep with us too, and then we could use the old tent as a store, they both refused. So at night Amets, Esti and I had the right hand side of the hearth to ourselves, and Kemen and Osané had the left.

I lay awake the first night gazing up at the new hazel frame, the carefully sewn hides and the birchbark lining up above. Through the smoke hole I could see the stars. Never, since I left my mother's breast, had I lain on the right side of the hearth. Now it was I, not Nekané, who lay down at night and sat by day in the right-hand place next to the cooking place behind the hearth. I was now the one who could reach everything I needed without getting up. I was the one who could tell everyone, even the men, to take their boots off when they came in, and all the other things they must do, or not do, inside my house. With only two women in the tent both Osané and I slept in the best places next to the hearth. 'Like two of the Wise already!' I said to her. Osané smiled.

Haizea said:

We got to Salmon Camp early enough to catch elvers. Ortzi and I always used to make elver traps together. Now I persuaded Itsaso to come with me. We cut birchbark and rolled six traps. Alaia gave us calfskin. We spoilt the first bit of skin making the holes too big and she was cross, but she let us have more. We made channels in the stony rapids along the edges of Eel Stream, just above the beach. We weighed our traps with stones and asked the Eel spirits to be kind to us. They listened, even though Alaia said the Year was too old. I believed my father more than Alaia. He said the Year counted on its fingers, and whenever it reached a hand-full it told the Eels to give themselves unstintingly. I could just remember it happening before. Now I wanted elvers for my father – he didn't get enough meat because of not being able to chew.

One day the elver traps were so full they were nearly all eel and hardly any water. We tipped the elvers into a rush basket. They nearly reached the brim. They wriggled and swarmed in circles of shining ripples, black and brown. It was like trying to pick up threads of water – they just slipped out of our fingers – so we cupped our hands and shoved wriggly scoops into our mouths. They tasted fresh and fishy, tickling our throats as they went down so we couldn't stop laughing. Itsaso laughed so much she fell down the bank; I stuffed the basket between some birch stems and rolled down after her. There's a ledge of grass down there, bright green from otter spraint. We lay on our backs giggling; above us bright birch leaves danced under the Sun.

When I was a child I thought all these things would last for ever.

Early in Salmon Moon Itsaso and I were picking mussels at Shellfish Narrows when we saw the salmon coming in. The tide had turned: the River was starting to flow the other way in soft surges of salt water. Down among the seaweedy rocks the pools were filling. Colder water swished round our ankles. My basket was full. I swung it on to my back and looked at the swirling tide. Dark shapes like twilight shadows flickered through the seawater.

'Itsaso! The salmon! They're here!'

We raced back to Camp, dodging between the oaks along the path above the gorge. Some of the women were back already, their baskets full. Osané was roasting pignuts in the ashes. Esti had a little scraper of her own and was helping Osané smooth out the ash. Osané gripped the back of her tunic with one hand to stop her falling in the fire. Alaia and Sorné were scraping the fat off a fresh deerskin. The stripped carcass of a young stag hung from my father's oak tree. The men were lying in the sunshine doing nothing – at least, they had nets piled all round them, and netting-needles lying on top, but that's not the same as working! You know how men are useless at getting any work done when they've just been hunting! All they'd done was take that stag from a trap – its antlers had got caught in the noose. You couldn't say that was hard work! But men always say they're tired from the hunt when they've been away for a day or two. The truth is they're worn out from making their own fires and cooking their own food. Actually what men do best in the world is lying in the Sun.

'The salmon have come! They're at Shellfish Narrows! The salmon are coming in!'

The men leaped up. Even my aunt Sorné put aside her work and struggled to her feet. I ran back to Shellfish Narrows with the men. They soon saw I was right. The salmon were rolling in with the tide, over the trap and through the open gap between the fences. From the cliffs of Shellfish Narrows we looked down on rippling silvery backs as the fish surged into the River. The men waded in upstream, pulling the withy gate across the gap in the upper fence, and wedging it between the stakes at either side. Sendoa and his brothers came and stood beside us, dripping. Amets and Kemen had climbed out on the other side.

Slowly the tide slackened. The flood eddied aimlessly between the cliffs of Shellfish Narrows. Small waves lifted the last fronds of seaweed at high water. A soft swell rocked to and fro, a hand's length above the lower fence of the fish trap.

'Now!'

Sendoa signalled across the narrows to Amets and Kemen. Kemen waded into the water beside my sister's husband. There'd been a lot of talk among the women last Year at White Beach Camp about Kemen not being much of a hunter when it came to catching birds. Some of them said he wasn't really much use to us. I was glad Sorné was getting a chance to see that wasn't true. Kemen grabbed his end of the lower gate and wedged it hard between the stakes. The waves funnelling between the cliffs were as tall as he was, but that didn't bother him. Amets felt along the bottom of the gate with his feet to check it was right down across the gap underneath. He stood on the frame and pushed it down with all his weight. A stone was stopping it. All at once Kemen dived head first like an auk and disappeared under the water. Amets was so startled he let the next wave slap his cheek and knock him off balance. Suddenly Kemen bobbed up next to Amets, and held up his spread palm so we all knew the gate was fixed.

Everyone said afterwards that Kemen must have had some Auk in him from the Beginning, to be able to dive and swim under water like that. Women are usually better at seeing what's under the sea, because we dive after oysters in the hot Moons. It's not as easy to keep your eyes open in the water as men think. You have to remember not to breathe as well. Most men never even try it – well, they have us women so they don't have to, do they?

Sendoa was shouting at us: 'You – Ortzi! Haizea! Bring down the spears! And you can get that net ready to drag the fish down to the lower gate. Keep it away from the spears though, whatever you do!'

Ortzi didn't want to work with a girl. Itsaso hadn't followed us back to Shellfish Narrows. Ortzi was angry that Sendoa was treating us both as children even though Ortzi had made himself a spear specially for Salmon Camp. He wouldn't speak to me, though it was hardly my fault. Everyone knows women can set nets just as well as men can, but when the salmon come we all have to pretend it's the same as hunting. That's because the fish give themselves so freely that all you have to do – nearly – is ask them to leap into your basket. Women have to be much cleverer when *they* go fishing, which we do all the rest of the Year, you may have noticed! But when the Salmon first come, and you couldn't fail if you tried, fishing suddenly has to be a man's work. I wonder why . . .

But that Year, when Ortzi was first lost to me, I never wanted to grow up and become a woman. I was pleased when the men let me help, even just pulling a net about. When I was a child I still believed everything they said!

We got five baskets-full from the fish trap in just one night. Some of those salmon were too heavy for Ortzi or me to lift by ourselves, so we had to work together. The men carried the baskets uphill through the oaks back to Salmon Camp. Ortzi and I had two salmon each, strung over our shoulders; even so, we were struggling to keep up. Just one basket of salmon kept everyone feasting for two days. We split the rest open and laid them on the rocks to dry. We made a smoky fire and set up a shelter over it to dry the deer meat. It would do for later – after all, we'd been eating deer all winter.

It's always good when the salmon first come. After eating white fish the salmon are so rich and pink and greasy – they fill you up like meat, until you're only fit to lie in the Sun and rest your bulging stomach. For a few days it's wonderful, and then you get used to it. By the end of Seed Moon you feel like one more salmon would make you sick. But isn't it good while it lasts! In the spring Moons there always seems to be more work to do than anyone can get done, but in Salmon Moon you just have to walk as far as the River and you'll always find more fish coming.

Salmon Camp is good for firewood too. You remember the big aspen that blew down by Green Loch? That Year we were breaking up the dead branches right through Salmon Moon. Aspen's not the best firewood, but that Year it saved us a lot of walking. That old aspen still gives itself. It started sending up new shoots from the fallen trunk. They were all in flower – it's the only aspen I ever saw flowering like that. We're still cutting wands from that trunk – it's gone into all our traps at Salmon Camp, and lots of other things as well.

It hardly rained in Seed Moon. The River went down, and stayed very low till the storm came. Most Years it's two or three man-lengths across at Salmon Camp. By the end of Seed Moon its bed was a bleached skeleton. Dried-out tufts of black moss sat on top of each naked rock, showing where the water ought to be. Usually the River sings its song loudly while we're at Salmon Camp, telling about the hills it's come from, the waters it's gathered on its way and the sea ahead waiting for it. It seldom says anything different: it's like an old man by the fire in winter, telling his same old stories till everyone knows them by heart. And no one knows why it's like that until the voice has gone, and only the stories are left – because then you realise that every one of those same old tellings carved its channel a little deeper into your heart.

We followed the salmon upriver. Above Salmon Camp the River splits and splits again into more streams than you can count. They curl between banks of yellow-green mosses, cradling little grassy islands in their current. Now the islands had grown stony beaches that dried up the streamlets wherever they tried to break away. We filed along the wood path, carrying spears, nets and gaffes. The rapids in the gorge had shrunk to milky trickles that wound to and fro among a waste of stones. Even the path through the marshes was almost dry. Usually you can see the falls, white as lightning flashes, tumbling over the ledges above Rowan Pool. But now, instead of roaring down, the falls just chattered like shaken pebbles.

In Rowan Pool the salmon were waiting for the water to rise. They couldn't get up the fall: in its shrunken state the River was ready to give its salmon to us without even trying to fight back. While they were stuck in the shallow pool we trapped them with nets, and hooked them ashore with gaffes and hands and any way we could. Still the rain didn't come.

'It's good for us,' my father said. He and I were resting in the Sun on the riverbank. He was making twine, twisting it against his thigh, the way he always did when he was sitting quiet. Below us thin water chuckled past in its bed of whitened stones. 'But not so good for the salmon. They want to get to the high pools as soon as they can.'

'The high pools are a lot further for us to walk.' I was growing lazy, what with the heat and so much plenty. I lay propped on my elbow. Below me the River rippled over the shallows like the patterns on a birch trunk under cloud-shadows. My father and I were sitting so still the dippers had flown back to fish the dark eddies on the other bank.

'If the salmon don't manage to spawn in Seed Moon, you'll be walking a lot further than the high pools next Year.'

I lay back sleepily on the riverbank and shut my eyes. 'But next Year is very far away.'

'That's what you think now.' I looked up and saw my father gazing down at me. 'When Seed Moon comes back again, little daughter, you'll remember my name?'

'But—' I sat up and stared at him. His words filled me with a fear I didn't want to face. The River laughed softly in its narrow bed. Across the glen a cuckoo called to its mate: 'Cuck – oo . . . cuck – oo.' Not long after, I saw the cuckoo itself, a long-tailed shadow silently passing over the glistening treetops.

'You may not hear my name spoken for many Years, Haizea. I think one day you'll be the one who first speaks it again. When that happens, you'll remember me telling you this.'

My eyes filled with tears. I'd been content. The salmon days had been long and pink and plentiful. I felt as if my father had flung me into icy seawater. Cold depths yawned below me, where giant sea-things lurked in the dark. I shivered. 'I never want your name to go out of the world!'

'It will pass quickly, Haizea. Meanwhile, you'll learn to be happy without it. Remember: the spirits never let the smallest Animal be lost. All this will come again.'

Osané said:

Everyone must be wondering by now what I thought of all this.

My son was born at Salmon Camp. The River had been very low. Right through Seed Moon there was hardly a cloud in the sky. Then one morning early in Salmon Moon the air lay so thick it made me tired to breathe it. We smelt rain. Kemen and Amets dug more earth from the ditch round our tent. Alaia and I laid extra stones in the hearth to lift the fire above the floor. We brought all our food inside. The others were busy round their tents too. When the clouds opened the water poured down in white streaks. Hail rattled on the tent hide. White light flashed round us where we sat, still damp and breathless from running for shelter. Thunder tore the sky apart like a tree splitting when it falls, then like rocks tumbling over a precipice and rolling round below.

Esti lifted the tent flap a little way. The dogs were huddled against the threshold, ears flat and noses hidden. A double flash lit the Camp – huge brown puddles, streaming water, tents bowed to the rain – then within a heartbeat the thunder crashed above our heads. Esti let go the hide, too scared to scream, and stumbled towards the hearth.

'Baby, it's all right. Come—'

Amets cut across Alaia, 'My daughter's not scared of a little storm – don't be a fool, Alaia! Are you there, Esti? You're not scared!'

'No!' That was the only word Esti had so far, but it served her for everything she wanted to say. She set her mouth, and, without glancing at her mother, climbed on to her father's lap, where she sat sucking her thumb.

Thunder rolled around the sky with never a space between. The rain was like a waterfall. Water spread across the floor: our ditches had overflowed. Water was coming through the heather where we sat. Our furs were getting wet. I felt cold and strange. Something fluttered in my belly. Only when the fluttering began to hurt did I realise that the baby inside me had been woken by the storm and wanted to come out. I had no voice to tell anyone. I sat still for as long as I could, while the brown water swirled across the floor around our hearth.

The hide over the door lifted. Rain spattered over us as People stumbled over the dogs and staggered in: Nekané supporting her man, Haizea with a basket clutched to her chest – 'Our tent's down!'

We made room for them. Water ran off their deerskins and soaked into our furs. They took off their boots and hung them upside down to dry. Haizea's basket was filled with moist chunks of salmon. 'We cooked it this morning. Nekané thought we mightn't have fire when the storm came.'

We brought out dried deer meat and berries as well. I thought I was hungry, but when I tried to eat the pains gripped my stomach. I felt sick. The lightning grew less, and now we could count more than a hand-full of heartbeats before the thunder followed. It growled around the far-off sky as if it didn't want to leave us. The rain streamed down.

It wasn't just the rain. 'Listen!' said Amets. 'The River!'

Birch and rowan cling to the sides of the Salmon River gorge, looking down on the rushing rapids. Our Camp is just above the narrows. It's in a grassy hollow, which slopes gently down to flat rocks where the stream widens out just above the gorge. Often we work down on the rocks, and cook our fish there. When we come back the next Year our riverside hearths have always been washed away. We seldom see floods in Salmon Moon, but now the River sounded very close.

'I'm going to see!' Amets handed Esti to Alaia and ducked under the hide. Kemen went out after him.

The rest of us looked at each other. Haizea scrambled to her feet. Alaia grabbed her by her tunic. 'No, you stay here! They'll come back soaked. There's enough water in here already!'

'But I want—'

'No!' Nekané so seldom told her daughters what to do that Haizea sat down at once, more in surprise than anything else.

'*Could* the River get into the Camp?' she asked.

'The River does what it will.'

'But surely—'

'It never has before,' said Nekané.

'But . . . ' Haizea looked fearful, then burst out, 'the sea hadn't ever drowned the lands of the Lynx People before, had it?'

No one answered. Water roared in our ears, but whether it was the rain or the River we couldn't tell.

Nekané must have been looking at me, because suddenly she said, 'Osané! Is that child on its way *now*?'

Haizea and Alaia swung round and stared at me. A pain gripped me. I gasped, and leaned forward.

'Who *is* this, who chooses to come into the world on a day like this? Someone brave, that I can tell! Husband, you'll have to get out of here! Go to Sorné's tent – if it's still standing. Haizea! Help your father across the Camp! Alaia, are any of those skins still dry? Osané, even a girl who won't speak could surely let her elders know about a thing like this! That's it, husband. Take this cloak! Now, out you go! Haizea, tell Amets and Kemen they must find somewhere else to stay! Alaia, is any of that wood dry enough to burn?'

I'd never found Nekané easy. I'd been very glad when Alaia suggested she and I make ourselves a summer tent. We had enough hides, and she said it would be good for us and our men to have our own tent. Of course she didn't mention I was pregnant in case the spirits heard, but I knew what was in her mind. It was lonely for Esti when our family were at River Mouth Camp. Alaia knew she'd pleased me from the way I'd got to my feet and set about scraping skins at once. We both worked hard making our tent: we each had strong reasons for wanting this change.

Even though I'd felt like that about the tent, I was very relieved when Nekané saw what was happening and took charge of my son's birth. Haizea came back soaked to the skin, and said the River had overflowed the gorge, but it wasn't coming any higher. The rain was easing off. By then I hardly heard her. All I knew was that when my boy lay in my arms at last, I noticed how everything was quiet except for the water dripping from the trees, and the swollen River. The hide had been pulled from the smoke hole, and the evening Sun was beaming into the red heart of our fire.

I loved my son as soon as I saw him. I was frightened no one would recognise him – every woman must fear that – but I was also frightened about who he might be. And if I were the one to recognise him, how would I tell them who he was? Perhaps it would be a name I wouldn't want to speak even if I had my voice. Perhaps – I often wondered about this during the Moons when my voice was gone – perhaps my voice had left me in the first place because she knew it was better for my story not to be told. So although I was happy I was very scared as well.

I needn't have been. When Nekané brought her husband to see my child, he stood looking down at him for a long while. When he smiled his face broke into more creases than I'd ever seen in it before.

'Bakar.' The quiet voice was rich with satisfaction. 'I've been waiting for you to come back.'

Alaia said:

Bakar was born in the tent that Osané and I had made. It was a good thing we'd made it so strong! I was very happy when my father recognised Osané's son as soon as he set eyes on him. Somehow I'd had it in my mind that we were expecting a little stranger – some soul from the Lynx People whom we'd never known. But of course Osané was our far-off cousin, and Bakar's name has lived among our People for longer than anyone can remember.

After Bakar was named Osané let me take him in my arms. 'Welcome back to the Auk People, brother,' I said to him. My voice trembled with joy. 'We're so happy to see you again, Bakar. You will always find food here!'

Since my mother had become Go-Between she hadn't been with her family much. She had to learn from Zigor, and that took her far away. I wondered if one day she'd be sorry she'd neglected my father so much in his last days. It seemed to me that learning from Zigor could wait, but Death never waits just because someone isn't ready.

Sendoa and Sorné left us at the end of Salmon Moon. My mother went with them: she wanted to go to Gathering Camp. It was lonely when they'd gone, but I was pleased to stay away from Gathering Camp. Now Kemen had joined our family we had enemies we'd never had before. It frightened me that one of them – Hodei – was Go-Between. Edur was angry with us too, and, though Amets didn't talk to me about it, I knew he was upset about losing Edur's friendship. Osané's family wouldn't speak to her at all after the night Kemen took her – not that Osané said anything anyway, but they'd made it quite clear they'd cast her off. When her brothers had met Kemen alone they'd spat and muttered curses. That was when I told Kemen it would be best if he didn't go out alone while we were at Gathering Camp. 'If you're with Amets or Sendoa,' I'd said, 'they'll just keep away.'

Kemen hadn't answered me. He'd turned to Amets and said,

'I think your wife is asking us all to be women! Perhaps she's tired of meat and doesn't want any men around because they just keep bringing her more of it!'

Osané of course had said nothing.

Haizea and I walked further every day to get food. Now that Bakar was born, Osané came with us; sometimes we spent half the day walking with our babies on our backs. We'd dug so many roots and taken so many plants in the woods that we started going along the shore instead – however long you stay in a Camp, the sea keeps on giving more food than anyone can eat. We found good places along the shore where we'd never gathered before. We set nets and caught sand martins above the beach, and trapped waders where small streams spread themselves across the sand. We managed to trap one otter; Osané used its pelt to line her baby's sling.

It got harder to find dead wood, so twice the three of us paddled along the coast and got driftwood from the beaches. We lashed it into big bundles, and towed it home when the flooding tide was ready to help us with our load. On other days we climbed above the trees and set traps for hare and ptarmigan on the slopes of Mother Mountain. One sunny day we climbed to the top of Mother Mountain, where we showed Osané the two peaks of Grandmother Mountain, lying between the High Sun and Morning Sun Skies. When we faced the other way we could make out, between the Sunless Sky and the Morning Sun Sky, the hills above Gathering Loch. There, in the far-off haze, men would be preparing for the great Gathering Hunt of the Auk People.

Haizea and I always climb to the top of Mother Mountain when we're at Salmon Camp. We do it because our father took us up there every summer when we were little. From the top of Mother Mountain he used to show us where everything was, right across the world. The Year Osané came was the first Year my father didn't come with us when we went to the top of Mother Mountain.

Amets hadn't said anything, but I knew it hurt him not to be at Gathering Camp. After all, he was – and is – one of the best hunters among the Auk People. He should have been at the great Hunt! Edur would be there, and Osané's brothers . . . so many friends and cousins would be there, but not Amets! We all had our reasons for keeping away from Gathering Camp that Year, but none of us spoke about them.

Or only to the spirits: the spirits listened to us. The spirits heard how we longed for the wrongs we carried with us to be put right.

Osané said:

I said nothing for two hands-full and three Moons. After Nekané brought my soul back, and I lay alone in the Go-Betweens' shelter, I tried to waken my voice. My throat hurt. My voice was so unhappy she'd fled my body. Then after two hands-full and one Moons my son was born. My voice wanted him to hear what she sounded like. At first she only spoke to him secretly. One day I was filling waterskins at Salmon River. I sang to my son as he lay in his sling against my heart. I'd seen him gazing at the lights that danced on the water, so I sang to him how at the Beginning there was just the one light falling from the Sun, and how it broke into many pieces when it hit the ground, and some fell into the sky and some into the water, and some still drift across the lands, always looking for a home.

While the River flows
While the River flows
Catching the light as it falls . . .

A shadow fell across us. I looked up. It was Kemen.

I stopped singing.

'I heard your song.'

I was silent.

'I heard your song.'

My heart spoke to him. He didn't know that, because I had no words.

Kemen moved the full waterskins aside, and squatted beside me on the riverbank. 'Osané, I'm very glad you have words for him. Couldn't you find even one for his father?'

My voice fled. I swallowed, searching for it in my throat. Something changed inside my heart and now I wanted my voice to come back. I couldn't force it. Instead, I nodded.

Kemen laid his hand on my knee. 'I heard you sing about the light drifting across the land, always wanting to go home.'

I looked away. The lights danced on the River. After a while I saw that the River was holding the song curled up inside it. I listened to the River, then I hummed the same tune under my breath. Then, very softly, fixing my eyes on the lights until I couldn't see anything else, I began to sing the words.

The song reached its end. I'd been looking at the sparkling lights so long I couldn't see the River any more. I could only see the patterns the light made inside my eyes.

'Osané?'

I kept my eyes on the River. I cleared my throat. I found my voice huddled inside my gullet. I forced it to remember.

He had to lean very close to hear me.

'Yes?' I said to him.

I'm glad Kemen was the first – it was different with my son –

he had no words of his own – he was still part of me – I'm glad Kemen was the first to hear me speak again.

Alaia said:

The storm had filled the Sun with new strength; the great rain had washed the sky deep blue. The nights were growing longer, and in the clear skies the stars came back to us. They told us the summer was almost gone, even though the days were hot. One afternoon we spread a bearskin cloak for my father so he could sit propped against his oak tree. Esti knelt between his knees decorating his leggings with rows of shells and different-coloured pebbles. Amets sat on a log a little way away, chipping new blades off a white-stone core. Haizea and I had walked a long way in the heat that morning. We lay back in the Sun and closed our eyes. All I could hear was the River flowing through the gorge, a blackbird singing in the oak tree and the steady knocking of stone on stone.

'What is it? Has something happened?'

Haizea's clear voice came into my dream. I jerked awake. Kemen was coming towards us, leading Osané by the hand. Why would he do that? He brought her over to the hearth. But it was all right: he was smiling – more than I'd ever seen him smile before.

'Osané would like me to tell you—'

I knew already what he was going to say. Osané's arm was round Bakar in his sling. She looked a little frightened, a little shy, but also as if she could smile too, so long as we were careful.

'—that her voice has come back to her.' There was a little tremor in Kemen's own voice as he told us. 'But her voice isn't very brave yet – I suppose it knows it belongs to a woman, and so it thinks it should tease us a little. So we have to be patient with it. Well, we know all about patience, living in this Camp full of women the way we do!'

'Well!' Haizea looked at me as she spoke. 'I think Osané's man just told us some very good news, Alaia!'

'I think so too,' I said smiling. 'And you all know how much I like asking questions! But I won't! I'll be patient. *I'm* not the sort of woman who goes round teasing People!'

I kept my word, but it was difficult. There was so much I wanted Osané to tell me. I got my reward two mornings later. Osané and I were by the River. Bakar lay on his otterskin kicking his legs. Esti was picking daisies and scattering them over him. Our fishing lines were all tangled – not by us: Haizea had been using them the day before – and we had to unravel them and tie on new hooks.

Osané said, 'Don't pull! There's another knot!'

My fingers slipped. A splinter of bone from the fishhook ran under my fingernail. Osané didn't see. I caught my breath and said very calmly, 'So there is.'

She began to undo the knot, then pointed at my hand. There was blood on my fingers. Osané reached for my hand.

I looked at her as if I didn't understand. I wasn't going back to this game.

'Let me see your hand. It's bleeding.'

It hurt when she took the splinter out, but I didn't care. I knew now I could get her to talk. I kept on being careful, though. If I'd frightened Osané's voice away again I think I'd have lost my temper completely. Kemen would have been furious with me, and that would have made Amets angry too. As it was, the spirits didn't tempt me further. Osané began to speak more and more. First we just spoke about small things we were doing – cooking, tending the fire, finding plants and firewood, catching fish. Then as the days passed we started to chat more easily.

All my questions were poised, waiting to spring. I waited cunningly for our talk to start going the right way.

Amets said:

When Deer Moon was nearly full the women went to Small Loch to collect rushes: they said they had to make new cloaks before the days grew any colder. When they'd gone my wife's father asked me to come into his tent. I sat facing my wife's father across the hearth. Soft rain pattered on the hides over our heads. It drifted through the smoke hole and melted away in the heat above the fire.

We sat in silence. I had bark-strings in my pouch. I thought about taking them out and getting on with the twine I was making. The only sound in the tent was the crackle of the fire, and faint birdsong in the trees outside. A breeze stirred the aspen above the gorge; it sounded like the rain. I had many things I wanted to do outside. The old man sat so still I found myself unable to make any move at all. The air was heavy with waiting. The spirits were very near, but I couldn't see them. It wasn't me they were watching for.

'Amets, I want to talk to you. My daughter may be telling you a different story. But this matter concerns me alone.'

'I'm listening.' I leaned so close I smelt his breath. It was the only way to hear him over the crackle of the fire. He didn't realise how much he mumbled now his teeth were gone.

'Death walks at my side, Amets. He's been speaking kind words to me ever since Bakar was born. I'm ready to go with him when he asks.'

'I thought this might be what you wanted to tell me.'

'You're not stupid, Amets. You're not a woman either, to fuss over me and make a noise. You know why I waited so long?'

'Because Bakar needed you. You had to be there in case no one recognised him.'

'I said you weren't stupid.' My wife's father gazed into the fire for a long while. I could see it made him tired to speak.

'Was that all you wanted to say to me?'

He waved his hand impatiently. 'No, it's not all!' Presently he went on, 'I knew – not that the spirits ever had much to say to me – but I knew – maybe he let me know it himself – I *knew* Bakar depended on me. Sometimes it felt like a huge burden he'd laid on me. At first I hoped he'd be your child. Only then our little Esti arrived.'

My wife's father leaned back and closed his eyes. When he'd rested a little he went on, 'After that I guessed I'd have to wait four or five Years or even more – I didn't want Esti weaned too early.' He coughed, and wiped his mouth with a shaking hand. 'That child of yours will live! I see long life and good health in everything she does. Then Osané came to us. When I saw she was pregnant I hoped – I allowed myself to hope a little – that I mightn't have to wait much longer. And that's how it turned out. So now I needn't wait any more.'

'We'll look after Bakar when you're gone.'

'I know.' It came out in a whisper; I only just heard him. He shifted his legs, moving stiffly as if it hurt him. When he spoke again his voice held a shadow of its old strength. 'You'll take care of my family when I'm gone, Amets. I knew when Alaia took you that you'd do that. Though . . . I was afraid after Bakar went we might lose you too.'

'I wouldn't have left Alaia to bring up Esti alone.'

'So you were thinking about it. But you might have left us and taken them with you?'

'Where to? I left my own family long ago.'

'You see – you did think about it. But now this family is growing again. You won't leave now.'

'No, I won't leave now.'

The fire was burning low. I fetched two logs from the pile at the door. I laid them on the glowing ashes. I wondered if there was anything else my wife's father wanted to say to me.

'Two more things,' he whispered, as if he'd read my thoughts. 'Bakar's father—'

'Kemen.'

'—Kemen. Through Kemen the spirits sent Bakar back to us. But Kemen brought us trouble. I lost my son in the same Moon that Kemen arrived. Now we have enemies because of Kemen. I never made enemies: this family has never had enemies before.'

'Kemen is my brother. His enemies are my enemies.'

'Then my children are forced to have enemies among their own People, even though they've done nothing to deserve it.'

I raised my hands to such spirits as might be listening. 'I'll look after your children' – I called him by his name – '*All* your children. I'll deal with anyone who calls himself their enemy. That I promise you.'

I think I set his mind at ease. He only had one more thing to say. He was very tired; he had to fight to speak each word. 'We've never stayed so long at Salmon Camp before. Soon it'll be too late to get round Fierce Point to River Mouth Camp.'

'There'll still be days of good weather.'

'But the sea – you can't trust the sea in Yellow Leaf Moon.'

'It's not yet Yellow Leaf Moon.'

He kept picking at the fur beside him. 'Death is waiting for me here in Salmon Camp,' he said at last. 'But that doesn't concern the rest of you. Amets, take them to River Mouth Camp while the sea still lets you through! If you get stuck here at Salmon Camp you won't get such good hunting. We mustn't let the children go hungry!'

'We could make a winter Camp here. Only our own family – Sendoa and the others – hunt on this side of Mother Mountain in winter. Sendoa wouldn't mind if we were here too.' I didn't sound sure, because I didn't like the idea any more than he did. River Mouth Camp was the best place we had, and if we didn't claim it soon, somebody else might think we weren't coming, and take it.

Alaia's father knew what I was thinking. 'Go to River Mouth Camp!' he urged me. 'Go now, while you can! I don't need you – any of you. If I can't meet Death without your help, then what have I lived for all these Years? Amets, take them now!'

I knew he was right, but I also had to think about what Alaia would say. Not that I let my woman tell me what to do, but it never works to force them against their will. They make too much fuss. So, knowing what Alaia would want on the one hand, and being urged by her father on the other, I finally gave him my word that whatever happened I'd get his family – my family – safely back to River Mouth Camp before Yellow Leaf Moon.

Kemen said:

We woke one morning to mist so thick we could barely see across the Camp. The treetops reached into the sky and vanished. We smelt damp earth and dying leaves, and the first breath of coming winter. The air had no songs in it. Amets and I got ready to go fishing.

'We'll take spears and gaffes,' Amets said. 'It's misty enough.'

'But as soon as the Sun rises he'll burn this mist off!'

'Not for a while. It's too cold. And the mist is very thick.'

I remembered that Alaia had told Amets to check the fish traps. 'We women have quite enough to do,' she'd said last night. 'There's no need for you two to go hunting tomorrow. We've still got half that dried stag meat left. Someone's got to lay the fish to dry, and turn them, and scrape that otter hide

– Osané and I will have to do that. And we need more sea-roots. I told Haizea and Itsaso they could go up and pick bilberries. And cloudberries, of course – your favourite, Amets – you know you don't want to miss those. The least you and Kemen can do is check the fish traps. Men are no use to anyone when they're not hunting!'

Why was I so happy when Osané's voice came back to her? I must have been mad! All I can say is the spirits were kind to me when they gave me a quiet woman! Now I remembered Alaia's scolding yesterday, I understood why Amets said we had to take fish spears even though it was going to be sunny. At least it made us look like men! Not that anyone was awake to see us off.

As we walked upriver a little circle of yellow appeared in the Morning Sun Sky. A thrush hidden in a willow began to sing. The pale circle in the Morning Sun Sky grew too bright to look at. The treetops across the River threw off the clinging cloud. Through the grey they took on red and brown and gold. Yellow light broke through and touched our hands and faces. We saw a smudge of blue beyond the cloud. Then all the day-birds burst into song as the Sun gulped down the last fleeing shreds of mist.

I'd been walking behind Amets with a heavy step. Now the autumn had come I often found myself thinking about the past. It was in Deer Moon – two Years ago now – that the sea took away everything I'd loved. My heart still beat to the pulse of the lost Lynx lands. The ways of my fathers still flowed in my blood. The same Moons brought different seasons to the Auk People. I could learn Auk lands as a man learns a new song from far-off cousins – even if he's never heard the words before he can still remember them – but in my heart I'd always be a stranger.

As I followed Amets I was thinking about a different River. My River was strong and steady. It didn't change its mood at the least whisper of weather from the hills above. It rose with the meltwater, as all Rivers must do, and shrank under the summer Sun, but it wasn't fickle. It didn't leap into spate, or dry to a skeleton of whitened stones, in less than a night, without a thought for the season. My River would let me fish from my boat early in the Year, as the ripples slid by on the currents that carried me down. I saw the brown surface of deep waters reflected in my heart. Gulls screamed overhead. I heard the steady note of the rapids, then I came down them in a swirl of water that played all round me in the shifting light. The trees above my head were taller than anything that grew in Auk lands, and they were still bare of leaves. *Our* salmon give themselves when we need them most. *Our* salmon come when the land is hungry. They come in greater plenty than Auk People have ever known, at the beginning of Young Moon – the Moon you Auk People call Limpet Moon. Before spring even reaches the land the Lynx People feast – feasted – every night on the rich pink flesh of the Wise Fish. When Sendoa told me that in Auk lands the salmon didn't give themselves until Seed Moon, I wondered what the Auk People could possibly have done to anger the Salmon so much that their spirits were prepared to let the People starve.

The Sun burst free of cloud, and I came back to where I was. I remembered that now I had a healthy son, a wife who spoke to me and a family I could trust. In Amets I had a new brother. I needed to speak to him, but now I could do it with a lighter heart. No one wants to listen to a man who's sorry for himself.

We'd stopped using the trap at Shellfish Narrows when the salmon stopped running. Now we set basket traps at the pool outlets upriver. Most days we caught a few grilse and brown trout, but the older salmon were too wily to be caught that way. We got more by enticing them in at night with fire-sticks, and that was more like hunting – any woman can empty a basket trap. It didn't take Amets and me very long. Our baskets were still nowhere near full when we'd emptied the last trap.

'This is no good!' Amets brushed away the biting flies that swarmed around his head. He dumped his basket on a strip of green turf below a clinging rowan, and laid down his spear. He untied the leather ember pouch that hung from his belt. 'We'll make a fire, Kemen, and smoke out these flies.'

Amets took oak-ember from its damp-moss wrapping, and crumbled dry fire-mushroom over the glowing wood. I collected rowan twigs and dry leaves, while Amets blew the embers into a small flame. Soon we were propped on our elbows, one on each side of a small fire. Leafy rowan twigs shrivelled on the flames and sent up clouds of smoke. The flies kept away. We split open a few trout, and stuck them on sticks to grill in the tasty smoke. Their juices ran down and crackled in the flames. They smelt good.

The trout tasted fresh and smoky all at once. The first one was so hot I had to jiggle it between my fingers as I bit off big chunks. I swallowed, and said thickly, 'Amets.'

'Yes.' His eyes were on the River, not on me. I found that easier.

'If we don't stop fishing here soon, the fish won't want to give themselves next Year.'

'We will stop. We'll go back to River Mouth Camp before Yellow Leaf Moon. It's going to be a hard winter. Every day more geese come from the Sunless Sky. The sooner we start hunting at River Mouth Camp the better. I want us to have meat when the bad weather comes.'

'That's what I was thinking. Only what about the old man?'

Amets told me what Alaia's father had said to him. It didn't surprise me. When he'd finished I knew he hadn't told me everything.

'That wasn't all, was it?' I asked. 'He's worried about me,

isn't he? He's worried about the enemies I made when I took Osané.'

'He knows you weren't given any choice.'

'All that means is that I needn't blame myself. Maybe I sleep with a lighter heart, but it doesn't change anything else.'

'Your marriage with Osané was Zigor's doing,' Amets pointed out. 'He brought this trouble on us. He must take the blame.'

'He's Go-Between,' I said. 'He sees more than we do. Or, if he doesn't, the spirits who guide him can see much further.'

'Perhaps.' Amets reached into the basket and took out two more fish. 'There's so few we might as well finish them.' He tossed a couple of slippery fish over to me, and laughed when I didn't catch them. I picked them up and slit them open, spilling out the guts. I ate the delicate red livers just as they were, and skewered the fishes longways to grill across the embers of our little fire. Amets laid on more rowan leaves. 'What bad spirit sends all these flies into the world?' he grumbled.

We ate our fish and lay quiet for a while. The Sun was getting hot. Amets began to breathe long breaths, with a little snort inside each one.

'Amets!' I said suddenly. 'Let me explain to you!'

'Eh?' Amets stopped snoring, rolled over and opened one eye.

'Listen, Amets! Are you awake?'

'I am now.'

'When I saw what happened at Gathering Camp last Year – when I saw how Edur wouldn't speak to you, and how Hodei would have nothing to do with your family – I don't care about the rest of Osané's family – they've plenty of enemies already and no one thinks much of them – but when I saw how much I'd hurt you and your family by joining you – I thought I should go away.

'I made up my mind to tell you this, and then leave. Osané

was safe in your family. You wouldn't let her starve. I didn't think she'd mind if I went. Remember she'd never even spoken to me! Sometimes she seemed to like me – you don't need words for everything. For all I knew she'd like another man just as much, or even more. I thought she'd be better off going to Gathering Camp this Year without me. It made me sad to think about it, but – with her not even speaking to me – I didn't see how things could get any better.

'Once we got to River Mouth Camp it was different. Our enemies – the enemies I'd brought on you – were far away. You needed me to hunt. You and I hunt well together. Everyone seemed happy. Osané began to smile more often. I watched her play with Esti, and I thought things might get better.

'I didn't know Osané was pregnant at first – how could she have told me? Not that she would have – everything in Osané's life is secret. Sometimes I . . . Anyway, when Osané was sick on the boat coming round Red Point it suddenly struck me. Then your wife looked back at me from the bows, and I saw she was wondering if a man would have the sense to notice what must have been so very clear to her.

'When I realised Osané was pregnant I couldn't think about going away any more. Our son . . .'

My voice trailed away. I found I couldn't tell Amets how Zigor's promise – it had sounded like a promise, or a threat – certainly as if the spirits meant that it should happen – had stayed in my mind. Zigor had told me that the names of my lost family would live again among the Auk People. When Bakar first lay between my hands I gazed into his face for a long while. Hopes and memories whirled through my mind. But all I saw in front of me was the little closed face, red and wrinkled, of a complete stranger.

Sitting there on the riverbank, I thought about how Alaia's father came and looked at my boy and recognised him at once.

Everyone was happy. What could I have said? Also, I wanted to love my son. *That*, I realised, was why I couldn't admit to Amets, or indeed to anyone, that Bakar wasn't the child I'd hoped for. I can say this now because all that has changed.

Amets probably knew what I was thinking. All he said was, 'Your son is one of us. A child without its father usually dies. Also, this family needs you at River Mouth Camp. It would be very bad for all of us if you went away.'

'But if it's true that I bring bad spirits with me . . .'

Amets spat into the River. 'You sound like Osané's mother! Anyway, there's no such thing as a bad spirit. If the spirits you bring are our enemies – well then, we have to make them change sides!' Amets reached over and slapped me on the back so hard I nearly fell in the fire; I caught his arm to steady myself. 'At least your wife speaks to you!' He gave me another great buffet on the shoulder. 'Some men would say that was good. I'm not so sure – I envied you the way you had it before! Plenty of sex every night – oh, we all heard *that*! – and no words battering against your ears all through the day. I wouldn't call that bad luck!'

In this way Amets made it clear he liked hunting with me and he wanted me in his family. This made me very happy. I didn't want to hurt them or make their lives more difficult. I didn't want to leave them either. I had too many things now which made me long to stay.

Haizea said:

I was with my father when he died.

I was glad about that. When my father said he wanted us to go to River Mouth Camp without him I cried. My father told me that when I was old I'd meet Death as my friend. He said that Death hears our first heartbeat in this world, and from then on he knows us. My father told me that neither People nor Animals want to recognise Death until he comes so close they see his face. Then they find he's a friend who's been waiting kindly for them all along. My father said his own name would come back into the world one day, and if I were there to meet him we'd be together again. He said it touched his heart that I was sad, but the sadness would pass as my life went on. He was right, but also wrong.

Deer Moon waned. Amets had promised my father we'd leave before Yellow Leaf Moon. Every day long strings of geese flew over us, all heading towards the High Sun Sky. Esti was usually the first one to hear the geese honking as they flew with the wind from the Sunless Sky. 'Geese! Geese!' she used to shout, waving her arms towards the sky. She always made us stop whatever we were doing and watch until they'd gone.

I told Esti about the Bird-spirit Woman far away under the High Sun Sky who keeps calling the birds to come to her, all through Gathering Moon and Deer Moon, and how when Moon of Rushes is over she lets them all fly home again. 'The Sun tries to go with the geese,' I told her, just as my mother had told me. 'He sees how the geese are free to cross the sky as the seasons change, and fly far over the horizon where no one can follow. The Sun can't do that because the Moon and Stars tell him he has to stay in his course just like they do. But every Year he does his best to fly away with the geese. He manages to go a little way – that's why in winter he rises and sets nearer to the High Sun Sky, and in summer he moves as far towards the Sunless Sky as he can. But he can't follow the geese, any more than we can.'

Esti loved stories. I told her how the cuckoo and the swift always left together, before any of the other birds, but one day the swift borrowed the cuckoo's winter cloak, and that's why the cuckoo always calls, 'Where is – my cloak?', and that's why swifts are always darting through the air, and never stop to rest, in case the cuckoo asks for its cloak back.

'The geese make me sad,' Alaia said. 'It's another Year gone into the dark – it's not as if we have so many.'

The swallows were gone too, and the starlings, and the rafts of auks in the bay. Salmon Camp was strewn with yellow birch leaves, brown oak leaves, blades of willow leaf with a tinge of green still in them, aspen, alder and rowan. I played with Esti in the leaves. We made pretend house circles and built up the walls of leaves. I helped her find acorns and hazelnuts, and she played at storing food inside her leaf houses. I knew we ought to be storing real food in our winter house at River Mouth Camp. The wind came and tore more leaves off the trees. The white-caps on the sea chased each other towards the Morning Sun Sky. I was frightened because it looked as if the sea would never calm down enough to let us pass Fierce Point before the winter came.

Alaia wanted to gather green rushes to make new baskets. It was a long way. I didn't want to go. Alaia said in that case I could turn the fish that she'd laid out on the rocks to dry in the sun, and she'd leave Esti with me. Esti could go without milk for half a day now, though if she cried while her mother was gone I couldn't easily comfort her. Sometimes Esti was angry because I didn't have any milk. She'd pull at my tunic as if I could find some if I tried hard enough. I chewed up hazelnuts and acorns and mixed them with water and a bit of fish with no bones in it, and she ate that. Every day when the weather was good my father sat leaning against his oak tree – there were still skulls in that tree from Animals that had given themselves to him long ago – while Esti and I played in the leaves. My father liked watching us. When we ate I made him take a little food as well, but he didn't eat it. What he wanted was water. Esti quickly learned what he was asking for. She liked to lift the waterskin for him and help him hold it. When we go back to Salmon Camp now I always greet my Father's Oak Tree as my friend. I call it my father's tree because it sheltered him in his last days.

I was decorating my clothes, squatting by the hearth close to my father. He'd just given me his necklace with all his wolf and bear claws, and I wanted to honour so great a gift by making the rest of my clothes look as good as possible. I already had a full set of cat claws, which Amets had given to Alaia and she had given to me. I had plenty of shells too. I took off my tunic and laid out my shells and cat claws in a pattern. Then I fetched Alaia's awl and needles and her best sinew thread from her basket and started making holes in my tunic. It was difficult. I decided just to sew the cat claws on to the deerskin and thread the shells on a string to make another necklace. I borrowed Alaia's hammerstone and started rubbing holes in the shells so I could thread them. While I worked, Esti was counting out acorns to a pretend family, and telling each one they were getting their fair share. My father was dozing in the Sun.

I remembered I hadn't turned the fish.

I looked up and saw my father had changed. His eyes were still shut, but now his mouth hung open. His face looked empty. Death had come for my father while I was decorating my tunic, and I hadn't even heard him pass.

Then . . .

No! I don't want to say any more about that.

Later we bound hazel wands to make a frame, and we wove willow across the top. We laid my father on his frame. We mixed ochre and painted his body red to remind the spirits that, although his life-blood no longer flowed through his body, his soul-blood still lived as much as ever. As I rubbed colour into my father's cold skin I told the spirits how much I wanted my father to come back. I begged them to send him back to me before I left my present life.

Amets, Kemen, Alaia and I each took a corner of the frame.

We crossed the River and carried it up the slope of Mother Mountain. My father had been a big strong man, but now he didn't weigh much at all. We built his platform high on the side of Mother Mountain where only small birch, willow scrub and juniper grow. Alaia chose the place because she said my father's soul would like to rise over the top of Mother Mountain and look across the sea to Grandmother Mountain with its two sharp peaks that reach up and trap the clouds. When we were little, and my father used to take us up Mother Mountain and tell us about the world we could see from there, he used to talk about Grandmother Mountain most of all. He'd been there when he was a young man looking for adventure.

We all helped make the platform – even Esti. My father lay on his back, facing the sky. We tied his body to the platform with twine. As we did so a high-pitched honking came from the Sunless Sky. We shaded our eyes with our hands and watched the geese come down with the wind. Hands-full upon hands-full of geese – more hands-full than you could count on the hands of all of us put together – had made themselves into arrows as wide as the whole hunting lands of the Auk People. The goose-arrows shot slowly across the sky, honking over our heads on their way to the far edge of the world. We heard their wingbeats in the frosty air. Past Mother Mountain and Grandmother Mountain they flew – past every winding path my father had travelled in his small life – past the Sun treading his endless way across the High Sun Sky. The Bird-spirit Woman was calling them out of the world.

We watched them until the Sun shone straight into our eyes and we couldn't look any more. When we came back to where we were, everything looked like twilight after the bright sky. Crows flocked around us. Two ravens eyed us from the crag. The hill waited for us to go away.

I laid my cheek against my father's cold forehead. Alaia took his hand and held it for a heartbeat. Then we left him.

At dawn the next morning we took the hides off the tents, and stacked the poles against my Father's Oak Tree. We laid turfs over the hearths. We gave Salmon Camp back to the Animals, and told them we'd like to come back when the Salmon came next Year.

We couldn't take our boat round Fierce Point so late in the Year. Wild winds drove the swell right up Mother Mountain Loch. Waves crashed on the beach, and funnelled into Shellfish Narrows. We didn't dare wait. With the wind on our beam we paddled across the loch at slack tide. At the top of each swell whitecaps broke against the boat-hide and drenched us. Esti was sick. The tide shoved us through the narrows between Mother Mountain Island and Cave Island. We paddled with all the strength we had across Cave Island Loch and beached in Sandy Bay. I was sweating with effort, and yet I was frozen. I've never been so glad to beach a boat as I was that day!

We slept that night in the cave at Sandy Bay. People had been there not long before. They'd left dry wood; I hope the spirits are forever kind to them! When I woke next morning I jumped up, pushed back the hides and gazed out to sea – when it's clear you can see the whole of White Beach Island from that cave, but on that day I could barely see to the other end of the sands.

We left our boat in the cave, and walked over the hill to River Mouth Camp. It's only a half a morning's walk usually, but we were heavily loaded. No one wants to travel with children if they haven't got a boat! At least we had the rain and wind behind us all the way.

We reached River Mouth Camp in driving sleet. You can guess how glad we were to get our fire going, and invite the friendly spirits of warmth and light and dryness into our winter house. I don't think anyone ever stayed so late at Salmon Camp as we did that Year, before or since.

FIFTH NIGHT: LOCH ISLAND CAMP

Nekané said:

Four Years passed after I took down Aitor's Drum. Hodei grew used to me being Go-Between. At Gathering Camp I never went near the Go-Betweens' shelter when the men were speaking to the Animals about the Hunt. That pleased Hodei. He accepted that when the men had left for the Hunt I'd go behind the Go-Betweens' hearths and hang my Drum with the others. The fourth Year, Hodei agreed that I could deal with the questions People had brought to Gathering Camp while the other Go-Betweens went to the Hunt. It was Hodei's turn to stay behind; of course that was why he agreed to it. When I sat alone outside the Go-Betweens' shelter I felt strong but not proud. If People had been troubled by spirits bringing illness or quarrels into their families, I knew my Helpers could do as much for them as anyone's.

By now People were used to a woman Go-Between. Anyway, I didn't look much like a woman any more. I'd burned my last woman's skirt on the fire at River Mouth Camp before my son Bakar was lost. I've worn my deerskins the man's way ever since. Over my tunic and leggings I had this cloak – the very one I'm wearing now. See how it's plaited from all kinds of reeds, rushes, grasses, bark-twines? See how they make patterns with their different colours? Yes, you can look – you little ones can touch if you like. I dreamed this cloak in Salmon Moon when I first went Go-Between. It took me until the end of that winter to make it. In my dream I saw how the colours of the different twines changed as I moved. Like this! I wanted my cloak rough and smooth, soft and shiny, dark and bright, thick and delicate – all these things at once. And so it is – no, don't stop her – let her feel it! That way she'll remember even though she's so small – the children and I don't have much longer together – I want her to remember.

When I dreamed my cloak I saw how little bright spirit-catchers made of shell and bone and stone glinted between the threads. Look, you can see them in the firelight now! I saw the snakeskin with the spearhead mark between its eyes woven into the plaited rushes down my back. No, you can't see that. I'm not going to stand up and turn my back on this warm fire! Remember I'm just a poor old woman. You'll have to wait until tomorrow. Anyway, I gathered everything I needed, and slowly I made my cloak until it was exactly how I'd seen it in my dream.

After four Years it was already much mended, but no one knew that, because as the Moons passed I gathered as many spirit-homes – claws and bones and teeth, polished speaking-stones, memory-shells, dream-webs, shining-light-stones, all with Animal souls sleeping inside – as any other Go-Between. Whenever I moved, the spirit-homes glinted and rippled in the light to show they were alive. I carried many other spirit-matters in my pouch. When I came among People they saw Go-Between, not Nekané the old woman. I looked as Go-Between as Hodei or Aitor or even Zigor, though no one could ever mistake any one of us for another.

At Gathering Camp the women often chose to come to me. People grew used to me travelling with Zigor and turning up at their Camps, however far away they might be. Now I'd finished learning from Zigor I went alone. People were always willing to take me over the sea from one Camp to the next, and so I learned nearly all the places where Auk People hunt. Sometimes the journeys were hard and dangerous. I was happy, although I missed my family. I missed my husband most of all. After he died I seldom went home. Our winter Camp was still small, but we had two good hunters, and everyone was healthy and strong. They didn't need me.

Four Years passed. Then, because of what Zigor told me in Light Moon, I went to Arantxa's camp at Loch Island.

I'd never been to Loch Island Camp. By good luck I met two of Osané's brothers at Flint Camp. I made them paddle me to Loch Island. They didn't dare refuse. They were bringing back a young stag they'd trapped near Flint Camp. It took up most of the boat; its antlers dug into my back as I crouched in the bottom of the boat between the two paddlers. At least I wasn't going to starve in Arantxa's Camp: I hoped that wouldn't be the best thing that could be said about my visit.

We set off up Gathering Loch at slack tide. Rain pocked the sea with as many silvery circles as there are stars in the sky. As we paddled out of the bay at Flint Camp the wooded hills turned from green to grey, then faded into mist. Cloud rested on the water, rocked by a sleepy swell. The sea pressed gently against the boat-hide; through the thickness of my cloak I felt the hazel-wands yield to it. Only the steady plash of the paddles, and the faint crying of far-off gulls, made any sound at all.

As we rounded Whale's Nose a sharp black fin cut through the water. Koldo lifted his paddle to point it out to his brother. It dived and surfaced again, much closer. Then another. Sleek black backs rolled through the swell. For a heartbeat I thought it was my Dolphin. But no – it was his far-off cousin the sharp-fin whale. Even so, I took it as kindly meant, that the Animals of the sea should remind me of their presence. Osané's brothers shrugged, and bent to their paddles again. Unless a Whale chooses to give itself, its riches are out of the reach of People. Koldo and Itzal were too young to recognise a gift beyond the power of a hunter to take.

The tide gathered strength. Itzal leaned back, trailing his paddle, eyes half shut as if he couldn't be bothered to steer. He was just a boy – he's learned now that it's not that easy to deceive an old woman of the Auk People! Koldo pretended to sleep. Those boys were in no hurry to take me anywhere – they wanted me to be quite clear about that! The flooding tide was kinder: now we could see the grey outline of land on each side of us. White water surged in a broken line against the rocky coast. Islands loomed out of the mist. The boys stirred themselves to paddle round the hidden skerries, deep into the heart of the loch.

Even before we reached Loch Island hostile spirits came out to meet us. They flew low over the boat, trying to beat me back. Osané's brothers said nothing, either to the spirits or to me. Silently I called upon my Helpers. My Swan came at once and flew into the cloud of angry spirits. He couldn't put them to flight, but after that they hung back, not daring to attack him. My Dolphin remained hidden. That puzzled me, but I didn't have the chance to think about it. Osané's brothers steered along the High Sun side of Loch Island, within a paddle's reach of a reef of glistening seaweed, and brought the boat alongside a rock. Koldo gripped a handful of trailing seaweed and held the boat steady. Their dogs leaped ashore, nearly knocking me over. The two young men said nothing. I was an old woman but luckily I didn't need their help. I stepped lightly over the boat-lip into slippery weed. I picked my way across to dry rock without looking back, leaving the young men to unload their meat and carry their boat ashore.

The dogs started barking as soon as I was on the island. A hand-full of children came running along the shore, baskets of shellfish bouncing on their backs. When the dogs reached me they leaped up and barked in my face. I knew they wouldn't dare hurt me. A little boy shrilly called them off.

'Argi,' I called to him. 'You know me! Come here.' He came warily towards me, the other children following. I took a shell-full of crab meat out of my basket – it was all the food I had left after my journey – and gave it to him. 'You can divide that between you. Now, I'm looking for Arantxa. Is she in Camp now? Can you take me to her?'

'Yes, Nekané.' Of course they all knew me from Gathering Camp. Argi took hold of my travelling cloak and started pulling me back the way he'd come. The other children stopped being shy and pressed round me. Now they all wanted to take part in bringing the Go-Between into their Camp. Seeing I was welcomed, the dogs trotted back to Camp ahead of us.

Many feet had trodden the path to the Camp so it was easy to follow. It led us through waist-high bracken, threading its way among rocky hummocks where late bees droned among the heather, through marsh-flats where the deer grass was already taking on a tinge of russet. I rounded a rock, and came upon a grove of aspens sheltering in the lee of a hillock. They whispered to me as I passed, with a soft pattering like falling rain.

I stopped in the shade of the trees for a hand-full of heart-beats, surveying the Camp where it lay in a hollow at the foot of Loch Island Crag. Everyone had heard the dogs, so the women were on the look-out. A beaver hide was stretched on a frame facing the Sun. I saw no fresh skulls in the trees. Arantxa, leaning over the hide, still had a scraper in her hand. No one was doing any work now. As I stood silently under the aspens, one of her cousins saw me and jerked Arantxa's tunic. When Arantxa looked round, her mouth fell open. All the cousins stared at me.

'Nekané has come,' said Argi with a flourish. That child always knew how to make himself the important one!

That brought them to their senses. Arantxa managed to welcome me, and Argi's mother brought me crab mashed up with sea-roots and limpets, roasted in dulse. I'd been travelling all day and I was hungry. The women pretended to carry on with what they were doing – scraping hides, grinding roots, twisting twine. But all they were really doing was watching me.

'You're all very quiet,' I remarked. 'Is your Camp always as quiet as this?'

Several of them burst into hurried talk, like the chattering of a sudden breeze through the aspen grove. Nothing they said was to the point. I knew what they were hiding from me.

'Your men are still away at Hunting Camp.' I made it a statement, not a question.

Argi's mother gave a guilty start, then tried to answer casually. 'Oh yes, they've gone to their Hunting Camp in the hills, towards the Morning Sun Sky somewhere. They'll be back in a day or two.' She stopped and put her hand over her mouth. She'd been told not to tell anyone that. 'Or longer,' she gasped.

'The sooner the better, as far as I can see.' I left it to her to decide whether I was being unforgivably rude about the lack of meat, or whether the spirits had given me insights too deep for her to fathom.

Soon Arantxa's sons appeared, with their deer slung on a pole between them. In the midst of sudden silence they carried it into the Camp and laid it by the main hearth. The women gathered round at a little distance. No one said a word.

Arantxa whispered to Koldo.

Koldo replied loudly enough for all to hear, 'No, mother! Your sons aren't much good – if we'd been proper hunters we could have brought you *that* many deer!' He held up both hands with all fingers spread. 'What we've brought you is so little it's hardly worth bothering about. You can have the hide, but all our cousins will have an equal share of meat. After all, there's not much – what difference does it make?'

Sudden talk rose in the air like flocking magpies. Itzal skinned the deer. He eased the last bit of hide from the back legs. In a heartbeat the women had cut strips of heart, lungs and kidneys and seared them in the flames. The Wise ones fed me first, then the eager children, then the pregnant women and the ones in milk and last of all themselves. Fires were built up, joints cut into strips, entrails cleaned, sinews twined . . . this one small deer was a lot more welcome than it should have been in Light Moon.

For the rest of that day I sat at their hearth. I played at twine patterns with a small girl who had toothache. After a while her mother was brave enough to ask if I could cure the pain. I unpeeled the dandelion leaves from the lump of birch-resin I always carry with me – my own teeth, what's left of them, are none too good – and gave her a bit to chew. Then another cousin asked me to hold her baby while she heated stones for the roasting pit. The child fell asleep in my arms. While I rocked the baby, one of Osané's cousins – I could see the like-ness, but this girl was a pale shadow of Osané as I'd last seen her – came and asked me, very quietly so the others couldn't hear, if my Helpers could make a charm for her to get preg-nant. Otherwise her man would leave her, she said. I asked her how bad a thing that would be. 'You could always send him away first,' I pointed out. 'Then the shame would be his, not yours. You'd soon get another man at Gathering Camp – one who might do a bit better at giving you a child. Had you thought of that?'

Clearly she hadn't. But then People don't. Usually all I have to do is to turn their troubles inside out and get them to look at the other side. I don't wake my Helpers for that. I never tell People, of course, how simple it really is. People like to think that their lives are very difficult, just as they like to think their troubles are unlike anyone else's. I travel around and I listen to People's stories wherever I go. I seldom hear anything new. When People are young they think everything is new. I'm old: I know that People have always cared about the same small things, and they always will.

In the evening Hodei and some of the other men came back empty-handed. The fresh skull of Koldo and Itzal's deer stared down at them through the aspen leaves. Its meat, roasting in the pit, would now have to feed more than four hands-full of mouths. Hodei nodded to me when he saw me, then strolled off to lay his unused weapons in the shelter. I didn't expect him to show surprise. After all, he'd know better than anyone why I was here, and if his Helpers hadn't told him I was on my way they must be fast asleep.

That night I lay next to the hearth in Argi's family tent and thought things over. If Osané's brothers hadn't brought meat we'd have gone to bed hungry. The hunting hadn't been going well anywhere. We'd had four hard winters, and even the summers had often been grey and wet. The Animals were unhappy. I was a guest at Loch Island Camp. I watched, and listened.

Next morning, as soon as the men had paddled across the strait to the mainland, I followed Arantxa to the spring. I'd miss my chance if I didn't speak to her before the main hunting party came back. The spring lay between two heather-covered outcrops above the aspen grove; I scrambled up the rocky path to where the water bubbled upward between dark-green rushes. Arantxa squatted on a flat rock which had been laid on the wet ground at the edge of the spring. She was holding the lip of the waterskin just below the surface so clean water could flow in gently.

'Arantxa! I'm here to talk to you!'

'Oh!' Arantxa dropped her skin, and lunged after it with a splash.

She tried to make excuses, but I wasn't having that. Luckily she was frightened of me. 'You've muddied the pool now anyway, splashing like that. You'll have to wait.' I looked her in the eye. 'You haven't asked me yet about Osané.'

Arantxa looked terrified.

'She's your only daughter. Surely you want to know how she is?'

Arantxa fretted with the waterskins. She held the one she'd just filled upside down and the water splashed all over her skirt. 'Oh dear, now look what . . .' She rubbed her wet skirt. 'Oh yes, I . . . yes of course. I mean . . . I didn't think you'd seen your family lately.'

'I see them when I can. I saw Osané much more recently than you did.'

'Oh yes, you . . . Yes, of course.' Arantxa had filled the waterskin again, and was trying to tighten the sinew-twine with trembling fingers.

'Leave those waterskins alone, Arantxa! We're not going back yet.'

'But they need . . .'

I took the skin from her, tied it firmly by the neck and laid it upright on the bank. 'They can wait. We're talking about Osané, Arantxa. You must be sorry never to see her at Gathering Camp. You'll be missing your grandson. Four winters now . . . and you've never even seen him.'

'Oh yes, yes. Little . . . little Bakar. Oh yes. Yes, of course.'

'Is that all you can say? You know, don't you, Arantxa, why Osané and her man don't come to Gathering Camp?'

'Oh yes. I mean no. No, no. Of course.'

'Have you lost your wits, woman? I'm talking about your daughter! No wonder she left this family! Well, *we* love her, I can tell you that!'

Arantxa burst into tears. There was nowhere to sit on the wet ground, and the midges that hovered around the spring were beginning to find us. I made Arantxa put down the other waterskin and come with me to the open clearing at the summit of the island. I sat her down on a rock among the dry heather. She was still trying to hold in her sobs. I looked round. There was a welcome breeze up here, and also I could keep an eye out for boats.

I put my hand on her shoulder, and said in a very kind voice, 'It's all right, Arantxa. I know how hard it's been for you. You must be so unhappy.'

Arantxa was so astonished that anyone would speak kindly to her that she sobbed harder than ever. 'Nekané, you do understand! I thought nobody ever . . . Oh Nekané, I did try! It was so hard! She was such a pretty child . . . of course I loved her'– I waited patiently while Arantxa put her hands over her face and wept – 'how could I ever want to lose her!' Here Arantxa broke into a storm of weeping. I hoped no one would hear. I didn't think any woman would dare come and meddle with me. It was lucky that the men were off the island. Normally they'd leave a Go-Between alone, but this family had too much to hide.

'You'll be very glad, then, to know Osané's well,' I said at last. 'She's happy with Kemen. Your grandson is thriving too.'

Arantxa sniffed hard, and wiped her nose on the back of her hand. 'Kemen!' she said with loathing. *Now* we were coming to the point. 'That man! Nekané, how *could* Zigor let that man steal my daughter!'

She didn't dare accuse me. If she wanted to take refuge in

blaming Zigor, it wouldn't hurt him, and it might help me. I left Zigor out of it. 'Kemen didn't steal your daughter, Arantxa.'

'What do *you* call it then?' flashed Arantxa. 'What right had he to take my child? She was promised to Edur! Kemen stole her! He stole her from Edur! He stole her from us!'

'What do you mean: *stole* her? Was Osané a baby at your breast? Was she your cloak or your knife or your needle? No, Arantxa, she was not. She was a grown woman! She wasn't yours to keep, or yours to give. So how could she be *stolen*?'

'Kemen *took* her!'

'Yes, and she took Kemen. Is that so strange?'

'But she never would if . . . She was *forced* to do it. She should have stayed with her family. Zigor had no right—'

'Forced?' I repeated. 'Osané wasn't forced! She chose to stay with Kemen. I was there that night, remember! No one held Osané down. If she'd wanted to leave my hearth she could have got up and walked across the Camp to yours. Why didn't you – *you* – her mother – come and fetch her home, if you had the faintest breath of a suspicion that she was *forced*? And where was her father? Why didn't he come and get her *instantly* if he thought she was being raped? But he never came near her! What kind of father is that? And why didn't her brothers ask her to come back with them, instead of hurling insults and empty threats at my family? Did *they* see anyone holding Osané back by force? No, Arantxa, they didn't. Nobody did. Osané could have returned to your hearth whenever she liked. But she didn't, did she?'

'But that man! Not that I blame *you*, Nekané,' Arantxa added hurriedly. 'That Kemen! He took her! He raped her! After that she was too ashamed to come! Poor child! Oh Osané, my poor lost child.'

'Oh do be quiet, Arantxa! Osané is neither poor nor lost. On the contrary, she has everything a woman needs, and you know exactly where she is. If you think she went with Kemen against her will, why didn't you say so when he took her? If Osané had said then that it was rape, the People would have made him give her up at once.'

'And then no other man would have touched her! You know that! You know why girls don't . . . You know what happens!'

'Edur didn't seem to know. He made enough fuss about wanting her back. You can't have worried about no one wanting Osané, Arantxa!'

Defeated, Arantxa subsided into whimpers. I looked at her thoughtfully. She was gazing helplessly out to sea. Her cheeks were wet with tears: her sorrow was real enough, not that I'd ever doubted that. I judged my chance had come. I said in an off-hand way, 'But Edur can tell me himself, can't he, as soon as the boat comes back from Hunting Camp?'

Arantxa leaped like a startled hare. She stared at me wildly. 'Edur? I . . . I . . .'

'Oh yes you do,' I told her. 'Edur's been at Loch Island since Egg Moon. And now I think you should tell me about the men he brought with him.'

'I . . . I . . . I don't know what you mean, Nekané! Truly, I don't know what you mean!'

'Come, Arantxa, you can do better than this! D'you think I don't know why you've welcomed the brother of your worst enemy to your own hearth?'

She turned so white I thought she was going to faint. She believed me, of course – I appeared to know so much that she thought I had the power to see anything I wished. I pressed the point home. 'D'you think I don't know why Edur brought Kemen's brother here? It seems a strangely long journey to come all the way to Loch Island, when Edur's own family have their summer Camps away under the High Sun Sky by Grandmother Mountain. You'd think Edur would have taken

Basajaun straight across to Kemen on Mother Mountain Island, wouldn't you? Because Basajaun must have asked Edur about his brother? Hodei realised what had happened at once, didn't he? Did you really believe that *Zigor* wouldn't see just as much as Hodei?'

'Zigor!' Arantxa gasped. 'Does he . . . does Zigor . . .'

'Of course Zigor knows,' I said impatiently. 'And I'm sure it's not really your fault. I told Zigor that. But you'd better explain it to me yourself.'

Arantxa wasn't quite as stupid as I'd thought. 'I don't see why I should break my word' – she stretched up her hands to the spirits – 'to tell you something you know already.'

'Your word to your husband, Arantxa?'

'And what's wrong with that?' she retorted.

I'd known all along we'd have to come to this. 'I think your daughter could tell you best what's wrong with that,' I said.

Arantxa took me by surprise. She really did faint. She gave a hiccupping gasp and slumped against my arm. I lowered her on to the turf. I still had some water in my waterskin so I sprinkled cool water on her face, and stroked her temples. A shadow crossed her face; I looked up and saw small clouds gathering, chasing one another slowly across the Sun.

Arantxa's eyelids fluttered. I had a heartbeat's memory of Osané, bruised and swollen, opening her eyes as I leaned over her in the Go-Betweens' shelter. I'd never seen any likeness between mother and daughter before. My heart both softened and hardened towards Arantxa. I couldn't doubt that she'd suffered too. But she'd let these things happen, and I could use that to deal with her now.

Arantxa tried to look as if she were still too faint to speak.

'Come on, Arantxa. You know you can't get out of it. We're not leaving this spot until we've talked about this.'

Arantxa wept. I put my arm round her and spoke to her as if

she were my little daughter. At first she was stiff and frightened. Then she laid her head on my breast and sobbed as if her heart were breaking. I made no move to stop her. There aren't enough tears in this world for all there is to weep about. This woman – whom I didn't like – but that was not the point – had suffered more than I ever had, more even than I did when I lost my son. I found myself thinking about my own husband. I remembered what a good man he was. No one realised how much I missed him. As Arantxa gave herself over to weeping, I felt a small prickling behind my own eyes. That was a good thing: Arantxa would have known if my sudden kindness didn't come from my heart. At last her sobs began to die away. She took huge shuddering breaths like a child that's worn itself out with crying. Her face was still hidden by the fold of my cloak. Suddenly a torrent of words flowed from her, just as I'd intended.

'My husband is so difficult! No one wants to come to our winter Camp! It's because of *him*. The boys – they hate being with us! Oroitz has a woman – he'll take her this Year at Gathering Camp. He'll go with her family. Of course they won't come back to us. And Itzal – less than a Moon ago Itzal fought his own father – Itzal struck his father! What can I do about it? It's the way he treats them – no one must know this, Nekané – I tried to say to *him*, "Itzal is a man, you can't –" And then of course he hit *me*. What can I do? And the boys – they've seen this all their lives. Itzal is a good boy. But Koldo – I worry about Koldo – he's the one most like my husband, and my husband seems to hate him for it! Nothing Koldo does is right. And yet he's the one who loves his father. But Koldo will leave too. Itzal isn't a fighter – he hates all that. He'll go too. And Oroitz – he hardly speaks to anyone. Oh Nekané, I worry about them so! But they'll all leave me. I know they'll all leave me, because of *him*!

'But my daughter!' I waited patiently while Arantxa's tears

got the better of her. 'My little girl! I always thought I'd have my daughter with me, even when the boys were gone. *He* said she'd have to stay. *He* said it was a good thing she was so pretty' – here Arantxa wept again – 'because she had to get a man who could hunt for us when the boys were gone. Nekané, the thing that frightens me – what I lie awake at night and think about – it's all right in the summer Camps – my family are all here too – but they don't like *him* either – it's never been easy – but I know – I've even *asked* them. I asked my aunt and my cousins – none of them want us to join their winter Camps. They won't have us because of *him*. And Ihintza – my own *sister* – Ihintza said. Ihintza said . . .'

'Try to tell me, Arantxa. What did Ihintza say?'

'She said she wouldn't have *him* in her winter Camp. She said – she said – "not while . . ." She said, "Not while I have unmarried daughters!"'

Arantxa flung herself face down on the turf and screamed. She beat the ground with her fists. I laid my hand on her back. I looked round – surely we'd be interrupted now! No one came. The small clouds had finished crossing the Sun, and were drifting inland towards the hills. Sunlight twinkled on the sea around us, and the far hills lay soft and blue. The landward breeze laid a gentle hand against my cheek, yet in its touch my bones felt a faint twinge of the Year growing old. I sniffed the air, laden with the honeyed scents of heather and bog myrtle basking in the Sun, but underneath I smelt the first sharp tang of fall. Another ending, and already I was growing old.

Arantxa kept on howling like a wounded puppy. Surely they'd come! But no. Then it dawned on me – I was unusually slow – there was something Arantxa had just said: Ihintza! Those women in the Camp knew quite well what I was doing. They weren't hostile after all. They were afraid. I thought of little Argi pulling me into the Camp. I knew his parents well. I'd known all these People since they were born. They were *my* People. My task suddenly narrowed down and I saw its edges clearly. The cousins here wanted me to help Arantxa – I wasn't sure if I could do that – it wasn't my main purpose. Whatever they thought about Edur bringing Kemen's brother – most of them probably felt it was nothing to do with them – they *wanted* me to listen to Arantxa now.

At last I got Arantxa to sit up. She didn't go on from where she'd left off; I didn't try to make her. She talked and talked about how they'd needed Osané to bring in a good hunter. They'd relied on some man thinking highly enough of Osané's beauty to wish to join their family. When Edur tried to take Osané, Arantxa couldn't believe her luck. I'd always thought Edur was stupid; everything Arantxa said confirmed this. Yet Edur had been clever enough, and angry enough, to think of bringing Basajaun here to Hodei, so as to get rid of Kemen. Whether Edur still hoped to get Osané I didn't know. If Edur were to get hold of Osané's child as well, then Kemen's son – my grandson Bakar – wouldn't live another Moon. But none of this could ever happen – Amets was Kemen's friend – Amets looked after my family now – Amets would never let it happen!

' . . . when Edur wanted her,' Arantxa was saying, 'I thought the spirits were being kind to us after all. I don't *know* why she wouldn't take him. She made my life so *difficult*! I never understood her, Nekané. She *knew* that if she didn't take a man who could hunt for us we'd starve. She knew the boys would leave . . . *He* made it all so difficult. We were so much alone always . . . What could I have done? My family – I still think they might easily leave us to *starve* . . . Only Edur . . . Osané knew that, and yet she . . . Her father was so angry with her . . . I didn't know what to do! There was nothing I could do . . . But she was my little girl, Nekané! I still can't believe . . . She was so lovely!'

'She's still lovely,' I said sourly. I let that sink in, then I said,

'You know she'd never have stayed near her father once she had the chance to get away.'

'Nekané, I miss her so much. Couldn't you persuade her at least to come to Gathering Camp this Year? I've never even seen her little boy! Couldn't you do that for me, Nekané?'

'Everyone will be at Gathering Camp this Year,' I told her. 'And now we're talking about Gathering Camp' – I didn't change my tone: I wanted to take her by surprise – 'Arantxa, if you don't want all the Auk People to hear who attacked Osané at Gathering Camp four Years ago – if you don't want the Go-Betweens to tell the People who did that – then you'd better tell me now why Edur brought Basajaun here. You'd better tell me everything that Edur said to your man.'

'But – but . . . I gave my word . . . I don't know . . . No one told me . . .'

I let her protest for a little, and then I said, 'It's not often a man gets cast out. A woman – almost never. I've seen many bad deeds forgiven, though never one forgotten. I've very seldom seen People cast out, even for a Year. I've never seen a man sent away from his People for the rest of his life. There are only two things a man can do which the People will never forgive – for which they'll cast him out for the rest of his life and never relent. Only two things. You know what those things are, don't you, Arantxa?'

She whimpered.

'One of those things is to let your parents starve. You know that, Arantxa. Your children may well refuse to live with you, but they know what evil the spirits would bring down on them if they let you starve. You *knew* you didn't have to be afraid of that. What you were really afraid of was being left alone with your man. Why don't you leave him?'

Arantxa said I didn't understand, and tried to summon up a sob. But all her tears were out of her, just as all my patience was now out of me.

'You know what the other thing is, Arantxa. Do you want all the People at Gathering Camp to hear who it was that attacked Osané? Do you want them all to hear the things that went on in your family? You know what that might lead to, don't you, Arantxa?'

'You give me no choice.' Arantxa stretched her hands towards the sky. 'I can't tell you everything, but everything I tell you is true.

'Basajaun and . . .' Arantxa mentioned another name, which no longer lives among us – 'left the Heron People in Limpet Moon. They travelled towards the Sunless Sky—'

'Who is . . .?' I also spoke the other name.

'He's Basajaun's cousin – Kemen's cousin. He's one of the Lynx People. Four young men came from under the Morning Sun Sky after the sea washed away the Lynx People's lands. One took a woman among the Heron People. He's still there. Basajaun said the Heron People accepted him. As for the two who've come here – I don't know. Maybe the Heron People told them to go away, or maybe Basajaun's story is true – that he grew restless among the Heron People and wanted to leave. He missed his brother – this is what Basajaun told us. He wanted to find out if Kemen was still alive. Kemen had told everyone he was going to Mother Mountain Island to find the Auk People because he had cousins here. I don't know about that: I think even if there were cousins long ago, it's too far-off for Kemen to call anyone here his kin.'

Arantxa's story had taken hold of her now, and it put its own strength into her voice. 'So Basajaun and his cousin made a boat and crossed the Wide Strait, heading towards the Sunless Sky. But the wind wasn't kind to them. It wouldn't let them through to Mother Mountain Island. They had to turn and run before the wind towards the Morning Sun Sky. They landed near Edur's winter Camp by Rapid Strait. Not that I was ever in any of these places – I'm just saying what Basajaun told us. They found a path, which led them to the winter Camp of Edur's family, just across the strait from Grandmother Mountain. Basajaun and his cousin walked into the Camp one day near the end of Limpet Moon. They brought as much bear meat as two men could carry. You know what these last winters have been like, Nekané! Even Edur hadn't had good hunting. Then one day these two strangers arrive, loaded with meat!

'Basajaun walked straight to the hearth where Edur's family were roasting saithe on sticks. His cousin couldn't choose but follow him because he was carrying the other end of the pole – that's how it always is with Basajaun and his cousin, as far as I can tell.

'According to Edur, Basajaun wasn't in the least afraid of walking into a strange Camp, loaded with meat taken in another People's hunting lands. He just said, "Here we are, two poor strangers seeking shelter at your hearth. Not only do we bring nothing – all we can do is beg you to be kind but perhaps we've already wronged you. I don't know if we got this little bit of meat in a place where you usually hunt. But if we did, then we'll do anything we can to make it up to you. It's not much, as you see. It was so easy to get, you probably wouldn't have bothered with it anyway. And you see how weak we are; we couldn't even carry much. It was hardly worth wasting the string to hang the rest of it, but we can fetch it tomorrow if you like. It's strung from a big pine tree – I expect you know the one. Maybe some of these strong men could help us. But if we'd known we were so near your winter Camp we wouldn't have taken so much as a limpet without telling you we were here first. As it is, we can only beg you to forgive us, and ask you to accept two useless strangers at your hearth, even if it's just for one night. It would be very kind if you shared this little bit of meat with us, so we didn't feel quite such a burden to you."

'Well, Nekané, it's not hard to guess how Edur felt about that! Edur had to listen to Basajaun speaking to that Bear's skull in his own Camp! To make it even worse, Basajaun gave the bearskin to Edur's mother, and she liked it so much she started giving those Lynx strangers food before her own son! At first the family thought these strangers were Heron People. The Heron People must have had a hard winter too. Young men might easily paddle across into Auk country and take meat if they could. The odd part was that they came and told Edur's family what they'd done. Why, Edur and his cousins could easily have killed them! That's what they'd have done if they'd caught them hunting – a sleeping bear too! A Bear in winter must give itself to the men whose Camp is nearest. I'm glad *we* live a long way from any other People. I think you'd have to travel for at least four days from here to get beyond Auk country. It's much better that way. Even Mother Mountain Island is too close to the Heron People for my liking.'

'A full day's journey when the sea is at its kindest,' I pointed out. 'No one would dare hunt so far into another People's country. But, Arantxa, you must know that men who live near another People are often more willing to fight. They get like that among their own People too. It gets into their blood. Your sons need to be wary of men like Edur, Arantxa!'

I shouldn't have spoken. She looked frightened, and her story almost lost its hold on her. 'Oh, I don't . . . I'm sure they won't . . . *My* boys haven't had anything to do with any of this. You saw yourself how Itzal and Koldo wouldn't go to Hunting Camp when my man took Edur and his cousin with the others. They said no, they'd rather go by themselves to Flint Camp. You know that – that's where you met them! Oroitz went, it's true, but Oroitz never minds what anyone does. I'm sure *he* won't get into a fight. At least . . . Nekané, I do hope not!'

'So Basajaun and his cousin brought this bear meat into Edur's Camp,' I prompted her.

'Oh yes – where was I? They feasted on the bear meat. Everyone felt well fed and happy. Then Basajaun asked about Kemen. Edur thought very quickly—'

'I don't believe it!'

'Did you say something, Nekané? Oh, I thought you did. Edur told the women not to chatter, and took over the talk himself. When the rest of the family understood what he was doing they didn't say anything either. Nobody let on that Kemen was Edur's enemy. Edur told Basajaun that Kemen had taken a woman – Osané – not just any woman, but a prize that any man alive would have been glad to win. He told Basajaun how Kemen had been marked by the Go-Between and accepted by our People. All this was true – so far as it went. Of course Basajaun thought it was very good news. The way Edur talked, Basajaun was left believing that everyone was so pleased with Kemen they'd certainly welcome his brother too. You may wonder, Nekané, why Edur misled Basajaun like this. When my man told me about it I wondered myself.'

'No,' I said. 'I'm not in the least surprised by anything you say. Go on, Arantxa!'

'Edur offered to take Basajaun and his cousin to Osané's family. Of course Basajaun assumed that our daughter, and Kemen too, would be here with us. Edur didn't say anything about how Osané was stolen from us. He didn't tell Kemen's brother how my daughter's own baby – my only grandchild – was a stranger to me, and I to him. He didn't tell Basajaun that Kemen had—'

'All right, Arantxa. I understand everything that Edur didn't tell Basajaun. Go on with your story!'

'But, Nekané, it's all part of . . . Oh, very well: Basajaun and his cousin set off with Edur as soon as the sea let them through. They reached our Bird Camp early in Egg Moon. They'd been travelling for many days' – Arantxa held up both hands with all fingers spread – 'I'm not sure just how many. The winds were unkind, but we were still at Bird Camp when Edur's boat arrived.

'Our Go-Between met them on the shore. His Helpers had told him something – I don't know what. But Hodei came running into Camp – he'd left them pulling up the boat – Edur had spoken to him secretly – I don't know how – Hodei told us Edur was there, with Kemen's brother and cousin. You can guess how everyone burst into sudden chatter and angry threats! Hodei held up his hands and yelled above the noise. He said if we wanted everything to be healed we must listen to him at once. He said this brother and cousin of Kemen's mustn't hear anyone shouting. He seized my man by the shoulders and shook him. I thought there'd be a fight. But the women – some of the men too – shouted my man into silence.

'"Listen!" Hodei said. "Listen to me carefully all of you – you must understand quickly. Listen!

'"Edur has brought Kemen's brother and cousin to us. The Animals made this happen. The Animals are unhappy. You've seen how little they give themselves. Why are the Animals avoiding us? Because bad spirits haunt us. We opened the way to the bad spirits when the rightness of things was broken. Ever since Kemen took Osané our winters have been bad. Do we want to be hungry? Do we want it to get worse? Do we want our children to start dying? We must get rid of these bad spirits! Good spirits brought Kemen's brother and cousin into Edur's winter Camp. Good spirits whispered in Edur's ear and told him to bring these People here. This is so that we can put right the wrong that was done when these Lynx People first brought their bad spirits into our lands.

'"But we must help the spirits! Listen – these People will be here in a heartbeat – listen to what we must do! We must treat these Lynx People as if they're our friends. We'll give them food, and let them stay with us. We'll hunt with them – Quiet, you! Listen to me, if you wish your children to live! – We'll hunt with them, I say, as if they were our brothers. We'll let them think that Kemen is our friend – *listen*, I tell you! – we'll tell them how sad we are that Osané and Kemen aren't here to greet them. And this – listen, you women – I know it's hard for you not to pour out speech like water as soon as a man even looks at you – this is what you must say: you must say that Osané and Kemen have been in this family since Kemen took her. Usually they live here with us. It's a sad chance that this summer they decided to stay with Kemen's good friend Amets. We'll all be very happy to see them when we meet at Gathering Camp – that's what you must say. Have you understood me?

"'You're saying you can't lie? Then don't lie! It's better if you women don't speak at all. If only it could always be so! These men won't ask you – why should they? Just let them believe what they think they see. Then the lie is in their own heads, and all you have to do is let it live. Smile at them. Agree with them. And don't let your children say anything either! Have you all understood that? Quiet now, get back to your work! They're coming now!"

'That's what Hodei told us to do. No one is happy. You must have seen that. People are unhappy because it's wrong to give People food and yet lie to them. Some People here are glad – they dare not say this to me, but I know it – that Kemen took Osané away from her family. Even my sister said that Kemen is a good man. How can Kemen be *good*, when he . . . But not everyone here thinks that Kemen brought bad spirits. Not everyone here wants to hurt him—'

'How much do *you* want to hurt him, Arantxa?'

Clearly no one had asked her that before. I heard her catch her breath. She looked around her as if she'd forgotten where she was. I glanced out to sea. The ebb had slackened. Out in the loch a ripple of darker water was beginning to flow the other way. An otter was swimming away from the rocks at the far end of the island: I could see the black dot of his head, and a spreading wake in the silvery water. In this sea I'd be able to see a boat from very far away. If anyone were coming to interrupt us I'd have plenty of warning.

'Forget what your man keeps telling you to think, Arantxa. How much do *you* really want to hurt Kemen?'

Arantxa said very quietly, 'I want my daughter back.'

'And who's stopping you having her back? Who is it who makes it impossible for her to see you, let alone stay with you? Is it *Kemen*?'

Arantxa said even more quietly, as if the words were being dragged out of her heart by a stubborn spirit, 'If Osané is truly happy . . .'

'Osané is happier than she's ever been before.'

' . . . then I wouldn't take Kemen from her.'

'For that kindness, Arantxa, one day the spirits may be kind to you.'

'You mean—'

'What I say. So finish telling me, Arantxa. Basajaun and his cousin have stayed in your Camp for almost a whole Moon, and they still believe that everyone here, including your husband, is their friend?'

'My husband most of all. Once he understood that the point of this lie was to get back at Kemen, he gave himself over to it more than anyone. He takes Basajaun and his cousin hunting with him. He treats them far better than he's ever treated his own sons. I told you, though, Itzal and Koldo won't have anything to do with it. I don't know what they think. They're angry with everyone, and certainly they won't talk to me. It's all been very difficult, Nekané.' Arantxa's face began to work again. 'Worse than you could possibly guess. With my man threatening me, and the rest of my family all furious with me – why *me*? – for dragging them into this, and the boys hardly speaking to me, and Hodei urging us on . . . Oh, Nekané, I hate it all so much!'

Hodei said:

I paddled Nekané across the loch to Sand Island so we could speak privately. Between scudding clouds the Sun threw showers of light across the sea. The wind from the Evening Sun Sky whipped against the tide, slicing the tops off the swell. Balanced between wind and tide, I paddled a straight course. Nekané sat behind me clinging to the boat-lip as each wave slapped our side, drenching us with spray. I paddled into the calm of a crescent bay and beached on the sand. Nekané climbed ashore and shook out her wet cloak. I carried my boat to the top of the beach and laid it in a hollow among the dunes.

We stayed on the beach where we could walk side by side. Flocks of turnstones flew up in front of us, skimmed over the sea and settled back to feeding as soon as we'd passed. Now we were out of the wind, the warm smells of land – pine, myrtle, bracken and seeding grass – greeted us. We turned at the end of the beach and strolled back again. Soon there were many sets of footprints in the white sand, lapped by the retreating waves – from my own bare feet and Nekané's sealskin travelling boots. Each row was a little lower than the one before, following the ebbing tide.

Nekané's a woman; I couldn't tell her everything my Helpers had shown me about the Hunt. But she's Go-Between too: I had to work with her. I wished Zigor had come. But Zigor had merely told Nekané that Basajaun and his cousin were at Loch Island Camp. You could say he sent her, except Nekané was no longer learning from him. She chose for herself. When I'd sent my message I'd hoped for Zigor, but I got Nekané. Aitor was at his family's summer Camp on Bloodstone Island. We wouldn't see him before Gathering Camp.

I had no choice but to work with Nekané. I had to talk to her before Basajaun and his cousin got back from Hunting Camp.

'The rightness of things has been upset,' I said to her. 'For four Years our winters have been getting worse. Meat is scarce. The spirits are unhappy. You know this, Nekané.'

'Yes,' she said. 'I know.'

'I keep asking my Helpers what the Auk People have done. Have we hunted too much? Have we taken more Animals than were ready to give themselves? Have we taken the wrong Animals? Have we failed to sing the Animals the right songs?'

'Yes,' she said. 'I've asked my Helpers about these things too.'

'*You* asked *your* Helpers about the Hunt?'

'Only as much as a woman dares to do,' she replied cunningly.

I let it be; we'd had this talk too often, and it always ended in the same place. Instead I went on, 'Have you learned, Nekané, what the Auk People have done to upset the rightness of things?'

'Yes.'

I didn't expect that. Rather than let her see my surprise, I waited for her to go on.

'Do you want me to tell you?'

'Of course I do, woman! If you know what's causing all this, why haven't you said so before?'

'Because . . . I don't know if you'll follow this, Hodei – you're always so certain about what you know, and what to do about it. You don't look at things the way a woman does – of course not – but too often it's the ones who've done no wrong who get most hurt.'

'Explain yourself!'

'Osané is your sister's daughter.'

'What of it?'

'Did you know that through all the Moons she was with us, until her son was born she never spoke a single word? Not to us – not to her husband – not to a soul. When Bakar was born she spoke to him. Kemen heard her. He was kind – Kemen is a good man, Hodei – and that gave Osané the courage to speak to us.'

'No, I didn't know this.' I frowned. 'What has Osané's silence to do with breaking the rightness of things?'

'Everything. Ask yourself, Hodei: what was the story Osané couldn't tell? I'm sure Zigor knew, but he couldn't say anything either. What would happen to Osané if People knew what she was hiding? What would happen to her mother and brothers if her story were told? *They* hadn't done anything to hurt anyone. Nor had Osané! Hodei, you saw how someone nearly strangled that girl. That man came close to murder. Have you forgotten to ask yourself, in these four Years, who that man could be? Aitor told the People he'd be found, but we've heard nothing more about it. Why did Osané never accuse anyone? At first she was hurt so badly it was too painful for her to speak. She took that as a sign. She talks to us now, but we don't ask questions. Perhaps it will always be too painful for her to speak.'

Nekané could hardly have been more direct. Arantxa is my sister. Her man was in my family. Nekané was our guest at Loch Island Camp. Even a Go-Between can't accuse a man of a wrong as great as that – a wrong that would cause him to be cast out for ever – if she's not seen it for herself. If her Helpers show it to her – of course that's a different matter. From the way Nekané spoke I realised that her Helpers hadn't told her about this. It was something she just knew somehow, in the way that women do. There are many ways of knowing: wherever Nekané had got her story, I had to listen to it.

'If what you say turns out to be true, it would be a wrong great enough to make all the spirits angry with us,' I said slowly. 'But you must know, Nekané, this isn't the path where the spirits have been guiding *me*.'

'I know.' I heard her take a breath. 'Hodei, in return I must say: you think angry spirits came here with these Lynx People. You think the angry spirits that brought the sea down on the Lynx People aren't yet satisfied. You think the Lynx People, not us, must have upset the rightness of things. But that's not the path where the spirits have been guiding *me*.'

'I can see that. But I have a story to tell too. Perhaps you should hear what Edur said to me.'

'Tell me!'

As I talked I watched Nekané to see what she made of my story. 'Two days after Edur brought Basajaun to Loch Island Camp he and I went fishing. I paddled out into the loch so no one could hear what we said. Edur told me how Basajaun and his cousin had walked into his family's Camp one evening carrying bear meat. "I could have killed him at once!" Edur said to me. "I knew where that bear slept! Of course I knew! A man could walk to that bear's lair between dawn and mid-morning from our Camp! I'd spoken with that Bear in Swan Moon!"

'"Keep still!" I said to him, "or you'll swamp us. Try to look as if you're quietly fishing. Now, go on!"

'"That Bear spoke to me in Swan Moon. I stood outside her lair. I saw how she'd pulled the brushwood across to shelter herself. I asked her to give herself to me. I spoke aloud so the spirits could hear me. The spirits all heard that sleeping Bear agree to give herself to *me*!" Edur's fist crashed down on the lip of my boat.

'The boat rocked under the blow. I grabbed my fishing line. "My boat asks you not to beat it so hard," I said quietly. "My boat wants to remind you that it's done nothing to make you angry."

'"That Bear was pregnant when she went to sleep." Edur spoke as calmly as he could. "I was waiting for the cubs. I wanted their furs. That Bear had promised to give herself – and her cubs as well – to *me*, when meat got short in Thaw Moon. What kind of hunter is Basajaun, to think I wouldn't know about a sleeping bear so close to my Camp? No wonder his family died, if he really thought a man wouldn't have a bear like that in his mind for the winter! He even handed the fur to my mother, as if *he* were giving a gift to her! It was a rare pelt – almost black along the back – the shoulder fur *this* thick! I was so angry! But as soon as I laid eyes on her body, that Bear spoke to me. She told me she'd always meant to give herself to *me*! She'd wanted *me* to hang her skull on my Tree! I asked that Bear if I should kill Basajaun then and there! No man would have thought it wrong if I had!"

'"So what did that Bear say to you?" I asked him.

'"Ah!" Edur thought himself cunning, but I'd seen his whole plan more clearly than he did before he even spoke. He'd done well, though. I didn't know he had it in him to think so fast. "This man – this *stranger* who killed a bear in my hunting land – this *fool* – he isn't the first one to wrong me! That Bear reminded me: his brother took my woman! The skull of that Bear said, 'Surely you've not forgotten *that*?' She said to me, 'Remember Osané, Edur! If you still want her, you can have her back!'"

'"*Was* Osané your woman, Edur? Had you taken her?"

'"As good as," he growled, not looking at me. "I want Osané back, Hodei! She was mine first!"

'"She has Kemen's child."

"'I don't care about that! It would be better anyway if all that blood were wiped out. Or else these Lynx spirits will be among us for ever. Listen, Hodei, when that Bear gave me my plan – she gave it me in a single heartbeat, while Basajaun still stood at my hearth showing us her hide – the hide from that bear which was ready to give itself to *me*—"

"'When that Bear gave you your plan . . .'"

"'She gave me my plan because I was thinking of our People. I was thinking of the bad spirits that came here with these Lynx People, and how these spirits have been preying on us. I was thinking that it wasn't enough just to kill Basajaun. It would be better if we wiped out these Lynx spirits from our lives all at once, for ever! That Bear showed me my chance. I would pretend to be friendly. I'd even pretend I was pleased to have the bear meat – in spite of those furs I'd lost! If I could make Kemen's brother think he was among friends, I could get him here to Osané's family – I could bring him to *you*, Hodei. If we could get these Lynx People to Gathering Camp we could confront them with all the wrongs they've done to us. With everyone to help us we could get rid of them. We could banish these bad spirits for ever and the hunting would be good again."

"'Do you care so much about the rightness of things, Edur?" I asked him. "Or is it just that one brother took your woman, and the other took your bear?"

"'I care most of all for the rightness of things." It was a lie: his words spoke my thoughts, not his. "Hodei," he urged me. "This stranger killed a sleeping bear on my hunting ground. Any man among us would have killed him for that! I've brought you this chance. These Lynx brothers have wronged us too much. We can accuse them at Gathering Camp. We can get rid of these spirits that are troubling us, for ever!"

'So you see, Nekané,' I finished, 'Edur's plan is to get rid of

Kemen and Basajaun together. I don't admire his reasons. But if these Lynx brothers have broken the rightness of things among the Auk People, then we must get rid of them. See how the spirits used Edur to bring Basajaun here! I say the spirits are showing us very clearly what we need to do. All this trouble started when Kemen came. This is why Edur's plan may be good. The People here don't like what's happening, but we must go on. We must get Kemen and Basajaun to Gathering Camp, and there we can get to the root of the matter.'

'And cut the root out when we find it?' Nekané asked. 'That's what you hope for, isn't it?'

'Of course. Why d'you think Zigor made Kemen swear that Lynx names would live among the Auk People, *and nowhere else*?'

'He said that?' Nekané was frowning.

'Zigor sees far,' I told her. 'What if Lynx names live among all the Peoples: Auk, Heron, Seal, Otter . . . ? Nekané, if I meet a man who shares my name, that man is my brother. The same spirits watch over us both, even though our Peoples may be different.'

'What of it?' asked Nekané. She was still frowning. 'It happens, and no harm comes of it.'

'Because all our Peoples are kin! Because in the Beginning two sisters came from Grandmother Mountain . . . you know that story as well as I do. But *Lynx* . . . who are they? Men who share Lynx names will be brothers. *Their* kinship will cut across all the careful threads that link our Peoples. They'll be strangers in our midst, belonging *first of all* to one another . . . I tell you, Nekané, Zigor sees far!'

Nekané stopped walking, and turned to face me. 'Hodei, you're taking this too far! It's true our troubles started when Kemen came to Gathering Camp. It's just as true our troubles started when someone nearly murdered Osané. Both these things happened together, after my son was lost. I've not forgotten that Bakar's disappearance was the real beginning, if only we could see far enough. But for now we have two different stories, and we can't yet see how they join together. We have to choose between them. I think we must do it, not by looking at the *outside* things, but by looking *inside* the souls concerned.'

I was furious, I admit. Was this woman teaching *me* to Go-Between? But then . . . perhaps I had listened too much to Edur, who can only think about the outside things. I turned away from her and stared out to sea. The tide swept past the island, heading for open water. The wind fought against it, slicing at each wave as it scurried onward. Clouds chased one another towards the distant hills, darkening the sky above our heads with their passing. Nekané and I would have to stay on Sand Island until slack water. By then the Sun would be dipping towards the Evening Sun Sky. That was how I'd planned it: I didn't want interruptions. We had fire, and there was plenty of food here. It would be foolish to waste this day – our one chance – on useless anger. I turned back to her and said as calmly as I could, 'Very well. These men will soon come back from Hunting Camp: the two from the Lynx People, and Osané's father. We now have two Go-Betweens here at Loch Island Camp. Why wait any longer?'

'Why indeed?'

Perhaps this was what she'd planned to make me do all along. It didn't matter. I said, 'You think one thing and I think another. But to ask "who did what?" is just to think of small matters. We're not Go-Between for small matters. We're here to speak to the spirits. If something has happened to upset the rightness of things for the Auk People, then we're here to put that right. We're not concerned with anything less.'

'I agree that we're here to speak to the spirits and make sure of the rightness of things. But I think the way to do that is to be concerned about *everything* less.'

'Perhaps it's the same thing,' I told her. 'Anyway, if we're to speak to the spirits, Nekané, we must stop arguing. We have today – and only today – to get everything ready.'

Nekané said:

The children were playing Blind Man's Buff when Hodei and I came back to Loch Island Camp. Argi was Blind Man. He groped his way towards us, arms stretched wide and ran straight into me. He seized me by my cloak.

'Guess who! Guess who! Guess who!'

Argi could tell by the shrieks of laughter that this was no ordinary catch. He ran his hands over my cloak.

'Guess who! Guess who! Guess who!' Everyone started to join in. The women were holding on to each other, wiping the tears from their eyes, they were laughing so much. Even Osané's brothers took up the chant. 'Guess who, Argi! Guess who!'

Argi's small hands clutched my necklace. He felt the oyster shells and the wolf claws between each one – the very claws that Kemen had given me, though no one here knew that. He screamed in triumph. 'It's her! It's her! I've caught the Go-Between!' He ripped the leather bandage from his eyes and gave me a gappy grin – Argi had no front teeth that summer – 'I caught the Go-Between,' he sang. 'I caught the *Go-Between*!'

The other children took up the song: 'Argi caught the Go-Between! Argi caught the Go-Between!'

They were still singing while everyone moved up to give the best places at the hearth to Hodei and me, and thrust full plates of mussels, scallops, crab meat and blueberries into our hands. 'Eat, eat! We've all had plenty. This is for you!'

It was hard to believe anything could be wrong. The after-noon Sun shone through the leaves and brought out the gold inside the green. A breeze trickled through the branches, making each tree sing its own song: hazel, alder, birch, aspen and one little oak. Dappled shadows drifted across the Camp. As the day wore on they touched us where we sat. The air above our heads was full of butterflies, blue and brown. Every now and then the children broke out into Argi's song. They'd gone to play on the shore, but we could still hear their laughter. The rest of the People lolled in the shade; no one was doing any more work that day. I realised why they all seemed so much happier: it was because I'd talked to Arantxa. They were good People. They wanted things put right. Yesterday I'd felt like a stranger among them. Now I felt welcome: an old woman sitting among my kin.

Just as the Sun left the clearing, the dogs jumped up and ran towards the shore, tails held high. The women got to their feet and took the stones they'd been heating out of the fire. They laid the hot stones at the bottom of the cooking pit, and covered them with birchbark. Then they fetched baskets of shellfish and sea-roots from a shady pit, and took off the damp leaves: it would be very bad to look as if they'd been expecting meat if there was none.

The children down on the shore were quiet. No one was running back to be the first to tell us what the hunters had brought. We glanced at one another.

The men came into the clearing. They carried their weapons. The dogs padded at their heels. The tail of children hung back, keeping out of the way.

Arantxa's man came over to the hearth.

'Welcome, husband.' The fear in her voice made me angry.

Arantxa's man looked suspiciously at me. I greeted him by his name. 'And these men are your guests at Loch Island Camp?'

Because I was Go-Between he had to lead them forward and tell me who they were. 'Basajaun, of the Lynx People.' He named the cousin too.

'You're Kemen's brother?' I said to Basajaun.

'Yes. You know him?'

'He belongs to my family.'

That startled him. 'To *your* family? But . . .' Basajaun wasn't one to write his thoughts across his face. He caught himself up at once: 'In that case, Wise One, I'm glad to call myself his brother.'

I didn't reply. Kemen didn't waste his words saying clever things that had no meaning. But if I hadn't had eyes to see, I'd have thought it was Kemen speaking. These brothers twisted their words the same way. Their tongue was Lynx. Kemen didn't make so many mistakes as he used to, but when I heard Basajaun speak I realised that Lynx words still lived in Kemen's tongue, and however hard he tried to speak like Auk People, they always would.

I let my gaze rest on the two strangers. Basajaun raised his brows, then he saw that everyone held me in respect. Perhaps he guessed I was Go-Between. He braved it out, but I could see he didn't like the way I stared at him. He was taller and stronger than Kemen. His hair was darker. He wore it in a long plait down his back. Kemen had plaited his hair the same way when he first came to us. I realised, looking at Basajaun, that Kemen now looked like one of us. Only in the heavy outline of nose and chin did I see a likeness. The eyes were different, and the thoughts inside the eyes even more so. All I read in Basajaun's gaze was a proud refusal to let me read – but that told me something. I turned to the cousin. The shock was like touching ice. In his eyes – blue like Kemen's – I read naked fear.

He knew he'd shown me too much. His eyes dropped. I watched how he looked down – how he moved – how he stood.

For a heartbeat the spirits drew aside the hide and let me see through a doorway I'd never entered. They showed me a hand-full of boys huddled under an oxhide. Blizzards swirled round them, wiping out the world. I couldn't see what spoke to them, but I read fear in every upturned face. In one I saw blind terror. What the test had been, and by what chance he'd survived his initiation – all this was closed to me. But I had my warning: terror in a man means danger for everyone who comes near him. I looked from the cousin to Basajaun, and from Basajaun to the cousin. It was very clear who was the strong one – which one led the way. But already my Helpers had shown me how to reach what was hidden in Basajaun's heart.

No one spoke about the lack of meat. The men laid their clean weapons in the shelter, and the women tipped their baskets of shellfish on to the birchbark in the cooking pit. When the shellfish were roasted they picked out the best bits for the men. They gave the razorshells and mussels that were left over to the children, but the women only got limpets. If things got no better, I thought, they'd have to leave Loch Island Camp within the Moon.

We finished our meal. Even the children were unusually quiet. They knew something was about to happen. When Hodei and I stood up, everyone's eyes followed us. Some looked hopeful; some looked afraid. Basajaun's face showed nothing. The other Lynx man sat in Basajaun's shadow, so I couldn't see what he was feeling.

In spite of everything, I smiled as I fetched my Drum from its sleeping place. I remembered how angry Hodei had been when he first saw that Drum. It was Zigor who'd sent me to find my Hazel Tree. I found it in the Moon of Rushes, far upriver under the Morning Sun Sky. The spirits showed me where my drumstick waited. I told them I was much too old to climb so high. The Hazel bowed down low, and I cut my drumstick. Hazel showed me a straight wand growing from its bole. It told me where to cut.

I'd already worked out how to get the hide for my Drum. It had to be done alone, but what kind of hunter was I – a woman, and old at that? After I got my hazel I went into the high birches and watched the deer for a long while. I saw what paths they took. I walked back to a place where I'd seen a fallen pine, and cut four spiky branches. I sharpened the ends with my knife. I carried my sharpened stakes up the hill to the deer path. I dug a pit, loosening the earth with my digging stick, and emptying baskets-full into a heap. Then I drove my pine stakes into the hard earth at the bottom of the pit. I wedged them with stones. I filled my pit with leaves. After a day and a night, a Yearling hind gave herself. I found her in the morning. Two stakes had run her through. I cut her throat and hauled her out of the pit. I drank her spirit as if I had been a man. I gave thanks as men do. I became a man that day, although I remained a woman.

I made fire. I opened my hind along her belly-line. I eased the hide away from the stomach. I took out the liver and cooked it while the blood was warm. When I'd eaten some of it – it was too big for one old woman! – I shoved my fists down the ribs, between skin and flesh. The hide came away sweetly. I stretched it on a frame. I built a shelter of birch boughs and laid moss over it. Now I had everything I needed for my Drum, I knew I'd be in this place for a long while. I hung my meat and dried it. My Hind gave enough meat to keep me as long as I needed to be at Drum Camp. I'd carried woman's-stone and ochre with me. I took the wand Hazel had given me. I ran my hands to and fro along its length. Gently I bent it to my will. I persuaded it into a circle. I sang as I bound it with rawhide. I sang until it forgot it had ever been a wand. A new spirit entered it: not Hazel, but Drum. I sang to my Drum as I cut willow and wove its base. I sang as I carved my drumstick.

I sang as I stretched my hide over its frame. I sang as I sewed it with sinew from my Hind.

I sang as I mixed colour and water on a flat stone. I sang as I wrote my helpers into my Drum: Dolphin and Swan, Hind and Hazel Tree. I sang as I wrote my long journey. I sang for the son I had lost. My Song wrote patterns I couldn't yet read, as it sang itself into my Drum. I sang to my Drum as it tightened in the Sun. I sang to it for two days and two nights until it was dry and taut.

Hodei had been furious when I'd hung that Drum in the Go-Betweens' tent at Gathering Camp three Years ago. But he saw that I hadn't written the Hunt, so he let it be. And now, here at Loch Island Camp, his Drum and mine together would wake the spirits. Neither of us had dreamed that this would happen.

Our drums awoke so quietly that People were only gradually aware of them. The spirits came as rain on water, rain pattering on hide, Rivers running into rapids. People hushed their children, threw the baskets of empty shells on to the midden and turned towards the hearth. The spirits grew louder. Children too young to be afraid began to clap as the spirits drummed. Their elders were slower: they knew that beyond the swelling water lies melting ice. The spirits spoke to men and women of wrong deeds uncovered, trapped water finding a way out, floods that sweep away good and bad without making any difference between them.

The Dark crept in and listened. The Fire shrank from the sound of the rain, and went out. The light was in the stars: the Evening Star, the Red Star, the Wolf, the Lynx, the Fox, the Red Deer. The River of Milk streamed across the sky. I remembered when I'd seen my son outlined against the winter stars. I thought of how he'd come back to me, how once again I'd held him in my arms. I saw that if my little Bakar were to live to become a man, we must make this world a safe place for him. And that, the stars told me, depended wholly on what the spirits said to us tonight.

Hodei and I sang to our Helpers as we drummed. The People clapped and sang. A Fox barked from across the water. The trees woke. Animals rustled through the grasses of the clearing. A Swan splashed into flight and rose above the loch. A Peewit tumbled through the air, bringing with it the smell of the high moor in Seed Moon. A star shot across the sky in the curve of a Dolphin's back.

The dead fire leaped up in answer. In one heartbeat the drums stopped.

Before anyone could move, the Go-Betweens struck.

Itzal said:

I was furious when Nekané loomed out of the mist at Flint Camp demanding that we take her to Loch Island. Of course I respect the Wise, but when she said she'd come instead of Zigor I was so angry I could hardly speak. This wasn't what Hodei had meant! I'd given Hodei's message to Zigor very clearly, and there was certainly nothing in it that suggested anyone at Loch Island Camp wanted to see Nekané.

I'd felt torn in two when Hodei sent me secretly to Zigor. I owed loyalty to my father. I had no right to betray him just because I hated him. When Edur arrived at our Camp with the two Lynx People I didn't understand why he'd come to us. My family were more likely to kill Lynx People than give them food, because a Lynx man had stolen my sister Osané. Hodei told us we must welcome them and pretend to be friends. As soon as they arrived we gave them food.

Yes, we gave them food. What was I to do? My father said

he'd take them to our Hunting Camps. I couldn't speak to my father about it. Not because he could hurt me – I was a man grown, and he couldn't touch me if he tried – but because I didn't want a fight. I'd hit him once. My family could have sent me away for that! When I struck my father they took me to Hodei.

Hodei made me go into his tent so we could speak privately. I was shaking with fear. I thought he'd say I must go away from the Auk People because I'd struck my father. But all he said was, 'Do you want to see your sister again, Itzal?'

'Of course I do!' I cried. 'Osané was my friend as well as my sister.'

That was true. Osané is four Years older than I. I owe it to her, not my mother, that I lived. When I was small she carried me on her hip when I was almost as heavy as she was. She took me with her when she went out for food. She kept me warm at night with her own body. She picked the lice out of my hair, and sewed shoes for me when it snowed.

I was snatched from Osané's side when they took me to Initiation Camp. I was so glad! I'd been old enough to go the Year before – just – but I hadn't been taken – I'd begged the spirits not to leave me behind again. I was terrified the men thought I wasn't fit. I knew no reason: I wasn't crippled, I didn't act like a woman, I'd done no great wrong to anyone – nothing like that. I worried about it because I wanted to leave my family more than anything in the world. I wanted it much more than most boys do, and so I feared all the more that it would never happen. But that Year they took me, and I became a man. When I came back I wanted to show Osané what they'd written on my back. Osané had gone. Someone had tried to kill her, and Kemen had taken her away.

I knew it wasn't Kemen who'd tried to kill her. I thought it might have been Edur. That confused me. Although I was now a man, I still felt like a child in many ways – I didn't know how to rescue my sister. I didn't even know if she *wanted* to be rescued. Edur had joined us at Initiation Camp, but he wasn't there to begin with. He wasn't with us when Osané was attacked. Edur took Amets' place after the Hunt. No one told us why. Edur was much harder on us than Amets had been, but we admired Edur more. We knew Edur was a great hunter, and he was generous about teaching boys who were quick to learn. He didn't care about boys who weren't quick. I did well, and I learned more from Edur than from Amets. I knew Edur was going to take my sister. I was proud. I showed off about it to the other boys. Edur didn't stop me. He just smiled.

So now I said to Hodei, 'Of course I want to see my sister again!'

'Then I'm sending you away.' I must have looked stricken, for he touched my arm. 'No, no, Itzal, not away from the Auk People. You struck your own father – the spirits saw you do that – but' – he looked at me, as if wondering how much to say – 'right is born from right, and wrong from wrong. This wrong wasn't yours in the first place, Itzal. The spirits punish People for what others have done before them – the spirits don't care which of us is which. But People – we can feel what it's like to be one another. I don't want to punish *you*, Itzal, but there's a wrong here that must be put right. Or the spirits will be angry, and destroy us all.'

'So what must I do?'

'To begin with, you must go towards the High Sun Sky, to Zigor's family. Can you find your way to their Camp?'

'Of course I can! I know where to go, and who to ask.'

'Very well. I want you to go alone. Leave quietly. Don't take any dogs. Cross the loch as if you were going fishing, and perhaps to visit some of the Camps on the other side. No one will take any notice. Then leave your boat and walk towards the High Sun Sky. Don't tell anyone why you're going. Find Zigor, and give him my message.'

'What must I tell him?'

'Tell him how Edur came here with the two Lynx People. Tell him Edur has talked to the men here. Tell him we plan to bring Basajaun and his cousin, all unsuspecting, to Gathering Camp. Tell him that we need to make sure Kemen comes to Gathering Camp too. Tell him we plan to bring all three of these Lynx men into the Hunt. But what the Lynx men will not know is that they will not be among the Hunters. Our plan is that the People shall cast them out, and hunt them to death, and none of their names shall ever live among us!'

I stared at him, open-mouthed. 'But . . .'

'What, Itzal?'

'These men . . . Kemen too . . . We gave them food! Every day we give them food!'

'I know that. Men often ask themselves, "Which is the greater wrong?" They think, "A man has wronged me; I will do him wrong." The spirits of the Animals don't set one wrong against another like that. They see only that wrong follows wrong. This is why they withhold themselves. This is why our People grow hungry. This is why it won't help us to kill these men privately just because they've harmed us. This is why only the Hunt itself can make right what has been made wrong. Do you understand me, Itzal?'

'I understand the message I'm to give to Zigor.'

'Tell him, then, that this matter must be dealt with before things get any worse. Tell him I ask him to come at once to Loch Island Camp. Tell him we must speak to the Animals about this plan, and find out if that's what they want us to do. Tell him that's why I need his help.'

Nothing could have been plainer that that. I gave Zigor this message very clearly. I travelled for a hand-full of days, going from one Camp to another, and in each place People set me on my way. I found Zigor at his family's Berry Camp, which lay far inland up a River I had never known before. I followed the River as it grew small and wild, chattering over stony shallows where dippers fished, tumbling over rocky falls, losing itself in reedy marshes, then climbing thin and quiet among the birches until it ended in a limpid spring. I stopped and looked around.

The Sun shone slantwise through the still trees. Bogbean and mint grew at the edges of a round pool. The bottom was lined with white stones that could only have been laid there by the hands of People. I saw a stony beach by the pool where many feet had walked. Above it the birch roots had been polished smooth along a winding path. The spirits of the spring hung lazily in the warm air, watching me. I carried no water because I'd been following the River all day. I untied my waterskin and, bowing to the unseen watchers, I shook it over the pool, squeezing the sides together. A few drops fell. The Sun caught them; the spirits were content with the little that I had to give. I squatted on the stony beach, cupped my hands and drank.

Zigor's Camp was less than a dozen heartbeats from the spring. I hadn't known I was so near. The breeze was taking the smoke the other way, the dogs were out and no one was at the hearth but the oldest and the youngest, all dozing in the late Sun. An old woman roused herself and gave me a roasted lapwing with bilberries and rowanberries. Hodei is my uncle, so I know what it's like to have cousins of every degree suddenly turning up wanting a Go-Between. That's why Go-Between families seem less curious about everything than ordinary People. No one spoke much, but their spirits had already greeted me kindly. I felt welcome. I basked in the Sun with the others, gazing into the blue distance and thinking about nothing much at all, until the afternoon wore towards evening, and the rest of the People drifted home.

Zigor barely greeted me when he came in. By then the women were roasting the carcass of a young deer on the spit. We ate until the Moon rose, and that night I slept at Zigor's hearth. In the morning he said curtly. 'You bring the message from Hodei?' So he knew already – the thought flashed into my mind – why had Hodei sent *me* – if Go-Betweens wish to speak there are easier ways than sending a man on a long journey – so why . . . ? 'Then come,' said Zigor.

I followed him uphill, away from the spring. The summit was a rocky outcrop where no trees grew. We looked out to blue mountains that lay far off under the Morning Sun Sky. The rocks were yellow with lichen. Zigor sat down, and gestured for me to sit too. 'So?'

I told him everything Hodei had asked me to say. Zigor raised his brows, and gazed at the distant hills. We were silent for a long while. I wondered if I'd said anything at all that Zigor didn't know already.

'And you, Itzal,' he said suddenly. 'You've told me everything that Hodei wanted you to say. What d'you think about it?'

'Me?' I stammered. 'I . . . I . . . does it matter what I think?'

'I'm asking you.'

I met Zigor's eyes. They were blue and hard. 'We gave these men food,' I told him awkwardly. 'We've eaten with them, as if they were our brothers.' I plucked up my courage. 'Does a man hunt his brothers?'

'Every day,' replied Zigor. 'Are the Animals not our brothers?'

I puzzled over that. Then I said, trembling a little – for Zigor was Go-Between, and very powerful – 'But the Animals *give* themselves. They choose!'

'And have these Lynx men not chosen, with every step they take?'

My words seemed to be dragged out of me. 'No.' It was terrible to find myself arguing with a Go-Between! What might he do to me? I cleared my throat. 'No! You can't tell the Animals lies, even if you try. But if People are told lies, they can't choose. Because . . . because they don't know what's happening. You can only choose about things you know. Telling People lies makes them weak.'

'Thank you, Itzal.'

I looked at him sideways to see if he was mocking me. A small wind nipped at my cloak. It blew Zigor's straggling hair across his face so I couldn't read his eyes.

Zigor said, 'Now you must go back, Itzal. Say nothing and do nothing. Keep out of things as much as you can. Tell Hodei that help will come very soon.'

'Shall I tell him you'll come?'

'I've told you what to tell him.' Zigor stood up stiffly. 'Now then, my women here are useless, as you see, and there may be nothing for us, but no doubt we can find you some scraps the dogs have left - if we can, we'll eat, and then you must set off while the day's still young.'

I was furious when half a Moon later Nekané turned up at Loch Island Camp instead of Zigor. My sister Osané had been stolen by Nekané's family. She was our enemy. Why had Zigor sent her instead of coming himself? Now Loch Island Camp was full of our enemies on every side. We had to eat with them as if they were our family. Wherever I turned, I felt as if I were living inside a lie. Two days after we brought Nekané, all the men came back to Camp. They brought no meat. That night the women got other food ready without anyone saying anything.

I was still breaking crab legs to get at their meat when everyone began to mutter. Koldo nudged me. 'The Go-Betweens have gone!' I shrugged – I wasn't going to show I was scared – and went on eating.

The sound was like rain. It couldn't be – the sky was deep dark blue, turning to night. There wasn't a Moon. The sound was a River, but there's no River at Loch Island Camp. One by one the stars came out. The sound was the Go-Betweens' Drums. They didn't frighten me – that's *true* – the Drums sounded kind to start with. My anger faded. I forgot what I had to fear. I lay back, snapping the spindly crab legs and sucking out the meat. I watched the stars turn around the one Still Star in the Sunless Sky. Where the Sun had set I could see the Wolf, the Red Deer, the Lynx and the Fox. The night was so clear that even the Cat showed herself, and dimly between the Lynx and the Fox I saw the Eagle Star, which only happens in the emptiest nights of all. The River of Milk, that was made when the Milk of the First Mother spurted across the sky in the Beginning, arched so brightly I could see the whole way plain.

The fire had gone out. We sat in the dark. People were dim outlines like the trees and rocks. Even the children were still. A fox barked on the mainland shore; my dog growled in its sleep. I heard the rustling of Animals on the move. On the ground, and in the air – at first I thought there were a lot of bats about, but bats don't lift your hair or brush against your skin. I felt a cold breath on the back of my neck, but when I swung round there was nothing there.

The Fox barked on the island. Now I recognised her: Hodei had been Go-Between at our hearth since before I was born. The Fox came nearer. She barked between the People and the dead hearth. I heard the harsh cry of a Swan. I didn't know that Swan. An empty shape swept over us. The spirits shifted in the trees, under the stones of the hearth, in and out of the cloaks of the huddled People. White waves curled against the hearth stones and gently broke. I saw the curve of a Dolphin's back. I'd never seen that before. A small patch of darkness tumbled against the stars. I knew what it was: I'd heard her song at our hearth from my earliest days. I strained my ears to hear it now: *pee-wit pee-wit pee-wit*.

Softly the echo came: *pee-wit pee-wit pee-wit* . . . Out of it our song grew, as it often had before. My voice was inside the chant. My heart followed. The spirits sang. The dead hearth leaped into flame. Firelight shone on our faces. The Go-Betweens drifted back to their places by the hearth. Nothing moved between our upturned faces and the stars.

The Go-Betweens struck like lightning. They seized someone from the huddled People and dragged him into the firelight.

'Speak, you!'

Hodei's spear was at the hollow of the man's neck. He stumbled as they pulled him forward. A flame caught at a log and flared. Light fell on the face of Kemen's cousin.

'Speak, you! Whatever it is, you must speak now!'

Our voices joined the chant, surrounding him. 'Speak, you! Speak! Whatever you have to say, you must speak it now!'

He looked over the Go-Betweens' heads, staring with wild eyes into empty space. I don't know what he saw – there was nothing there as far as my eyes could tell – but I felt cold terror coming from inside the emptiness. So could everyone else. The People shrank back, though I don't think any of them knew what that Lynx man was staring at, any more than I did.

He stammered in terror. 'The Dolphin . . . it wasn't me! It wasn't us!'

'Then who?' The Go-Between's spear was at his throat. A thread of blood trickled down his neck. 'Speak, you! Whatever it is, you must speak now!'

'Me and Basajaun! No! Don't kill me! No! No! No! It wasn't us . . . it wasn't us . . . we didn't kill the Dolphin!' He was babbling now, shrinking away from the blades. We were all round him. He had nowhere to hide. 'The Dolphin . . . when we . . . when we came . . . We didn't take the Dolphin! When we . . . The spirits knew . . . No! No! No!'

The song was lost inside his screams of terror. A shadow leaped to its feet beside him. It was Basajaun. 'What he says . . . It happened far from here!' cried Basajaun. 'The Dolphin . . . it wasn't where the Auk People hunt. It was far from here!'

The flames in the hearth cowered low and blue.

'The spirits don't know "far" or "near".' The spear was at Basajaun's throat now, forcing him back. 'Speak, you!' Men pulled Basajaun away. The other man was on his knees, sobbing with terror. 'Speak, you! Whatever must be said, say it now!'

His whisper came like dry leaves in the wind. We all leaned forward to hear. 'We took where we did not kill. The spirits of the stranger refused to hear us.' He whimpered, and grovelled on the ground.

'Speak, you!'

Basajaun lurched forward from the shadows. Men forced him back. The Go-Between prodded the other man with his foot where he lay in the firelight. 'Speak, you! Say what must be spoken!'

'We ran away.' Everyone strained to hear the hoarse whispering. 'We took what we needed, and then . . . we didn't . . . we ran away.'

'For the spirits there is no "away".'

The man lay still. Slowly he crawled to his knees. His voice came back to him. He said quite clearly, 'The Heron People knew nothing of this. But the spirits . . . In the end they made us go away. Kemen had gone. He went away long before. My brother wasn't there either . . . He took a woman among the Heron People . . . they marked him as their own . . . He was nothing to do with this. Basajaun and I were alone. We came here. We followed Kemen. We came to the Auk People, who are our far-off kin.'

'You did wrong! You brought angry spirits among us. You took where you did not kill, and the spirits refused to hear you.

You ran away. You did wrong, and you brought that wrong with you to the Auk People. Is that so?'

The man cried out in terror, 'We did no wrong to anyone here!'

The fire went out.

Hodei spoke to us all. 'You all heard what this Lynx man said! They took where they did not kill! The spirits refused to hear them! Is this the wrong that's been done, do you think? Is this why the Animals refuse to speak to us about the Hunt?'

Basajaun faced Hodei. He seemed quite at his ease, not scared at all. 'Aren't you making too much of too little?'

Everyone gasped. Hodei was my uncle, but I'd never have dared to speak to him like that when he was Go-Between!

Hodei's voice showed no emotion. 'How so?'

'How were we to know what the Animals here wanted us to do?' said Basajaun. He sounded quite friendly and sensible. 'In the lands where we Lynx men used to hunt, the Animals didn't ask us to do anything different if they gave themselves without a hunt. We found a dolphin – this was under the High Sun Sky where the Heron People hunt. We took its meat back to the Heron Camp where they'd given us food. We thought they'd be pleased. They were angry because we didn't know we should have given that Dolphin fire as well as thanks. We didn't know that's what the People under the Evening Sun Sky must do if there's been no hunt. The Heron People thought the spirits would be angry, and that's why my cousin is so frightened. But the spirits have forgiven us! We know that for certain, because the Animals give themselves to *us*! That bear by Edur's Camp under Grandmother Mountain gave herself to us! So you see it can't be us. *We're* not what's making your spirits angry. It's very easy to blame the strangers among you. But is it right? Are you quite sure it's right?'

'The spirits know everything. That's why they can't let us do what we find easy.'

'Then they must be telling you it's not us! Your spirits surely say you can't blame us!'

'What you say is true.'

For a heartbeat Basajaun stared at Hodei. He'd been ready to fight, and suddenly his enemy had vanished like the morning mist when the Sun rises. Then Basajaun smiled, and held up his hands towards the spirits: 'The spirits hear me! If my cousin and I failed to give thanks in the way the Auk spirits require, we're very sorry. We'll do whatever the Auk Go-Betweens tell us. We want nothing more than to make things right with your spirits. That I promise!'

'The spirits are pleased to hear what you say.' Hodei was watching Basajaun closely. 'When we get to Gathering Camp they'll hold you to your promise.'

Hodei sounded quite satisfied. I didn't like it at all. I was sure there was more to this than Basajaun made out. I'd always thought Hodei was much cleverer than me. I still thought so. But . . . that other Lynx man had been terrified. He was still terrified: he'd got up off the ground now, but as far as I could see – he'd retreated into the shadows again – he acted like a man who feared for his life, even without being questioned by a Go-Between. If they'd simply made a mistake, why hadn't they gone to a Go-Between and asked him to explain to the spirits? Why didn't they make gifts to the Animals to say how sorry they were? Some wrongs are easily put right. But Hodei seemed to think Basajaun was talking sense. I expected a Go-Between to be much cleverer than me. Perhaps there was something I'd missed.

Hodei turned to the People again. 'The spirits heard what these Lynx men said tonight. You People heard everything too. You heard us speak about the Dolphin. That Dolphin knows what happened. That Dolphin is waiting for things to be put right! There's another Lynx man in the lands where the Auk

People hunt. We haven't reached the end of this story yet. One strand is here, at Loch Island Camp. Another strand lies with Basajaun's brother Kemen, who took Osané. There may be other strands. All these strands must be plaited together. Now Salmon Moon has gone into the dark. When Gathering Moon is halfway to full, all these strands will be brought together. At Gathering Camp the spirits will make things right at last.'

After Hodei had spoken, the Go-Betweens hid their drums and the spirits went away. A woman fetched fire from one of the tents. She rekindled the fire in the outside hearth. People stood up and stretched. Children cried and were carried to bed. The women laid turfs on the fire. I went off into the trees to piss. Someone whispered to me as I passed.

'Itzal! Come over here! Edur wants to speak to us!'

We stood in the shadow of the birches. Edur said, 'We have to watch these Lynx men. We have to have eyes like kestrels and see everything they do. I think these men know something about running away! We're not going to let them run away now. There's half a Moon until Gathering Camp. We're not going to let them get away from us!'

Koldo said, 'We've thought of that. Oroitz and Zeru are already down at the boats. They'll keep watch.'

'I'll be in the tent with the Lynx men,' said Edur. 'They won't get past me! If they do, I'll put on a woman's skirt tomorrow, and start collecting shellfish!'

'They can't get away without a boat,' I said. 'Basajaun might be able to swim to the mainland. I doubt if that other one could. But if we hunt on the mainland we'll have to stick to them like limpets.'

'And if we fish with them we make sure there's another boat close by.'

'I'll sleep by the boats as well,' I said.

'If you like.' It was clear Koldo didn't think it made any difference where I was.

Edur was kinder, but then he wasn't my elder brother. 'You keep your eyes open, Itzal. You're usually the quickest to catch a scent, and you can run the fastest. But we won't let it get to that.'

As I went softly down to the shore, a fox barked on the mainland shore. A little owl hooted softly, flying low over my head. I found Oroitz and Zeru in the shelter of a half-turned boat. I crawled in beside them. They agreed I should take the third watch. I wrapped my cloak around me, and wriggled down among the pebbles until I'd made a sleeping place. It was like being at Hunting Camp. But this wasn't exactly a hunt, unless . . . I started thinking about the message Hodei had given me to take to Zigor, but my thoughts were drifting away like falling leaves, and I couldn't hold on to them any more.

Sixth Night: Gathering Camp

Haizea said:

Little Bakar was shy when he saw all the People at Gathering Camp. Esti was used to it: her parents brought her here every Year. Esti grabbed Bakar by the hand and led him off to play with the cousins. Bakar dragged his feet, but we all know it's hard to stand against Esti. When I went upriver to fill the waterskins I passed a group of shrieking children and barking puppies playing tig among the oaks. Esti was tig. She didn't see me. She tore past me up the bank, flushing out a huddle of little boys. Bakar came hurtling down with the rest, squealing as loudly as any of them.

That freed me from looking after the children. Alaia now had Alazne at her breast, and always had lots of things she needed to do. Osané never seemed to be busy, but she was pregnant. Her baby would come before Deer Moon went into the dark. Also, Osané had plenty to worry about now we were at Gathering Camp. She and Kemen had kept away for four Years, and Osané hadn't seen any of her mother's family in all that while. She hadn't thought of going to Gathering Camp until a hand-full of days ago, when Nekané had arrived at Berry Camp.

Nekané had said that Basajaun was among the Auk People. She told us what had happened at Loch Island Camp – or rather, she only told us some of it. Go-Betweens always know more than they say. She said to Kemen that this Year he must come with the rest of the family to Gathering Camp and find his brother.

Kemen looked very happy when he first heard that Basajaun had come. I suspect he only realised later that this might make things even more difficult than they were already. My sister and Amets were more anxious than Kemen was. I found them talking about it when I went for wood. They stopped speaking when they saw me come round the woodpile with the empty basket. Then Alaia said, 'There's no reason why Haizea shouldn't hear what we're saying, Amets. She's a woman now. She'll hear more than we do when we get to Gathering Camp. She's young – she's free to go where she pleases. No one has any quarrel with Haizea. I think I should tell my sister what you just said.'

Amets hesitated. Then he said to Alaia, 'Very well. Speak to your sister.'

'Haizea,' Alaia turned to me, 'we're worried about what's going to happen at Gathering Camp. You heard our mother say how Edur took Kemen's brother and cousin to Arantxa's family at Loch Island Camp. I can see why Edur didn't bring them here – I'm sorry to say he's quarrelled with both Amets and Kemen. Amets has tried to make it up; Edur still thinks my man wronged him. But Edur could easily have kept the Lynx cousins with his own family until Gathering Moon. Nekané obviously knows why Edur took Basajaun to Osané's family at Loch Island Camp. She *must* know – she went Go-Between with Hodei while she was there. What journey did Nekané and Hodei make when that happened? There's a lot our mother isn't telling us, Haizea!'

I stood and thought. Then I asked Alaia something that had

troubled me for a while. 'Why is Edur still so angry with Amets, Alaia?'

Alaia glanced at Amets. I saw her reading his face – I could see nothing in it – and then she answered me. 'Do you remember that when Amets brought Kemen into our family it was Amets' Year to take the boys to Initiation Camp?'

'Yes, I remember that.' I still had nightmares about my cousin Ortzi being snatched from my side.

'It was Kemen's first Hunt with the Auk People. He went with Edur. Afterwards Edur took Amets aside and told him what a good hunter Kemen was. Edur *liked* Kemen. He *encouraged* Amets to invite Kemen into his own family. Amets wanted to bring Kemen to our family himself, so Edur at once offered to stay at Initiation Camp in Amets' place.

'When Edur came back with the boys, Kemen had taken Osané, and they'd *both* come into our family. Edur thinks Amets had it all planned. He thinks Amets deceived him while he did Amets a good turn. Amets has tried to explain what happened, but Edur won't listen. He won't even speak to him.' Alaia glanced at Amets and added, 'It makes things very hard for Amets at the Hunt. It means —'

Amets quickly put his hand over Alaia's mouth.

'My husband doesn't want me to talk about that. But he and I are worried, Haizea, now that Kemen's brother and cousin are with Edur. Why did Edur take them to Loch Island Camp? Arantxa's family are our enemies. Edur knew that. Amets and I think there may be a plot to get rid of the Lynx men. I'm sure Nekané knows what's going on. You can see she's worried – we can all see that. But Amets and I don't think Nekané is really anxious about Kemen. She's thinking about something else – something far away that the rest of us can't see.'

'She's Go-Between,' I pointed out. 'She and Hodei will have been thinking about why the Animals won't give themselves.

That's why Go-Betweens don't think about their own families much.'

'That's *it*! Amets, I told you my little sister was very wise! Haizea, I hate to say this – but I'm not sure we can trust our mother to be loyal. Of course, she'll never let anyone harm Bakar. I sometimes think he's the only one of us she cares about. I'm not sure she'd protect Kemen. And if anything happened to Kemen . . . Or even Osané . . . I think Nekané loves Osané. Perhaps you *do* love People more when you've saved their lives. But I'm not sure I'd trust Nekané even to protect Osané. The only thing I'm quite sure of, in my heart, is that she'll always look after the little boy.'

I stared into the empty wood basket at my feet, and thought some more. Then I said, 'Supposing she was right?'

'Right? Who was right?'

'Supposing . . .' I spoke slowly, because my sister's husband was listening, and I didn't want to sound impertinent or foolish. 'Supposing . . . supposing that these Lynx People . . . Alaia, have you never thought about it being *true*? Some great wrong has upset the rightness of things – Hodei says that every Year at Gathering Camp. I mean . . . maybe it's not for me to say this? But every Year Hodei calls upon the People to speak. You've heard him – how he calls on us to speak what we know. There are those among us who know – every Year Hodei says this – who know what it was that upset the rightness of things. I'm only a woman – I *don't* know, but even when I was still a child – and that's not very long ago – I saw how when Hodei calls on them, the People jump up and tell everyone all the small foolish things they've done. I don't think that's the point. When I was a child I heard People saying that angry spirits from the Lynx People had come among us. We *do* know that the Lynx People's spirits were angry – they washed away the Lynx land and drowned all the People. Kemen never meant us any harm

– *never* – but it *was* just when he came that our brother Bakar was lost. What I'm saying is . . . supposing it's *true* that it's Kemen – and his brother and cousin too – who've upset the rightness of things? Supposing that *is* why the spirits of the Animals have to withhold themselves? What then? Our mother is Go-Between. If what I say is right, what's she supposed to do about it?'

I don't think I'd ever said so much to Alaia before, and certainly not when her man was listening too.

Amets said to Alaia, 'I think your little sister is learning to talk some sense, Alaia! Maybe she'll turn out to be worth the bother of bringing her up. We have all the trouble of feeding our Go-Betweens, who hardly ever do any useful work at all, and then we forget what they're for when we need them. Kemen's my friend. He belongs in this family. His enemies are my enemies. But if there are wrongs that go deeper than I know, we'd better find out what they are. Then at least we'll know what we're up against.'

I said to Alaia, 'Your man probably won't ask you what we women keep chattering about. But if he does, remember to tell him that some of us women hope that this Gathering Moon will see everything sorted out. If the Go-Betweens are giving all their attention to putting things right, we'd better trust them to get on with it. I heard a man say that's why Go-Betweens' families give them food when they don't do much work for us. I think that man talked sense.

'I want to see Kemen and Osané at Gathering Camp like the rest of us. If our Go-Betweens find out what spirits the Lynx People brought with them, then they can fight those sprits, or, better still, they can make them change sides. Then the spirits would leave Kemen and Osané, and the rest of us, in peace to get on with our lives. When I was a child – when my father was alive' – I couldn't hold back my tears any more when I said that – 'this family didn't have any enemies. I want to see it like that again.'

I'd meant what I'd said, but now we were all here at Gathering Camp I had a sinking feeling in my stomach. Sometimes when I walk through the trees alone when the mist is down I feel a prickling at the back of my neck. Every stirring twig sounds like a prowling bear; every rustle among the leaves could be a pack of wolves; a twisted root looks like an adder under my foot. Usually, though, I walk in the dark or the fog or the blizzard and I feel nothing but the smells of the trees, the songs of the birds and the cold touch of the wind in my hair. It all depends what mood the spirits are in. That Year at Gathering Camp the spirits lowered above the hearths. Wherever I walked I felt invisible bowstrings drawn taut behind me, their arrows aimed at my back.

It was better at High Clearing. It was good to be young, and able to walk away from our families – from everyone's parents telling us what to do, and everyone's little brothers and sisters trying to follow us about. It was good to climb up through the woods until the trees were no higher than our middles, to the high places where we could gaze into the blue, and see the rocky heads of the mountains. When we got to the Clearing the Sun was scarlet in the Evening Sky, setting the hills aflame. Lapwings called across the moor, flapping their way to roost. The spirits had studded our green ground with harebell, tormentil and eyebright, like sewing different shells on a plain deerskin to make it beautiful. Marsh-grasses were laden with seeds like reddish feathers. Scarlet rowanberries shone so bright they seemed to sing. A chill breeze off the hill kept the flies away: the air was clear and cold as springwater. It smelt untouched, after being down in the woods where the smells of Animals, People and fires mingled by the muddy riverbanks.

We dumped our baskets of food, and rebuilt our shelters

under the rocks, where the heather was thick enough to sleep on just as it was. There were hazel wands left from last Year, and fresh willow and bog myrtle to thatch the roofs. When we'd made our sleeping-shelters we trampled down the bracken in the flat place between the rocks to make our dancing-place. We cut away the turfs where we'd set them last Year, and underneath we found our blackened hearths inside their rings of stone. We'd collected dry wood on the way up, and quite a few of us had brought fire. At High Clearing Camp we could speak to the spirits about the Fire for ourselves, with no one else to interfere. We laid all the fires we'd brought in the central hearth and set kindling to them, and then we took fire from there to the other little hearths around our dancing-place.

I'd stayed at High Clearing as much as I could the Year before. Then, it was to be with my friends – Itsaso was still with us then – but this Year there was more to it than that. I wasn't the only one who was running away from the forebodings that haunted all our hearths.

The second night in High Clearing we did the Taunting Dance: girls in the middle facing outward, and boys on the outside facing us. Last Year it had been my favourite. We linked arms and circled round, trying with all our lungs to out-sing each other. We yelled our insults loudest when our victim came round opposite – it was a great ripple circling around, first far away, then roaring through us:

> Ortzi tried to sleep with a girl
> So he did!
> So he did!
> But he couldn't get it up
> No he couldn't!
> No he couldn't!
> He can't even see where he put it

It's so small!
It's so small!

The boys sang back:

Zorioné wants a boy
So she does!
So she does!
She tried to take Ortzi
That's what she did!
That's what she did!
She put her hand down his . . .
She made it sit up quick!
She made it—

'I *never*!' Zorioné was so angry she forgot the whole point was to take no notice. She screamed as loudly as she could over the chanting. 'Ortzi is a *caterpillar*! I never did! I never . . .'

The circle of boys collapsed into laughter. We turned and yelled at Zorioné. She'd lost us a point, and now they were winning. But we soon recovered:

Arrats is a very little boy
He looked for a girl
He looked for a girl
She thought he was her baby
That's why she let him
That's why she let him
Suck her . . .

Now the boys were back on their feet again. They didn't wait for us to end our turn:

Haizea looks at Itzal
She wants him to
She wants him to
Put it inside her
So she does!
So she does!
Itzal, why don't you?
Itzal, why don't you?
She wants you to!
She wants you . . .

Zorioné had already lost us a point. I looked over the boys'
heads at the oak leaves shining under the Moon. I shut my ears.
I tried to make my heart follow my eyes. I tried to be outside
that circle. It wasn't just the boys that were betraying me. My
belly churned in a way that my head didn't want to listen to.
The whole Taunting Dance is about feeling like that – of course
that's why it's everyone's favourite – but the boys were getting
too clever. My legs felt weak. A flame I never wanted lit licked
at my insides. A cruel spirit dragged my eyes back to the grinning boys as they circled past me.

  I saw Itzal. He sang with the others. He looked straight at me.
  Then it was the girls' turn:

Itzal why don't you?
Here's Haizea!
Here's Haizea!
Take her under the trees, Itzal!
If you can!
If you can!
Or we'll know it's much too small . . .
Won't it stand up?
Won't it stand . . .

The circles were taking us in opposite directions. I glanced at Itzal. He caught my eye. He saw I wasn't singing. He saw how I couldn't make myself sing that song. I hadn't lost a point in the game, but I knew I'd lost a point to him.

Kemen said:

Basajaun came to Gathering Camp four days after I did. It was strange to be at Gathering Camp again. I looked up at the Go-Betweens' mound where so much had happened to me four Years ago. In daylight it was smaller than I remembered: just a green wart-shaped hillock in the middle of the hearth circle, with smoke rising from small fires at the top. Children were scrambling up to the top, then rolling down the steep slopes, shrieking with laughter.

At first we thought everyone had arrived – Arantxa's tent was pitched – but it turned out her sons had come on ahead, bringing Hodei with them. I hadn't seen Arantxa's sons since they'd threatened me at Alaia's hearth four Years ago. Now they were keeping out of my way. I didn't mention them to Osané, and she didn't say anything to me. I met Hodei in the oak-wood the day after we arrived. He nodded curtly.

I stood in his path and greeted him with the respect due to a Go-Between. 'Nekané told me your family have taken my brother and cousin to your hearth,' I said. 'I'm grateful that you've shared food with my family. I was very happy when Nekané said we'd meet here at Gathering Camp.'

'You surprise me,' said Hodei dryly. 'But the spirits protect fools – we all know that. That's if the fools are truly as simple as they make themselves out to be.'

'I never pretended to be clever,' I said humbly. 'I know that the Auk spirits treated me kindly when they accepted me as their own.'

'Then mind them well,' grunted Hodei. 'For who knows – they may still be watching you.'

After I'd spoken to Hodei the waiting was easier than I'd feared. I was reminded on all sides that the Auk People – except for a certain few – thought of me as one of them. Amets and Sendoa had been telling me that for four Years. On the other hand, they'd never encouraged me to come to Gathering Camp. They knew it was better if I stayed away. I hated lurking in the shadows. I wanted to meet whatever lay in wait for me, and fight it face to face. Whenever I said so, Sendoa shook his head, and said the spirits weren't ready for that. I knew by Amets' silence that he agreed. My friends had their families to think of. And when I spoke to Osané about it she fell to her knees, clutching my cloak, and begged me to stay away. 'Just a little longer,' she said. 'That's the only thing I'll ever ask of you, Kemen. Just give me a little longer.' I never let my woman rule me, you can be sure of that. She wouldn't dare try. But I didn't want her voice to leave her again. I'd also had my son to worry about: if Osané lost her milk he'd die. I settled it with myself that while Bakar was at her breast I'd leave things as they were.

Sure enough, in the very Moon that Bakar was weaned – the next child was on the way, but of course we didn't speak of that – Nekané joined us at Berry Camp. She told us she'd met Basajaun – that she'd just come from Loch Island Camp – that my brother and cousin were coming with my enemies – with Edur and Osané's family – to Gathering Camp – that within a Moon I'd meet Basajaun at the Gathering.

I wanted to see my brother – of course I did! At least . . . Basajaun was my brother – my one link with the People of my birth – of course I was glad to have news of him after so long. Now he was with my enemies. Nekané said Basajaun didn't know that. My enemies were using him. If they meant to do him wrong it would be because of me. Basajaun was quick to act – never willing to wait and see. Although he was my brother he wouldn't understand the path I'd taken – not as Sendoa and Amets understood it. Unless he'd changed . . . Years had passed since we parted. I might have changed too, more than I knew. I didn't know what to think.

A keen wind came from the Morning Sun Sky, bringing freezing rain. Whitecaps scudded across the loch. Leaves streamed from the trees, caught up in the gusts that blew them seaward. No newcomers would arrive while the gale lasted. People shifted their tent doors to face the Evening Sun Sky, moved their fires to the inside hearths, and hung their strings of fish and meat over everyone's heads. Baskets of roots and shellfish were piled up so there was hardly anywhere to sit. That didn't stop People visiting. When I lifted the door hide to peer out I saw bent figures running across the rain-swept clearing. I watched them lift a door hide, barely stopping to call a greeting, and duck inside out of the weather. More often than not they were heading our way. Our hearth was always crammed with People wanting a word with the Go-Between. Usually they had to make do with the rest of us, because Nekané had gone off somewhere.

Either our hearth was crammed with children or there were none; the little pack from Berry Camp all went off together, and soon found plenty more cousins to join them. I think they visited every tent at Gathering Camp, cleaning up People's food as they went like a swarm of ants. I was very glad when Esti seized Bakar's hand and led him off with the rest. My boy never looked back; he'd forgotten about his mother's milk already.

We hardly saw Haizea. She came in, ate, slept, ate again and left. She had hardly a word to spare for anyone. No doubt they'd made their own shelters at High Clearing. Alaia scolded her for not bringing food.

'Alaia, we've got *plenty* of food. When I was young and free I had other things than food to think about at Gathering Camp.

I think you did too!' It was so unlike Osané to add her voice to any argument that everyone looked up.

Amets was lying in the bed place behind Alaia. His infant daughter Alazne lay prone against his bare chest, her head against his heart. Amets roared with laughter and grabbed Alaia with his free hand so she fell backwards beside him. 'That's right! You hear what your woman says, Kemen! I think she knows something! I think these women of ours remember more than they let on! We'll have to watch them, Kemen! They know too much!'

'Amets! Now I've spilt these shells everywhere! Let me sit up!'

'So!' I put my hand up Osané's warm back under her deer-skins – she was leaning forward, picking bogbeans off their long runners – 'What's all this you're remembering, then?'

'Ow! Your hand's cold! Stop it, Kemen!'

'I *did* bring food.' Haizea looked round at us as if we were so many worms under an upturned stone. 'Alaia, it was me that brought all those flounders hanging there—'

'No you didn't! You brought flounders two days ago! They didn't last long! Those aren't—'

'Oh!' Haizea leaped to her feet. 'I don't need to eat here! So there!'

She grabbed her cloak, ducked under the tent flap, letting in a shower of raindrops in a swirl of air, and was gone.

Amets and I went out before dawn next morning. The wind had died. We took our bows and arrows, net and snares, and crept out, leaving our women asleep. There were brown puddles all across the clearing, but the rain had stopped. No one was about. Pink-footed geese made great arrowheads above our heads, heading towards the High Sun Sky. The air had changed: it smelt of the Open Sea. We headed uphill. Amets wanted to take me to the Great Marsh that lay beyond the hills, where, he told me, 'The Swollen River leads between one loch and the next. It's the best place for duck anywhere around Gathering Camp. It takes less than half a morning to get over the hill. We could even get back tonight – but why should we? I think we might have our own Roast Duck Camp by the Swollen River, Kemen!'

I was glad to get away; it was hard waiting every day for Basajaun. Amets had often – very often – described how his dog, as well as all the other things he could do, knew how to lead duck straight into a trap. Amets had wished – very often – that I could get a pup from the same litter. There was no chance of that, as Edur's bitch was the mother. I was happy with the pup I'd chosen, which was one of Sendoa's. 'And,' I said to Amets, 'I reckon your dog sired this one anyway. It comes to the same thing.'

'In that case,' Amets had said, 'my dog can teach yours. *If* he can get duck to follow him – at least we'll find out who his father is!'

'If it were that easy, there'd be a lot more angry men in this world!'

Amets had roared with laughter. But he didn't forget that my dog and I needed a lesson. So now we were wandering deep into the marsh, our dogs leaping through the water behind us. We brushed through bullrushes and reeds, and waded thigh-deep across creeks and patches of open water. Here and there we came to islets covered with birch and willow scrub growing so thick we couldn't scramble up to dry land. The reeds thinned out; the bare wetlands were red as an otter pelt, with gleams of water here and there. I gazed, eyes half shut, until I began to make out the rounded shapes of many ducks, thick as leaves in fall, scattered across the floodlands. The rushes round me whispered among themselves while the wind stirred them.

'This way!'

I followed Amets. We came to a creek that wound across the

flats until it lost itself in spreading waters. Amets' dog stopped on the bank. It watched Amets, ears cocked. My dog looked this way and that, at me, at the other dog, at Amets and at me again.

Amets pointed to the gap in the rushes where the stream flowed out. He spoke low, close to my ear. 'We spread the net there, inside the rushes. You take this end. You'll stay here while I wade across. Then we'll drag it up.'

'How far?' I whispered.

'Not far – less than a man's length. Just enough for the rushes to hide us.'

'And the dogs?'

'Ah!' Amets held his dog by the muzzle and looked in his eyes. He spoke to him softly. The dog stood poised, tail high, straining to be off.

I told my dog to follow. I told him – but this part was without words – not to shame me.

As soon as Amets let go, his dog trotted away. My dog followed. They didn't follow the creek. Amets' dog was making a wide curve across the flats, so as to come on the ducks sideways. I had to take my eyes off the dogs to get our trap in place. Amets unrolled the rush netting, and we set it across the creek. Then we crouched, one on each side. I peered through the rushes.

The dogs, Amets' dog in front and my dog following, came into sight, trotting up the bank towards us. Every few paces Amets' dog stopped and lay down. Amets' dog didn't glance at the ducks. My dog stood behind him: *he* never took his eyes off those ducks. I heard him whine. I whistled him to lie down, as loud as I dared. I willed him not to shame me. Slowly my dog lay down. Amets' dog trotted forward a few paces, and lay down again. Two heartbeats later, my dog followed.

I saw the ducks. Sure enough, they were swimming *after* those dogs. They weren't being driven. They were curious – you listen to what I'm saying, you children – those ducks just wanted to see what happened next. Well, isn't that about as foolish as you can get? Just tagging along, wanting to know what happens next . . .

Sure enough, those ducks swam up the creek. They watched those dogs push their way into the rushes. The ducks wanted to see why. They followed. They swam into the rushes. They swam under our net – and then . . . We pulled it tight! Like this!

Amets can't say now that I don't listen to what he says! And I can't deny that Amets' dog is clever – almost as clever as Amets says he is!

Amets and I walked back over the hill next morning, each of us with four plump ducks dangling from his shoulder, and two more in our bellies. We came by the highest hill so Amets could show me all the islands. The Sun climbed as far as he could into the High Sun Sky: now it was Gathering Moon he was starting to get tired. The waves were still chasing each other down Gathering Loch, but they'd lost their white caps. We reached the shore not far from Gathering Camp. The tide was low enough for us to walk along the beach. We came round the rocks and saw two loaded boats paddling towards Gathering Camp. Sunlight sparkled on the water. I shaded my eyes. The boats bobbed up and down so I couldn't see.

'Amets, they must be from Loch Island Camp!' My voice sounded hoarse and strained. 'No one else could have got here so soon after the gale.'

'Where are your wits, Kemen? For all we know they're from Bloodstone Island, or even further out. They could have camped anywhere between here and Flint Camp while they sat out the storm.'

I knew better. I broke into a run, slipping and sliding over the wet rock. The boats were well ahead. They reached Gathering Camp beach before I did. Amets shouted at me to wait. I couldn't.

I arrived all out of breath. They were pulling up the empty boats. Their gear was piled on the beach. The men turned the boat over and laid it down. They stood up and turned away. I saw my brother.

'Basajaun!'

He ran towards me. I held him to my heart. We stood, holding each other by the elbows, searching each other's faces.

Basajaun, my brother!

He hadn't changed. The lines from nose to upper lip had hardened – were familiar – only it was my father who had deep lines like that, not Basajaun. My brother's eyes were the same, the colour of hazels in fall, green turning to brown. I looked into them. I couldn't read his heart. He *had* changed. His beard was cut close to the skin, in the manner of the Auk People. His lynx-skin cloak was worn and sea-stained – all the fur rubbed off the collar – he still wore it the Lynx way, fastened on the right shoulder with a pin of polished antler. A picture flashed across my mind: our mother's hearth in Fishing Camp – the smell of root-cakes baking – my mother turning them with her digging stick, burying them in the ashes – and Basajaun sitting on an upturned log, shaping and polishing that very pin. And now – now I wore deerskins sewn by an Auk woman, fastened at the neck with a rawhide string. That same woman had threaded my necklace, made from the teeth and claws of the bear I'd not yet killed when last I saw my brother. Osané had also plaited my hair for Gathering Camp – in the Auk way. I looked at my brother and saw how I had changed.

Nekané said:

More People had come to Gathering Camp than usual, because, in all the places where Auk People hunt, the Animals were refusing to give themselves. Now the Hunt was delayed because of the gale. Soon there wouldn't be enough food at Gathering Camp for so many. Everyone knew the crisis would come when the Go-Betweens spoke to the Animals about the Hunt. Either the rightness of things would be restored, or the Auk spirits would change sides and destroy us.

I walked on the edge of a precipice. I trod slowly, step by step. Between each step I gazed into the chasm below me. If I fell I was lost for ever. None of you realised that. You knew I was taking risks. You knew that this Gathering Camp would either see everything lost, or everything healed. You had some idea of the task that lay before me. What you didn't know was that my very name was in danger.

Some People thought that the wrong had been done when I went Go-Between. We all know there's only one way to get rid of a Go-Between: their name must die. I'd seen men – and some women too – making signs as I passed. Not just signs to keep away bad spirits, but signs that threatened me directly. No spirit had heeded those signs, but People's wishes have great power, and if these enemies of mine had known what to do they could easily have bound a weak spirit to work against me. Everyone knows – I'm not giving anything away here – that even a weak spirit can cut the thin thread between a journeying Go-Between and their sleeping body. If that happens, the Go-Between can't get back into the world. I didn't let myself think about that. Luckily only another Go-Between would know how to bind a spirit in such a way, and it hadn't taken me long to realise that even if my fellow Go-Betweens didn't love me, they wouldn't betray me either.

I was already shaken by grief. At Loch Island Camp, when Hodei and I made Kemen's cousin show us where his soul had journeyed, I saw at last why my Dolphin had been waiting for my call. I didn't yet see how the wrong had happened, but I saw who'd caused it. I saw enough to tear my heart in two. When we came back to our bodies, Hodei and I agreed we'd both been right. He'd picked up my strand of the story, and I'd picked up his. Now we were able to twine the two strands together. We tested the rope we'd made. We made it rise up straight so we could climb to the top. It bore our weight; we found no weakness in it. Until then we had been – not enemies – but not friends. We'd circled around one another like two wary dogs who meet when their families come together, not knowing – because dogs' memories are short – that they were born of the same mother not so many Moons ago.

Now Hodei and I worked together. In spite of my fears I felt strong. At Gathering Camp Zigor and Aitor listened to what we had to say. I sat with them. We roasted spirit-mushrooms on the hot stones of our hearths. We waited until everyone had gathered. Daylight faded into twilight. Hearth fires flickered. The smell of food hung over the clearing. The Evening Star shone like a white pebble in the dusky sky.

I was Go-Between, but because I was a woman I had no part in speaking to the Animals about the Hunt. I knew how men muttered among themselves, saying that I couldn't really be Go-Between because whoever heard of a Go-Between that didn't speak to the Animals about the Hunt? Nothing had been said openly. But now we had to answer that question, because the answers to the other questions were wrapped up inside it. That was why it was I, not Hodei or Zigor or Aitor, who first took up the Drum. That was why I called on the women.

'Come, you women!' I cried as I drummed. 'Stand up, you

women! Now the Dance is for you! This Year you women are making the Dance! Come, you women! Come! Come! Come!'

All around the Go-Betweens' mound, the women hung back, glancing at one another. At every hearth women looked round at their men. The men dropped their eyes and said nothing. However angry, or puzzled, or fearful those men were, what could they say? I had three strong Go-Betweens at my back, silently watching everything I did.

'Come, you women! Come! Come! Come!'

My sister Sorné got slowly to her feet – she was old, like me – and shuffled into the empty clearing below us. Haizea jumped up beside her. I might have known it: that daughter of mine has such courage! They clasped hands and walked slowly towards the mound.

Aitor, Zigor and Hodei had been standing behind me, in front of the Go-Betweens' fires. Now they moved back into the shadows. From the foot of the mound the Go-Betweens' fires must have looked longer than usual. Only the four Go-Betweens on the mound could see why that was: there were no longer three linked hearths, but four. Four fires blazed into flame, fed by sticky pine branches. The crowd whispered like aspens in a breeze. Now they realised what had changed. Their sighs and mutters were like the wind whistling to itself in a high corrie.

Ten heartbeats passed.

My niece Itsaso ran forward from her new family at one of the far hearths. Hilargi leaned on Sendoa as she heaved herself to her feet. Sendoa gave her his hand as she stepped over her basket into the clearing. Esti left her mother's side and ran to join her aunty. I was amazed when Zigor's niece Zorioné came from the other side of the clearing, pulling her two sisters with her.

Osané stood up – even in the midst of my drumming I felt the wave of courage that swept her on – and seized Alaia's hand. One hand cradling her bulging belly, Osané dragged Alaia forward. The women clapped as I drummed. The dance rippled round the forming circle.

My Drum quickened. It beat a path. All the women were on their feet. My Drum gave them no choice. I glimpsed Arantxa's terrified face in the flickering firelight. My Drum searched out the way as it went. This dance had been done before, but not in the present life of anyone here. This dance was a tale passed down from the Ancestors along with stories of trouble, fear and want from a past so distant it had crumbled away, leaving no more trace than the bones of the People laid lovingly to rest on their platforms among the hills.

But the song had stayed alive. When I began to sing, my voice came echoing back from many throats. It grew like the wind. Every woman of the Auk People knows that song. We sing it whenever a girl becomes a woman so that it never dies. No man in that gathering had heard it since he was a little boy. If any of the men remembered, it could only have been like a fragment of a dream.

> Where clouds gather
> On Grandmother Mountain
> Water springs from her breasts
> Water streams from her caves
> Water flows to the sea
> Where clouds gather
> I am your daughter
> Grandmother Mountain
> I am your daughter
> Grandmother Mountain
> Where clouds gather . . .

Something crashed in the Go-Betweens' hearths. Black smoke billowed upwards. The footsteps of the Animals drummed behind me. They had no dance in them. They were rock falling. They were Aurochs charging. They were the sea sweeping over the land. Hooded shapes leaped from behind the mound and tore through the dancers. The drums banged without speaking to each other. The song broke into separate drops like a River going over a precipice. The dance stumbled. It lay dead on the trampled ground. The order of things fell to pieces.

The women fled, leaving a clear space before the mound. The men rushed forward, then stopped in their tracks. They could go no further. The dance had drawn a line round the clearing. The People felt where the line was. They gathered, men and women together, in a ring behind it. Only the four Go-Betweens on the mound stood inside the circle. The hooded Animals had gone. The four Go-Betweens stood side by side – not in our usual place behind the Go-Betweens' fires, but in front of them. Moonlight fell on the faces of the People. Our faces were in shadow. There was nowhere for anyone to hide.

We waited until the silence began to hurt. A log crackled in the fire behind us. Then Aitor raised his voice in lament:

'The rightness of things has fallen to pieces! The Hunt is broken! The Animals refuse to speak to us about the Hunt! The Animals aren't listening to the Hunters. They listen to the women. The spirits won't come to the men of the Auk People. A great wrong has been done, and the spirits refuse to come to us.

'We men are no good! Our women asked the spirits to come. Our women had to do that because our men are no good! The spirits listened to the women. The spirits have come! The spirits are listening to us now! Our women are better than we are!

'We men are shamed! Can our women speak to the Animals about the Hunt? No! No woman can do that! We men must put things right with the spirits! We must put things right before the Moon sets tonight!'

The People all turned towards the Moon with a soft sound like a breath let go. In two days Gathering Moon would be full. She'd just come clear of the hills between the Morning Sun Sky and the High Sun Sky. The stars turned pale. The dark fled and hid under the trees as the Moon rose higher. In the clearing it was as light as day.

'Before the Moon sets tonight, that wrong must be put right! Before that Moon sets, your Go-Betweens must speak to the Animals about the Hunt! If the Auk People are to live another Year, that wrong must be put right!'

Now Hodei was calling on them: 'You think first of your families, as People do. You think about your sons, your fathers, your brothers, your nephews, your cousins. That's the right order of things, when all things are right. Now there is a great wrong, which threatens not just your own family, but the whole of the Auk People. A great wrong has come among us! Now you must think of the Auk People, not just of your own family! If anyone has anything to speak, speak now!'

The spirits came into the Drums and beat our cry into the hearts of all the People: 'If anyone has anything to speak, speak now! Speak now!

The People took up the chant: 'Speak now! Speak now! Speak now!'

Three men leaped into the clearing. They jumped up on to the Healing Place halfway up the mound. Their heads were level with the four hearths. The firelight fell on their faces. Osané's brothers, Koldo, Oroitz and Itzal, stood before us.

The drumming died away. Only the heartbeats of the People carried the beat: *speak now! speak now! speak now!*

Zigor cried out so everyone could hear: 'Koldo! Oroitz! Itzal! Speak now!'

The eldest spoke for them all. Koldo hadn't the voice of a Go-Between. He sounded sullen. I could hardly hear him.

'The men of the Lynx People brought this wrong. We three know. One of them stole our sister. Edur brought the other two to us. We know they did great wrong from things that were said when they were with us. We saw when the Go-Betweens spoke to the spirits at Loch Island Camp. These men were cursed when they came to us. Their People did great wrongs and the spirits washed their land away. Now they've brought those bad spirits here. Those bad spirits want to kill us!'

We Go-Betweens know there is no such thing as a bad spirit. We know there is no such thing as a wholly good man either. Itzal understood this better than Koldo. I saw that he was trembling. Oroitz didn't meet our eyes. Only Koldo was quite sure that everything he said was true. I beckoned to Itzal. 'Come here, Itzal!'

Itzal glanced at his brothers. He climbed slowly up to us. He looked at the four hearths and his eyes widened. 'Come here, Itzal!'

Hidden between the cloaks of the four Go-Betweens, Itzal knelt at our feet, shaking like a leaf about to fall.

Zigor spoke first. 'What wrong did these Lynx People do, Itzal?'

Itzal swallowed. 'Kemen stole my sister!'

'Did you see him do it?'

'No, but—'

'Then what do you know of it?'

'My brothers saw . . . my father . . .'

'Your father and brothers told you to speak against these men?'

'No!'

'You were a child, Itzal. What did you know?'

Itzal glanced up. Hodei was his uncle. Zigor had often spoken to him kindly. Itzal sought the faces of friends: there were no faces. Only the empty shapes of the Go-Betweens hung over him, blotting out the stars.

'I knew I loved Osané!' Itzal blurted out.

'You loved your sister.' The voice was dry as a stone. 'Was she raped, Itzal? Is that why you want to protect her?'

He was crying, grovelling in the turf at our feet.

'Was she raped?'

'You were a child, Itzal. What did you know? Was she raped?'

'I can't say! No! No! Yes! No! I can't say!'

'Then why did you say you could speak? Get out!' Zigor kicked him savagely. Itzal curled into a ball. Hodei kicked him in the back. Itzal rolled out into the firelight. He would have jumped up and fled, but Aitor gripped the neck of his deerskins. 'Stay there! You came into this circle! This isn't finished yet!'

The Go-Betweens faced the waiting People.

'Send these Lynx men forward!'

Basajaun and his cousin were shoved across the clearing, and pushed up to the Healing Place.

After a heartbeat's pause Kemen stepped forward. Amets and Sendoa tried to come with him, but Kemen pushed them back. 'No! You mustn't be part of this.'

Amets tried to protest, but Kemen took him by the arm and spoke to him quietly. I saw Amets raise his hands to the spirits; I knew very well what Kemen had asked him. That pleased me: if Amets had promised to look after little Bakar, my grandson was as safe as he could be.

The three Lynx men stood below us on our right. Koldo and Oroitz stood on our left. Basajaun folded his arms and stared with contempt at Arantxa's sons. Koldo and Oroitz dropped their eyes.

'Oroitz!'

Oroitz jumped. He'd thought he was safe now.

'Oroitz! Did you give food to these two men' – Aitor pointed to Basajaun and his cousin – 'when they came to your hearth at Loch Island Camp?'

Oroitz hesitated. He couldn't look at Basajaun. But there was only one answer. 'Ye-es.'

'You gave them food. Were you deceiving them when you did that?'

There was only one answer to that too. 'Ye-e-es.'

'You forced the spirits of your hearth to tell a lie?'

Oroitz was silent. Koldo opened his mouth to speak.

'Quiet, you! Oroitz, where is your father?'

Slowly Oroitz raised his arm and pointed into the darkness, in the direction of Arantxa's tent.

'Is your father alive, Koldo?'

Koldo stared. 'Yes!'

'Is he mad?'

'No!'

'Is he ill?'

'No!'

'Then why are you here without him? Is he ashamed?'

'No!' Koldo and Oroitz cried out together.

'No? Perhaps he's just dozing then? Perhaps his sons hunt so well for him that he's eaten too much meat? Perhaps he's sleeping quietly in his tent? No? Well, well – we won't disturb an old man in his dreams. Basajaun!'

Basajaun stood with his arms folded and his lynx-skin cloak thrown back over his shoulder. He stared up at Aitor with the same contempt in his eyes that he'd shown to Arantxa's sons. Then his gaze dropped. His arms fell to his sides.

It was my turn at last. Basajaun wasn't expecting me to speak, and he started in surprise.

'Basajaun,' I said. I was glad that in spite of everything my voice held firm. 'Basajaun, the dolphin beached on the white strand – whose was it?'

He didn't answer. Over his head I saw the Moon look down. She cast her shadow, and laid Basajaun's head at Osané's feet, where Osané stood in the crowd between Sorné and Alaia.

'I don't know what you're talking about,' Basajaun said at last.

He stood braced, like a deer that catches an alien scent, ready to dodge if we pursued him any further. It shocked him when Aitor and Hodei leaped down to the Healing Place and seized his cousin instead.

The People hadn't expected that either. A woman cried out. The shadows of the trees hid the People. When I glanced up I couldn't see them, but I could feel them surrounding us, watching everything we did. They were our People. We worked for them. They gave us strength.

We held the young man down between our cloaks. We hid him from the People and the light. We smelt his fear. We called on him by name.

'You tell us about that dolphin now,' I said. 'Or we'll kill you.'

'No, no! I know nothing! I did nothing! Leave me alone!'

Aitor grabbed him by the hair and pulled his head back. Zigor's knife was at his throat. 'We might kill you now. Or – we could make certain your name never comes back into the world. We could do that. You know how we'd do that?'

'No! No! No! I did nothing! I didn't do it! Ask Basajaun!'

'Kill him now!'

'No! I did nothing! No!'

Zigor drew his knife across the young man's cheek. Blood ran down and soaked into his hair. 'Then speak!'

'I didn't kill him!'

'He told you his name?'

'No! I didn't know who he was!'

'But when he was dead you stripped him. You read what was written on his back.'

'I didn't kill him!'

'What did you find written on his back?'

The man stank of fear. It ran down him in cold sweat. He was a broken reed in the hands of the Go-Betweens. Did he know that he must die? I willed not. We needed him to hope a little, to have something still to lose.

That boy still hoped, because at last he whispered, 'Auk!'

Aitor let go. Basajaun's cousin sank forward, his hands pressed to his eyes. In the air around us I felt a long breath let go. The People were one, watching us. They were a great Animal surrounding us, like a mountain cat curled in its lair around its kittens. We were doing what must be done, for the sake of our People. They gave us strength.

We crouched above the Lynx man. Hodei said, 'Now you'll speak about why you were on that beach. You'll speak about how you came to be in lands where the Auk People hunt. You'll speak about how you met him, and you'll speak about just how it was that this Auk man died.'

He couldn't speak above a whisper. We leaned into the smell of his fear. 'Basajaun took another man's woman. He took her the day after Kemen left to find the Auk People. He waited till Kemen had gone . . . He knew Kemen wouldn't . . . This was five Years ago. The Heron People sent us away. Not all of us – not my brother – it wasn't his fault – they let him stay.'

Zigor's knife stroked his throat. He gasped. 'We took a boat . . . We paddled towards the Sunless Sky . . . towards Kemen . . . Kemen . . . he went to look for Auk . . . We followed . . . A kind wind took us . . . We paddled fast . . . the Year was growing old . . . Yellow Leaf Moon . . . we sailed into Auk land . . . deep into Auk lands . . . without meeting anybody.'

He looked up at us. He couldn't see our faces. 'I did nothing . . . nothing! There are kind spirits . . . will you let me live?'

'Speak what you have to speak!'

Perhaps he thought that was a promise. He went on in a rush of words. 'We beached on a white strand. We were hungry. We didn't know the land. The Animals saw we were strangers. They refused to give themselves. We were hungry.'

The People leaned closer, straining to listen. I felt their nearness. They couldn't see what we were doing up on the mound. They couldn't hear what the Lynx man said. They couldn't follow us on this journey, but they trusted us. I felt their strength.

'We walked on the white beach. We were looking . . . needed . . . Animal paths to lead us . . . all marsh . . . We saw . . . a rock on the white sand. We came close. Not a rock . . . a dolphin . . . high and dry . . . beached. It smelt fresh. Our knives . . .'

Aitor jerked his head back hard. A blade nicked his throat. 'Go on!'

'We came . . . we found . . . footprints . . . dog . . . a man alone . . . ashes in the sand . . . lit from tree-mushroom . . . thyme stems . . . a white stone . . . That Dolphin . . . already given itself. Thanks given . . . already given . . .'

'Go on!'

'We walked round . . . He'd stripped blubber . . . ribs cut . . . meat was gone . . . footprints . . . a path . . . under the trees . . . He'd gone to hang the meat . . . We found it later . . .

'He'd gone . . . We were hungry. We took . . . We wouldn't have taken it! Not all! We heard the dog . . . The dog barked . . . His dog . . . The dog . . . Basajaun was cutting meat . . . The dog . . .' The words died into a sob.

He cowered from Zigor's knife, whimpering like a beaten puppy. 'Speak, you!' – that was Hodei – 'The dog?'

'His knife . . . Basajaun . . . he was cutting . . . The dog leaped . . . His knife . . .'

'Speak, you!' The knife moved. Blood trickled over the blade.

'No! No! I will . . . I am . . . The dog . . . He ran . . . one man . . . His dog lying . . . on the sand . . . His dog . . . He saw the . . . I had meat . . . And Basajaun . . . His knife red . . . He saw the . . . His dog . . .'

'Speak, you!'

'I will! The dog . . . faster . . . He was angry . . . He saw . . . and . . . and . . . Basajaun had . . . in his hand . . . the blood . . . I didn't do it! It was Basajaun! Basajaun did it! I did nothing! I tell you, I did nothing!'

'What did you do with his body?'

My voice wasn't my own when I asked that. My body wasn't my own. I was high up and far away. It was a Go-Between – not me – not Nekané, whose only son had been dead five Years – who said to that coward so coldly, 'What did you do with his body?'

In the end we made him answer me. 'We hid it in the marsh.'

Osané said:

I'll do my best to tell you this. If I can't . . . if I find I can't . . . I'll tell you as much as I can.

We women danced. The spirits came. I never thought I'd do that dance before the Hunt in my present life. I couldn't dance very well because I was eight Moons pregnant, but even so the dance took me. I'd always been so light on my feet . . . but what did it matter? We clapped to the Go-Betweens' drums. We sang that song before the men . . . it was like stepping into the Beginning. We were the ones to save the Hunt. The spirits filled us with strength. I thought we'd made things turn. I thought when we danced that now the men could ask the Animals about the Hunt. How could I have forgotten the fears that lay on my heart? Ever since Nekané brought the news from Loch Island Camp I'd been so frightened. I saw too many endings, and none of them good. When I danced I forgot. When we danced we were in the Beginning. Everything seemed right.

I came back into this world when I saw my brothers stand in the Healing Place before the Go-Betweens. I remembered everything. I covered my face with my hands and dared not look. It broke my heart to see Itzal there. I'd just found him again. I'd not spoken to him since he was a child. Only yesterday we'd met secretly in the hazel grove. That was because he didn't want to see my man, and I didn't want to see my parents. But now everything was right between him and me. If it had only been the two of us . . . as it was, our meeting had left me more fearful than ever.

Then the Go-Betweens asked . . . The Go-Betweens said . . . Aitor said to Oroitz, 'Where is your father?'

I learned to cry without a sound when I was very small. Alaia knew. Alaia put her arm round my shoulders. Sorné saw us. She put her arms round me too. The children – Esti – Bakar – you were there too. You were with us, standing in the Moonlit circle around the Go-Betweens' mound. You clung to our cloaks. Oh, Bakar, do you remember? Sometimes I've hoped so much you don't remember . . . and yet . . . I see now that it must all be remembered in the end.

The shadows of the People hid my tears. Besides, no one was watching me. If I hadn't had Alaia and Sorné to hold me I'd have fallen. Everything that I'd dreaded for so long . . . Please . . . I'm sorry . . . No, no, don't . . . This must all be remembered. I can tell you now.

When I looked up I couldn't see what was happening. The Go-Betweens had gone. Oroitz and Koldo stood in the clearing. They looked so alone they might have been dead. The fire on the mound was hidden by an empty space. My eyes were dragged to that space. In it I saw darkness that moved and fluttered at the edges where the Moonlight caught at it. That darkness had swallowed my brother.

When the spirits had done with Itzal, he rolled out from underneath. For a heartbeat I thought he was dead. He lay still. He crawled away as if he'd been beaten. No one looked at him except me. I saw him stagger to his feet. When he stumbled down to the Healing Place and stood beside my older brothers they didn't even glance round. Everyone was watching that empty space which hid the fire.

Two other men were in the Healing Place. They stood opposite my brothers. I looked at Kemen. I looked at Basajaun. They were too much alike . . . I wished they looked more different. My man would have been safer if they'd looked more different. The Moonlight wiped out colour – wiped out warmth – so that the way those two men stood, the outline of their faces – the cruel Moon forced everyone to see – which wasn't true in daylight – how beneath the ordinary things that make us know one another – these two brothers looked very much the same.

The Go-Betweens' fires blazed above them. The Go-Betweens were up there, throwing on more logs. Sparks flew up and died in the Moonlight. Shadows leaped to their feet. Wind soughed in the oaks as the spirits breathed. A bundle lay before the Go-Betweens' hearths. In the tricky light I couldn't see. Kemen ran up the mound and rolled it over.

'Dad-da! That's my dad-da!'

'Hush!' I tried to put my hands over Bakar's eyes. I didn't want him to see. He wriggled free.

'That's Dad-da!'

'Yes, Bakar,' Sorné said. 'That's your brave father up there. You watch him, and be proud!'

Bakar pushed my arm off his shoulder. He stood up straight.

He watched everything that happened. After a while he let Sorné take his hand. But he didn't glance again at me.

The Go-Betweens were drumming. They took no notice of Kemen kneeling on their ground. I saw my man's face outlined in the firelight – the familiar line of nose and jaw – suddenly strange to me now I saw his brother in him. I glanced at Basajaun. He was watching Kemen, but even as I looked he turned away. Kemen's hands were on that strange bundle. I couldn't see what he was doing.

The Go-Betweens drummed. Spirits flashed in the Moonlight, red and yellow and gold. The spirits twirled above our heads. The oak tree tops bowed as the spirits passed over them.

Kemen held the bundle in his arms. He struggled to his feet, pulling it with him. The fire lit them from behind. As it rose, the bundle took the shape of a man. Kemen got the man's arm round his own shoulder. He walked his cousin down the mound to stand by Basajaun. In the Moonlight the face of the young man whose name has gone out of this world was black with blood.

The spirits rose over the Go-Betweens' heads as they drummed. They swooped over the People. They showered down Red and Yellow. They shot back to the Go-Betweens like arrows made of fire. The spirits dipped over my brothers' heads as they passed. None went near the Lynx People. The air over their heads was empty space.

The drumming stopped, sudden as a stricken bird. The spirits sank behind the fire.

Aitor faced the People. He spoke to us all.

'Listen, you People! The spirits have come!'

I was terrified. I hid my face.

All round me People were echoing Aitor's words 'The spirits have come!' they whispered. 'The spirits have come!'

'Now!' cried Aitor. 'The spirits will show us the wrong that was done! Nekané's Helpers told her this long ago, but only now is their message plain.'

The Go-Betweens' drums murmured behind the hearth, echoing every word he spoke. I clung to Alaia. I hid my face against her shoulder. I knew too many things; I was terrified of what the spirits might tell the People. I wanted to run away and hide.

'Listen, you People! Five Years ago Nekané's son Bakar went alone from River Mouth Camp. He took his young dog – he was training him to hunt birds. They walked along the shores of Long Strait towards the High Sun Sky.'

I raised my head. I began to listen to what Aitor was saying. He was talking about Bakar, who had been Alaia's brother – Bakar, my little son. Perhaps I'd been wrong to be so frightened after all.

'Bakar and his dog came to the White Strand at the foot of the marshes. The tide was going out. They found a dolphin high and dry. It was a strange dolphin, sinuous and thin, with a stripe along its side. The dolphin still breathed when Bakar found it. Bakar plunged his knife into its blowhole. The Dolphin gave itself to him.'

'The Dolphin!' the People began to mutter. 'The Dolphin!' I heard them whispering Nekané's name.

What had the Dolphin to do with Kemen, or my brothers? I didn't know anything about any dolphin. I was still trembling, but I dared to look up at Aitor through the wreathing smoke. Perhaps I'd made a mistake; perhaps I had nothing to fear after all.

'Bakar laid a white stone before the Dolphin.' Aitor held up something that gleamed white in the Moonlight. 'This stone! This stone you see here! He lit a fire with tree-mushroom, and burned thyme, because the Dolphin gave itself freely, without a Hunt. The Dolphin breathed the smoke.'

I felt the People round me draw in a great breath, as if they too were one Animal.

'The Dolphin breathed in the smoke. It didn't go away at once. It watched Bakar strip away its blubber and roll it up. It watched him cut through its ribs and take meat. That Dolphin gave too much meat to carry. Bakar took the meat to a stand of birches a little way away. He hung it to dry out of reach of Animals, and went back to get more. His dog ran ahead.'

A baby wailed. The cry rose, thin as Moonlight, out of the silent crowd. There was no whispering now. The story was twining itself around the hearts of the People. We couldn't move or speak. The story had caught us.

'Bakar heard the dog bark. He started running. He came out of the birch-wood. The dog was racing towards the dolphin. Bakar saw two men by his meat. He tore across the sand. The dog was faster.'

'No!' 'No!' 'Bakar!' 'Bakar!' 'Bakar!' 'No!' The cries of the People echoed round the mound.

'Bakar reached the dolphin,' Aitor shouted above the noise. 'His dog lay dead. Both men had blood on their hands. They'd been taking meat. One man held a reddened knife.'

'They took his meat!' 'Bakar!' 'Bakar!' 'Bakar!' 'They took his meat!'

'They'd stolen his meat,' cried Aitor. 'His dog lay dead. Bakar pulled his knife.'

Aitor whirled round to face the Lynx People. 'Will we strip these men? Have they scars on them? I think they have! I think Bakar of the Auk People left his mark on them! There were two of them, and one of him. The Dolphin saw that fight. That Dolphin knows that Bakar left his mark on these men!'

The crowd broke into a roar like a great wave on jagged rocks. In terror I cradled the child in my belly; I thought the People would rush forward and knock us down. The noise washed over me. Was I the only one, out of all the Auk People, who felt for a heartbeat as if that wave were crashing down on *me*? This story had nothing to do with me – except for my son . . . my own Bakar! I wanted more than anything in the world that this story should have nothing to do with me!

'Listen, you People! Listen!'

The Drums crashed. 'Listen, you People! Listen!'

The People grew quiet enough for me to take my hands from my ears.

Aitor's voice sounded soft as a snake as silence crept back into the crowd. 'That Dolphin gave himself to Bakar of the Auk People! That Dolphin could still smell the thyme which Bakar burned for him. That Dolphin saw these two men steal Bakar's meat and kill his dog! That Dolphin saw these two men kill Bakar! That Dolphin saw these men throw Bakar's body into the marsh! It saw them take their boat and flee! Those men knew the tide would wash away all trace of what they'd done.'

Screams and taunts washed over us as Alaia, Sorné and I were shoved towards the Healing Place. We gripped the children tight. Not the width of a hair stood between those Lynx men and death. 'No! No! No!' Now the screams were my own. 'Not Kemen! Not my husband! No! No! No!'

'Stop!' The spirits whirled round Aitor's head. Men stopped in their tracks. Slowly the quiet settled. I looked up, and saw the oak trees far above in the Moonlight, tossing in a gentle breeze I couldn't feel down here.

'Listen to me!' Every face turned towards Aitor. 'You see this man? You see him? This man Basajaun wronged the Heron People. That's why he left Heron lands. After he'd killed Bakar he didn't dare stay in Auk lands either. He sailed to another Heron Camp where he wasn't known. His boat was full of dolphin meat. The Heron People were hungry. They didn't ask questions.'

The crowd muttered, and fell silent. The story swept on, and caught us in its wake.

'The Dolphin knew where Bakar's body lay hidden in the marshes. If that Dolphin hadn't watched, Bakar's spirit would be buried still. How could the Animals see him? Those men – those men you see standing there – had hidden his body away from the clean air, where no spirits would find him! That was worse than killing him! Bakar had wronged no one! You see these men? You see them? What kind of cowards can these men be?'

The crowd surged forward with a huge roar. It broke against the sides of the mound and fell back.

Aitor held up his arm. Spirits flashed from his open hand. 'Be quiet, all of you! Wait! This story is almost at its end. Treat it with respect – it's getting old! Just wait a little longer!'

'Now listen: that Dolphin saw Bakar's danger. But Dolphin didn't know the marshes – he'd never hunted there. Swan knew. Dolphin spoke to Swan, and Swan took Bakar's spirit from where it lay, and flew up with it out of the marshes. Swan ran across the water, splashing with every step – a man's spirit is heavy, and not used to flying – then took off into the air.

'Dolphin and Swan searched through the lands where the Auk People hunt. They found Nekané. They helped her. At last, these *murderers* – these men you see here – came back – finally driven out by the Heron People – as the spirits knew they would be. At last the spirits are able to speak. This is why the Animals won't speak to us about the Hunt! It was *these* men – these you see standing here! They caused it all!'

Amidst the screaming, jostling crowd I clung tight to my son. I held him to my heart. I looked in horror at my husband and his brother, alone up there on the Healing Place. This crowd

– my own People – wanted to kill Kemen! Whatever I'd feared at the beginning, it had not been this!

Kemen didn't look at them. While Aitor was telling his story Kemen had covered his face with his hands. Now he stretched his arms up to the spirits and gave a great cry. 'Oh, Basajaun! Basajaun, my brother!' Kemen beat his fists against his chest. 'Oh, my father! My father! Oh, my fathers of the Lynx People! Oh, Basajaun, my brother!'

Kemen's cries died away. He pressed his hands against his face.

Basajaun's right hand clasped the hilt of his knife. He threw back his head and met Aitor's gaze. He looked as fine a man as Edur. Edur is a great hunter. But Basajaun wasn't a hunter any more. Basajaun was the Animal at bay.

Zigor's harsh voice broke across my thoughts. 'These men have wronged the spirits of the Auk People! Now they must give back what they took, or die for ever! Our spirits say to them: "Choose! Choose now!"'

He looked down at the three Lynx men. 'Choose now! Either your names go out of the world for ever, or you give yourselves! The sea took the land where you hunted. You brought your angry spirits here! You stole meat! You did murder! Yet the spirits of the Auk People are kind. They let you choose: will you give yourselves, and put right the wrong you did? Or will your names die forever?'

I pushed Bakar into Sorné's arms. I shoved Alaia and Sorné aside. I knocked over the children in front of me. Heavy-footed, I ran to the Healing Place.

'No! Not Kemen! Kemen didn't! Kemen's my husband! Kemen's one of the Auk People! He did no wrong!'

Nekané and Zigor ran down to meet me. They seized my hands and swept me upward. I couldn't run as fast as them. My legs gave way. The wind carried us. Moonlight glinted on the trees below. The sky was cold. Strong hands held me. We flew so close to the Moon I felt her warmth. I'd never known that Moonlight could be warm. On earth we only see it like the fire from a far-off Camp on a different island.

The warmth of the Moon was kind. Before I hated my mother she held me to her breast. Because she kept me warm I lived. Only later . . .

'What happened later, Osané?'

The voice was kind. I looked down. I saw the dark shapes of islands in a wrinkled sea. I saw a string of islands. On the highest island I saw our Camp in Egg Moon. In the Moonlight I could see very far. I saw many eggs lined up. I saw my mother hold each one to her ear and shake it. She laid them in the fire and smoothed the ashes over them.

On that island a little path leads uphill through the bracken. The bracken swishes when a man walks through. The bracken . . . I was still a child.

'What happened later, Osané?'

'I can't tell you that!'

The hands slipped. I thought I'd fall. I caught my breath as they turned me. The sky was cold. Gathering Camp lay far below. The Moon shone into the clearing. Kemen's cry hung above the treetops. 'Oh, Basajaun, my brother!'

'Itzal said that man raped you. Shall he die?'

'No! No! He did no wrong!'

'Your brothers say that man raped you. Must he die?'

'No, no! Not my husband! No!'

'Itzal said that man raped you.'

'No! No! It wasn't him! He knew . . .'

'What did Kemen know, Osané?'

'He knew – I couldn't speak – I never said a word . . .'

'But he knew . . . ?

'He knew I'd been hurt.'

'Who raped you, Osané?'

Bracken fronds brushed our feet as we flew. The bracken swishes when a man walks through . . .

'That's where it began, Osané. Then in the end he tried to kill you. Would you let Kemen die for *him*?'

I was falling into the bracken. I was a child. I was crying, 'Oh, my mother! Oh, my brothers! Koldo! Oroitz! Itzal! Why didn't any of you save me?'

'Who raped you, Osané?'

The bracken swished. I saw Kemen's hands covering his face. 'Not Kemen! It wasn't Kemen! Kemen never did me wrong!'

'Who was it then, Osané?'

I was crying . . . I cried out . . . How can I tell you this? Even now, how can I . . . No, don't, leave me alone . . . I can speak. All this must be remembered. I can tell you now.

I spoke my father's name.

Seventh Night: Gathering Camp

Esti said:

I remember this part. So can he – can't you, Bakar? We remember because we were scared. We clung to Alaia. It was worse for Bakar – it was his own mother out there with the Go-Betweens! He was crying: 'Mamma, Mamma!' Of course, Osané couldn't hear him. No one else took any notice. Bakar buried his face in my mother's shoulder. 'Alaia, Alaia! I want my Mamma!'

Osané cried out her father's name.

We didn't know what it meant. There was a lot of shouting.

They dragged Osané's father into the clearing. He'd been hiding in his tent. They pulled him up to the Healing Place. They forced him to face the Go-Betweens. I thought the Go-Betweens were cruel. I didn't know . . . I thought they were being cruel to him like they'd been cruel to Osané. He was Bakar's grandfather. Bakar didn't know him. I'd known *my* grandfather but I didn't remember him. Haizea and my mother often told me stories about how my grandfather and I used to love each other. I'm sure it's true but I don't remember any of it. My grandfather hasn't come back into this world yet. I hope he will while I'm here. I want to know him. Bakar's grandfather was still in the world, but he was no good to Bakar. I thought he might as well have been dead. Later, when I understood, I wished he had been.

That night – oh yes, I remember that night. I saw a man sent away for ever. Most People get through a whole life without seeing that. I'd been back in the world for less than seven Years. It's the worst thing I've ever seen.

I still dream about it. In my dream I'm alone. My People have cast me out. I have nowhere to go. I can find food. I can build a shelter. I can make myself a cloak. But why would I bother to live in an empty world? The Animals are there. They don't know I've been cast out. The spirits are there. They don't care whether I've been cast out or not. But I'm not an Animal or a spirit. I belong to the People. If the People won't have me back, the world is as empty for me as before the Beginning.

When things go badly for me I have that dream. Not very often – usually things are good. But if I'm sad, or angry, or lonely, then I have that dream. The dream began the night I saw Osané's father sent away. His name has gone out of the world. He won't come back. That means my dream can't go away.

He was a big man – bigger than my father. He didn't fight. There were too many men holding him down. Maybe he wouldn't have fought anyway. It wouldn't have done any good.

Zigor's words struck like a spear. The big man seemed to shrink. He looked like an Animal too wounded to run.

Zigor cried out, 'Look at your sons! Look at them!' He paced to and fro above Arantxa's sons. Angry spirit-lights whirled around his head. The young men cowered.

'See Koldo, Oroitz and Itzal – your sons! Shall the People cast them out?' A great gasp rose from the People. Oroitz and Itzal clutched one another's arms in terror. Zigor never looked round. 'You! You're their father! Should Koldo, Oroitz and Itzal be cast out? What could anyone do to deserve that?'

Zigor stood over Arantxa's husband, and swung his arm round to where Arantxa's sons stood open-mouthed in horror. 'You won't say? Then I'll tell you! Listen, every one of you! Hear this: two things only deserve that a man should be cast out! Only two things! One of those things is to let your parents starve!'

Itzal had covered his face with his hands. 'You are no father to them!' cried Zigor. 'They owe you nothing. They must never give you anything in this world again! No, even if you starve, Koldo, Oroitz and Itzal must never give you food again!'

He turned round, and pointed straight at the cowering man. 'The other thing you know. If a man takes his daughter, his sister or his mother he will be cast out! Cast out for ever! If a woman willingly takes her father, her brother or her son, she will be cast out! Cast out for ever! But if she's raped, it makes his wrong the worse. You raped your daughter! Once would have been wrong enough. You did it often – how often none of these People can bear to think. She was a child! Osané has done no wrong. You wronged her! Not only Osané – every one of the Auk People now suffers for the wrong you have done.'

Zigor called the man by name.

'You hear your name? You will never hear it spoken in this world again. I call you by your name, and tell you to leave us. Go! You no longer belong here! Go where you will – the world is wide – but never come near any of the Auk People. Seize him!'

All I could see were men's backs. All I could hear was People shouting. From their midst came a shriek that cut me to the bone. I clapped my hands over my ears. I couldn't make it stop. Shrieks echoed through my head, high and broken, like a pig being eaten alive.

'Mamma!' Bakar screamed. Alaia let go of both of us. We were crying.

Then Osané was there too. Bakar clung to his mother. He was howling. I held on to my mother. I didn't like her running off like that, even to fetch Osané. All four of us clung to each other.

Later I saw that man again. He was alone, crouched on the ground, whimpering. His back had gone away. The place where it had been was black and shining. His back had turned into blood.

I didn't know what it meant.

Later I understood. They'd taken their knives and scraped away the marks that said who he was. Now he wasn't one of the Auk People any more.

They sent him away.

The People fell back to let him pass. No one wanted to touch him. He staggered towards us. He'd picked up his deerskin tunic. He was holding it in one hand. Blood slid down his bare arm; it dripped from his wrist. Alaia pulled me out of his path.

He saw Osané. She held Bakar's face against her shoulder so Bakar couldn't see. I was the one that saw. I saw how that man looked at Osané as if he were an Animal about to die. He didn't ask for anything. I couldn't see her face. I don't know if she gave anything back.

All the noise had stopped. The silence was terrible. No one spoke or moved.

He walked away. The People parted to make a path for him. Only his dog wanted to follow him. Edur held him by the scruff of the neck until his master was out of sight. No one spoke until Osané's father had gone away into the darkness of the woods.

Only the dog kept whining. Edur tied him to an oak sapling. The dog went on howling long after the men had gone to the Hunt. Neither Arantxa nor her children made any sound at all, but the dog howled enough for all of them.

All night long the dog howled for his lost master. Later I got to know that dog well. After a while he started following Itzal around, and so Itzal became his master. That dog settled down, but every Year when we came to Gathering Camp he'd leap out of the boat before we'd even landed, tail high, and rush ahead to the clearing, barking with excitement. Osané's father still lived in that dog's heart; it was the one place left where no power on earth could wipe him out.

Nekané said:

At my back I heard the footsteps of the Animals, softly at first, growing louder as they drew near. Now the three Drums behind me were beating out the footsteps of the Animals. My Drum joined its voice to theirs. I listened to the footsteps of the Animals, and I drummed what I heard. No woman had done that for as long as any of the People could remember.

The footsteps drummed louder. They came from the very edges of the clearing. The ground shook under my feet, beating out the footsteps of the Animals.

The three Lynx men stood on one side of the Healing Place, and Arantxa's three sons on the other. All but Basajaun stood with bowed heads. Itzal had his hands over his ears. Kemen kept his face covered. Only Basajaun outfaced the spirits. The spirits swirled round the six men, making fiery patterns in the air, winding the men together in ropes of blood. The Animals caught us in their footsteps as we drummed. Through our Drums they beat out the pulsing cords that held those men together. I raised my head and saw how the red cords stretched back to the Beginning, and disappeared into the hidden Years ahead.

Aitor cried out.

The Drums stopped.

The footsteps vanished. Feeble echoes of their beat stuttered from the gathered People, and died away.

Aitor held his hands up to the spirits. To us he was a black shape outlined against the fire. The People on the far side of the fires had to strain their eyes to see him through the wreathing smoke.

Aitor spoke. 'These men standing here are shamed by the spirits. Every one of them has cause to be ashamed. What will we do with them now? Do we want men who are shamed to live among us?'

The People were silent for many heartbeats. Then someone stepped into the Moonlight from my own hearth. I peered through the smoke, but only when he spoke did I recognise him.

Amets looked up at the Go-Betweens and said, 'We've no choice, Aitor. Show me a man who says he's not ashamed about anything and I'll show you a liar. We're all shamed. I can tell you what I'm ashamed of myself.'

'Why would we want to hear that?' said Aitor coldly. 'But speak if you must.'

Amets faced him firmly. 'Edur once did me a good turn. He stayed at Initiation Camp in my place. He lost his woman because of that. That was my fault. I didn't mean it to happen. But it did. So I'm ashamed.'

'What's that to me?' said Aitor. 'You made a mistake. Why whine about it now?'

'Because, Aitor,' – Amets sounded angry, and no wonder – 'you may be Go-Between, and know a lot of things I don't. But *I* know that every man here – and woman too, perhaps, though I don't know much about what *they* think – has some reason or other to feel shame. The spirits are showing us that all these different shames are joined up. Why punish Arantxa's sons and not anyone else? You could say what happened in their family wasn't their fault. I left my own parents long ago, but I can tell you one thing – I'm glad they weren't like Arantxa and her man. Koldo, Oroitz and Itzal, I can see why you're ashamed, but I don't think anybody here wants you to carry the blame for ever. I'm not Go-Between, but I'm a good hunter, I'm one of the Auk People and I have daughters of my own. And now I've said one part of what I think.'

All round the clearing People shouted and stamped and clapped their hands. Men surged forward and surrounded Arantxa's sons, pounding their backs and shaking their arms. When Aitor raised his arms to speak again the men fell back to the edges of the clearing, taking Arantxa's sons with them so they were lost in the crowd. Only Amets still stood before Aitor, with the three Lynx men on his left.

'Well,' said Aitor, with a glint of a laugh in his voice. 'You've settled that matter, Amets. It looks as if we all agree with you. So what's the other part of what you think?'

Amets jumped up to the Healing Place next to Kemen and pulled his hands away from his face. 'This man,' he said. 'Kemen.' He turned Kemen to face the People, holding Kemen's hands so he couldn't hide his face.

'What about this Lynx man?'

'No!' Amets grabbed Kemen's tunic by the neck and ripped apart the grass twine that fastened it. He tore the deerskin away so Kemen stood naked to the waist. Amets swung Kemen round so everyone could see him. 'Look at him! Look at his back! Is that Lynx? Is that Lynx?'

People muttered. Someone called out, 'I read Lynx, inside the red stripe!'

'*Inside*! And on the outside' – Amets turned the unresisting Kemen in a circle again so everyone could see his back – '*Auk*! And now read this!' Amets pulled his own tunic over his head and flung it away. He turned his back to where the voice had

come from. 'What do you see? A man born into the Seal People
– read that, inside the red stripe – and below it – what? Doesn't
it say *Auk*? Am I Auk, or not? You People can read what's
written here – I can't see it – what does it say?'

Amets had no enemies anywhere, except what his association
with my family had brought him. The People shouted so loud
that the rooks woke in their nests, and rose up squawking.

'Auk! Auk! We read Auk!'

Even Edur was shouting with the rest. When Amets showed
Kemen to them again, the shouts were almost as loud as before:
'Auk! Auk! We read Auk!'

Sendoa and his brothers ran forward to surround Kemen,
but before they could take him back into the crowd with them
Aitor held up his hands. 'Wait!'

Everyone froze. Amets and Sendoa were holding Kemen by
the arms, one on each side. They stood sturdily before the Go-
Betweens, and made no move to let Kemen go.

Aitor said to Amets, 'You would say, I suppose, that just as
Arantxa's sons are shamed by their family through no fault of
their own, this man too is shamed by his family though he
himself has done no wrong?'

'That's what I say.'

I watched Amets curiously. I'd never seen my daughter's easy-
going husband in this mood. My own man used to say that,
although he never worried Amets would be unkind to Alaia, he
wasn't sure he trusted Amets to stand up for her. It wasn't that
he was weak – Amets was a brave hunter, and very strong – but
more that he mightn't take an important matter seriously enough
to bother. I wondered what my husband would have said if he'd
seen Amets standing up to the Go-Betweens, looking as
dangerous and truculent as a newly wakened bear.

Kemen tried to pull away. 'Amets . . . Sendoa . . . I can't let
you do this. I'm ashamed . . .'

'That's what I'm saying.' Amets didn't look at Kemen. He kept his eyes on Aitor, as if the Go-Between were a boar about to charge. 'Aitor, Zigor just told us that there were only two things a man could do to be sent away from his People for ever. Kemen is one of the Auk People, and he's done neither of those things. He's ashamed because his brother and cousin have murdered an Auk man. But Kemen *is* an Auk man, just as I am. His own son, Bakar, is the very one who was murdered when he was here before! Kemen has to live with his shame, just as the rest of us do. We don't punish each other for what our families do. How can we? We're of one People: we're all related to each other's shame. I can't let you People wrong Kemen. He's my brother. If you wrong him, you wrong me.'

Aitor said, 'You're a good man, Amets. People will listen to what you say. From now on Edur will know that you're his friend. You're right: Kemen is one of us. But he also comes from these Lynx People. The Lynx spirits he brought here with him have brought us grief and pain. Since he came, the Animals have refused to give themselves. Was that because Bakar was murdered? The murder wasn't Kemen's fault. But the Lynx People's lands were swept away, these men fled towards the Evening Sun Sky, and all that we've suffered followed from that.'

'Wait!'

I'd been surprised already by Amets. But that *Alaia* should come forward and brave Aitor, with all the People watching her, astonished me more than anything else could have done.

Alaia's voice shook, but she faced Aitor as bravely as her man had done, and said, 'I'm one of Kemen's family too. Bakar was my brother. Even though he's come back as Osané's son, I'll always miss the brother that I had – that's what Bakar first was to me. But listen: if Bakar hadn't been killed, then my mother wouldn't have gone Go-Between. If my mother hadn't gone

Go-Between, Osané would have died when her father attacked her. That wrong would never have been put right. Supposing that had happened – the Animals might have been so angry they'd never have given themselves again. If Bakar hadn't died, that's what would have happened. And Osané would never have married Kemen. But she did, and so Bakar came back to us. And Kemen is Bakar's father, and Kemen has made Osané happy, instead of her being dead. Bad and good are all mixed together, just like with everybody else.'

Now Edur ran forward into the firelight: 'But what about these murderers? You're all talking about Kemen . . . Kemen this and Kemen that . . . We've heard quite enough about Kemen. What about these other Lynx men that I brought here? What do we do with them? Decide that, and we'll know what to do with Kemen. Kemen hasn't said anything for himself. Is he going to be loyal to his brother? Will he share what happens to Basajaun?'

Kemen raised his head. 'Yes,' he said, in a voice so low most People couldn't hear him. The crowd muttered, asking each other to repeat what Kemen had said. 'Yes!' repeated Kemen louder. 'Edur's right. Basajaun is my brother! Basajaun was my grandfather! Basajaun was the uncle of my grandfather, and my father's cousin, and his cousin's son. Basajaun was my far-off cousin's newborn child! And the Drums just now – they beat out the lines of blood that tie me to the Lynx People. My father told me that my grandfather was a good man. Basajaun was a good brother to me. When the sea swept over us Basajaun saved my life. I can't turn my back on Basajaun. Whatever you do to him, his name will live in my heart. I can't change that.'

Basajaun turned his head and looked at Kemen. Neither brother made any move. I think – the Moonlight was tricky and I can't be sure – I think Basajaun smiled.

'In that case,' said Aitor, 'for as long as you live, Basajaun's name won't die.' Aitor turned to Amets. 'You call yourself Kemen's friend?'

'I certainly do!'

'Then seize him!'

Amets looked startled.

'You and Sendoa – and you – and you – seize him! Bind him! Carry him to the Go-Betweens' tent! You want him to live? Then seize him, I tell you! Do as I say!'

Sendoa ran up and twisted Kemen's arm behind his back, forcing him to bend over. 'You hear the Go-Between, Amets! Fetch ropes! Bind him!'

'What . . . ?'

'You fool!' shouted Sendoa. 'You don't want him to die with his brother.' Kemen twisted backwards, and Sendoa fought to keep his grip. 'Fool! Amets! Help me! Don't you see, man! It's the only way to keep him out of it!'

Amets couldn't think that fast. He hung back. Koldo and Oroitz rushed forward to help Sendoa instead. A mass of People, including Alaia – *she* wasn't stupid – grabbed Amets and forced him back before he could move to help Kemen. Kemen kicked Oroitz in the groin. His fist smashed into Sendoa's face. Sendoa fell to his knees, blood pouring from his nose. Kemen's cousin lurched forward to help him. Swift as a snake, Basajaun struck down the man's raised arm. I saw the frightened question in the cousin's eyes. Basajaun didn't trouble to answer it. He just held his cousin back, gripping his shoulders, until the Auk men had overpowered Kemen. Edur bound Kemen hand and foot to a big birch branch, pulling the ropes tight with vicious knots. I hid in the shadows when they carried Kemen up the mound and dumped him in the Go-Betweens' tent. As soon as they'd left him there, I crept back to see what happened next.

Only when Aitor turned to Basajaun did I see a glimmer of understanding in Amets' face. 'Your brother is out of this,

Basajaun. He wouldn't be a man if he didn't try to help you, but we've made it impossible for him to do anything.'

Basajaun nodded. 'For *that* – I thank you,' he said, as coolly as if it were he, not Aitor, that was Go-Between.

'Now,' said Aitor, 'I say to you two Lynx men what Zigor said to you before: choose now! Either your names go out of the world for ever, or you give yourselves! You did murder! Yet the spirits of the Auk People are kind. They let you choose: will you give yourselves, and put right the wrong you did? Or will your names die for ever?'

Basajaun held his head high. He showed neither fear nor sorrow. He looked Aitor in the face, and challenged him: 'My name will never die!'

Aitor met his eyes. 'Are you so sure of that?'

'Oh yes.' Even though he had to look up from the Healing Place to meet the eyes of the Go-Between, Basajaun seemed much the taller man. 'You heard what the Drums were saying. You know very well that whatever you do, my name will live in this world. You can't make it die!'

I thought of my son, dying at the hands of this man, alone on the white beach beside the Dolphin that had given itself to him. Now Kemen, one of my own family who shared my hearth, had told everyone that Basajaun's name would stay alive in his heart. Yet Kemen was now Bakar's father. Five Years ago Zigor had made Kemen swear that Lynx names would live among the Auks, and nowhere else. Zigor hadn't known then about Basajaun, but the spirits had known everything all along. Although I'd been Go-Between five Years I found myself without any wisdom to deal with this matter.

No one asked me to be Wise, which was just as well. I was a woman, and had nothing to do with what followed.

Zigor said, 'We promised that before the Moon set we'd speak to the Animals about the Hunt. We must do that now, or the Animals will go away and leave us.' Zigor stepped out of the smoke and came round the Go-Betweens' hearth to where everyone could see him. He held something in his hands. It looked like a branch from a tree. 'Now we'll speak to the Animals about the Hunt! Men, come forward!' He dismissed Alaia with a flick of the hand. She fled, and hid herself among the women.

The Animals were stirring. I stepped quietly into the shadows beside the tent.

Men flooded into the clearing. Their song surged forward like new tide over ebbing water. The men stamped their feet along with the footsteps of the Animals, as the Go-Betweens' Drums led them onward.

Always when the dance began, I'd creep away from the Go-Betweens' tent and go down the dark side of the mound, away from the fires, and round by a little woodland path to join the other women by the hearths. Now I stayed where I was. The men danced the footsteps of the Animals. They danced Cat, Marten, Boar and Deer. They danced Aurochs, Wolf and Bear. They danced Lynx. Their stamping shook the ground. Never had I come so close to the Hunt as this. The part of me that was woman was too afraid to move: if I was not Hunter, I must be Hunted. As each Animal danced before my eyes I felt the terror that comes before the giving in. I had no wish to give myself, yet I couldn't take my eyes away. Terrified, I crouched in the shadow of the Go-Betweens' tent.

I saw Zigor lift the branch. It was no branch: I recognised the antlers. I gasped in fright, but I was neither man nor woman now. I was Go-Between, and the spirits didn't hurt me.

I saw the Hunted. He never flinched. When they brought the antlers he didn't cower. He towered over most of them, but he didn't bend his head to help them. Unlike an Animal, he met their eyes. Like an Animal, he knew the only way was to give himself before he was taken.

Edur placed the crown of antlers round Basajaun's head. He was the only man tall enough to reach. Edur pulled the mask down over Basajaun's face. Basajaun's green eyes glittered through the slits. The footsteps of the Animals beat from the heart of the earth. The press of stamping men hid the Hunted from the eyes of all but the Hunters. Except they had forgotten me.

Even under the weight of the antlers Basajaun held his head high. I'd almost forgotten the other one, a pale shadow at his side. No one took any notice of him. I think he was past caring himself whether his name lived or died. I looked at him and felt a sick wave of fear that for a heartbeat rocked me off my balance. From Basajaun I felt no fear at all.

Edur knotted the last strap. The hands that restrained Basajaun fell away. For a heartbeat he stood still, perhaps not realising he was free.

Then he leaped.

He went straight up the Go-Betweens' mound, surprising all his pursuers. He leaped over the fires and ran for the dark space behind the tent, where there were no men to hold him back. Only I was there. He crashed into me as he landed, flung me aside and shot away down the dark side of the mound, into the shadows under the trees.

Kemen said:

My arms and legs were lashed to the branch behind my back. I tried rolling on the wood to break it; it was too thick. I strained against my bonds until my wrists and ankles bled, but Edur had used thick strips of rawhide, and he'd done his work thoroughly. They'd blindfolded me too. I don't know why: I couldn't have freed myself even if I could see. I knew where I was. I'd lain blindfold in this same place before, only then it was full of People. Now I smelt only the closeness of imprisoned air.

I was so full of grief and anger, I felt I had to break out or die, but for all my struggles I lay helpless as a baby that doesn't want to be born. And about as much use: my mouth was filled with bitterness that I lay trussed like a pig on a spit when Basajaun needed my help as he'd never done before.

The ground beneath my back shook with the footsteps of the Animals. I heard them all: Cat, Marten, Boar, Deer, Aurochs, Wolf, Bear, Lynx . . . Lynx . . . and . . . something else. The close air round me rippled with a current I'd never felt before. My skin prickled. I smelt strange excitement. I smelt fear.

I'd been in this place before. Not when I lay under Zigor's knife a hand-full of Years ago. I went back long before that. I smelt the sweat of huddled bodies. Before my blinded eyes I saw strips of hare meat roasting over a heather fire that sparked and hissed, then flared up, catching the faces of the listening boys in sudden flashes. I smelt their excitement; I also caught a current of cold fear.

'A man can also give himself.'

Even the snow-laden wind that had buffeted our tent seemed to hold its breath, waiting for what came next. All these Years later, I remembered exactly what our teacher had said to us: 'A man is not an Animal. He doesn't know the spirits as the Animals do. But the spirits know him. If the spirits mark him, they can take him for their own. They can save him by forcing him to give himself. He is still man, but also, for a little while, he is Animal as well.'

Long ago, in the high snows where the Lynx People have – had – their Initiation Camp, I listened to that quiet voice telling us how it was done. Even then the story sent a cold trickle down my spine. But I was very young: I didn't understand how we still live in the Beginning, even though the Years have carried us such a long way away. How could I know, caught on the cusp between child and man, that one day I'd lie bound and helpless, listening to the footsteps of the one Animal that is not Animal? How could I dream that the Hunted Man would be my own brother? I couldn't: through the Years that followed my dreams told me many things, but they'd never given me any hint of this.

I lay, wide-eyed under my blindfold, until the last footsteps died away. I don't know if I slept. A strong wind started to blow from the evening sky. The trees roared like the sea. If Basajaun were making inland, towards the drowned lands of the Lynx People, the wind would be behind him, blowing away his scent and helping him on his way. Perhaps the spirits were on his side. But later, in the stillness before dawn, I felt no wind at all. Perhaps it had already done its work. I heard faint movements outside the tent. The soft sounds faded into whispering leaves. A dog howled. I sniffed the growing dawn seeping into the tent. A blackbird sang above my head. Doves cooed in the wakening woods. My anger and grief were spent. What I wanted more than anything in the world was to piss. How long would they leave me here? I was thirsty too, but there was nothing to be done about that.

It hardly mattered. Basajaun was gone. Auk dogs were on his trail. Auk men were hunting him to his death. This was Auk hunting land; the Auk men had dogs and spears and arrows. Basajaun had nothing. He couldn't escape. Perhaps he was already dead. Where would his spirit go now? He and my cousin – they were Lynx, not Auk. How would Basajaun's spirit find its way through this strange land?

I tried to think of Osané. She'd suffered last night too. I thought of her unborn child, and hoped – as well as I could hope anything – that the baby had come to no harm. I thought of my little Bakar. How much had he seen, or understood, of his parents' shame? In one night my son had seen his mother's father stripped of his name and sent away for ever, and his father's brother sent to his death. I wanted to find my boy and take him in my arms and make sure he was all right. I wanted to comfort Osané. I wanted my friends to be my friends and not my deadly enemies. I wanted to lay out my brother's body where the spirits would find it, even if I couldn't save his life. But more than all that I wanted to piss. But shame myself I would not. I lay still and waited.

Gathering Camp started to stir. Shrill childish voices mingled with birdsong. Fresh smoke rose. Women called to one another across the clearing. A dog whined. It wasn't a nursing bitch or a pup. I knew how that dog felt. He and I were the only hunters left in Gathering Camp. We'd suffered the same loss; I wondered what it was like to be him. Dogs live halfway between People and Animal. We People know them very well, and yet we don't know them at all. At least that dog could piss if he wanted to, and not think anything of it. I envied him that, and hoped someone had brought him water.

It was Zigor who came at last. I was so glad it wasn't Nekané I almost smiled when I heard his voice. He cut through my bonds – I'd tugged at them too hard for him to undo Edur's knots. Zigor rubbed the blood back into my legs until I could stand. I was stiff with cuts and bruises from the fight last night, and when I tried to walk my ankle gave way. Zigor let me stagger outside to piss. I wasn't in a fit state to fight or run, but I would have done, had I not known already that it was all too late. I let Zigor lead me back into the tent, and when he offered me his waterskin I drank deep. Zigor watched me as if he were a duck sitting on her eggs, and I a lynx about to spring.

'Am I your enemy after all?' I asked wearily. 'What d'you think I'm going to do?'

'The only enemy you have now is yourself,' said Zigor. 'You're one of my People, and it's my job to save you from your enemies.'

'From myself?'

'Exactly.' Zigor had picked up the strap Edur had used to blindfold me and tossed it away. 'I think you can see well enough without this now.'

'You know what it was I saw?'

'Your brother showed me the Lynx People understand as much of these matters as we do.'

'They taught us about it at Initiation Camp.'

'All People are kin, if you go back to the Beginning.'

'I know that.'

We sat in silence for a while. Zigor made no move to leave me. Then I asked him, 'Is Osané all right? And my son? Have you seen them since?'

'Bakar is very well. Osané knows how to survive.' Zigor glanced at me under heavy brows. 'So do you, Kemen.'

'It seems I'm made to survive,' I said grimly. 'I don't have much choice.'

'Oh, you have choice,' said Zigor. 'Don't tell yourself lies. You're not the sort who gives in.'

'You mean my cousin? It wasn't fair on him.' Suddenly I found my tongue was loosened. I never meant to confide in Zigor, of all men, but the words seemed to come tumbling out of my throat like water over a fall. I don't know what trick he used to make me speak. 'My cousin's not clever,' I told him. 'He never learned to think like the rest of us. When he was little, Basajaun used to protect him. He wouldn't let the other boys tease him. Basajaun never showed kindness where he didn't love. And he never loved where he didn't respect. So it wasn't that. It was because my cousin was family. He was born weak. No one thought his mother could rear him. She was the one that named him. People said it was a pity she ever recognised him. He had a good name – I knew fine men who had that name, but they're gone now. The sea took them and left him.

'It wasn't his fault he was weak. He went to Initiation Camp the Year after I did, even though he was born two Years before I was. He was weak and silly when he went away. Many People thought he'd never make a man. But he came back. He was still weak and silly. But something else had happened. If you breathed in the breath that he'd breathed out, it touched your lungs like ice. His fear was like the snow in a north-facing corrie that never melts. And yet he lived. He found a way to live with fear.'

I'd been sitting cross-legged, gazing into the empty hearth as I talked. Now I swung round and faced Zigor. 'None of this was fair on him! You think my cousin didn't matter! You think he was weak and afraid. You saw him as hardly a man at all! Didn't you? Didn't you?'

'No,' said Zigor quietly.

I took no notice. 'Well, you were wrong! My cousin knew fear in a way that men like us never do. It weighed down his heart. He had to carry it with him wherever he went. He knew he wasn't strong like the rest of us. He could see it was a joy to us to be alive, but he hardly ever felt that joy himself. Sometimes he did . . . I remember . . .' I shook my head. 'Never mind that. We were just boys, and it was long ago, in a land that's gone. But he was happy sometimes, in the past when we were young.'

'Don't forget that,' said Zigor.

I didn't understand – not then – why he said that. 'You're Go-Between. I'm not. You think I'm just a stupid man who sees nothing. But I knew my cousin and you didn't. Now you've killed him. His name has gone. Basa . . . my brother's name will live. You said that; you let him give himself. Don't think I won't mourn for . . . my brother. I do! I always will! But at least you People recognised him! But my cousin – you didn't even see who he was. You didn't give a thought to what happened to *him*. You've left nothing of him at all!'

'That's not true.'

'What?'

'You remember him,' said Zigor.

A sob rose in my throat. I killed it there, because Zigor was watching me. I knew what he could see. I looked away. There was nothing I could do. The hunters were long gone. I knew in my heart that everything had already happened. I'd never see my brother again. I'd spoken of my cousin, but I had nothing to say to Zigor, or anyone else, about my brother. I felt more than my heart could hold. My thoughts whirled inside my head without anything to hold them down.

Basajaun had killed Bakar. Bakar lived as my son. If the Auk People had not hunted Basajaun down, it would have fallen to me, in the rightness of things, to make sure of the death my brother owed my son. What would I have done then? Because of the Hunt, I would never know. The spirits had been kind, because now I need never think about what I'd have done if the matter had been left to me. Except that my heart was so tired I could think of nothing else.

Amets said:

We set off before dawn, men and dogs together. Ortzi and I left from our hearth. With Ortzi at my side I felt strong. I was with a grown man like myself. I'd never seen Ortzi in that way before that morning.

Only Nekané and Sorné were up and about when we crept from our tents, took our spears and bows and arrows and left the clearing. They looked the other way. The tents were silent, but we smelt a wakefulness in the air different from any other Year. After Basajaun and his cousin had fled into the wood the women had watched the Dance for longer than usual. When the Dance and the fire died down, the boys were seized and carried off into the woods. The rest of us had slept a little. The Hunt stayed awake. A wind rose off the sea, blowing clouds over the stars. A man who didn't know these lands would be tossed by the wind, unable to see or sense where he was. If he found his way through the trees it could only be very slowly, with many mistakes. The Camp stayed watchful all through that short night. The wind died; the trees stood still enough to hear a twig crack. We knew that the women were aware of our leaving, but they kept their silence, and we kept ours.

I had the cleverest dog. Some men say I'm the best man with dogs round here; I say I know how to choose the best dogs. After that boar killed my old dog, when Bakar and I last hunted together, Edur gave me the pick of a litter he'd brought to Gathering Camp. The pup I chose wasn't the biggest, but I watched how he got through to his mother's teats by wriggling his way in where he wasn't expected. That was the dog for me. Now that pup had grown to be a dog in the prime of his life – still fast and strong, but wise too. Never did I think I'd chosen the best dog to hunt down a man! I didn't want to lead the Hunt against my brother Kemen's own brother, but there was no doubt that I had the best dog. I had no choice.

Basajaun's quiver, pouch and ember bag lay where he'd left them by Arantxa's hearth. My dog sniffed Basajaun's things. I watched him make up his mind. Then, while Basajaun's belongings were shown to the other dogs in turn, I took my dog to the place where Basajaun had leaped out of the dance and run across the Go-Betweens' mound. The wind had blown hard in the night: there'd be little smell left in the air. But the ground would hold it. My dog cast about this way and that around the Go-Betweens' tent. He snuffled in a drift of last Year's leaves. His tail went up. He raised his nose and gave a short bark. He ran down the back of the mound and into the trees.

The paths around Gathering Camp are all criss-crossed. People pass to and fro; while we're there the Animals who keep the paths open for the rest of the Year retreat deeper into the wood. It's hard to follow the trail of one man across a big Camp. That very man will have come and gone often as he lives his life from day to day. Many others will have gone the same way. People-smells hang in the air. We People read our own smells as a presence: we can say there have been many People and dogs in a place, or only a few. If it's not long ago, we can guess at how long they stayed, and what they did while they were here. Dogs are much cleverer than that. Their noses tell them every story that passes their way as clearly as you hear the words I'm speaking now.

My dog soon found how Basajaun had run in a half circle round the Camp, just out of sight under the trees. Then he'd done just what I'd have done in his place: he'd headed down-river to the marshy place where men shit. He'd trodden through the shit, tracking to and fro in the stickiest places, splashing his way through murky pools. The dogs were muddled. The air itself said nothing: it smelled of the sea it had just come from, and had no other tale to tell. Even my good dog couldn't tell where Basajaun had jumped into the River. We knew that's what he'd have done though – it's what any man would do.

The River grows big and dangerous long before it reaches Gathering Camp. All the more reason for Basajaun to cross it if he could. We looked at the sweep of brown water; it was just about low enough for a strong man to cross – if he were desperate. I leaped in. My dogs and Edur, with Arantxa's sons, followed me. The other men waited – we didn't need all of us muddling the trail before the dogs found it.

Edur and I stood, dripping, on the far bank. Arantxa's sons waited for us to speak. I had an idea Basajaun would head upriver because that was harder going: he'd think we'd expect him to take the easier way. Edur wasn't so sure. He thought Basajaun would make for the boats. Basajaun wasn't to know, argued Edur, that our dogs were already guarding the boats, with old men and boys watching over them, before ever the Dance began. Basajaun wouldn't know that a hand-full of men had run to join them as soon as the Hunted one had left the dance. But I thought Basajaun was clever enough to have guessed.

In fact it was those men guarding the boats – Sendoa and his brothers – who killed Basajaun's cousin. He'd slipped away before Basajaun made his great leap out of the dance. He knew no one would be looking at *him*; sure enough he got clear away and crept down to the shore. He wasn't as clever as Basajaun. He thought he'd found an unguarded boat. He turned it over and was groping for the paddle there wasn't one, of course – when they seized him. Sendoa said they didn't expect him to fight much. But he did. He fought like a Lynx, with hands and feet and teeth and nails – they'd have let him draw his knife but he never gave them a chance. Sendoa cut his throat and that ended it.

The dying man's blood spurted over Sendoa's chest. Sendoa dropped the body, threw off his clothes and ran into the sea. He plunged headfirst into the waves, then splashed himself all over. He pummelled his deerskins in the salt water until every spot of blood was gone. While he was doing that, his brothers rolled the Lynx man's body on to a hide, and dumped it on a makeshift platform above the shore. They took care not to touch anything that belonged to the dead man. As soon as they'd finished their work they all stripped and washed themselves in the sea, until they were sure there wasn't a drop of blood left on anyone. No one wanted the spirits who'd watched over Kemen's cousin to start following his killers! Those spirits would make bad enemies! The Auk People would never have got rid of them either, because that Lynx man's People were all dead, and his name had gone out of the world for ever.

That was before the Hunt began. It didn't matter: that man was never going to be part of the Hunt. He was your cousin, Kemen – I know you don't like me to say this – but that man was nobody, even while he bore his name. He didn't matter. Anyway, before the Hunt began he was out of it.

I was right: Basajaun never looked for a boat. He was a strong man. He pushed his way upriver right through the rapids until he was above the watering place. Maybe some of you little ones haven't been up there: before the River reaches Gathering Camp's watering place it threads its way through flood plains, meandering between little pools. The higher pools were made at the Beginning – you can tell by the shelving shores of rock – but the two lower pools were built by beavers. The land is open: after the beavers drained the marshes to make their pools, we People made the wide meadows by burning off the birch saplings and willow scrub every few Years. Now aurochs and deer make for the open spaces, and that saves the hunters many a long journey into the higher grazings.

The dogs and I followed every meander, searching for a scent. A little band of cows and calves were grazing two hands-full of ten paces away. The watch cow stared at us as we came near. The cows lying down got to their feet. Mothers lowed to their calves. The herd kept its eyes on us until we'd passed, but it didn't bother to move. They knew no Aurochs had agreed to give itself that day.

Before the River reaches the beaver meadows it tumbles down from the watershed between Eagle Crag and Sharp Peak. White falls force their ways through broken crag and loose boulders, then lose themselves in airy pools. We sent the dogs ahead on either side – Basajaun could have doubled back on his tracks and come ashore on the High Sun side after all. He could have headed up any of the many side streams that tumbled from the ridge. Some of the men kept to the near bank; some crossed over and followed me. The dogs searched to and fro across the rocky ground, sniffing among sallow willow, bilberry and bog myrtle. I was worried the dogs might have missed something – but how could Basajaun have fooled dogs like ours in open meadowland? There were no trees to climb into – no way of hiding his scent at all.

Zeru's dog on the far bank gave a warning bark. Next thing we knew, half the dogs on the far bank were in full cry. The dogs on our side stood still, ears cocked. I glanced at my dog. He sniffed the air. He scratched his ear. He trotted on up the hill. The other dogs turned their heads this way and that. My dog gave a sharp bark. Doubtfully, the others followed.

Zeru and his brother were running downhill after their dogs. Sendoa's dog hadn't moved. Sendoa signalled across to me: 'No!'

Men and dogs vanished into the trees. We heard dogs barking, and a sudden silence.

Across the River Sendoa traced a flowing Animal in the air with his two hands: 'Otter!'

Koldo and I glanced at each other. 'That dog of Zeru's has a mind like an empty basket!'

'Most dogs can't think sideways,' I said. 'When did we ask them to hunt a man before?'

'Lost children?'

'Ah, but then they're looking for their own.' I glanced down the glen once more before turning to follow Koldo. Itzal was already well ahead, running uphill as light as a cat. 'Here's Edur! Here come his dogs!'

Oroitz wasn't far behind the dogs. 'We got as far as the boats,' he panted. 'We didn't pick up anything.'

Edur came up next, looking glum. Surely Basajaun couldn't have outwitted us so easily! The dogs trotted on, nosing the ground this way and that along the banks, which were rising now to the gorge that cuts its way down from the watershed. I looked down at the white water – narrow enough here for a man to leap across – and the steep cliffs where rowans clung between the rocks. A strong man *could* push his way up through the falls – the River wasn't in spate – but he'd be risking his life. A hunted man faces greater risks than a few falls of water – but if Basajaun had still been struggling upstream he must have come out before the long fall below the ridge. Up there the rock is sheer and slimy with moss. Even the falls we'd already passed would be hard to climb. He'd have the water in his face and the rock was slippery. He'd be climbing through swift water by touch alone. All the while he'd be losing his lead on us.

Yet his plan made sense. Soon after he'd leaped out of the dance, the Moon had set. The stars were hidden: he'd been travelling in the dark. The wind would have pushed him off course even if he'd known the woodland paths as we did. There was only one certain path away from Gathering Camp, where a man might feel his way through unfamiliar lands however dark it was, and where his smell would be washed away. The wind had brought rain with it – but from the sea, not the hill. Spate was a risk, but an unlikely one. Yes, it made sense.

I heard dogs behind me. Sendoa and his brothers were coming up from the beaver pools, running to catch up. Soon Edur's dogs had overtaken the men and joined mine, sniffing the high banks, stopping short at the edge of the gorge. I waited for Edur. As I stood there, the Sun cleared the hill and touched me with its finger. The morning was growing fast. The Hunted had had daylight on his side for longer than I cared to think.

This was Auk land, not Lynx. He'd never been in this place before in his life. He had no dog and no weapon. The Auks would be shamed for ever – we would never thrive again – if he got the better of us now.

My dog gave one sharp bark.

That bark spoke to the stillness. That bark was the beginning of the Hunt.

The dogs milled together and were off. I spared two heart-beats to glance down the gorge and see where Basajaun had climbed up. Yes – it could be done, just. But he must have had light to see by. When he'd stood here the day must already have been breaking. We weren't so far behind him after all.

'He's heading for the watershed.'

'Yes.' I shaded my eyes so I could see the dogs running straight into the morning Sun. 'He'd see the Black Lochan from the top,' I said. 'Either he'd keep on the High Sun side and head uphill—'

'Or he'd go for the Sunless side,' said Edur, 'and follow the water down. Or he could break off uphill towards the Sunless Sky –'

We whistled the reluctant dogs to wait, and broke into a run. Every man dropped to the ground before he reached the col, and edged forward on his stomach, his dog crawling at his side, until we were over the ridge. Only then did we cautiously raise our heads and look down.

The two divers that winter on Black Lochan weren't in sight. It might have been Basajaun who disturbed them . . . it might not. A hand-full of hinds grazed just below the summit of Sharp Peak – it was too far away to see clearly, but they showed no sign of anxiety. High above the eagles were soaring. They'd be watching us – maybe they could see Basajaun too. The young one was still in its nest on Eagle Crag, but the eagles stayed high in the sky. They knew no Eagle had agreed to give itself that day.

We let the dogs creep downhill ahead of us. Soon they were sniffing along the shores of the Black Lochan – of course Basajaun had taken the chance of throwing them off the scent. He'd have known from the lie of the land there'd be water down there, but his first sight of Black Lochan must have seemed like a gift. But he'd have been in a hurry . . . sure enough, the dogs picked his trail up quite quickly, on the High Sun side of the loch under Eagle Crag. I watched my dog lead the way across the screes towards Black Corrie. I whistled him to wait. The dogs gathered at the foot of the screes, ears alert. Perhaps they wonder sometimes why we don't get down on four legs and run properly – life with men must seem like one long wait. A man hunt was better than usual for them – they're used to staying at heel until the final chase.

'That's our man,' I breathed in Edur's ear – out of habit, for a man can no more hear like a deer than he can scent like a dog. 'I *knew* he'd do the difficult thing – the thing we wouldn't find obvious.'

'That's his mistake,' breathed Edur. 'For if he's on Eagle Crag we have him. He's climbed into his own trap.'

'If we're quick enough. He'll be down the other side—'

Edur slid down the heather off the ridge. Off the skyline, we quickly divided into three bands. The fastest runners – except for Arantxa's sons – and their dogs went with Sendoa. They had to get above the precipices that faced the Evening Sun Sky, and fan out on the far side of Eagle Crag before Basajaun could climb down. Edur led the next band, with its dogs, across the head of the Black Lochan, to head round Eagle Crag on its morning side. I took Arantxa's sons – they're fast climbers – and we scrambled after our dogs as they picked out Basajaun's trail across the tumbled scree. Sometimes they lost the scent

– in spite of the dangerous slope, Basajaun had jumped as far as he could from boulder to boulder – a lot further than most men – but it didn't matter. Now we knew what our quarry was doing.

If he were still on the summit he'd see every move we made on the open ground. Sendoa and Edur had a thin cover of birch and willow scrub, but they were moving too fast to go un-noticed. A pair of ravens rose from the crags above Edur, croaking the news of men passing. Two young stags and an old one moved out of the birches beyond Sendoa, and drifted away over the hill. They didn't hurry any more than the Aurochs had done. They knew no Deer had agreed to give itself that day.

If Basajaun were watching he'd see how the trap was closing round Eagle Crag. If he were still stuck up there he'd be sorry he'd made the less obvious choice. He might now be racing down – the High Sun side of Eagle Crag was a trap – he wouldn't see the cliffs from above – he'd be hurrying – sliding down the scree slopes – could easily meet his death over a precipice – a deer running into a trap – but if he managed it – if he broke out before Sendoa and Edur met – he'd have to run fast – the chase would be on again.

If that happened – I was thinking all this out as I panted uphill among the boulders – even if he were a match for our fastest men he'd tire long before the dogs did. Even as I climbed, I hoped it wouldn't come to that. The dogs would pull him down and tear him to pieces – and yet – if the spirits wanted it . . . Hadn't Bakar's dog been killed before his master, and flung away into the marsh with Bakar's body? I remembered how Bakar and I had made a platform for my old dog after the boar killed him – how we'd laid him there as if he'd been a man. If Basajaun were forced to give himself to Auk dogs in the end, he'd surely know why.

Arantxa's wiry sons climbed faster than I did. They were two man-lengths ahead of me. The dogs were in front of them, scrabbling on bare rock. Dogs can't climb like men: Oroitz and Itzal were right on their tails. I followed as fast as I could, swinging myself up by small birches that grew out of islets of solid soil among the scree. Nothing grew on the loose rock up above. I wiped the sweat out of my eyes and glanced up. Two ravens flew up as the dogs approached. They circled overhead, waiting to see what we did next.

A rock rattled down the mountain.

Before I could shout, the rock struck. Oroitz' dog was crushed under it. Oroitz went flying. I reached the man first. His leg was doubled under him. Another rock crashed down the boulders. I ducked, hands clutched to my head. It missed us by several lengths.

'He's up there!'

'Scatter!' I whistled to the dogs. They fanned out across the screes into a hand-full of small shifting targets. The men followed them, except for Koldo and Itzal, crouched over their brother.

A rock the size of my head tumbled between me and Arantxa's sons. 'Scatter!'

'We can't leave him!'

'He's safer if you do!'

Oroitz said through clenched teeth. 'Amets is right. Get away from me!'

'But . . .'

I dragged Itzal away. 'Scatter, you fool! He'll leave the wounded man – it's the rest of us he needs to stop. Go that way – go up by the gully if you can!'

Under the crag I was out of sight. Another boulder crashed behind me. I flattened myself against the rock. He'd know I was down here. He couldn't reach me. My dog whined at my heels. It was too steep for a dog, but I knew where I could climb. I was in too big a hurry to heave my dog up with me. I needed both hands as it was. I took off my bow and quiver and laid them by the dog. I slung my spear across my back so it was out of my way. I told him to wait. His tail went down. I heard him whining as I scrambled up. I couldn't see Itzal or Koldo. I couldn't climb like them, but if they got to Basajaun ahead of me they didn't have the weight . . . If anyone was to take on Basajaun at bay, it had better be me.

I reached the worst bit. I curled my body over the hanging rock. Last night's wind was still strong up here – it tried to catch me off balance. I clung to the rock face. Basajaun would see me from above if he'd found the nick in the ridge. I begged the spirits not to let him find the place. He couldn't send a boulder down from there, but he could throw stones . . . My left hand scrabbled for a hold. I knew it was there. I'd done this before. But I hadn't been hurrying – and there'd been no wind. My head was turned the other way – I couldn't see. I couldn't reach – I'd forgotten to get my right foot into the next hold – a little crack on the far rock. I slid back, feeling for the place. My toes felt their way, hampered by my sealskin shoe. I found the hold – I thought it was the right place, but I was curled over the rock and I couldn't see. If my foot slipped . . . but I had to hurry. I shifted my weight. My toes gripped the edge of a crack. I pushed myself up, reaching for the left hand-hold. No . . . no . . . yes! There it was. My fingers gripped a little stony edge. I got a hold. My right foot slid, and kicked out at empty air. I shoved upward with my left foot, and threw myself over.

I'd have been faster going round by the easy way. I pulled myself over the rock, ran up the last length of scree and on to the ridge. The wind swept in from the sea and drowned all other sounds. I found the head of the gully where I'd seen Itzal going up. There was a bit of shelter in the dip. He wasn't there.

The ridge is barely the length of a man above the gully. I looked to the Evening Sun Sky and the Morning Sun Sky and back again. Both ways the ridge was empty. I saw where Basajaun had thrown down the boulders. Either he'd run back to the summit when he sighted Itzal and Koldo, or – he'd know he'd be trapped that way – he'd seen the precipices on the Evening side – he could have headed down the High Sun slopes to get away. Had he attacked Arantxa's sons? Had he seen the lines of men moving round to cut him off? Where were Itzal and Koldo?

In a heartbeat I'd made up my mind. I ran for the summit, against the wind. From there I'd be able to see. I leaped up the last crag and stood at the edge, looking down the High Sun side of the hill.

Basajaun was there.

My heart leaped to my throat. He was here! He was running across the scree, rocks sliding as he went, dragging him downhill. Just as I'd thought, he was trapped because he couldn't see down. Then I saw Koldo. He was running across the sloping rock above Basajaun as easily as if he were on level ground with no sheer drop below. Itzal must be below me, hidden by the jutting crag on which I stood. That's why Basajaun was running away from me. He couldn't see Koldo heading him off. He wouldn't hear any of us against the wind.

There was one place he could still get down – the scree chute we call the Dogs' Path. It's very narrow – he'd never see it from above – the gap in the rock might make him chance it. If he did . . . I scanned the foothills of Eagle Crag below me. No sign of man or dog. A cloud of starlings had risen from the birches below the evening end of the crag. Edur was sure to have got that far. I peered into the Sun for any clue to where Sendoa might be. I saw none.

I ran back along the ridge, and slid noisily down the scree.

I wanted Basajaun to hear me, in spite of the wind. He did. He looked back, hesitated, scrambled up the scree until he was level with me, ten lengths away. Then he leaped for the top of the crag. There he stopped. He watched me follow him across the scree.

I'd never faced a man at bay. He'd picked the high ground, just as I'd have done. He had solid rock under his feet. I had scree. So far he was the winner. There was empty air on three sides of him, a wild wind knocking him off balance, and no way out except by facing me. I had my spear in my hand and my knife at my belt. The wind was with me. He had – I saw as he stood there – a fresh hazel wand. I had Koldo coming towards me on one side, and no doubt Itzal on the other. So far I stood to win.

I came within a length of Basajaun and stopped. Koldo jumped down lightly beside me. I unhitched my spear and balanced it between my hands. Itzal slid to a halt on my other side in a clatter of stones.

Basajaun stood on his pinnacle of rock watching us. The two ravens circled behind him, waiting. Basajaun flexed his hazel wand between his hands. He'd had no chance to fashion it into a weapon, but it could sweep a man to his death if it caught him off balance. His feet tensed on the rock. In a heartbeat he would spring.

One on each side of me, Itzal and Koldo notched arrows to their bowstrings. Basajaun was within two man-lengths of them. There was nowhere he could go. I watched him watching them. His eyes showed no expression at all.

I aimed my spear at his chest. This would be the easiest kill I ever made. Some stubborn spirit held my arm back. Everything he'd decided had been just what I might have done myself, and yet he'd failed. He'd been trapped by his own cleverness – by so clearly *not* doing what an Animal would have done.

He met my eyes. No man does that to another man unless they're equals, and the closest of friends or brothers. Wolf is the only Animal that looks into a man's eyes like that. I lowered my spear. I couldn't help it. The spirits refused to let me kill a man who looked at me as if I were his brother.

Only the spirits know what might have happened if I'd met Basajaun alone. But no man can out-stare three men at once. Nothing I saw touched Itzal or Koldo.

I was still looking at Basajaun. I saw the arrow in his throat.

I saw the second arrow quiver in his chest. I saw the ravens fly upwards. I heard them croak.

I saw him fall.

Itzal said:

Koldo and I had no idea what was going through Amets' mind. We saw him balancing his spear, ready to throw. We saw Basajaun about to spring. Amets was out of breath with running. I thought that was what made him a heartbeat too slow. The kill was ours.

We slid down by the Dogs' Path and met the others. Our own dogs had run round the hill and joined the pack. We told the other men how Oroitz had fallen. Zeru and his brother went to bring Oroitz off the hill. I'd have gone too, but Edur and Amets said I must stay because I . . . because I . . .

I've never told you this before, Kemen. We've lived as brothers for six Years, and I've never told you. Now that we're telling everything that happened, I have to say this: it was I who struck first. The kill was mine.

The dogs found Basajaun's body at the foot of the crag.

I looked down at him. His head lolled from his body. The stump of my arrow snagged in his throat. He lay arched, broken backwards across the jagged scree. My brother's arrow pinned his torn deerskin to his chest in a welter of blood. His right hand still clenched his unbroken hazel wand. The stones around shone scarlet, winking in the morning Sun. I'd never spoken to Basajaun while he lived, but we'd stood opposite each other in the clearing the night before, while the Moon slowly sank across the loch. We'd been tested before the People together, he and I. Shame had touched us both. Now I lived, and he lay dead.

I looked up. Our greatest hunters – Edur – Amets – Sendoa – they were all waiting for me. The kill was mine.

I pulled the stump of my arrow from Basajaun's throat. I thrust my fingers into the wound. I cupped my hands and drank his blood. Koldo did the same. My brother and I smeared each other with the blood that held Basajaun's strength. We claimed it for our own.

I took my knife and slit his hide along the belly-line. I opened his body below the ribs and cut his liver free. My brother took embers from his pouch and made fire. We roasted his liver in strips. There was enough for every man to eat. The strength of Basajaun flowed into us. We stretched up our arms and gave thanks to the spirits of the Lynx, who had given us Basajaun so that the Auk People might live. The blood of Basajaun was our blood. Our hearts were his.

Everyone waited for me to speak. I thought for a heartbeat. I made up my mind. 'The kill is mine. No one gets any more meat from it. He was a man: we must give his body back to the spirits as if he were one of our own People. Since he didn't give any of his things away, all that he has on him stays with him for the spirits to find.'

I looked down at Basajaun's outstretched body, and the bloodied opening where I'd taken his liver. I thought about how he'd tried to get away from us. He'd had speed and cunning and strength, and he'd used all those things. If he'd known the land as we know it, he'd have got away. Men and Animals are the same: they belong to their own hunting lands, and nowhere else. If Basajaun hadn't been a stranger to the Auk spirits, they wouldn't have been his enemies. He never even tried to make them change sides. But that was only because of who he was. In a heartbeat I knew what to say next.

'It's a long way to carry him, but there are plenty of us here to do it. We'll make his platform by Lynx Cave on Cat Mountain. That's what the Lynx spirits want us to do. When we danced Lynx last night they heard us. Lynx belongs in our hunting lands just as much as any other Animal. Now we'll give him back to Lynx.'

Edur slapped me on the shoulder so hard I staggered on the loose stones and nearly fell across Basajaun's body. 'Quite right, Itzal! And come to think of it, there's quite a bit of Lynx in you and your brothers too. There's not much bulk on you, but the way you ran and climbed today – I think you got those Lynx spirits to change sides somewhere!'

I wasn't sure I wanted anyone to see Lynx in me, after all that had happened. But of course I was glad to have Edur's praise. I'll never forget the things he taught me at Initiation Camp, after Amets left. To be honest I was sorry when Osané didn't take him. I'd have liked to have Edur in my family. But that's all in the past – I'm happy where I am.

We got hazel from the woods and made a stretcher. The weight was nothing compared to a full-grown aurochs or stag or boar. We cut more birch and hazel wands in the woods at the watershed. We crossed the watershed and climbed the slopes of Cat Mountain until the trees thinned. We pushed uphill through old bracken, heather and bog myrtle, over spines of rock ablaze with lichen, right up on to the moss-covered slopes below Lynx Cave.

We raised Basajaun's platform about three man-lengths below the Cave. There was no soil to drive the poles into, so we wedged them with piles of stones.

I looked up at the dark entrance to Lynx Cave and spoke to the spirits inside.

'You Lynx spirits gave us this kill. If he'd been Animal the Auk People would have feasted in your name. We'd have raised his skull over our Camp to watch over us. But it wasn't an Animal I killed today. It was a man – a Lynx man. He belongs to you while his name's out of the world. We're giving him back to you. We want you Lynx spirits on our side. We want all you Animals to give yourselves again. We've only taken his liver, even though we've been hunting all day and we're very hungry. He was a man, not an Animal. Even his heart belongs to you. I'm talking to you, Lynx, listening up there in that cave: you can come out when we've gone and take whatever you want. This man is yours!'

Everyone stood in a circle round the platform where the dead man lay. We all faced Lynx Cave and raised our hands to the spirits. There was no movement from the cave. The spirits hung in the air above us. They leaned down so low they almost touched our stretching hands.

And that was how Basajaun died.

As for the Antlers: we found them the next day, wedged between two rocks in the rapids. Either he'd stuck them there on purpose so they wouldn't get swept away, or the spirits of the water held them safely for us until we came to claim them.

Zeru and his brother splinted Oroitz' leg and got him off the hill. They did my family a great service that day. If it wasn't for their skill, my brother Oroitz might never have walked again. As it is, he hardly limps, although his leg sometimes troubles him in winter. But then, my brother Oroitz has seen quite a few more Years than I have: maybe he's already getting old!

I don't think I have anything more to give to the story. You all know how I took Haizea – or perhaps it was Haizea that took me – don't snigger like that, you three! Wait until *you* find yourselves up at High Clearing! You won't be children for ever, you know! Anyway – when everyone left Gathering Camp that Year, Haizea and I went away together. We made our Lovers' Camp in the hills above the trees, facing the Evening Sun Sky. From our tent door each evening we watched the red Sun fill the sky with flames, until he dropped so low that the waves which break at the edge of the world seized him and doused his fire. No People have trodden those distant shores since the Beginning, but in the fall of that Year the far edges of the world seemed to draw nearer to me. Alone in that high place with Haizea, I was as close as ever I've come, in this life anyway, to the Beginning.

Deer Moon waxed and waned. Hail clattered on the tent, and covered the hides with rime as thick as my hand – this thick! Haizea and I scraped the snow off our hearth each morning and woke our sleeping fire. We trapped hare and ptarmigan and snow buntings, but the Animals were withdrawing into the cold, and didn't want to give themselves. The Year was telling us to go back to our People. So I went with Haizea to River Mouth, and we joined her family. That was my first winter at River Mouth Camp.

I was happy. I'd made a great kill. I'd been treated with honour by the finest hunters of the Auk People. Now I was going to hunt with Amets all the Year round! And Kemen – I soon found out how much I could learn from Kemen. I missed my brothers, but all three of us were ready to find women of our own, and new families. Now I had Haizea for my woman! What man among us wouldn't envy me that! Haizea and I now lived with her sister and Amets, and my sister Osané and Kemen – my sister who'd been out of my life for five Years. I had my sister back again, and I had a nephew to get to know too – yes, you, Bakar!

I was a happy man. That first winter I spent with Haizea will live in my heart for the rest of my life.

Eighth Night: River Mouth Camp

Haizea said:

Deer Moon had gone into the Dark when Itzal and I came back to River Mouth Camp. On our way we stopped at Zeru's Camp on the Morning Sun shore of Long Strait. Zeru lent us his old boat because he was making himself a bigger one. Itzal said that if the sea wouldn't let us cross Long Strait so late in the Year, we could go to Zigor's Camp for the winter. I could tell Itzal liked that idea. Neither of us suggested going back to Itzal's family. I didn't want to stay at Zigor's Camp one bit. After all that Itzal had been through at Gathering Camp, you'd think he'd be more scared of Zigor than I was. But it was quite the opposite: Itzal seemed to think now that Zigor was his greatest friend. Men are very strange!

While we waited for a kind wind I called on the spirits as often as I dared – I didn't want them to get fed up with me – begging them to let us cross. I wanted to take Itzal home. I didn't want to go anywhere else. The spirits teased me for four days. Then early one morning, just as the tide was slackening, the wind dropped and the swell went down. We crossed Long Strait as fast as we could paddle, between one gale and the next.

Oh, but I was happy to set foot on Mother Mountain Island! I'd never been away from it so long. We left Zeru's boat at Sheltering Island Bay – it was far too late in the Year to paddle under the wild cliffs of the Sunless shore to River Mouth Camp. We walked over the hill to River Mouth Camp, hand in hand wherever the path would let us walk side by side. I showed Itzal where Mother Mountain rose beyond the River Mouth hills, far away under the High Sun Sky.

At last we stood looking down, over the heads of the tossing birches, to my beloved River. Yellow leaves swirled upwards as gusts of wind swept over Mother Mountain Island from under the Evening Sun Sky. Lichen-covered trees glowed pale green through the dusk. Flocks of geese, and swans like scattered flakes of snow, grazed on the red salt flats of River Mouth. Far beyond the islands, the Sun was dropping into the sea in a blaze of pink and orange. Twilight crept across the windswept lands below us, and mixed with it . . .

'Itzal, see the smoke? Down there, look! That's River Mouth Camp. Look, look! We're nearly home! See the smoke?'

Itzal spat out the husk of a lily-seed. 'Uh-huh.'

I glanced at him. I was getting to know him better every day. It dawned on me that he wasn't surly because he was angry, but because he was scared. His family had hardly been the best of friends with my family. Before I could tell him there was nothing to be frightened of, a picture of my sister Alaia flashed into my mind. Alaia would *never* tell Amets not to be frightened. I watched Itzal, and bit my lip. He was scowling into the wind, his wolf-fur hat pulled down tight over his ears. What would Alaia do now, if she were me?

'They'll have been expecting us days ago,' I said, as if I'd not noticed anything. 'Especially Osané. Osané'll be looking out for us most of all. And maybe—' I stopped short. If Osané's child was still waiting to be born, no bad spirit was going to hear about it from me.

Itzal made a face that might have been a smile. 'Maybe.'

'Come on! This way!'

Turfs were built up over the outside fire when we got to River Mouth Camp, but smoke streamed from the roof of our winter house. The walls had been patched with fresh turf. Even as the wind whisked the smoke away I caught the whiff of oak logs. I pulled the hide from the door.

'Alaia! Osané! Esti! Is that you, my Bakar? Mother! I didn't know you were here!'

I hugged each one as I spoke their names. Osané's belly was bigger than ever. Amets and Kemen watched us with big grins on their faces. When I grabbed Itzal's hand and pulled him into the winter house after me, Amets jumped up. He took my man's hands and shook them hard. He thwacked Itzal on the shoulder. 'Welcome to River Mouth Camp, Itzal! Welcome to this family!'

Kemen hung back for a heartbeat, then he stood up and took Itzal's hand in his. 'Welcome to our family, Itzal,' he said quietly.

I knew it was hard for Kemen to say that to Itzal. But now Osané was hugging her brother, the children were clinging to my legs, shrieking in delight, and Alaia was saying to the baby, 'Here's your aunty Haizea, Alazne. Give a kiss to your aunty Haizea! Here's Haizea!'

Over the noise Amets was shouting, 'You can see what our women are like, Itzal! We can't keep them quiet! I don't know what we've done wrong, but they never take any notice of us at all! I hope you'll show us how to manage them better!'

They'd all been eating shellfish while they waited for the ducks and eel meat that were roasting in the ashes. The ducks smelt very good after our long journey. As soon as Alaia and

Nekané had pulled them apart and laid the meat on the hearth-stones, everyone leaned in and took their share. I saw Kemen choose one of the duck legs and toss it over to Osané. I couldn't help wondering if Itzal would ever be doing that for me. Would I ever be pregnant? It seemed impossible – back then!

The faces of my family shone in the firelight. Light flickered across the hides hanging behind them – soft wolf-fur, russet otter pelt, pale brown deer, mottled sealskin – winter furs to warm us through till spring. The hides swayed in the draughts that eddied between the doorway and the smoke hole. Oak-smoke swirled above our heads and pierced my heart with its smell of older winters. Faces that I'd never see around this hearth again swam inside my eyes. They filled my heart with tears. For a heartbeat Bakar was once again the brother I'd lost; I saw my little nephew Bakar through a watery blur as if he were far away. Much closer, I saw my father as he was when he lived among us. I saw how my niece Alazne lay curled inside her father's arm, half asleep, and for a little space I was Alazne, but also myself – Haizea – as I'd once been.

The Year before last, when we were at Salmon Camp, Alaia and I had climbed up to my father's Death Place. All that was left of his platform were sapling stems rotting into the ground, half hidden by long grass, and a greener patch of ground starred with eyebright and tormentil. When we felt amongst the flowers we found shards of long bones, cracked open long ago and stripped of marrow. Broken bits of skull, green and rotting, were matted over with new grass. The Birds and Animals had come so many Moons ago that all trace of their work had vanished. We combed the soft grass with our fingers, scratching at the soil underneath. We found four knuckle bones still lying together, and a scattering of finger bones. We stretched up our arms to the spirits who watched over my father's Death Place and told them what we wanted to do. We gathered up the small bones, and wrapped them in a little bag of woven grasses.

We left two of those bones under the hearth at Salmon Camp, my father's Birth Place, and six more we carried with us to River Mouth Camp. Two of those bones are at White Beach Camp now – it was I who wanted that. Now, sitting by the hearth at River Mouth Camp with Itzal beside me, my heart went out to my father's bones where they lay under the hearth-stone. I looked up at the wolfskin swaying against the wall. For a heartbeat my father's face hovered between pale fur and pink firelight. Before I knew what I was seeing, my father had gone.

Osané leaned into my line of sight to lay another oak log on the fire. She moved awkwardly with her great belly. A wild hope filled my heart: the presence of my father was so strong tonight. I thought the spirits were telling me . . . they *were* telling me . . . I'm not Go-Between: the spirits didn't tell me wrong, but the way I read them was wrong. Part of this story is still waiting to happen. It won't be told here and now – maybe it won't be told for a long while. The older I get, the less I worry about it. Everything that needs to happen will happen. My father always said that.

We all sat staring into the fire for a long while. No one spoke. We were happy to be together again. The fire licked at the oak logs. Little blue flames mingled with long orange ones that flowed over the wood like water over a fall. A sliver of bark caught and crackled, then flared upwards like a sudden burst of summer.

Amets stirred, and laid Alazne down on the bearskin behind him. He shook his arm: it had gone to sleep with holding her for so long. He looked across the hearth at my man, and said, 'Kemen and I are going to Seal Bay tomorrow, Itzal. We've taken plenty of pups already, but these women say they want more seal fat. They've been telling us the children need it now that the cold days are coming. They keep telling us all this deer meat's no use – they must have fat! I think these women of ours plan to eat the best fat themselves until they're round and plump, so we'll want to have more sex with them! One way or another, they'll wear us out long before Limpet Moon! You'll come to Seal Bay, Itzal? Good. And you can bring your woman too, if you like. The more People the better.'

Men are always glad to have our help with the sealing. I suppose they think it's not as clever as real hunting – or maybe it's because they've done so much hunting all through Deer Moon they're feeling too weak and tired to manage without us. I wanted to go to Seal Camp. I also wanted to be at River Mouth Camp when Osané gave birth. For all I knew, the baby would wait until we got back from Seal Camp anyway. I said aloud, 'Itzal, you can tell your friend that your woman will be glad to come along and show you men how to catch a seal or two.'

Our Seal Camp is less than half a day's walk from River Mouth Camp. It's a long sandy bay facing the Evening Sun Sky. When we came over the hill the sea roared in our ears. We looked down on strings of white water curling across the bay. Great waves chased each other onward, then broke like thunder on the white sand. There was no wind now: those waves were remembering some storm far out in the Open Sea, further out than People could ever take a boat in winter. Waves like these would be crashing against White Beach Island, sending clouds of spray right over the island. I thought of White Beach Island – my Birth Place – hidden out there in the Open Sea, empty of Auks and of People. No one could reach it now. Only the spirits could be quite sure it was still there. That was a strange thought: I found myself wondering about it, so I didn't listen to what the men were saying.

In Deer Moon some of the seals move inland over the dunes when the beach gets too crowded. Kemen knew the seals here better than any of us, even though he'd only been in our family for five Years, because every Deer Moon when the rest of us had been at Gathering Camp, Kemen and Osané had come to Seal Camp. Each Year, when the rest of us arrived at River Mouth Camp, we'd found plenty of seal meat hanging in the shelters, and seal hides already stretched to dry. This Year, of course, it hadn't been like that.

Kemen and Osané had made themselves a winter house at Seal Camp, high above the breeding grounds so as not to disturb the seals, but close enough to keep a watch on them. There was barely room for four of us to lie down in their turf house. Wood was already piled by the hearth. I lit the fire from my embers. We ate and dozed until low tide, just before dusk. We'd hunt in the last of the daylight; there'd be no Moon tonight.

When the Sun dipped towards the sea we set out, carrying barbed spears and knives. We didn't take dogs. A bitter wind came from between the Evening and the High Sun Skies, so we took the ridge on the Sunless side of the bay, keeping on the far side of the skyline, out of sight of the seals. We crept down the gully next to the stream and came out on the beach. We chose big stones and shoved them in our belts. The curve of wet sand gleamed like a fallen Moon in the last of the light. Far down – the tide was at its lowest – the waves shone through the dusk like white flames as they curled and broke. The wind carried the chill of night between its teeth. The sand was covered with seals. From here they looked like shining rocks.

Itzal and I watched Kemen and Amets creep down to the sand. They were hidden from the land by the dunes. They ran along the high tide mark where the sand was firm. The seals on the sand stirred and grunted. They humped towards the waves. Soon they were all swimming. Their dark heads came up through the waves, watching the men run over the seal-scuffed sands.

Kemen was ahead. Neither Amets nor Kemen could run as fast as Itzal and I would have done! But Itzal was a stranger, and I was a woman. We did as we were told! Amets and Kemen ran ten man-lengths twice, and stopped. Any further, and the wind would have told the seals inland beyond the dunes, that there were men between them and the safety of the sea.

Itzal and I sped three man-lengths across the sand. We crept up through the dunes, crouching low. I led the way: I was a woman, but Itzal hadn't hunted here before. There were marks all through the dunes where many seals had pulled themselves up from the beach. A big male otter had crossed their tracks since, heading towards the Sunless Sky. Wind had carved the soft sand into ridges like mountains, with sharp edges. Sea had swept through the sand-valleys and left wet ripples. Little islands of couch grass clung together by thin ridges between the channels. There were circles written in the sand where the wind had made the grasses dance. Itzal and I crawled up the last dune-island, and lay flat on our stomachs, our faces hidden by the spiky grass.

Dusk was falling fast. The green land was much darker than the white sand. I gazed until I could see. Seals were spread across the muddy grass, thicker than stars in the sky. So many seals! But soon at least two of those seals would give themselves, if our family was any good at all.

The seals had been out of the water for a while. Their fur was dry so they were all different colours: grey and black and brown and mottled. I recognised a few from last Year. I didn't know every one of them the way Kemen did. They snorted and snuffled among themselves. Half-grown pups lay close to their mothers. Young bulls shoved each other around. A few got too close to the cows where they clustered round a big brown bull. The bull bared his teeth in warning.

Itzal nudged me. He barely moved his hand, but I followed his pointing finger. Then he wrote the outline of a big humped seal in the sand under his hand, and marked the ones round it, so I knew which one he meant. It was the big brown seal lying next to his cows. I swallowed. That seal would be strong! You can die from a seal bite – it's the most dangerous bite there is. That's the spirits making sure it's not too easy for us to hunt seals on land, even though the seals' own hunting grounds are in the sea.

I knew why Itzal had chosen that seal. This was his first hunt with my family. He had to show what he could do. I had to do my best to help him. I'd have preferred him to pick an Animal that was more my size, but I didn't say anything.

It was growing darker. Itzal and I crouched, spears ready.

An owl hooted. Amets!

Itzal and I sped towards the seals. I saw Kemen and Amets spring from their hiding place. I ran after Itzal. At once the seals were humping over the mud, sliding down the dunes – bulls, cows, half-grown pups – all melting away as fast as you could think.

We leaped between the brown seal and the sea. He dodged Itzal. I stood in his way. He bared his teeth. I saw down his red throat. He reared, bigger than me and much, much heavier. I aimed my spear. Itzal swung round. I thrust for the seal's throat, just as it turned on Itzal. My spear glanced off its shoulder. Itzal's spear was in its neck. The seal fought. It tried to bite. The barbs held the spear firm in the wound. Blood poured down. I thrust my spear into its neck as hard as I could. The seal twisted. It tried to bite. I pushed as hard as I could. The seal was stronger. In spite of its wounds, that seal still fought to get to the sea.

I let go my spear. I grabbed that seal above its hind flippers. Its skin was warm. Its harsh fur was slippery. I got a grip on its flippers and flung my weight backwards. The seal dragged me. I dug my heels in. I held tight.

Itzal let his spear go. He clubbed the seal hard on the nose with his stone. Itzal's hands were wet with blood. He struck again. I held on as hard as I could. I was scared that seal would reach round and bite me.

At last that great seal gave itself. It lay dead. Itzal pulled out his spear.

Itzal's hair had come loose. He pushed it out of his eyes, smearing his face with blood. He stretched his arms up and spoke to the Seal spirits. Then he turned and grinned at me. 'Is this good enough for your family, Haizea? Will they want me now?'

I sat in the mud where I'd fallen. I was still clutching the seal's back flippers. I grinned back at him over the bloodied body of the seal. I nodded.

Alaia said:

Osané's second son came into this world much more easily than his brother Bakar had done. It's often like that with a second child; the first makes the way easy for them. Birth is just the beginning: the spirits tend to be kind to younger children all the way along. Life's easier for my Alazne because her sister Esti is there to make her path smooth for her. I know what it's like to be Esti – it was the same for me when I had my sister Haizea to look after. Anyway, this boy of Osané's – yes, that one there – look at him now! He may well laugh at me! He gets everything just the way he wants, and he knows it! He's always been the lucky one!

This boy here – sitting between Bakar and Alazne – this boy slipped into this world six Years ago, just as the Sun dipped into the sea on the first night of Yellow Leaf Moon. I caught that boy, wet and slippery as a fish, and held him between my hands. Esti cut the cord, using a blunt knife to stop the bleeding. Nekané held the cord for her. Esti cut very carefully, using both hands to hold the knife, while Alazne sucked her thumb and watched, round-eyed. Then I laid this boy of ours in his mother's arms.

I got to my feet, cramped from crouching for so long. I pulled back the hide from the door. The winter trees stretched their bare arms towards the sky. Over their heads I saw the sliver of Yellow Leaf Moon, thin as a nail paring, soaring clear of their clutching hands. On my right the swollen Sun slid into the sea, staining the water scarlet. On my left the thin Moon rose cool as a fish in the deepening dark. Next to the Moon, the Evening Star sang its welcome to Osané's hidden boy.

The winter house sheltered our nameless one, but even though they couldn't see him, the Stars, as they shone out one by one, sang their welcome to him. I stretched my arms up to the kind spirits. I'm not my mother: I don't usually hear what the spirits say – at least, not plainly – not like words whispered in my ear – which is how they speak to Nekané. But that night – just that once in all my life – the spirits sang to me as if I too were Go-Between. They told me, even before any of us knew who he was, that this boy would be happy among the Auk People for as long as he lived.

Next day the men and Haizea came back laden with seal meat slung on poles. As soon as the dogs greeted them, we ran to welcome them. I was carrying Alazne. Esti and Bakar ran faster than I did. I shouted after them, 'Don't speak before the spirits! Remember who listens to us all!'

When I caught up with the children, Amets and Kemen had put down the seal they'd been carrying. Esti sprang into her father's arms. Kemen caught Bakar and swung him high above his head. Bakar squealed in delight.

Itzal and Haizea laid down their load as I came running up.

Esti was shouting, 'Dada! Dada! Tell him – tell Bakar's dada! He's got a—'

'Amets!' I broke in. 'Don't listen to that child! But your friend may be asking why his woman isn't out here to welcome you!'

Kemen saw me smiling. He put Bakar down. He ran like the wind towards the winter house. The children clustered after him like a string of puppies.

'Osané . . . ?' gasped Haizea.

I smiled at Itzal and Haizea. 'Osané is very well. Go in and see her! And perhaps one of you . . . I can't say more. But one of you may know . . .'

Haizea turned and ran like a hare into the winter house.

When I came in, Nekané was at the hearth, telling everyone not to crowd so close. Osané clasped her baby to her breast. She looked frightened. Could any mother not be frightened? All the family were here. If someone didn't recognise her boy now, he would be cast out.

'Let them all see him!' There was no pity in my mother's voice. There never is, on these occasions. But then, what use is pity? The spirits arrange things as they will.

Osané's son lay in an otterskin lined with eider down and sphagnum moss. Osané unwrapped him, brushed his skin clean and laid him naked on her lap so everyone could look at him.

'A boy!' Haizea leaned forward to look into his face.

Red and wrinkled as a skinned seal pup, the baby, freed from his wrappings, kicked his legs and waved his arms. There was nothing wrong with him. I heard Kemen take a long breath. He didn't take his eyes off this new son.

Haizea caught the baby's flailing heels. 'He's strong!' She stared into the baby's eyes, frowning. I saw no gleam of recognition in her eyes. Many heartbeats passed. Haizea bit her lip and sat back on her heels.

I met my mother's eyes. We glanced round at the other

faces. Amets and Itzal looked at the baby, at Kemen and back to the baby again. Amets looked blank, and Itzal puzzled. Haizea's face was a mixture of disappointment and hope. The children looked round at everyone, wondering what would happen next. Only Kemen's face was hidden behind his hand.

I remembered how the Stars had sung to welcome Osané's boy. I looked at his little kicking body, strong and perfect. Surely the spirits hadn't been cruel enough to send us a stranger! Surely there'd be at least one in this family who'd recognise Osané's boy!

Osané's face crumpled. She picked up her son and clutched him to her heart. 'No, no, no!' She rocked herself to and fro, clinging to her baby. She began to sob. 'No! No! No!'

'No!' Kemen's arm was round her. 'No, Osané, listen to me! It isn't that . . . It isn't . . .'

'Kemen!' My mother's voice was harsh as a raven's. 'You recognise your son! What are you thinking of? Would you risk his life, you fool!'

Bakar began to cry. He climbed on to the bench and clung to his mother.

'Hush! Quiet, all of you!' My mother turned to Kemen. 'You know him! You do know him! You *must* speak! Would you risk his life – *again*?'

Kemen took his son from Osané. He held him between his hands. He looked into the baby's crumpled face.

'Basajaun,' he whispered. 'Oh Basajaun, my brother!'

Nekané said:

Now we're getting near the end of this story. Now you've all heard how Basajaun became one of the Auk People again. You children must never forget the words you've heard us speak.

Never! Bakar and Basajaun – you need to remember them most of all. I've often told you there's no such thing as a bad spirit. All spirits are good, but sometimes you have to make them change sides. You two – Bakar and Basajaun – after all that happened between you long ago, you're here as brothers. As brothers you must be loyal to each other all your lives long. However or whenever you meet one another again, you must always remember that you were once brothers. That's why *all* you Auk People listening to us tonight must remember the story we've been telling you. Because if these two brothers should ever fight again, the spirits will take us straight back to that long-ago killing. If that happened – if brother were to turn against brother – the Auk People would suffer for it for as long as we remain in this world.

But the story of the Lynx People in Auk lands isn't quite finished. It's growing late, but there's only a little more left to tell.

Kemen said:

When I recognised my son, I didn't want to tell you who he was because I thought you'd kill him. Thoughts whirled through my head. He was already more than a day old. If I kept quiet for two more days, it would be too late to cast him out. If he lived four days, the spirits would count it murder if anyone tried to take him from his mother. I had wild thoughts of speaking his name in the last heartbeat before it was too late to recognise him, but already too late to kill him. Because as soon as I looked in his face I loved him. I wanted him to live!

I heard Osané's cry. Out of pity I had to speak. I spoke Basajaun's name.

No one said anything for many heartbeats.

Alaia took my son from me. She looked into his eyes. 'Basajaun, we welcome you to the Auk People. You will always find food here.'

A breath softly touched my forehead, as if the winter house itself sighed with relief. Inside my heart the spirits of the Lynx People laid down their weapons. All these Years those spirits had been poised to leap to my defence. I hadn't even known it until now.

Osané said:

When Kemen recognised my baby I burst into tears of relief. I'd been terrified no one would know him. I'd tried so hard to recognise him myself, but his face was closed to me. Also, I had my own reasons for being afraid to know the truth. Now it seemed as if all my fears were put to rest.

As the Year went into the dark Basajaun thrived. Snow came early, but we had plenty of meat hanging in the shelters, stores of roasted nuts and enough seasoned wood to last until Dark Moon. Amets made a sledge and we brought in lots more wood without even having to carry it home – now I had another baby on my back I thanked the spirits for that! Soon we had to make an extra shelter, we had so much stored wood.

Bakar could find plenty of food for himself now. He wasn't the baby any more! Nearly every day he and Esti went out together. They'd been bringing home baskets of shellfish as soon as they could walk. They knew how to spear flatfish, and fish for saithe with lines off the rocks. That winter, when the fish left the shallows, the children got very keen on catching birds. Robins, tits, blackbirds, finches . . . all the small winter birds that come close to People's Camps looking for scraps. Esti and Bakar used their slings and pebbles – they scorned nets and snares. Kemen caught them keeping count. They'd notched up every hand-full on a birch trunk. Amets and Kemen were so angry! I'm sure neither Bakar nor Esti have ever boasted about finding food again after what their fathers said to them! But I was secretly glad that they hadn't yet learned the hard way that it's not our own cleverness that feeds us, and we can only thank the spirits with all our hearts for every single thing they give.

But that winter the spirits were pleased with us, and the rightness of things was restored at last. As we sat round the inside fire in the long dark, we sang joyful songs because it was good to be alive. We told stories about Birds and Animals and People. We told how all things came to be in the Beginning, and everything that had happened to the Auk People since. When the Sun came back in Swan Moon, we greeted him with outstretched arms as we stood in the snow. Our fire flared as high as it could to welcome the Sun. The slanting rays of the morning Sun reached between the bare trees and touched our fire with a brighter flame than any earth-born fire could make.

After a while I began to notice that my man wasn't as happy as everyone else. One day, soon after the Sun came back, I left Basajaun with Nekané, and went with Kemen to empty the eel traps. We walked by the River where it wound through the salt marshes. The snow on the River path had been trodden into ice, so we walked beside it, making two new sets of footprints in the blue-white snow. I'd stuffed our sealskin boots with dried moss. We walked fast until my fingers and toes tingled with warmth.

Now we could see the whole wide sky. Freezing wind blew from the hills. We smelt more snow. Three of the traps were empty, but there were two eels in the last trap. We tipped them into the basket and tied the lid down tight. Kemen swung the basket on to his back. I set the trap back in its channel. Icy water flowed over my wrists. I weighed the long trap down with stones. We clapped our frozen hands together and swung our arms to and fro. My hands were so cold I could hardly pull my gloves back on. I stood with the wind behind me, pressing the soft hare-fur against my cold cheeks.

'Come on,' Kemen said. 'Let's get back before it snows again.'

It was easy to walk side by side over the snow-covered salt flats. This was the chance I'd been waiting for. 'What's troubling you, Kemen?'

He stopped short. 'What do you mean, Osané? What should be troubling me?'

'That's what I don't know. That's why I'm asking.'

'I don't know what you're talking about.'

Of course, being a man, that's what he would say. I didn't let it put me off. 'I think you do. Whatever it is, it won't go away unless you do something about it. I think you'd better tell me.'

'There's nothing to tell.'

He tried to walk on, but I stood in his way. When he pushed me aside I grabbed his arm. 'Is it about Basajaun?'

I thought he was going to hit me. I ducked away. I held my other arm across my face. But I didn't let him go.

'Osané! Don't do that!' He struck my arm down. I'd made him really angry. 'Have I ever hit you? *Ever?*'

'No. But I've been . . .' I hesitated: that wasn't what I wanted to say. 'But I've never asked you to . . . I've never tried to make you speak before, Kemen, if you didn't want to. But if it's about my son, you must tell me!'

I did get him to speak in the end. He told me everything. I wasn't as anxious about it as he was. Not at first, anyway. But as Swan Moon wore on I had too many chances to think about what he'd said. Slowly the trouble grew inside my mind. I'd told Kemen I'd think it over. Now it seemed to be up to me to decide what we should do. But I didn't have an answer, any more than he did.

Before Thaw Moon rose from the dark the answer came by itself.

My uncle Hodei walked into River Mouth Camp at dusk. There was no wind; the sky was clear. We were sitting round the outside fire for the first evening that Year. It was good to have the open sky over our heads again, and not a smoky roof. Kemen had shot a swan from his boat that morning, and we were roasting it on a spit.

Itzal was the first to see Hodei. He leaped to his feet. 'Uncle!' He ran to Hodei and gripped his hands. 'What . . . How . . . ?' Itzal mastered his astonishment. Hodei was Go-Between, after all. Itzal stammered the proper greeting. 'You are welcome to our hearth, Hodei. There is always food here for you!'

Only Nekané showed no surprise. The rest of us were as astounded as Itzal. No one crossed Long Strait in winter! Hodei's winter Camp was far away under the hills of Gathering Loch. But Go-Betweens can travel whenever and wherever they please, because their Helpers speak to the spirits and open the closed ways for them. Even the sea will do as they wish, if the spirits desire it.

Hodei held me by the elbows and looked into my eyes. 'Is all well with you, Osané? Your mother sends you her greetings. This is a hard winter for her.'

I didn't answer that. I met my uncle's gaze boldly, and said, 'Everything is very well with me. My son was born on the first night of Yellow Leaf Moon. His father recognised him.'

'Yes,' said Hodei.

I realised as I spoke that Hodei knew already what I was going to say. 'He is Basajaun.'

'Yes,' Hodei said. 'Perhaps when we sit by the fire you can show this new little one to his old uncle?'

I wasn't fooled by that sort of talk, but I led my uncle to the fire as if he were an old man and needed my arm to help him – this Go-Between who'd just crossed Long Strait in Swan Moon, and found his way across Mother Mountain Island to our River Mouth Camp, where, as far as I knew, he'd never been before! Not in his body, anyway. I helped him sit down upwind of the smoke. Nekané moved along to make room for him. 'Well met, Hodei!' she said. 'Perhaps these girls of mine will give you a bit of this swan that's roasting here. You see how poorly we live when we're alone! I should have taught my daughters how to feed this family better. Now I'm no use to anyone – I'm just a poor old woman, as you know – we have to rely on these young ones. So we may have to starve together, you and I.'

While Nekané was talking, Alaia took the swan off the spit. Soon the steaming meat was piled on the hearthstones. Alaia handed a choice bit to Hodei, and then everyone leaned in and took their share.

We all wanted to know why Hodei had come, but even the children knew better than to ask a guest questions until he'd eaten his fill. And this guest was Go-Between – you can't ask a Go-Between questions anyway. Hodei seemed content with us all, so it didn't look as if any of us need worry. He'd spoken kindly about my little son even before he sat down – he wouldn't have done that if he'd come because of Basajaun. I felt no fear. I looked up at the sky, my heart filled with thanks, as I chewed the meat off my swan-bone. The night was clear as spring-water, the stars strung together like drops of dew on huge cobwebs strung across the sky. Star-webs hung from spiky branches. Under the Sunless Sky green spirit-lights rose and fell like saplings moving in a far-off wind. The night smelt of damp earth where snow had lain. No one spoke while we ate. Beyond the crackle of the fire the swollen River sang of snow melting in the hills. Amets threw more wood on the fire. Flames leaped hungrily. Light flowed over the tree trunks so they shone like shadows of the spirit-lights above.

Hodei was here. He was Go-Between, but he was also my uncle, and his presence here was kind. Tonight even the far-off Stars were kind. I found myself thinking about Kemen's secret fear. I considered the strange arrival of my uncle. I looked at these two things together in the clear light of the Stars, and I saw what I should do.

Hodei said:

I travelled far in the worst of winter to speak to Nekané. The news I brought was no secret, so when her family had given me food I told them all what had happened. I didn't tell them why I'd set out at once for Mother Mountain Island. No one asked.

When I'd eaten I looked up at the wintry stars. I said, 'How close the stars are tonight! See how they cluster round our fire! Those Stars know what I've come to say to you. The spirits of the sky are joyful because one of their own has come back to them. For a little while at least, they have him back.

'Nekané, you know what I'm about to say. As he lay dying I saw your Helpers watching from the smoke under the roof. I saw the Swan's wing spread over him to protect him. A shaft of sunlight pierced through the smoke-hole. Through it I saw the curve of the Dolphin's back through the wreathing smoke.'

Nekané said, 'At first I was more afraid of him than I ever was of you or Aitor. In the end I loved him well. He taught me spirit-ways. He spoke harshly but in his heart he was kind. He held nothing back. Whatever the spirits gave him, he was willing to give again.'

'He gave himself,' I said. 'Over and over again he gave himself for the Auk People.'

My niece knew who we were talking about. 'Is he dead?' A sob caught in her throat. 'He saved my life, when he fetched Nekané to me long ago. You're not saying he's dead?'

Esti whispered to her mother. I raised my voice in lament before Alaia could whisper back. 'One of the Go-Betweens of the Auk People died with the Year that's gone. He died when Swan Moon went into the dark. The greatest of our Go-Betweens is gone from us!'

One by one they joined my chant. We sang for him, just as we'd sung in his own winter Camp above Gathering Loch. The Stars hovered above the bare trees. The spirit-lights heard our song. They filled the sky with white-green Rivers. They flowed from the Sunless Sky to the River of Milk. High over our heads they made a song of their own out of colours. Red spirit-fire flamed above our little People-fire on earth. The spirit-lights took our lament and filled the sky with our song. The Stars remembered him. His name was among them. They kept his name alive while it ceased to live among the Auk People.

At last our song ended. Amets fetched a bearskin from the winter house and threw it over the sleeping children where they lay by the fire. The women piled on more logs.

'Hodei,' Amets said when he'd sat down again. 'Nekané may know everything, but you have plain men like me to deal with in this family too. Tell us what happened! How did he die?'

That was a question I could answer. I told them how Zigor had gone to hunt geese. He'd left before dawn, and crept out with the tide. He'd hidden in a frozen channel in the marsh and waited for the geese to come grazing as the tide drove them in. He'd lain in the frozen creek for a long while. Nothing new in that – but Zigor was an old man. Older than he thought, perhaps. When he got back to his winter Camp he was soaked to the skin, and chilled through. A Go-Between has enemies as well as Helpers. A fierce fever-spirit seized the chance to enter him while he was weak. It burned in his veins. Zigor was old but he was strong. For four days he fought that spirit. He spoke to that spirit aloud, so everyone could hear. On the second day Zorioné grew so frightened by the spirit-battle being fought inside her house that she sent her man to fetch me from my winter Camp beyond Gathering Loch. I arrived on the fourth day. I could see how Zigor's strength was ebbing with the tide.

I followed Zigor into the spirit-world. He was aware of me and spoke to me. I didn't tell the family at River Mouth Camp what he'd said. I said to them, 'I was able to travel with that great Go-Between a little way on his journey out of the world. I went with him as far as I could. I spoke his name. Then I left him and came back to this world. His soul was slowly leaving his body. His skin stretched over his skull, so thin the bones of his face seemed bare already. Harsh breaths filled the winter house. Zorioné took his hand as soon as I let go of it. She wept silently. The children sobbed aloud. As night fell, the harsh breaths stopped at last. I looked up through the smoke hole. I saw that great Go-Between's Helpers lean down. I saw them lift his soul. I saw his soul rise up through the smoke hole and fly into the dark.'

I was not the only one who wept for Zigor at River Mouth Camp that night. We sang many songs for him.

The next morning my niece asked to speak to me privately. She led me up the Look-out Hill behind River Mouth Camp. As I followed her I felt the spirits of River Mouth clustering round me. I spoke to them without words. They welcomed me, although I'd never stood on Look-out Hill before. I was interested to see how Auk lands lay from this new viewpoint. Basajaun slept under Osané's wolfskin tunic, snug against her warm back.

Osané looked out over the salt flats towards Sand Island. I followed her gaze. People often find it easier to speak without looking at each other. I waited until she was ready.

'Uncle, I need your advice. Maybe your help.'

I'd failed to help Osané in the past. I thought she might hate me for that. I was happy to find she still trusted me. 'This is about Basajaun,' I stated.

'Yes. No. I think so.'

I waited.

'I was so relieved when Kemen named Basajaun.' Osané gazed out to sea. The wind blew her hair across her face and she brushed it away. 'I didn't recognise him. No one did. Kemen wasn't there. They'd gone to hunt seals. Then he came back. He recognised Basajaun.' Osané glanced at me sideways, then looked away. 'I was glad because it meant my son could live. Only later . . .'

'Later?'

'Kemen was worrying.' Osané brushed her hair out of her eyes again, and faced the wind. 'I could tell. I knew it was about Basajaun. I made him tell me . . .'

'Yes?'

'He promised . . . I didn't know . . . Kemen promised Zi . . . him that's gone. When they wrote Auk on his back, he – the Go-Between that's gone – he said to him – he said, "The names of the Lynx People will live among the Auk People. And nowhere else."' Osané shot another glance at me. 'Kemen hadn't told me that before. But that's what he promised the Go-Between: *"and nowhere else"*.'

So Osané knew already why I'd come. I hadn't even spoken to Nekané yet. 'Are you telling me that Kemen hasn't kept that promise, Osané?' I asked aloud.

'I don't know! Don't you see, Uncle, that's just it! How can I know? How can Kemen know? He didn't even think of it when Zi . . . when the Go-Between spoke to him. He couldn't! Only later . . . and then he forgot. I think he wanted to forget. But then Basajaun came, and that made him start worrying about it all over again.'

'Worrying about *what*, Osané?'

'The other cousin.' Osané met my eyes and gave me a level look. 'Don't tell me you've never thought about it, Hodei. Four of them came from under the Morning Sun Sky. One cousin stayed among the Heron People. He took a woman there the very night they arrived. Seven Years have passed since then. Who knows whether Lynx names now live among the Heron People?

'Kemen promised the Go-Between something he couldn't do. That's why he thinks the Auk spirits are angry with him. He's afraid they'll punish him. He's afraid they'll take our son away. That's why he wanted to go back to the Heron People and find out.

'I said – down there on the salt flats, I said to him – "Kemen, you're mad. Suppose your cousin does have children with Lynx names, what are you going to do about it? Kill them? Steal them away and make them into Auks? Run away? If you did any of those cowardly things you'd make the spirits far angrier with you than they can possibly be now. The spirits know you were forced to make a promise no man could keep. They might forgive you that. They won't forgive you if you kill or steal from your own kin!"

'Kemen said, "Of course I'm not going to kill or steal! But if I went to find my cousin, at least I'd know the truth!" "You'd know nothing at all," I told him, "because, for all you know, hands-full and hands-full of Lynx names may be alive today, hunting in lands you've never even heard of. That thought should make you glad! Just because you had to make a stupid promise that no one could possibly keep, you're hoping that all your kin are dead for ever! Can that be right? Of course not! No good spirit would love you for wishing that! It was a bad promise you made. The best thing you can do is forget all about it. Everyone else has!"

"'Including all the spirits who heard me make that promise?" was all Kemen would say.

"'The spirits couldn't have meant you to keep a promise as stupid as that!" I protested.

"'No, but you don't understand! You can't see a meaning in it, and I can't either. But there has to be one! The Go-Between said it – he must have had a good reason, even if we can't see it."

'He can't forget about it, Uncle. And now I worry about it too. Are the spirits angry with us after all? Did the Go-Between that's gone mean something important that we can't understand? Hodei, will you help us? Please, Uncle, could you ask the spirits not to hurt Basajaun?'

'Have you spoken to Nekané about this?' I asked her.

'Kemen made me promise not to.'

'But you didn't promise not to speak to me? Is that it?'

She returned my smile, radiant as the Sun coming out from a dark cloud. 'You can make it right, Uncle? You can make it right!'

I put my hand on her shoulder. 'Anything I can do for you, Osané, I will do. I owe you more than you can ever ask.'

Amets said:

Nekané and Hodei went Go-Between that evening. I was furious. After all we'd lived through – after everything we'd done to put things right – we had to go picking over these dead bones and bring the whole thing back to life again. I'm not Go-Between, but I've hunted long enough to know when the spirits are happy to leave things alone. I said so. I told Hodei, 'When Alaia's father died he asked me to look after this family. That's what I've done ever since. I welcome any guests who care to come to River Mouth Camp. But I expect them to remember they're in *my* hunting lands, Go-Between or not.'

Hodei opened his mouth to answer. I hadn't finished. I went on telling him: 'We've been through all this already. Kemen is as much Auk as I am. His kin – if any live – are Lynx People. My kin are Seal People. We both brought good blood to the Auk People. People are always the better for new blood. Young men will travel. The spirits made things that way in the Beginning. No one ever said to me, "Amets, I think you'd better go back under the Sunless Sky and just make sure all your cousins among the Seal People are dead for ever." No one suggested to *me* that would be a bright idea! They wouldn't dare! I'd have knocked their heads off if they'd even whispered such a wicked thing. If you *want* to bring bad spirits among us, I can't think of a better way of doing it than punishing a man because his People have strong blood and many children. If we Auks want to rid this world of People, we might as well make short work of it and cut off our own pricks!'

'Amets!' Hodei roared at me. 'Stop shouting! Will you *listen* to me for one heartbeat!'

'I've listened enough! And I never heard—'

'Amets!' shouted Alaia. 'Stop it! That's not what he's saying! *Listen*!'

'As for you, woman—'

'Amets! Amets!'

Even that young upstart Itzal joined in the shouting. He and Kemen and Alaia were all holding me back. 'Amets! Listen to the Go-Between! Amets! That's not what he's saying!'

In the end it was Alazne's sobs that brought me back to my

senses. I turned my back on them all and picked her up. 'It's all right, little daughter! Don't cry! I'm not angry now – at least, not with *you*.'

Kemen said, 'Amets – brother – no one could be more loyal to me than you. I know it. But listen, please. I *want* Hodei and Nekané to speak to the spirits. I *want* my mind set at rest. Please, listen to what Hodei's saying to us. He's on our side. The spirits are on our side! Please, listen to what he says!'

I let Hodei tell his story again. I glowered at the fire while he spoke. I didn't look as if I was listening. I was, of course. I heard everything he said.

'I didn't tell you this last night, but I came here to speak to Nekané about this very thing,' said Hodei. 'The spirits told me at Gathering Camp that the child in Osané's belly was a stranger. The Go-Between who's left us knew it too. We weren't worried. That other Go-Between reminded me how the spirits promised Kemen that Lynx names would live among the Auk People. We agreed that a Lynx stranger would be as welcome among us as – as our little Esti here.' Hodei smiled at my elder daughter. 'Don't look so frightened, Esti! You came to us as a stranger. Your father recognised you. Now your name lives among us.'

Esti spoke up. *She* wasn't scared of a Go-Between! 'It lives among the Seal People too! Dada says so! Esti belonged to his family where he was born among the Seal People. She was the mother of his mother. And now she's me!'

'And you are Auk,' agreed Hodei. 'And so our lives roll on, caught between the Beginning and the End.

'I went to my winter Camp,' Hodei went on. 'I was happy. I thought that the rightness of things had been restored at Gathering Camp. The Animals gave themselves. The winter was kind. Then the message came from Zorioné that my fellow Go-Between lay dying, and wished to see me.

'As I hurried towards the High Sun Sky the spirits spoke to

me. They recognised my sorrow, but they showed me how that Go-Between's task was done. Through him, more than any other, the rightness of things had been restored. Why should he linger in an ageing body, when all he'd worked for was fulfilled? I wept as I walked, but I felt no anxiety.

'Only when I knelt at his side did I realise that anything was still wrong. When Osané spoke to me yesterday I already knew what she was going to say. I'd heard it already, from the mouth of a dying man troubled in his mind. He reminded me of Kemen's promise: "Lynx names shall live among the Auk People. *And nowhere else!*"'

'"I thought I was clever," the dying man whispered. "That made me blind. The spirit who told me to say those words was cleverer than I was." He struggled to catch his breath. He tweaked my sleeve with restless fingers. "Hodei!"

'"I'm here," I said.

'"There's no such thing as a bad spirit. No such thing . . . Hodei!"

'"I'm here."

'"You have to make them change sides . . . Hodei!"

'"I'm here."

'He gripped my hand. I waited while he found the strength to speak. "Hodei, you must . . . I made a mistake."'

Hodei looked round at us all. Our faces shone in the firelight. I'd forgotten to look as if I wasn't listening. Hodei's next words echoed my thought:

'You see what a great man he was, the Go-Between who's left us. Those were the last words he spoke in this life: "*I made a mistake.*" Only the greatest of men can bring themselves to say that.'

For a while we all thought our own thoughts. Then I said, 'I agree with that. But as I said before, I'm just a hunter. I'm not Go-Between. What was this mistake? Was it a mistake to force a promise from Kemen that he couldn't possibly keep? Is that what the Go-Between meant?'

Hodei looked me in the eyes. This was my hearth, not his. The Go-Between's gaze pierced me though. I think he searched my soul and saw everything inside it. But this was my hearth, not his. I stared him out.

'Amets,' Hodei said to me at last. 'You hide nothing, and you want nothing hidden. If you were Go-Between, you'd find it much harder than you realise to drag everything into the daylight. How should I understand, any better than you, the words of a dying man?'

'Because you're Go-Between,' I growled. 'We feed you enough!'

'Amets!' I ignored Alaia's shocked whisper, just as I ignored Nekané's mocking laugh.

Hodei took no notice of the women either. This was between him and me. 'Amets,' he said. 'You want me to say, "The Go-Between made a mistake when he made Kemen promise '*and nowhere else*'." You want there to be no doubt about it. Well, I'd like that too! But how can I say it? For all I know, the mistake was to let Kemen become Auk. For all I know, the mistake was to let any Lynx man live at all!'

I leaped to my feet. I wasn't the only one. Everyone was shouting at once. Only Kemen and Nekané sat where they were and didn't say a word.

'Stop it!' shouted Alaia. 'Stop it, all of you! You're terrifying the children. You two – you call yourselves men, I suppose! Then stop frightening us! You're supposed to look after us, not scare us to death!'

What could I say to a guest when my woman had spoken to him like that? I had to laugh. I shook Hodei's hand up and down and clapped him on the shoulder. 'Hodei, what kind of Camp have you come to? We let our women have the last word here, as you can see. You thought we were hunters, until you saw this! Well, perhaps we all make mistakes sometimes.'

'That's true.' Hodei's cold gaze went through me like a spear. He searched my soul. I let him. Deep down I was still chuckling when I thought of our unruly women. As Hodei said himself, I had nothing to hide. At last Hodei spoke: 'Amets, this is your hearth. We two Go-Betweens wish to speak to the spirits, here and now. The spirits will answer your questions better than I can. Then we can put the matter to rest for ever. I want that – we all want that – as much as you do. Will you let Nekané and I speak to the spirits from this hearth?'

I looked round at my family. Every face was turned to me. I searched each one. It was quite clear what they all wanted. 'Yes,' I said to Hodei, looking him in the eye. 'You can make your journey from my hearth, if you think that will put things right at last.'

Nekané said:

Night fell. Thaw Moon was a little curl of light above the tree-tops, paler than the Evening Star. The stars under the Evening Sun Sky were cloud-hidden; the salt wind smelt of rain. We fed the fire with dead leaves and pine branches until it crackled and smoked. Dark crept among us and wreathed around the hearth. The children knuckled their smarting eyes. Bakar began to cry. People were blurred shapes moving through shadows. I fetched my Drum from its sleeping place. I came back to the hearth and took Basajaun from his mother's arms.

Osané clutched my arm as I held her baby. 'You won't let the spirits hurt him!'

'He's as safe with me as with you, Osané.'

People hear what they want to hear. My words comforted her. She let me take her boy. I tied his sling inside my cloak so both my hands were free. Hodei and I stood downwind of the fire. Beyond the smoke we felt the eyes of the People turned towards us, although there was nothing they could see.

I awoke my Drum. As soon as it began to beat, Hodei's Drum echoed back to mine.

We drummed the heartbeats of the earth. Our Helpers came. Fox barked from the wood behind us. Swan's wing gleamed through a mist of smoke. Through the wintry air came the honey-smell of heather, like a shaft of light in a dark cave: *pee-wit pee-wit* called to us from far-off summer moors. Even as my Dolphin rolled through the unseen sea, I glimpsed the shadow of Snake gliding through the hearthstones. She coiled herself once around my feet, and vanished. A breath of cold air sighed against my cheek. That Snake had led me on many journeys; I knew I would never see her likeness on this earth again.

My Drum never faltered. For Basajaun it was the familiar beat of his mother's heart. Too young to fear the spirits – too young to have forgotten – he fell fast asleep.

Stars surrounded us like glittering fishes when Dolphin dives into deep water. Deeper and deeper we flew, into the high darkness. We drifted among the stars. The stars go down deep as the sky itself: no earth-spirit ever reaches the far depths of the sky beyond the Moon. At last we turned and saw our earth far-off, which the spirits gave to Animals and People at the Beginning. We looked through the web of stars that held us. We saw how the kind earth stretched from sea to sea. We saw shores and woods, rivers and lochs. We saw how the mountains divided one part of the earth from another, and how the waters flowed away from the hills towards many different hunting lands. We saw Birds and Animals living joyfully on the earth below us. We saw how they spoke with the spirits, and how the spirits knew every one of them. We saw how the People lived on the earth among the Birds and Animals. We saw how the spirits watched them, even though the People had forgotten how to speak to the spirits in the way they did at the Beginning.

I gazed far away to the drowned lands of the Lynx People under the Morning Sun Sky. I saw white beaches, and the waves breaking. I couldn't see who moved across the earth. When I tried to peer into the darkness the stars dazzled me. I looked towards the Sunless Sky. I saw rocky islands rising from the Open Sea. Those were the hunting lands of the Seal People. But even as I looked the cloud came over, like a hide drawn across the door, and hid the islands from me. I turned to the High Sun Sky. I saw the sharp ridge of Grandmother Mountain outlined against the stars. She wouldn't let me see beyond her. The hunting lands of the Heron People were closed to me. But when I looked down at the hunting lands of the Auk People I saw with the eyes of the Swan that flies from the Sunless Sky. I saw the white-fringed coast and the salt flats beckoning, and gleams of water shining in the folds of the hills. I saw smoke rising from many hearths. Every one of those hearths was open to me. There were no names among them that I did not know.

'Anyway, why shouldn't we?' A shrill voice broke into my mind like a shower of freezing rain. The voice was clearly arguing. 'I thought we were all cousins anyway. It was two sisters that came from Grandmother Mountain to begin with. And *my* name comes from the Seal People. You *told* me so. So everyone's our cousin anyway. Anyway, why can't we have cousins wherever we like?'

At my ear I heard Hodei's mocking laugh. 'I think we have our answer, Nekané!'

Esti said:

I've heard that story so often. I don't actually remember saying those words. But the others all say that I did. My father says we were sitting by a cold fire, because the Go-Betweens had smothered it in wet leaves. I was complaining – so he says. He was trying to make me understand what the Go-Betweens were doing, and why Nekané had taken Basajaun with her. My father also says I was born arguing. Well, that shows he doesn't always speak the truth! All I can tell you now is that I don't remember.

This story is nearly finished now. My grandmother – Nekané – says the story began with my birth, and that I should be the one to bring it to an end. You've all listened very patiently. This is the last night of Gathering Camp. Tomorrow my family are going back to River Mouth Camp. River Mouth Camp is my Birth Place. Four of my grandfather's bones lie under the hearthstones there. I don't remember my grandfather, but everyone in my family tells me I loved him. And he loved me.

The Go-Betweens asked us to tell this story because last winter Edur met some Heron People hunting on the slopes of Grandmother Mountain in the Moon of Rushes. One of the Heron hunters had just been initiated – a Year ago now. His name was Basajaun. His father was Ekaitz, Kemen's cousin of the Lynx People, who took a woman of the Heron People. This young hunter, whom Edur met, has the same name as my cousin who's sitting over there, giggling and poking his brother and making trouble, as usual. Probably this other Basajaun of the Heron People is a bit more sensible. Anyway, now the other Basajaun has Heron written on his back.

That's what Edur told us all when we got to Gathering Camp, and that's why the Go-Betweens asked us to tell you this story.

We've finished it now. In the story I have the last word. Maybe that's not fair, because I'm not the most important person in it. But the story began with me, and my grandmother says it has to end with me. Something Haizea said when it was her turn makes me think the story isn't over yet. Haizea says there can't be an exact end to any story. Every story really started at the Beginning – wherever you begin telling it from – and it can't be properly finished until we come to the End.

My grandmother says there are many more lives to be lived before the End.

Author's Afterword

The Mesolithic era in Scotland tends to be passed over in deafening silence. Six thousand years of human occupation – from the last Ice Age until the agricultural revolution of around 4000 BC – are usually represented in histories and prehistories by a maximum of a page or two on Scotland's hunter-gatherers, with comments on how little we know about them. I was drawn to the early inhabitants of my country partly because, unlike ourselves, they left so little trace of their long presence. They lived long before agricultural peoples built stone circles like Callanish or villages like Skara Brae. My initial ignorance was great, but I soon discovered popular misconceptions were even greater. I've often been asked 'Could these people speak?' 'Did they have fire?' or 'Did they have any art?' I wanted to show that in evolutionary terms seven or eight thousand years is almost nothing. In other parts of the world people were already farming. These people were genetically the same as us; only the world they inhabited was different. Sometimes it seems so far away and long ago it's like looking down the wrong end of a telescope.

My search for these early peoples led me along various paths. I began looking at familiar Hebridean and West Coast landscapes in a different way. I considered what I'd seen and read of Inuit, Native American and Sami traditions. I read about peoples in places I've never been to, like Mongolia, Australia and South Africa. These parallels helped me to see my own country through the eyes of people who were hefted to their land in a way that I can never experience myself. Mesolithic people wouldn't have needed a separate word for 'nature': everyone – people, animals, birds, fish, mountains, rivers, seas – would have co-existed in the same holistic world.

Nor were Mesolithic lives necessarily as 'nasty, brutish and short' as Hobbesian theory would have us believe. The stereotype of grunting cavemen wielding clubs lingers on, although recent hunter-gatherers have lived rich lives in marginal areas where no one could possibly practise agriculture. Resources must have seemed infinite before agriculture took over all the prime land. Mesolithic Scotland seems to have provided a living as plentiful as that enjoyed by, for example, the Native Americans of the north-west coast before their way of life was disrupted for ever. Mesolithic people in Scotland shared their land with red and roe deer, pig, wild cattle, wolf, bear, beaver, otter, fox and perhaps squirrels. Rivers were full of salmon and trout. All kinds of birds inhabited sea, cliffs, marshes and forests. Shores were rich in shellfish. The sea teemed with fish. Ray Mears and Gordon Hillman, in their TV programme on survival, have indicated the tasty variety of plants available for gathering, even through the long winters. I am not suggesting that Mesolithic Scotland was a Rousseau-esque paradise full of noble savages, but all the evidence suggests that human life was about far more than mere subsistence. People could make decisions about their lives, just as we do, based on social and spiritual considerations, and not just the material imperatives of where and how to find the next meal.

There's little material evidence of the hunter-gatherers of

Mesolithic Scotland. The shell middens of Oronsay, caves near Oban and on Ulva, locations on Islay, Jura, Mull, Coll, Rum and Risga are the main west-coast sites. Microliths – tiny stone blades and points – are indicative of a Mesolithic presence. Food remains and tools of bone, shell and antler, and a few postholes where tents were once pitched, are really all that is left. The only human remains are odd finger-bones from shell middens. There is nothing in Scotland like the fishing traps, villages or cemeteries of southern Scandinavia. In a Danish Mesolithic grave a newborn child was found resting on a swan's wing. At Starr Carr in Yorkshire archaeologists unearthed stag antlers attached to a mask. Their purpose remains a mystery; I've incorporated them into my fictional narrative. There are no such indications of spiritual or symbolic life in Scotland. That could either be because soil conditions are too acid, or because burial practices were different. My premise, as a story-writer, is that wherever there are people there will be emotions, rituals, metaphors, stories, art . . . in other words, a constant search for meanings.

Hunter-gatherer cultures all over the world share remark-ably similar spiritual practices that express deep affinity with the land to which they belong. Shamanistic religions are closely allied to hunting economies. My Go-Betweens' spiritual prac-tice is based on my readings in shamanistic spiritualities from many different parts of the world. To be Go-Between is to enact a role rather than to belong to a class. Go-Betweens have their own sort of power, but it operates through the natural world, within an egalitarian society. Forms of social control in hunter-gatherer societies sometimes strike me as being remark-ably civilised and effective. However, if I'd been born eight thousand years ago, I would almost certainly have had fewer years in which to enjoy the cultural benefits on offer.

In all the long years of Mesolithic Scotland we know of only one definite historic event. This was the tsunami that struck the east coast following an underwater landslide off the coast of Norway in *c.*6150 BC. I took this tsunami as the catalyst for my plot, and used first-hand accounts of the 2004 Boxing Day tsunami as the basis for Kemen's story.

I use Basque names for my characters because, although no one has any idea what languages were spoken in Mesolithic Scotland, Basque is thought to be the only extant language of pre-Indo-European – which is to say, pre-agricultural – origin on the western seaboard of Europe.

Most of my novels have maps. There's no map in this book, partly because sea levels have changed in complicated ways: land around the Scottish ice cap lifted up after the huge weight of ice melted, while sea levels everywhere were also rising. But, more importantly, there shouldn't be a map because my characters imagined their land in other ways.

Mesolithic people, like hunter-gatherers today, attained a level of environmental understanding and practical skills far beyond the reach of our own culture. In trying to imagine Mesolithic lives, I looked for, and sometimes attempted, hunter-gatherer skills that are still practised today. I'm grateful to Peter Faulkner from Shropshire, who helped me to make my own coracle from hazel, willow and hide. Enid Brown of Scotlandwell explained how to harvest wild honey, and Eric Begbie from Clackmannan worked out my wildfowling strategies. Mark Lazzeri of Assynt, Douglas Murray of Aboyne and John Love of Uist contributed to the deer hunts, and Callan Duck of St Andrews to the seal hunting. I am indebted to Maurizio Bastianoni in Umbria for sharing his expertise in boar hunting. Bill Ritchie of Assynt advised on fishing, and Tess Darwin, Mandy Haggith, Linda Henderson, Pete Kinnear and Agnes Walker all contributed their gathering skills and ecological knowledge. Jonathan Sawday skippered the initial voyage up the Sound of Mull and Loch Sunart, and he and Martin Montgomery supplied sailing directions throughout the book. These people not only helped me to write this novel, they also helped to alter permanently my own perceptions of land and sea, and how to live from them and with them.

I quickly discovered that, although Mesolithic Scotland is a closed book to most of us, there is a dedicated core of experts in the field. Both Caroline Wickham Jones of Orkney and Steven Mithen of Reading University welcomed a novelist on to their digs on Orkney and Coll respectively. The bit of hazelnut shell I found on the dig at Long Howe, and its implications for the early history of Orkney, have been one of the most exciting parts of this journey. I'm used to writing fiction, and in contrast that hazel shell was so *real*. Other archaeologists and geographers who have helped me on the way include Sue Dawson on the tsunami, Kevin Edwards on the Mesolithic environment and Karen Hardy on technologies. Clive Gamble of Reading University kindly read part of the manuscript.

A residency at the Civitella Ranieri Foundation in Umbria, Italy, provided crucial uninterrupted writing time early in the project. I finished the novel in the ideal surroundings provided by a fellowship at the Rockefeller Foundation Bellagio Center on Lake Como, Italy.

I am grateful to all these people who helped me to envision a Mesolithic world. Caroline Wickham Jones answered questions and read drafts with undiminishing enthusiasm, besides providing bed, board and library for weeks on end. And thanks, as ever, to Mike Brown for support in everything from coracle-making to copy-editing.